W9-ANM-024

The cat was mostly black, its fur filthy, matted and coming out in tufts. Overweight—no doubt from feeding on rats and refuse—and much stronger than it looked, its eyes glittering with pure outrage. One mistake and the furious feline could claw his eyes out and use his abdomen as a scratching post. In a way, the nasty fur ball reminded him of his ex-wife. She'd been a bad pussy, too.

He said it aloud, testing his voice in the stillness of the room. "Bad pussy. You're a bad pussy, aren't you?"

The cat spit. Attempted to rake his arm into ribbons with its back claws.

"I'll take that as a yes." He tossed it across the room where it landed on an area rug and skidded to a stop. It turned to hiss at him, then made a beeline under the massive Napoleon III desk that dominated the office. No doubt it would be found there in the morning, poised to rip the crotch out of some unsuspecting police officer's pants. He wished he could be around to witness the chaos, but wishes, as his sainted mother often said, wouldn't get the dishes done.

He surveyed the room once more, carefully inspecting each detail of his handiwork. The game had begun. It wouldn't do make a mistake so early in the contest.

The dead woman lay on the floor, naked except for a string of pearls around her neck and a diamond stud in each earlobe. The jewelry belonged to her, and while he'd thought about taking the necklace or earrings as trophies, he knew if they were found in his possession, his identity would be discovered.

He allowed himself only one trophy from his first victim. . . .

Gordian Knot Books is an imprint of Crossroad Press Publishing

Copyright © 2015 by Laurie Moore & Russell Davis
Cover illustration by Dave Dodd
Design by Aaron Rosenberg
ISBN 978-1-941408-74-2 — ISBN 978-1-941408-75-9 (pbk.)
For information address Crossroad Press at 141 Brayden Dr., Hertford, NC 27944
www.crossroadpress.com

First edition

MURDER INK

A DAKOTA JONES, P.I. MYSTERY

BOOK 1

LAURIE MOORE
&
RUSSELL DAVIS

MURDER INK

A DAKOTA JONES MYSTERY

BOOK 1

LAURIE MOORE
&
RUSSELL DAVIS

Acknowledgments

Laurie Moore:

When my co-author, Russell Davis, told me about a concept he came up with and sent the outline he wrote while sitting in an airport terminal, I jumped at the chance when he asked me to write the story because of my "Southern voice." It's not often one gets the opportunity to work with such a talented and prolific author, and I didn't want to miss out on a chance to collaborate with my former editor.

I'd also like to thank my husband for putting up with the editing process and taking care of everything else so that I would have time to write.

Russell Davis:

Without the help of my wife, Sherri, *Murder Ink* would have been a book without a song. Her assistance in planning, and willingness to listen to my ranting and raving during the outlining process was invaluable. That she's waited patiently for this work to appear in the world is a testament to her understanding of what a strange business we work in; that she worked patiently with me—and still does—is a testament to her future sainthood.

I'd also like to thank my co-author, Laurie Moore, for joining me on this journey. Long ago, I had the distinct pleasure of being her editor on a number of novels. Even then, I knew I wanted to write with her—she carries a level of passion and energy into every story she tells, and I can't think of anyone who I believed would be better able to help me bring Dakota Jones to life.

Prologue

He loosened the twine on the bag and reached inside for the writhing, hissing animal. Protected by heavy leather gloves and thick sleeves, he withdrew the giant cat without fear of drawing back a shredded limb. He held the enraged animal by the scruff of the neck, taking great care to keep it at arm's length. An uglier, nastier looking creature had never walked the Earth.

The cat was mostly black, its fur filthy, matted, and coming out in tufts. Overweight—no doubt from feeding on rats and refuse—and much stronger than it looked, its eyes glittering with pure outrage. One mistake and the furious feline could claw his eyes out and use his abdomen as a scratching post. In a way, the nasty ball of fur reminded him of his ex-wife. She'd been a bad pussy, too.

He said it aloud, testing his voice in the stillness of the room. "Bad pussy. You're a bad pussy, aren't you?"

The cat spit. Attempted to rake his arm into ribbons with its back claws.

"I'll take that as a yes." He tossed it across the room where it landed on an area rug and skidded to a stop. It turned to hiss at him, then made a beeline under the massive Napoleon III desk that dominated the office. No doubt it would be found there in the morning, poised to rip the crotch out of some unsuspecting police officer's pants. He wished he could be around to witness the chaos, but wishes, as his sainted mother often said, wouldn't get the dishes done.

He surveyed the room once more, carefully inspecting each detail of his handiwork. The game had begun. It wouldn't do to make a mistake so early in the contest.

The dead woman lay on the floor, naked except for a string of pearls around her neck and a diamond stud in each earlobe. The jewelry belonged to her, and while he'd thought about taking the necklace or earrings as trophies, he knew if they were found in his possession, his identity would be discovered. He allowed himself only one trophy from his first victim.

Something small and almost impossible to detect.

A single lock of hair no more than an inch long.

In this case, a dark curl that looked almost wet when he clipped it from her head. It would smell like her for many days, and to touch it or look upon it would remind him of her and why she needed to die. Banded with care and tucked into a small glass vial, the hair was her essence—and a reminder of why he needed to play the game.

Sex between them had been consensual, and he'd been certain to use two condoms which were now carefully packaged in a plastic baggie for later disposal. He shaved his entire body, including his pubic region, so finding his hair on the corpse would be difficult. Since he wore a wig, his own hair neatly plastered against his scalp beneath a hair net, everything that could be done to shield his DNA from the cold scrutiny of the medical examiner had been done.

The faint light of a street lamp slanted through the window, illuminating the slender wooden handle of the stiletto he'd used to kill her. It protruded from the center of her throat like an obscene goiter. Nothing connected him to the weapon, and he'd worn rubber gloves beneath the leather ones the entire time he'd been in the room.

She'd asked him about that, and he'd shrugged and smiled. All charm, and oh so shy. "Guess I'm a bit of a fetishist," he'd said, doing his best *aw-shucks* voice. "I like the feel of the latex against my skin." That part, at least, had been true.

When he killed her, her eyes opened wide in pained surprise, a second intensity granted at the moment of their shared orgasm. He remembered the feel of her heat against the latex, the erratic pulsing of her fading heart beneath his chest. In that moment, she'd achieved the only perfection of her worthless existence. In death, as Poe had once intimated, she was perfect. Others in her profession would soon follow . . . links in a chain of perfect, necessary deaths.

He smiled, admiring the last bit of his handiwork—the henna

tattoos that decorated her torso, wrapping around her breasts. Complicated designs that, when unraveled, would reveal musical notations, actual note sequences and lyrics, embedded within Celtic diagrams. The music was also part of the game: the one set of clues he would leave the police. Should they put in the legwork to figure them out, he might eventually be caught and stopped.

That, too, was part of the game. He accepted the notion that he *should* be stopped. He had to give them a shot, no matter how long a shot it was. According to law, even necessary deaths like this prostitute's were illegal. An unfortunate reality of society. Of course, *should* and *would* were different concepts.

He wouldn't be stopped.

Couldn't be stopped.

He picked up his case and gave the room a final once-over, ensuring that it appeared exactly as it was supposed to. Satisfied, he stepped out the door of the dead woman's office and locked it behind him.

Walking down the dark hall toward the exit, he imagined the ugly cat he left behind as a calling card. Sitting under that fancy desk, waiting, thirsty, hungry, and mad as hell. Flea-bitten, mangy coat attached to an anvil of claws and teeth. In a couple of hours, it would be yowling at the top of its lungs; and if he got lucky, it would begin dining on Celia St. Claire's open throat, further compromising the crime scene. By the time sunrise rolled around, someone would make a call. Eventually, the police would come out to investigate.

What they would find would be two bad pussies.

One would be dead, and another that should be.

And both provided one last clue about the next move in his game.

Chapter One

"Of course I know the place. Everybody in Phoenix knows it. It's a blight on the moral landscape of Maricopa County. What does this have to do with me? It's my day off." And then, a long, drawn-out, "No. Anyone in custody? Suspects? Hamilton said what?"

Dakota Jones cracked open one gray eye. Kris's strident tone jarred her fully awake.

"Oh, that's just great," Kris huffed. Which meant not so great. "Gallows humor will land my partner in the Internal Affairs hot seat one of these days. Do me a favor. Don't repeat what Hamilton said, okay? Let's hope the press doesn't quote him in tomorrow's edition."

Dakota shifted her gaze to the alarm clock. The digital readout flashed neon red numbers—7:18 A.M. She groaned into her pillow. The delicious idea of slipping back into slumber flitted into mind, but Kris's words hung in her ears. Someone had died, that much was certain. And since Kris happened to be talking *about* homicide detective Hamilton Stark, instead of *to* him, that meant she had the police dispatcher on the line.

Dakota absorbed the one-sided exchange taking place down the hall, and didn't like what she heard. Phoenix had another murder. And even though cavalier, condescending Hamilton Stark drew the short straw to work the Thanksgiving holiday, Kris would have to go in.

Nothing says "the Universe loves to twist the knife" quite like having your life partner run off with her police partner on your six-month anniversary, Dakota thought.

So much for the non-traditional candlelit dinner of tamales, slathered with homemade chili con carne and fresh salsa, she'd made the night before. So much for slaving over a hot stove to impress her lover with all her favorites, plus flan for dessert. Kris, Phoenix's ace homicide investigator, loved it when Dakota showcased her domestic talents. For some reason, to Kris, a good meal always translated into hot sex once they adjourned to the bedroom.

But today, there was nothing like the shock of murder to clear the head, and this unexpected development ruffled Dakota's perfect Thanksgiving plans. With a resigned sigh, she rolled out of bed, slid into her silk kimono, and cinched it at the waist. Lately, getting time alone with Kris was like trying to grasp smoke.

Rain tapped the window. Thunder rocked the walls. Even with skeins of rain, the view of the mountains was no less spectacular than it was the first time Dakota'd seen it, standing on this slice of land at Heaven's Urn, going over the blueprints to her new home with the contractor. The slow, misty drizzle turned fierce, pelting the red Saltillo roof tiles on the adobe mansion. Dakota paused to reflect on her surroundings. Who would've thought a gal from the wrong side of town, living a kind of white-trash existence where relatives are often your dates, would end up picking the right numbers on the winning lotto ticket?

She made her way through the sprawling adobe mansion toward the kitchen—a cheery room with turquoise walls, aqua appliances, and wooden Oaxacan folk art animals in festive colors that lifted even her sourest mood. On the way to the coffee maker, she gave Kris a peck on the cheek. She started to throw a compliment the detective's way—to mention that Kris looked especially yummy in the new blue shirt Dakota bought her—but her companion waved her off like a pesky gnat. Her mouth opened and closed like a fish as she redirected her attention to the caller on the other end of the land line. When it came to the Phoenix Police Department, Kris was crisp, efficient, and all business.

"I knew this would happen." Dakota's harsh whisper made her thirty-three-year-old live-in slide a hand over the mouthpiece. "I knew we couldn't have a romantic Thanksgiving together." Hamilton Stark—the kind of man who erupted out of people's nightmares and into their real lives—would probably do a dick dance once he heard Kris would assist him on the call. "Why is it *you* always get stuck working holidays? I thought the old man was assigned to work today."

True, being thirty-nine didn't mean Hamilton Stark had one foot in the grave. Still, she could hope. She referred to the arrogant investigator by the pejorative term because he rubbed her the wrong way. And because he possessed the dashing good looks of a Ken doll. That he seemed physically fit, lithe, and determined to woo Kris back for another meaningless fling only complicated their already tense relationship. An unbidden image of the two detectives sprang into mind, causing Dakota to imagine what it might've been like for Kris to slip into the sack with the aging investigator—back in her days of gender confusion—before Kris figured out the best man for her was a woman.

Hamilton Stark. She almost spat the name. The man played a big part in the Phoenix Police Department as to why she and Kris couldn't be open about their relationship. While his contemporaries eased gracefully into middle age, Stark still swaggered around with a frat-boy persona.

A cruel thought crept into what had instantly become an ugly visual. In the bedroom scenario Dakota's mind conjured up, the terminally tense and uptight Hamilton would've needed a pill for erectile dysfunction. Unlike most men, who'd be calling their doctors if their erections persisted more than four hours, Hamilton Stark would be calling his friends.

Even injecting that artificial twist into the melodrama playing out in her head didn't erase the misery she felt when she thought of Kris and Hamilton between the sheets.

Dakota shook off the reverie. As a couple stuck in the research and development phase of their relationship, this should've been a happy day for them. Punishing herself with wild conjecture only made her stomach clench. Besides, she did a lot of reading. And according to American women, the average erect penis is only four inches. Hamilton Stark could probably be compared to a light switch. How big was *that*?

"How come it has to be you?" she hissed. "How come the old man can't just work the crime scene himself? You've worked cases alone. He's only doing this to screw up our holiday."

"Not so loud." Kris un-muffled the receiver and mimed *I love you*. She grabbed an invisible pencil and scribbled into the air.

Dakota pulled open a drawer and handed over a pen, followed

by a notepad with letterhead that read: *Runaway Investigations*, with *Dakota Jones, Owner* centered beneath it. Bookend images of a boy and girl flanked the name of her business. Kris snatched it from her grasp.

"Ready to copy," Kris announced to the caller. "Details?" Bouncy brown hair bobbed as she took notes. A tiny frown creased her forehead, then vanished just as quickly. Then her voice shrilled. "Where?" Her gaze cut to Dakota—and not in a good way.

Dakota did a subtle lean-in to read the notes. As usual, Kris's hen-scratch penmanship had all of the qualities of a serial killer on meth. Dakota reluctantly wandered away to fill the coffee maker with water and toss in a pre-measured packet of Kona grind. Her eyes flickered to a bar stool draped with Kris's blazer and shoulder holster. *Bra, panties, clothes, gun.* That's how it worked around here. Once the phone call ended, Kris'd be out the door, and no amount of tempting food offerings, or the playful flashing of breasts would delay the inevitable.

Building on her irritation, Dakota mocked Hamilton, imitating Kris's whiny partner through fisted eyes, crybaby noises, and exaggerated hand gestures. " 'Help me, Kris. I can't function without you. I can't do Shineola if you're not here to guide me.' " While strangling the air in front of her, she abruptly checked herself— *Who's the big baby now?*

"Stop it," Kris mouthed without sound, and addressed the dispatcher. "Who's our victim?" The pen hovered above the paper.

Dakota flipped on the switch to the coffee maker. The top-of-the-line beverage machine gurgled to life.

"Who?" The unexpected surge in Kris's tone sliced the air between them.

Dakota whipped around. Rosy pink cheeks, a by-product of Kris's northern European ancestry, had drained of color. Her poker face shattered.

"I'll get right on it." Kris replaced the telephone receiver in its cradle. Dropped her gaze and massaged her temples. "I have to go in."

"Can you at least have a cup of coffee with me first?" Dakota left off the rest of the sentence—that it wasn't like Kris worked as a paramedic, speeding across the streets of Phoenix to save a life; it wasn't like the victim would actually revive. Her conscience whispered, *Shame on you, shame on you, shame on you*. She only had these selfish thoughts because Kris was heading out to be with Hamilton instead of spending time with her.

"No time for coffee. I'll probably end up working two shifts because of this, so don't hold dinner for me." Kris shrugged into her shoulder holster and fastened the buckle. Pulled at the pinpoint oxford until it no longer bunched beneath the weight of the gun. Smoothed the front of her khakis with her palms. Slid into her blazer and pulled a cell phone from her pocket.

Thumbing the keypad, Kris stared at the digital display before whipping it up to her ear. "Stark? K.C. The dispatcher filled me in. Why didn't you call me yourself?" For a moment, Kris listened, alternating between head bobs and wrist flip-flops that indicated her partner was giving her a hard time. "I'm on the way. It'll take both of us working non-stop if we want to get through in time for Thanksgiving dinner. What?" She fell silent. Again, limpid brown eyes cut to Dakota. "You don't have anywhere to go?"

Dakota's eyes widened. "Don't you dare invite him here."

"He doesn't have anywhere to go," Kris whispered.

"That's because he's a jerk." Dakota kept her voice low, but still loud enough where he might hear. "A lot of people are alive only because new technology's made it easier to get a death penalty conviction."

Kris pressed the air in a downward motion. She mouthed, *I'll take care of it.*

Dakota mouthed, *You'd better.*

"We can always set an extra plate. No, we're not having turkey and dressing. We're having good old-fashioned Southwestern cuisine—the kind I love."

Kris winked, then fixed Dakota in her gaze. A little eyebrow-wiggle said *Show me.* Dakota pulled back a swath of fabric and bared one breast. Kris's eyes closed to half-mast. She made a little hand-motion, *Come here.*

Dakota shook her head, *fat chance.* Covered herself and headed to the refrigerator for Half & Half. Kris should be standing up to that partner of hers, not letting him cow her into giving up her day off.

Between pauses, Kris kept her voice even and metered. "A stabbing. Nude. Nope, nothing but a string of pearls and a pair of diamond studs in her ears. Uniforms got a call about ten minutes ago. Reporters probably heard it on their scanners, which means we need to figure out what we're going to say so we don't look incompetent—or callous—if the camera crews beat us there. The victim?" Kris let out a weary sigh. "Yeah, they got ID on her."

I'm sorry, she mouthed to Dakota.

"I think whoever did this knew her. This killing was up close and personal." Her voice went testy. "What do you mean, *How do I know?* You second-guessing me? Look, it's clear from the description she was posed." This time, Kris's eyes bulged. "Don't be crude. It's a tragic death. It's not 'one less hooker in the city.' "

Dakota arched an eyebrow.

Might be interesting to watch a home video of Hamilton's mom when she was pregnant with him. Bet she'd be holding a longneck.

"You're jaded, Hamilton. Maybe you could use a career move. I hear that position in Burglary's still open." Kris returned the phone to her pocket without a good-bye. Clearly, Hamilton *Let's-Party-In-Your-Pants* Stark hung up on her.

Dakota laid down the gauntlet. "You shouldn't have invited him. Trying to get the guy to accept our relationship and assimilate into our lifestyle as a friend is like trying to teach an ape how to hold a pen; eventually he just gets frustrated and sticks you in the eye with it. He's not coming over here."

"He declined. So we're good?"

"Not good—you still have to leave. But, better," Dakota grudgingly admitted.

Kris's expression changed. Worry lines in her forehead relaxed in compassion. "There's no good way to tell you this."

"Save it. I cracked your code." Said in a huff. "You have to work. I get it. I'll eat by myself—again." When Kris didn't bolt for the door, Dakota added, "Isn't this the part where you have to dash?"

Kris's voice went bedroom-soft. "Let's sit."

"You're not going to try to turn this into some sort of Shakespearian tragedy so I'll feel better about you caving into Hamilton's demands and blowing off six months together, are you? Well, don't bother. I'm fine with it—" meaning not-so-fine "—but one of these days, maybe sooner than you think, I won't take a back seat to the old man." Common sense signaled her to stop right there. To resist speaking thoughts that were hotwired to her tongue. *You can't un-ring a bell*, her mind inwardly shouted.

Kris inhaled deeply. Her shoulders wilted. "Please sit down."

"I mean it, Kris." Dakota's pulse throbbed in her throat. "One of these days you'll decide to stand up to that jerk, hopefully before you arrive home to find your stuff on the front lawn—on fire."

"Please sit. This isn't about me anymore, or about what I have to do right now. This could affect you, too."

Chills crawled up Dakota's arms and prickled the nape of her neck. Kris had turned pale, and her miserable expression suggested bad news all around. "Whatever it is, just tell me straight out."

"The city's latest homicide is Celia St. Claire."

Chapter Two

Harsh truths should be sugarcoated. News of Celia St. Claire's murder did more than suck the breath out of Dakota's lungs. It reduced her to tears.

Celia St. Claire ran Fantasy Escorts Unlimited, a high-dollar entertainment service catering to wealthy, discriminating businessmen looking for fun while visiting Phoenix. The telephone advertisement clearly stated the firm's purpose was to provide escorts for unattached males who needed a trophy girlfriend to appear with them at business functions, galas, the ballet, theater, and other similar events. Or not. Fantasy Escorts Unlimited happened to be one of those don't-ask-don't-tell places that law enforcement largely overlooked because Celia St. Claire paid skyrocketing property taxes on her downtown, zoned-historical building, spent lavishly on herself and others, and donated large sums of money at the end of each year to projects the city had a hard time funding. More importantly, she operated her enterprise with discretion. Celia protected her clientele.

Before Dakota became the sole proprietor of Runaway Investigations, back in a previous life, she'd worked at Fantasy Escorts Unlimited under an assumed name.

Anyone seeking companionship needed only to contact Celia St Claire and be willing to pay the hourly rate—a six-hour minimum charged whether you used the entire time or not. And if they desired a youthful looking twenty-eight-year-old who stood five feet eleven and weighed in at one hundred fifty pounds, with a mass of black curls that tumbled well past her shoulders and all the curves and tawny, lean muscles of a *Sports Illustrated* bathing suit model, they had only to request the services of Pussy Galore. Dakota'd chosen her call-girl alias for good reason: The "Goldfinger" character's intense dislike of men suited her personality to a "T." If a customer wanted a good spanking—or worse—Pussy Galore could handle the job.

Now, Dakota hiked up a pair of skinny-legged jeans, scampering clumsily as she trailed Kris into the marble foyer.

"You're not coming with me." Kris headed for the front door. "I don't care that you knew her. I've got a job to do and I can't have you underfoot."

"She was my friend," Dakota called out with the petulance of a five-year-old. "She took me in. I owe it to her." Barefooted, Dakota stuffed her tank top into the waistband, followed by the tails of a loose-fitting shirt.

"She wasn't your friend. She made money off you." Kris grabbed an umbrella. When she opened the door and saw that the rain had subsided, she put it back into the porcelain stand. "You owe her nothing."

"There has to be some kind of mistake. Celia can't be dead. I just spoke to her." As soon as the words tumbled out, Dakota wanted to reel them back in. Kris had expected her to cut all ties to her past. It was part of the agreement when they decided to play house—a term one might refer to as a deal breaker.

The detective closed the door until only a sliver of light sliced through. "You did what?"

"I'm sorry. There was nothing to it. I didn't think I should tell you."

"Damned right you should tell me. We agreed."

"Babe, she only called to warn me. Some weirdo came in asking questions about me. She thought I should know."

Kris's eyes ignited with fury. She had to suspect the man was a former customer.

"It's not what you think"—words tumbled out in a rush—"it was a warning. I didn't want you to worry."

"*Didn't want me to worry?*" the detective taunted her. "What else are you keeping from me, Dakota?"

"Nothing. You know everything."

Without warning, Kris grabbed her by the collar. Pulled her close and tongue-kissed her. Dakota's blood turned to sand, pouring into her leaded feet like the last grains seeping through an hourglass.

Lightheaded, she returned the kiss. As Kris's fingers peeled off Dakota's shirt and roamed the contours of her body beneath the tank top, the front door clicked shut behind her.

"You have to trust me," Dakota purred, then nipped the detective's neck with a series of little bites . . . bites that turned hungry . . . then ravenous as Kris maneuvered her against the door and pressed herself against her.

"I want to. Believe me, I do." She pushed away and adjusted her holster. Assessed Dakota through admiring eyes, naked from the waist up, and tracked a finger beneath her pouty lower lip. "But now I have to leave."

"I hate that you're spending our six-month anniversary with him. He needs to get a life."

"Can't be helped."

Dakota scrunched her face in disgust. "I can't stand him. But then, I have my reasons. And you know good and well what they are." She challenged Kris with a wicked look.

"He has a girlfriend—that's what I was trying to tell you. They met a few weeks ago. Apparently, she had to leave town on a family emergency, but he said they picked up a spiral ham and the trimmings from one of the cafés. He plans to eat that, and watch what's left of the football game when he gets off."

"What's she like?"

"I don't know. He hasn't introduced her, yet. But he talks about her a lot, so that's a good sign the relationship's moving in the right direction, don't you think?"

What Dakota thought—and would never forget—was that Hamilton had done his dead-level best to humiliate her in public.

Six months before, Kris and the old man had spent lunch huddled together, snuffling with laughter, at a bistro table in the same popular café where Dakota routinely dined. She'd tried to ignore them; to pretend they were talking shop. Tried to convince herself that their conversation had nothing to do with her. But Hamilton Stark got a little too loud for comfort. While other diners paused, mid-bite, fascinated by what he had to say, Dakota wanted to shrink in size until she could hide behind the saltshaker.

"Hey, K.C.—you wouldn't by chance have a thing for Bond girls, would you?"

"Bond as in James Bond?"

"Double-oh-seven. See that alley cat over there? Calls herself Pussy Galore. Ain't that a hoot?"

"We've met. Only back then, she was a two-bit whore parading up and down Twenty-seventh and Indian School Road."

Dakota shivered, recalling that dreadful encounter.

It's a wonder she and Kris had ever gotten together after that humiliating experience. And they wouldn't have, either, if Kris hadn't been ashamed enough of her behavior to slip a business card with her personal phone number and *Please call me* scrawled on the back on the way out the door.

It wasn't because Kris left money at the register to cover Dakota's tab that made her dial that number. Nor did she do it out of curiosity, or with any expectation of an apology. It took way more than that. As the detective sauntered past the table, they exchanged looks, and the raw spark of sexual intensity radiating from Kris's luminous brown eyes betrayed her scornful words. Connection made, Dakota picked up on the signal: *Sexually ambiguous Kris had the same interest in women that she did.*

She didn't expect an invitation to dinner at Kris's modest stucco home, either. After a couple of shots of Stolichnaya, dinner turned into a game of slap-and-tickle. It wasn't until later, when they fell into bed together, that Kris mentioned the PD's *Don't ask, don't tell policy,* and confided in her about the one-night-stand with Hamilton Stark.

Hours later, in a tangle of sheets, with their glistening bodies sandwiched against each other, and sweat-dampened hair plastered against their necks, Kris spoke to the dark.

"I don't want you to go."

"I don't want to go, either. But if you ever take a cheap shot at my expense or talk down to me in front of your colleagues, you'll never see me again."

"I'm so sorry. Let me make it up to you."

And she did. And they were still together.

"I really have to go, Dee." The detective brushed her aside and slipped through the opening, quickening her gait until she was sauntering toward her unmarked patrol car.

Beyond the rock garden, Dakota shifted her attention to a ratty car parked across the street. Hair prickled at the nape of her neck. Residents of Heaven's Urn drove high-end autos. And while most of the maids rode the bus, only gardeners, or contract workers in trucks with company logos on the driver's door, typically rolled through the gates in beat-up vehicles. It was odd, if not completely abnormal, to see such a car parked in this ritzy community—on Thanksgiving, no less—and something of a concern since Celia St. Claire's phone call. As Kris fired up the engine and rolled out of the driveway without so much as a backward glance, Dakota closed the front door.

She made her way through the living room, an enormous open space with buttery-soft leather furniture and coral walls stippled with black paint that suggested a deranged schizophrenic wielding a paint brush had gone off his meds and dotted the walls to resemble the skin on a Gila monster. Still, she liked spending time curled up with a good mystery in front of the double-sided, stucco fireplace. From her place on the love seat, she could glance past the glass doors to the inflatable plastic shark floating in the swimming pool.

The newspaper. She'd forgotten to get it.

Dakota returned to the front door wearing a pair of doeskin moccasins, custom colored and hand-beaded by an ancient woman from the Yavapai-Apache Nation—one of the many perks associated with being rich: Flash the right amount of cash and a famous artist could be coaxed out of retirement.

Halfway out the door, the telephone shrilled. She skirted a console table with a fruit cornucopia set up near the entrance and picked up the nearest cordless.

Despite the weighty sadness over Celia's murder, she infused a chipper lilt into her standard greeting. "Runaway Investigations, Dakota Jones."

"Thank God—Dakota." Relief turned to tears as the caller mainlined sobs down Dakota's ear canal. "Did you hear about poor Celia? She's dead. Stabbed in the throat. Who'd do such a thing, Dee?"

The upwardly-corkscrewing voice belonged to Cyn Evans, who dressed up as Catwoman at Fantasy Escorts Unlimited. Yet, away from the escort service, sitting around in Gap clothes, waiting to have her hair and nails done at *A Cut Above the Rest*, Cyn lived an uneventful life as a former *Yamboree*-coronated "Yam Queen" from Gilmer, Texas. Kris would ID her true name soon enough.

Catwoman's words disintegrated into unintelligible speech. In less than thirty seconds, she'd gone from run-of-the-mill hysteria, to what sounded vaguely akin to speaking in tongues.

"Cyn? Calm down. I can't understand you. Talk slower."

"You gotta help me." Cyn's marginally cosmopolitan speech slipped back into its default setting—a thick Texas drawl. "I think I'm next."

Next? The news jolted her. "Why would you say that?"

"For the last couple of weeks, I've felt someone watching me." Cyn broke into sobs.

Dakota moved to the kitchen, to the notepad and pen Kris left on the countertop. "Listen to me, Cyn. I need you to stay in control." She picked up the ballpoint and held it inches from the paper. "Was this a customer?"

"I don't know." Cyn's ability to remain cool, calm, and collected was short lived. A fresh swell of panic washed over Dee's former colleague. "Lord Almighty, what am I gonna do? I don't wanna die." Out of words, she panted into the mouthpiece.

"Where are you?"

"In the back seat of a patrol car, talkin' to you on my cell phone." Uh-oh.

Kris would blow a gasket.

"Pay attention, Cyn. Do you see any homicide investigators?"

"Just a couple of suits." Followed by a couple of sniffles.

"That's them." She visualized Hamilton Stark in a navy blazer and slacks; with a silk cartoon tie held in place by a tiny gold hand-cuff tie tack.

"I need your help, Dakota. I need you to find out who's after me. I'll pay you."

Dakota fidgeted with the pen. She wanted to help the girl. But Kris wouldn't have it, and this wasn't the type of case she normally took on. Cyn Evans needed a second set of eyes—like a bodyguard—the brawnier, the better.

"I investigate runaway kids. I don't take adult cases."

The fantasy escort tuned up in protest. "But the newspaper said you found that old man. The mayor gave you a gold key."

True. That came after she got her picture in *The Tribune* standing next to Mayor Jane Roman at the ribbon-cutting ceremony for the children's hospital. She'd never expected the new wing to be named after her; she merely hoped a generous donation might ensure that they chiseled a quote into a sandstone block leading into the play area: *Every kid has the right to a happy childhood. ~Dakota Jones.*

"Every now and then I get missing person's calls to find people with Alzheimer's. I accept those cases because they might as well be kids. What you're asking is way out of my league."

Cyn yowled. "But it *has* to be you. There's nobody else I can trust."

"Those homicide detectives—one of them is a . . ." Dakota hesitated. How much information should she volunteer? ". . . friend of mine. Kris Carson. She's wearing khakis and a dark blue blazer. Tell her what you told me and she'll help you, I'm sure of it."

"Oh, Jesus. That's her, headed for the car right this second. I've gotta go."

"Wait—don't tell her you called me," Dakota yelled, but she was talking to a dead connection.

Cyn Evans had already thumbed off her cell phone.

"Ah, hell," Dakota announced as the coffee maker quietly gloated in fumes of Kona-roast. Kris would spit galvanized nails. "Note to self:" she said to the room at large, "When Kris tries to browbeat me, remind her Celia spent a great deal of time and money helping me reinvent myself."

Celia'd been on a first-name basis with several Maricopa County judges, and a couple of attorneys owed her favors. One of her lawyer friends drew up Dakota's name change motion, Celia covered the filing fee, and the attorney represented her in court. With her new name—Dakota Jones—and the winning lotto ticket, she'd been able to assimilated into Phoenix's high society, and run with the city's social elite.

Yes, Celia'd made money off of her, but she'd also helped her along the way.

Dakota returned to the front door, stepped out to retrieve the morning paper, and drew in a breath of clean air. The rain had stopped, and everything smelled crisp and fresh.

Without warning, she saw an advancing blur out of the corner of her eye. A hulking figure rounded the tall, thick clump of pencil cacti next to the porch.

Gripped by the thrill of terror, she stood, marooned, unable to react.

An odor of hatred so strong it whipped her breath away hit her nose before her startle reflex kicked in. A rangy-smelling man closed in on her. His mouth was feral. Spectacular eyes of an unexpected shade of blue hardened into an assassin's gaze.

"Wha—?" She said this on a whoosh of air.

Dakota recoiled. She took in his looks at a glance. Burn scars deformed much of his face, and what the scars didn't cover, the furrows lining his jowls did. He stood well over six feet, and probably tipped the scale at two hundred pounds. The only thing this landlocked pirate needed to complete the swarthy image was an eye patch to go with the long, curly, unkempt hair and graying black beard.

"Heaven's Urn is a gated community. How'd you get in?"

"Told the guard I needed to see you. That is, if you're D. Jones." He was holding a page torn from the telephone book, with a red circle drawn around Runaway Investigations. His eyes slewed to the letters on the mailbox.

He seemed vaguely familiar. An old client? Surely not. Fantasy Escorts Unlimited had a high-dollar clientele. Celia might've given him a fried egg sandwich if he'd come to the door hungry, but that's about it. Was this desert rat the man Celia warned her about?

While her brain misfired over possible scenarios, Dakota struggled with the effort of speech. "What do you want?"

"My daughter, Annie. She's gone."

"I'm sorry to hear that." His steely stare sent chills racing up her spine. "Did you contact the police?" Not that she cared. At the moment, she had a bigger problem—the music had stopped and she didn't have a chair. She'd left the front door ajar.

Her amphibian survival brain took over. Now she just wanted him gone before he shoved her inside, shut out the neighborhood, body-slammed her to the terrazzo tile floor, and turned her into tomorrow's headline.

He shook off her suggestion. "Police don't give a damn. She was just another delinquent to them. Will you help?"

Every alarm in Dakota's internal radar system went off. She struggled to find words that would convince him to leave without harming her. Every fiber in her body screamed danger; sixth-sense and hunches be damned, she wouldn't do business with him even if the story was true.

"Look, I don't know who sent you here, but I can't help you." Her eyes narrowed. "I don't believe I caught your name."

"You didn't catch it because I didn't give it to you."

"Don't play games with me." False bravado came off as insincere. She should run. Head for a neighbor's house screaming bloody murder if he followed her. The next-door neighbor—Derek-something—he might be home.

Unexpectedly, the man buried his face in dirty, un-manicured hands.

Aw, Jeez. Made him cry.

Quit blubbering.

Oh, good grief. I'm paranoid because of what happened to Celia.

"Look," she said, digging deep to wring out a modicum of tenderness. She still couldn't place him, and it unnerved her. "You seem to know a lot more about me than you're willing to tell me about yourself, and I'm not accustomed to carrying on long conversations with people I don't know. So what'll it be? Ready to tell me your name, or not?"

He uncovered his face. Radiating waves of contempt, he fixed her with a hard stare. The tears he'd shed were of the crocodile variety.

"Travis. Travis Creeley." He stuck out his big, calloused hand for a shake. She refused the offer with a flat stare. "You must be . . . what? Thirty? Thirty-one?"

She let the silence speak for her.

"You could help me. I know you could."

"I'm sure there are other private investigators who're just as qualified. You should look through the telephone directory until you find one you like."

"I did. I picked you."

Dakota wanted to tell him she only worked when she wanted to these days. That she could afford to be choosy about the cases she took on. That it didn't matter how much money a person offered since she didn't charge for her work. And that a million in singles wouldn't sway her decision not to work for him. She took in his presence. The sound of his gravelly voice. This *had* to be the man Celia tried to warn her about.

"Look, I'm sorry." *Meaning, not sorry.* "I wish you the best of luck, really I do. But this isn't going to work. So if you don't mind, I'm here to get my paper . . ." She took a few steps and he made no move to stop her. As she bent to reach for *The Tribune,* she kept a close eye on him.

"If I could just come inside and explain—"

"No. This conversation is over." She pointed to the junk heap parked at the curb. "Make a U-turn and take the first right to get out of here."

"But she could be out there, dead. I have to find out what happened to Annie." His eyes glinted. His brow furrowed. He seemed poised on the precipice of another fake crying jag.

Dakota swallowed hard. "I want you to leave." Outwardly, she moved toward the front door and squeezed the handle. But mentally, she prepared to turn him into a reproductive cul-de-sac by drop-kicking his family jewels into the next county if he so much as flinched. "Don't bother coming back. If you want to know what happened to your daughter, file a missing person's case with the police."

She rushed inside, slammed the door, and threw the deadbolt half-expecting him to hammer a fist against the wood separating them. With her back to the peephole, she listened to the beat of her thundering heart.

Chapter Three

"The department isn't taking this seriously. Especially the Chief," Kris said. She glanced at the black tuxedo Kit Kat clock ticking away in the kitchen, its tail swishing back and forth as the seconds slipped by; its eyes moving from side to side as if pulling all-night surveillance. Kris shrugged out of the shoulder holster and eased it onto one of the dining chairs. She draped her blazer over the chair back, slid into her seat and gave a wary headshake. "Hamilton really pissed me off today. I was photographing the scene. It was ghastly, Dee. Nobody should die that way, and I said so. And then Hamilton said, 'You think Phoenix will fold with one less prostitute?'" She let out a long breath. "Reporters were crawling all over the place. I could've pistol-whipped him."

"Wish you had," Dakota mumbled. "Is that the general consensus of the PD?" She poured Kris a glass of merlot. On her way to the head of the table, she nabbed a tamale, peeled off the shuck and dipped it in salsa.

"Of course not. And don't lump me in the same category with the rest of the cretins. Murder's murder. Nobody has the right to cancel someone else's ticket." She belted back the wine and stuck out her glass for a refill. Dakota obliged. "But I have to tread softly when it comes to picking fights with the brass. Same reason they can't know you and I are together. Chief Forster would find a way to get rid of me. Or make my life so freaking miserable I'd quit." She sighed heavily. "So, how was your day?"

"How was my day, you ask? Lovely." *Meaning not so lovely.* "I had a woman accuse me of trying to steal her husband just because I returned his phone call and asked to speak to him."

Kris shook her head. "Well, if we're keeping score, you're not the only *femme fatale* around here who can attract men. Today, while booking a suspect into jail, I had to tell an inmate arrested for domestic violence that, no, he could not use his one phone call to call me at home."

"It gets better. We ran out of sweetener, so I drove to the convenience store. On the way home, I got a flat tire. While I was waiting for Triple-A to come fix it, the gods were kind enough to grace me with the sight of an old geezer jogging past me wearing nothing but a pair of short-shorts. The image of his balls swinging to and fro underneath like a pendulum is forever burned into my retinas. The Triple-A guy said somebody kicked the valve stem. Top that. "

"Don't mess with me right now, Dakota, it's been a rough day—a day where every-damned-time I turned around, I was envisioning you as Pussy Galore, going down on two men at a time."

Whoa. Way to skip your meds . . .

For no good reason, Kris pushed herself back from the table. "Dammit, Dee, why'd you have to do that? Couldn't you have found another way to make a living?"

The heat of shame rose to Dakota's cheeks. "Don't attack me for something I did before we got together."

"Every time I'm around those people I see your face. It's bad enough to watch men drooling over you when we're out in public, but to be inside the whorehouse where you used to—"

"*Used to*, Kris. Past tense. And don't call it that."

"—brothel—"

"Don't call it that, either."

"—I don't have enough bandwidth to deal with this right now."

"Fine. We don't have to talk about it if you don't want to. Besides, Cyn Evans pretty much filled me in."

Oops.

Can opened, beans spilled.

Kris jumped up from the table with such force her chair tipped over backward. Her chest heaved. Neck veins throbbed. "What do you think you're doing talking to my witness?"

Dakota splashed merlot into her glass, letting her lover blow off steam while she swirled the bouquet and sniffed it. How many times would she be made to pay for the same mistake? Even the legal system provided for an end to bad decision making—*res judicata*—where one couldn't be tried over and over for the same offense. But apparently Kris had never heard of *res judicata*. And if Kris, with her cop mentality, kept up these accusatory comments and refused to allow the statute of limitations to run on her time at Fantasy Escorts Unlimited, well then, they just weren't going to make it as a couple.

"Don't raise your voice to me, Kris. I'm not your dog." The silence stretched a few beats. "Cyn called me from the patrol car. Maybe next time you and the old man ought to frisk for cell phones before you give witnesses the cuff-and-stuff treatment."

Kris's eyelashes fluttered in astonishment.

As Dakota related the details of Cyn's phone call, Kris righted the chair and wilted into the seat like a deflated blow-up doll with its mouth still shaped into an "O." The detective eyed the wine bottle and extended her hand in a *gimme* motion.

With a tight smile, Dakota slid the merlot across the table. This time, Kris upended the bottle and guzzled until she drained it. For several minutes she sat in silence. Then her eyes took on the glaze and sheen of fine chocolate.

Her tongue loosened.

"It was horrible, Dee, just awful." Her eyes welled, and her lids rimmed red. "I keep seeing that stiletto sticking out of her neck. He posed her naked, too, with her legs splayed out in death for everyone to see. It made me feel degraded for every woman who's ever been at the mercy of a man.

"I keep seeing the look on Hamilton's face, so clinical, so pensive. As if by scrutinizing her snatch, he could divine who the killer was." A tear slid off to one side and sluiced down her cheek. "This case has all the earmarks of a serial killer."

The air between them grew thin, as though the oxygen had been siphoned out of Dakota's lungs. "You have *other* cases like this?"

Kris sniffed. "No, but the whole thing felt staged and set-up. There was even this big, raggedy-eared tomcat that sprang up out of nowhere, and mucked up the crime scene trying to get out."

Dakota frowned. "Celia didn't own a cat. Didn't keep animals of any kind. Allergies."

"It scratched your friend, who dresses up like Catwoman, which I found to be ironic. Would've clawed me, too, if she hadn't warned me in advance. And I think one of the uniforms had to get a tetanus shot."

"You mean rabies. A rabies shot."

"No, tetanus," she repeated, more emphatic the second time. "While he was trying to get away from the cat, he took a header down the stairs and sliced his arm on a rusty nail. I'm telling you, the crime scene turned into sheer chaos. There's something else . . . did your old boss wear henna tattoos?"

"Celia wouldn't hire a girl with tattoos. She thought they looked trashy."

"Bully for Celia," Kris mumbled uncharitably.

"Hey—Celia had standards." Said defensively.

"Sure she did. A madam with a golden heart."

"Now look who's speaking ill of the dead. You're no better than Hamilton when you act that way."

"You're right. I'm better than that." Sufficiently cowed, Kris said, "There were henna tattoos on her torso and breasts. With weird symbols that looked Celtic—I'm having that checked out by a ritualistic crimes expert—and a poem." She fisted her pants pocket and removed a piece of paper, then un-quartered it and held it out for Dakota to inspect. "I sketched it. See what you can make of this . . ."

It took a moment to process the swirls and curlicues in the pattern. Because of Kris's penmanship, it was hard to tell where the drawing ended, and the disturbing hen-scratch began.

Impatient, Kris pointed at the crude sketch. "Look at this. See what it says?" Without waiting for an answer, she repeated the written script. " *'Can you hear me? Are you sure you're there alone?'* I couldn't make out the rest of the words because I would've had to move her breasts, and the ME didn't want the corpse touched. So I can't be sure what our psycho wrote until I get copies of their pictures."

Dakota had no idea what it all meant. "Where'd Cyn find her?"

"Room two. You remember," Kris oozed sarcasm, "the one with the director's chairs, the old desk from the set of that old TV series, 'Dynasty,' and the casting couch?"

Once again, Dakota felt the weight of Kris's judgment. She could almost hear her screaming *How many times did you use that room? How many men did you audition for?*

Dakota swallowed the golf-ball lump building up in her throat. "After you left the house this morning, some guy showed up in our cactus garden. Sprang up out of nowhere like a giant-sized gnome. Said his name was Travis Creeley. I think you should check him out. Might be the guy Celia warned me about."

"What'd he look like?"

"Creepy."

"What kind of build? Tall? Short? Stocky?"

"Big enough to hunt grizzly bears with a toothpick. He had shoulders like a water buffalo. And a back wide enough for a saddle." She ran down a detailed description of Creeley, as well as a thumbnail sketch of his wish list. "I told him to call the cops."

Kris gave an almost imperceptible nod. "Don't have anything to do with him."

"Don't worry."

The phone bleated.

"I'll get it. Fill your plate." Dakota stuck her nose into the steam coming off the chili. "I didn't fix your favorites for nothing." She took a quick gulp of wine and pushed her chair back from the table. Taking long strides, she reached the cordless before the answering machine engaged. "Runaway Investigations, Dakota Jones."

"D. Jones. Dakota. Nice name. How long have you had it?"

Chills scrambled up her arms.

Travis Creeley.

"What do you want?" She darted Kris a look. Visibly stiffening, Kris rested her fork against her plate.

"I want you to take my daughter's case." Heavy breaths rasped in her ear.

"No. I have a full schedule. Like I told you, go to the police."

"The police can't help me. Only you can help me, Dakota. Will you help me?"

She hung up the phone and tapped in the number on the Caller-ID display to block it.

"Who was that?" Kris picked up a half-eaten tamale and held it inches from her lips.

"Nobody."

Not true.

Now Dakota wondered if Creeley *had* been an ex-client. She couldn't remember everyone she'd had sex with. This wouldn't be the first time a guy turned stalker on an escort.

Not the first time at all.

Chapter Four

Friday morning, Dakota touched a fingertip to Kris's nose. "Wake up Sleeping Beauty."

"Sleeping Ugly, more like." Kris groaned and rolled away, taking the covers with her.

"It's the biggest shopping day of the year. If we get to the opening ceremony at the new mall early enough, I can buy you a gift." When Kris didn't respond, Dakota crawled over her and shimmied up face to face. "Don't you want to know what I'm getting you?"

"No."

"Sure you do. Ask me."

Kris blinked against the sunlight slanting through the shutters. "Okay. What?"

"Crotchless panties." She vogued a sultry smile. "And something else. A surprise. I predict you'll love it."

Kris pulled the covers over her head and mumbled something unintelligible but vaguely threatening into the sheets. Then she raised her voice. "Why would you do that? You know I don't wear crotchless panties."

"No, but I do."

Kris tossed back the down comforter. "Gee, Dee, you sure know how to deliver a wake-up call. Now I'll be thinking about that instead of what the dignitaries are saying."

Dakota headed for the bathroom. "I don't understand why we even have to attend," she called over her shoulder. "Can't we just skip the whole thing and catch a movie?"

Kris pushed herself up on one elbow and rubbed her eyes. "The Chief told me to go." She trapped a yawn into her sleeve.

"Why didn't you tell him you had plans?"

"I did. He suggested I might rethink them if I ever wanted another promotion . . ."

Dakota drowned out the rest of Kris's explanation with running water and a toothbrush.

Fifteen minutes before the ribbon-cutting ceremony, they arrived at the new mall in Dakota's sapphire blue Jag. A large crowd had formed around a temporary stage out in the parking lot. Phoenix's lame-duck mayor, Jane Roman, along with Mayor-elect David Wilson stood near Police Chief Donald P. Forster, acting like the best of friends—which all but the politically uninformed knew they were not.

A handful of concession stands dotted the parking lot. With a "Be right back," Kris took off toward one with the shortest line.

Dakota felt the beginnings of a smirk angling up one side of her face. The mayor-elect might serve one term in office—after that, he'd be the lame duck, even if she had to personally bankroll his opponent.

Radiant in her tailored red suit, Mayor Roman looked as if she'd stepped out of a Vogue advertorial. Her short, flattering coif didn't have a hair out of place; her carefully made up face had just the right amount of blush. At five-feet-four inches in heels, she could've been easily dwarfed by the Mayor-elect or the Chief of Police, but Mayor Jane, as Dakota liked to think of her, was a native of Phoenix and a force to be reckoned with.

On the other hand, David Wilson, a tall, impeccably dressed black transplant from Baltimore, had run on a platform that included cleaning up vice crimes and gang violence; Mayor Jane had campaigned on her own record—a history which included taking a tough stance against illegal aliens, the Mexican drug cartel, and organized crime. Apparently, on election day, her constituents thought she told them to go "boat," not "vote", and they all left town for a regatta at Lake Mead.

Dakota shivered. It'd take a chainsaw to cut the tension.

Kris returned with a soft drink in each hand.

The unexpected shrill of an amplifier cut the air, forcing the crowd to plug their ears with their fingers. A man adjusted the volume after a mic assessment, *Testing one-two-three*, and the Mayor took her seat between Bible-thumpers Wilson and Forster. When mall security arrived with the owner and CEO, the program got underway.

Dakota gave the crowd a casual scan. She drew in a sharp intake of air and grabbed Kris's arm. She could've sworn she'd spotted Travis Creeley, and tightened her grip. "He's here."

"Who?"

"Creeley."

On instinct, Kris craned her neck to look—a ridiculous move, Dakota thought, since she had no idea what Creeley looked like.

Dakota pointed at the horizon. "He's wearing a hat." An equally ridiculous observation, she realized, since half of the men had their heads covered with ball caps, fedoras, and the occasional Stetson. "Follow me."

She grabbed Kris's hand and tugged, but her partner shook free. "Not in public, Dee." The detective's eyes cut to the platform—*the Chief.*

Mayor-elect Wilson had assumed his place on the dais. He pulled the mic out of its sleeve and launched into a rip-roaring speech about how to clean up the city. Dakota forged through the throng of people. When she looked over her shoulder to gauge Kris's reaction to Wilson's comments, she'd lost her in the swell of the crowd. She didn't glimpse the detective again until a round of applause made her turn. With the shindig obviously concluded, Kris ascended the stairs. Mayor Jane met her halfway down, and the two descended the steps huddled in conversation.

A childlike yip cut the air, reminding Dakota of the anguished cry of a coyote pup. But the only "coyotes" roaming around Phoenix were of the human variety from Mexico who smuggled other humans across the United States border for money. Dakota jerked her head in the direction of the screech.

Across the parking lot, a tow-headed girl struggled with a man in a ball cap and heavy jacket.

Not cold enough for a coat like that.

Can't see his face.

The man pulled the child by the wrist toward a car, a vintage '90s, Chevy Lumina with missing molding on the left passenger door.

Intuition snared her in its grip. Dakota dropped her soda and sprinted toward the girl. "Hey—what're you doing?" she cried. To the girl, she yelled, "Do you know him?"

The man had a vice-grip on the youngster. No amount of thrashing could free her from his grasp.

"I want my Mommy!"

"Let her go," Dakota shouted.

A look of sheer panic settled over his face. She broke into a dead run. He unhanded his quarry and jumped into the Lumina. Without thinking, Dakota threw herself at the car. She landed with a thud and sprawled across the hood. Tires screamed against the pavement. As she hung on for dear life, muted screams of "Mommy, Mommy, Mommy," echoed in her ears.

The kid disappeared into the crowd as the man powered down the driver's window. Having an angry woman plastered against the window had apparently foiled his plan and blocked his view. When he stuck his head through the opening, Dakota belted him with her fist. Fury reddened his eyes. Wheels rolling, he fended her off with a clumsy swat. She made a desperate claw at his face, raking her talons across cheek to chin. The car rammed into hard, unyielding metal—a light pole—and Dakota instantly lost her grip. With the angry crunch of metal-on-metal still ringing between her ears, she slid off the hood and tasted the asphalt.

Before she could pull in a deep breath and shake off the effects of her heroism, Dakota came face-to-feet with a couple of uniforms. Each grabbed an arm and hoisted her upright. A third officer and two security guards trained their weapons on the driver. He raised his hands in surrender as Phoenix police swooped in and got him in a takedown.

Reporters covering the grand opening jogged over with cameras rolling. Kris rushed up, her wide eyes wild with concern.

"Well, I'll be damned." A sneer worked its way up the side of one officer's face. "If it isn't Phoenix's richest lobby Lizzie. How's it going, Pussy Galore? Long time no see."

Oh, no.

It was bound to happen, running into a client. But this one liked to role play. Had tried out his latest Judo moves on her while trying to seduce her into switching teams. As the beat cop in Celia St. Claire's district, the chintzy bastard had worked a sweet deal for himself that allowed the proprietor of Fantasy Escorts Unlimited to fly under the radar and stay in business. Cheapskate never paid her for her time, and their liaisons turned into borderline rapes. It was all she could do to suffer through their play sessions.

A drop of sweat slid down the small of Dakota's back and into her panties. She locked eyes with Kris. Her lover's jaw went taut, and she turned away.

Curious bystanders flocked to the scene.

"Move along," Kris flashed her badge. "Show's over." When nobody moved, she walked toward the lookie-loos, pushing the air in a sideways motion, menacing them with her presence. Rubber-neckers scattered.

Dakota dusted herself off.

Mayor Jane seemed to materialize out of the ether, popping up in front of her like a freshly-picked pepper.

Instead of asking Dakota if she was all right, she pinched the sleeve of the loudmouth officer. "You like your job?" she asked sweetly.

"Beg your pardon?" He blinked, either unaware or too stupid to realize where this was headed.

She flashed a grin at the cameras. As if communing with an old chum, getting ready to mug for a photo op, she linked arms with him and spoke out of the side of her mouth. "I asked if you liked your job."

"Yes, ma'am."

"Apologize." She looked up with the calm, beseeching expression of a woman who'd just asked her fiancé if he'd spring for the larger of two diamond solitaires.

"Do what?" Eyes bulged in their sockets like two champagne corks ready to pop.

"Apologize to Ms. Jones. Say, 'I'm sorry, Ms. Jones, I made a terrible mistake. I didn't recognize you.' Say it."

He inclined his head toward Dakota. "I didn't recognize—"

"No-no," she interrupted, "say you're sorry. That you made a mistake. You *did* make a mistake, right?" It was a rhetorical question. "You bet your ass you did. Because *I'm* not accustomed to making mistakes. I *fix* them. Or *fire* them. Now try again."

"I apologize," he said grudgingly.

"No-no. You're *sorry*. Sorry-sorry-sorry. You're a sorry officer. *Very. Sorry.* Let's try it again, shall we?" Said with the most engaging of smiles.

He stammered out a grudging apology, with Mayor Roman coaching him until he got it right. She scrutinized his nametag and addressed him in a soft, ladylike voice. "If I ever hear you speak to Ms. Jones that way again, you'll be pulling that marksmanship pin out of your ass. Got it?"

"With bells on." He suddenly remembered he had something better to do, and churned up dust getting back to his assignment, while his partner skulked off in his wake.

For all anyone else knew, the Mayor had invited him out for beer and barbeque.

Mayor Jane linked arms with Dakota. "Hello, dear. So nice to see you here on the biggest shopping day of the year." She abruptly halted the conversation to exchange pleasantries with several people lingering in the area—*"Love the shoes, dearie. Think they'd look as good on me as they do on you?" "What a cute little baby; she certainly favors you, doesn't she?" "Have you finished your Christmas shopping?"* and *"I hope Santa Claus stops by the mall today,"*—before returning her attention to Dakota. "Of course, I'd prefer to think you and your friend Kristina came out to support me, seeing that the sharks are circling the water, and all." They strolled several yards away from the arrest scene before stopping, and Mayor Roman appealed to Dakota in earnest. "How've you been, Dee? Everything okay? How's business at Runaway Investigations?"

"Good. Everything's great." She shot Kris a wicked glare. Instead of shame for not rushing to defend her from the rogue cop, Kris arched an eyebrow that translated, *Just how well do you two know each other?*

Photographers swarmed the celebrities, clamoring for a photo op.

"You seem uncomfortable, Dee. Oh, come on, dear, why so glum? Don't pout. Give the people what they want." The mayor winked. "Everyone loves a hero."

While Kris looked on, bewildered, Dakota and Mayor Jane mugged for the cameras.

Chapter Five

Around seven o'clock that evening, after charred chicken remnants were scraped off the barbeque and the dishes had been cleared; after leftover grilled poultry was stored in a little plastic tub and tucked away in the refrigerator, the phone rang.

Business might be dead at Fantasy Escorts Unlimited, but at Runaway Investigations, it boomed.

Dakota stuck her head inside the Jack-and-Jill bathroom, a restful hideaway with a travertine marble shower, complete with waterfall, and a spa tub. She found Kris reclined in a bubble bath with cucumber slices over each eye and a half-empty wine bottle balanced on the rim of the tub. U-2 blared over expensive recessed speakers, keeping the lip-syncing detective blissfully ignorant of the intrusion.

"I'm leaving." Dakota fingered her keys until she flipped to the one for the Jag.

"For good?" Kris came halfway out of the water. Cucumbers dropped into the suds, floating to the surface like gill-green smiley faces in goblet full of Alka Seltzer.

"The Spencers—our neighbors two streets over—called about their missing daughter. I'm heading over to talk to them. Don't wait up."

"Dee, stop." Kris stood as hydro-jets continued to churn bath water into foam. She grabbed a towel from the side of the tub and unfurled it. Bubbles melted off her flesh, bursting in all the right places.

Dakota inwardly winced. It had been three days since she'd experienced the strength of those thighs. A low-voltage current ran through her body.

Those Jujitsu classes paid off. My girlfriend ought to be illegal in every state but Nevada.

"About what happened this morning," Kris said, "I never meant to hurt you."

"You never do." Dakota turned to leave but Kris switched off the stereo. "Anyway, I'm off to see what the Spencers need. If that guy Creeley calls again, tell him you'll send a couple of goons to break his thumbs—oh, I completely forgot—" she thunked her forehead with the heel of her palm "—you're out of the *Let's-take-up-for-Dee* business."

"You're right. I have no excuse. I should've taken up for you. But defending you in public exacts a high price. Can you honestly say I'd be more attractive to you if I were lounging around the house, unemployed? Because that's the price, Dee. You know how much I love my job. It'd kill me to lose it."

She stepped out of the tub and padded across the cheetah-print cowhide rug. Backed Dakota against a mirrored wall and slipped her arms around her waist.

"It won't always be like this, Dee," Kris said, her warm breath caressing; her nose nuzzling the nape of Dakota's long, graceful neck. "I promise."

Jake and Lorraine Spencer opened the door to their daughter's bedroom, flipped on the light switch, and stepped aside long enough to let Dakota inside.

"What the . . .?" Wide-eyed, the rest of the words slid back down Dakota's throat. She inventoried the room in a glance. After the parents' description of the missing youth, she'd expected to enter a condemned area. But the girl's room—while decidedly different than what she'd anticipated—had been well-maintained, with the latest in computers and other electronics.

Laura Ann Spencer's sanctuary contrasted starkly with the rest of the house. Unlike the Spencer's dining room, it was free from frescoed walls adorned with wrought iron candelabra crosses, and replicas of missions made of clay on the marble buffet. Instead of a Bible on the bedside table, like the one opened for display on a wooden stand in the Spencer's living room, Laura Ann's reading material leaned toward the writings of Dante and Edgar Allen Poe.

The walls and ceiling had been painted black; the bedcovers were black, and a large black area rug covered most of the parquet floor tiles. The room had all of the gloom and despair of Hell without enjoying all the fun experiences it took to get there.

With a fluff of short blonde curls haloing her head, Lorraine Spencer stopped short of crossing the threshold. She appeared quite the angel, in her gauzy gold silk hostess slacks and matching blouse, poised at the precipice of iniquity.

"Laura Ann got involved in the Goth movement about six months ago. At first, we tolerated it as normal teen rebellion. But she grew more sullen and morose as time went on. The day after her fifteenth birthday, she took off like a bat." The girl's mother heaved a weighty sigh.

"I still don't understand why she ran away," she went on, picking at her manicured nails until the cuticles were bloody. "We threw her a big party at the Country Club the night before. Rented the grand ballroom and invited all our friends—nice people. Upstanding citizens whose kids Laura Ann grew up with. Kids who go to the right schools. I spent twelve thousand dollars on that damned dress—" veins corded in her slim neck "—let me show you." She crossed the threshold with purpose in her step. Strutted to the closet and yanked open the door to reveal a ballooning white silk masterpiece befitting a debutante. Or a bride. Or a giant marshmallow-shaped balloon for the Macy's Thanksgiving Day Parade.

"Eleven hundred ninety-eight bugle beads sewn across the bust line. Eleven ninety-eight." Her voice corkscrewed upward. "Know how I know that?" Her eyes glinted. "I counted them, didn't I, Jake?"

Note the gloomy nod from the quiet man.

Laura Ann's mother fisted a wad of skirt and shook it. "That's right. I counted them. And do you know why? *Do you?*"

Time for a head bob.

"You're damned right," she snarled, fist on hip. "Because after my daughter left, I counted them twice to keep from going stir crazy."

Jake Spencer slid Dakota a sidelong glance. "She did count them." His gaze flickered to his wife. "Sat in the great room, peeled back the plastic dry-cleaner's bag and counted them one by one."

"You ask me," Lorraine Spencer went on, "the designer owes

me two bugle beads. At ten dollars a bead, he gypped me." She unhanded the dress. It unfurled with a nasty crease. "I'm sorry." The woman wilted like a hothouse flower. "You didn't need to hear that." Her hand went to her small bosom, as if checking for a heartbeat. "It's just that I get so angry when I think about Laura Ann's grand entrance. We had it all planned out, you see; how she'd enter the ballroom as the orchestra struck up 'There She Is' . . . you remember, the Miss America song?" Her eyes demanded confirmation.

"Right," Dakota said. "I get it. Cute. Like a theme song."

A theme song from Hell, for a kid straddling the fence of alternative lifestyles.

Lorraine Spencer's face flamed. "She popped in right on cue. But not in this dress." Her eyes misted. "Know what she was wearing? Do you know? *Do you?* Oh, come on, Ms. Jones, let's not stand on ceremony. You don't need to adhere to the social graces of pretense. You've lived in this community long enough to hear the talk, right? So you probably already know."

Big headshake.

"Then let me tell you."

The woman glided toward Dakota until she stood inches away.

"Black, steel-toed, lace-up boots. Black Mafia-looking overcoat. Black eye pencil smudging her eyes and a paper-white face, like she'd been dead a year. With a big black teardrop drawn on one cheek with eye liner. And that doesn't even begin to cover it—" she fanned her palms in a no-motion "—oh, no, not by a long shot."

"Lorraine, settle down. No sense working yourself into a tizzy." He turned to Dakota. "She's upset, as you might imagine. We both are." Jake Spencer played the part of the supportive husband but Dakota had her doubts. The year before, in Heaven's Urn, rumors buzzed of infidelity.

Lorraine Spencer talked over him. "Settle down? You want me to settle down? This is *your* fault, Jake." She whirled on Dakota. "She wore melted-on, black leather hot pants, and a black bustier with holes cut out. At first, I thought it was a bad joke. That the *'reveal'* was part of the garment. But no. Her nipples showed through, and she'd gotten them pierced with silver hoops. She sauntered in wearing fishnet thigh-highs rolled down just above the knees. Two thugs escorted her—absolute gutter trash. My daughter said, 'Hello everyone. Glad you could make it. Eat, drink, and be merry. For tomorrow's just plain fucked-up.' " The distraught mother burst into tears. "Is that enough background for you? She embarrassed the hell out of us in front of our friends."

"That's true," echoed Laura Ann's father, picking up where his wife left off. "Lorraine fainted in her champagne. By the time we revived her, our daughter yelled, 'You can kiss my lily-white ass, Daddy. You and all your corporate bullshit . . . and you, Mom, you're nothing but his fucking puppet." She shot us the finger, pivoted around and stomped right back out, leaving a roomful of people, slack-jawed, and clutching bosoms."

Dakota picked up a magazine, *Blue Blood,* and thumbed through it looking for dog-eared pages or notations. Nothing.

"I know what you must be thinking," Jake Spencer said. Slight of build, the sandy haired little man adjusted wire-rim glasses against the bridge of his nose. He had all the makings of a computer geek, right down to the vinyl pen protector jutting up from his shirt pocket. If someone didn't know better, they might think he worked as a programmer, trouble-shooting software glitches. And that'd be a mistake: Jake Spencer owned Spen-Soft, Inc.

Meaning he probably paid cash for the sprawling, two-story adobe in Heaven's Urn.

Dakota turned. "What am I thinking, Mr. Spencer?" she said airily.

"Jake. Call us Jake and Lorraine. You're thinking she was into Satanism, violence, white supremacy . . . but she wasn't. Laura Ann got into the Goth movement for the shock effect."

Actually, Dakota didn't think that at all. Still, with all the Celtic trappings, the heavy silver cross and Egyptian Ankh, dog tags with *"Synthetic Darkness"* embossed on them, and Laura Spencer's home address underneath—not to mention the dog collar with spikes lay-ing on her dresser—a really good investigator couldn't turn a blind eye to this pseudo medieval world of dark images.

Dakota traced a finger over the cross. "Was she depressed?"

"She cut herself." Lorraine darted a secretive glance at her hus-band. Dakota suspected she was about to reveal the layers that made up the complex personality of Laura Ann.

"Your daughter was a cutter?"

Jake Spencer's jaw torqued. "That was just to get attention. Lots of kids do it. Like I keep telling my wife, it's experimental. Kids experiment."

"It was a cry for help. She's mentally ill and needs treatment."

Maybe you're both mistaken.

Perhaps she did it to release overwhelming emotional pain.

Dakota selected her words carefully. "The act of cutting's often symbolic." Up went their eyebrows. "Maybe she did it to feel something. Superficial cutting's often an outward manifestation that serves as a release for emotional pain. Cutting allows her emotional wounds to heal."

"Nonsense." Spencer braced his arms. His dubious glint tracked her as she examined the dog collar, turning it over in her hand. "That kid was happy. The black clothes, the hang-dog looks? All for show. She had anything she wanted. We gave her a Mini-Cooper and got her a hardship license before other kids her age got cars and driver's licenses. All she had to do was ask."

"Did you spend much time with her?" Dakota's eyes flickered from husband to wife. Neither made eye contact.

"I probably spent too much time at the Country Club," Lorraine conceded. "But I play competition bridge with my friends, and it wouldn't do to miss. And Jake plays golf," Lorraine added, dodging the look and spreading the blame.

"I see." Dakota let two simple words deliver her disdain. "You said on the telephone that you put up flyers. Where?"

"Around the neighborhood; near her school; in the malls she frequents," said Lorraine.

Dakota replaced the dog collar, swept past the foot of the bed, and picked up a picture frame off the matching night table. The girl in the photo looked nothing like the oil painting hanging above the Spencer's fireplace of the mousy-haired kid with the cherub cheeks, done in the style of Lord Frederick Leighton's "Desdemona." From the chaotically-styled, shocking red clown hair, white face with black vertical lines penciled above and below her eyes and thin; drawn-on eyebrows and black lipstick . . . clear down to her black clothing and buckle boots . . . the young lady in the photograph seemed drenched in angst. And she appeared to have Celtic tattoos encircling her left bicep and right ankle.

Dakota returned the frame to the same spot next to a small black light—a spit-shined outline surrounded by a thin film of dust. "Was Laura Ann having trouble in school?"

Her parents answered in unison.

"Yes." Mom.

"No." Dad.

And, we have a tie game.

Dakota's gaze flickered between them. She decided she liked Laura Ann's mother better. She'd been less argumentative, and her responses seemed more genuine. She settled on Lorraine to get her take on the matter. "Which is it?"

"Laura Ann developed early. Kids—boys especially—picked on her because of it. After a while, she quit trying."

"Nonsense. Laura Ann made decent grades. The teachers liked her."

"No she didn't. And the teachers were scared shitless of her. So were the kids. It's like she had leprosy." Lorraine Spencer's cement exterior cracked. She burst into tears and wept, uncontrollably, into her hands.

"Maybe you need to take a moment," her husband suggested, making this seem optional, like the Nazi party. "Come back when you pull yourself together."

Lorraine Spencer slunk out of the room.

As Dakota glanced around, she barely restrained a sigh. "Mr. Spencer—Jake. If you'd allow me to look through your daughter's belongings . . . if I could go through her stuff, alone . . . maybe I can find something that'll help us find her."

"So you're taking the case?" He did a bobble headed head bob, as if he'd already convinced himself she'd do it.

"I'll let you know once I'm through nosing around."

"Have at it." He pulled the door shut, closing himself off from view.

Dakota toggled the black light and watched the tube glow purple. She went for the overhead light switch and flipped it off. Immediately, a picture took shape on the ceiling. She slipped out of her flats and climbed onto the missing girl's bed. Lay on her back with her face skyward and studied the intricate artwork that had previously remained invisible.

Even the parents probably didn't realize it was there.

The face of despair looked down upon her—an eerie self portrait of Laura Ann Spencer; or maybe this was Synthetic Darkness, Laura Ann's alter-ego—with the same vertical lines and penciled-on brows as the photograph. Thin, gossamer threads of a spider web had been stenciled across her head, intertwined with curly-cues. Faeries and gargoyles acted as sentinels in each corner. At first, nothing leapt out at her. It seemed little more than a strange drawing made by a disturbed young girl. Then, Dakota closed her eyes for a few seconds, and listened to the cadence of her own breaths. When she opened her lids, the mirage-like curlicues incorporated into the spider web that she'd previously mistaken for decorative touches, now formed words: *Can you hear me? Am I getting through to you?*

An internal switch flicked on inside her.

Where'd she heard that phrase before?

She closed her eyes tight.

Think, Dee, think.

Her carefully-shadowed lids snapped open like roller shades. She sat bolt upright. Chills swarmed over her body.

Can you hear me?

Those words showed up tattooed on Celia St. Claire's breasts.

Unexpectedly, the door snapped open. Jake and Lorraine Spencer stood in the opening, back-lit by the incandescent glow of the hall lights.

"So will you take the case, or not?" he asked.

Dakota slung her legs over the side of the bed and slipped into her shoes.

"I'll take it," she said. "But you may not like what I find out."

Several hours later, Dakota searched the computer, examining the information streaming across the screen. While buffing up on the Goth subculture, she checked out a nude photo of the missing girl that popped up on SinisterSisters, a Phoenix-based website linked with Alterna-porn.

The photo suggested Laura Ann might be confused about her sexuality. The lens of the camera certainly captured the missing girl in the most compromising of positions, with a rough-looking lesbian caught simulating sex on Laura Ann with a large cross.

It was impossible to tell, from the sexually explicit picture, whether Laura Ann had been a willing participant. From the hungry look in her eyes, she certainly didn't appear to be doped-up on drugs or alcohol.

Then again, willingness be damned, the missing girl was a minor, and the State of Arizona had tough laws against child pornography.

But the most unnerving discovery came around midnight when Dakota stumbled on a Goth *Personals* website. A photo posted of Laura Ann Spencer engaged in another sexual liaison revealed a familiar face.

Fiona McHugh—one of Celia's girls, who took on the comic book persona of Spiderman's girlfriend.

Another employee of Fantasy Escorts Unlimited.

Chapter Six

Since the Spencers last saw their daughter when they dropped her off in front of the local coffee shop, Jitterjava, Dakota began her Saturday morning investigation by flashing the girl's photograph at the employees and customers. Shoe-horned into a pair of high heels, and wearing a muted olive green angora pullover and matching wool knit pencil skirt that caused her eye color to deepen, she ordered a mocha latte, took the café's copy of *The Tribune* off an unoccupied table, and seated herself in the corner where she could scan for kids Laura Spencer's age. An older man in his fifties seated himself nearby. When she crossed her legs and the hem of her skirt rode up her thigh, she caught him sneaking a peak. His eyes took on a speculative gleam. When he realized she'd noticed him staring, his face cracked into a grin and he sheepishly looked away.

During lulls in activity, she scoured the front-page follow-up story on Celia St. Claire's death that suggested the madam had ties to the Mafia. Dakota did a heavy eye roll. She skipped to a comment attributed to Mayor-elect Wilson. According to the Baltimore transplant, the victim's "unfortunate lifestyle led to her death."

And why quote that pompous idiot, a newcomer who'd probably never even met Celia?

A Goth couple with matching purple hair cuts paused outside the glass doors. The male stood over a cigarette urn, sculpting the last of his roll-up into a point. A long exhale of smoke trailed them inside as they strolled, arms linked, up to the counter. They wore matching black trench coats, had lightened their faces with white foundation, and rimmed their eyes heavy with dark liner. Dakota slapped the newspaper closed. She waited until they paid for their cups of espresso, and settled in at a table, before she approached them.

"Excuse me, have you seen this girl?" She flashed the latest school photo Laura Ann Spencer's parents had given her.

They spoke in stereo.

The young man said, "No."

The girl said, "Synthetic Darkness. What a slitch."

Slutty bitch. The term had popped up in the previous night's Internet search while mining the information highway to Goth subculture.

The girl's companion shot her a wicked glare. She back-peddled. "We haven't seen her."

"She's not in trouble," Dakota slid the photo back into her purse. "I'm a private investigator, hired by a law firm that specializes in probate."

No response.

Hello—anybody home?

"Death cases."

They stared at her through a couple of salamander eye-blinks.

"People die?" she prompted. "Their estates go through probate?" She searched for signs of intelligence, and got dead fish looks for her trouble.

"Laura Ann—the girl you know as Synthetic Darkness—was named as a beneficiary in a client's will. She stands to inherit a lot of money."

"Like she needs it. Old man climbed the scrotum-pole and got the green, that's wikkid."

Dakota cocked an eyebrow. A smug smile settled over his pale face. He had to know she didn't understand a damned thing he just said.

The punk's eyes glinted. "What's the name of the law firm?"

Dakota dropped her purse. Bent over to pick it up in an attempt to flash the guy some cleavage and buy time. She concocted a legal firm and delivered it with mock innocence.

"Chase, Hsu, Fleesim and Settle. I do contract work for Mr. Hsu. You've probably heard of him . . . maybe you caught his late night TV ads? . . . Wears a funny little hat and big tortoiseshell glasses?"

What the hell? At least she didn't say she worked for Dewey, Cheatham and Howe.

The girl gave an almost imperceptible nod.

"Well, look, if you happen to see Synthetic Darkness would you call me? We just want to distribute the money. Might even be a reward in it for you. Never can tell." She couldn't very well give them business cards for Runaway Investigations, so she tore a sheet from a notepad, and jotted down both private and cell numbers for each of them. In a gesture of friendship, Dakota stuck out her hand. "Can I get your names?"

"Cryptkeeper." The boy extended his fingers in a palsied shake.

"Fractured Soul." The girl had the grip of beached marine life. "Good hunting."

"Scary Christmas and a crappy New Year to you." Her companion, again, with a blank, scary expression.

She didn't expect to hear from them again.

After finishing the news article on Celia St. Claire, Dakota purchased a snack. Once she had a muffin and her Sudoku book in front of her, she felt tied off to a safety line.

When a second wave of Goths drifted into the coffee shop, Dakota launched into a pre-rehearsed speech. The canned spiel fell on deaf ears, but the sight of Laura Ann Spencer's photo brought flickers of recognition to their eyes. Wordlessly, they fixed her with intentionally blank looks that screamed *Goth wall of silence*, ordered their coffee and turned their backs to her in a collective shift. After an hour of dead-ends, she decided on a different strategy—the morgue.

To eliminate the possibility that the runaway might be logged in as "Jane Doe," laying in a cooler with a wad of cotton stuck up her rectum and a tag on her toe, Dakota headed for the ME's Office for an impromptu meeting with leading forensic pathologist, Dr. Gus Stone.

She wheeled the Jag into a parking spot allocated for visitors, and noticed Kris's patrol car slotted into a reserved space near the front door.

In a way, the prospect of bumping into Kris filled her with butterflies. She wanted to run into her, casually, in a public place where protocol dictated they'd have to behave themselves. Especially since Kris ended up alone in their King-sized bed the previous night. It wasn't that Dakota didn't want to sleep with her; but after returning from the Spencers, and spending hours surfing the Internet looking for Synthetic Darkness, she'd ended up crashing in the guest bedroom.

She barked out a chuckle, remembering how curiosity prodded her into learning how Laura Ann Spencer settled on a name like Synthetic Darkness. When she stumbled across a website that translated ordinary names into Goth, she entered Laura Ann Spencer into the search bar.

Synthetic Darkness popped up on the screen.

For grins, she ran Kris Carson through the site's search engine. The result evoked an extended horselaugh that caused her to topple out of her chair and roll on the floor, peddling her feet like a roach drenched in insecticide.

Demented Whore.

She pulled herself upright and resumed her search. On impulse, fingers moved over the keyboard. She typed Dakota Jones and tapped the *enter* key.

Homicidal Maniac.

Chilling. As if they'd inadvertently dashed into each other's phone booths and stumbled out with their Goth capes on and their identities reversed.

Dakota popped open the car door and slung out a leg. Admired her pedicure through peep-toe Ferragamos and wondered if Gus Stone would even talk to her. Caught her reflection in the side mirror and thought, *Why wouldn't he?*

After all, she'd brought along a generic release signed by the Spencers. A formality, she'd hinted, that could be used to acquire Laura Ann's school and medical records. There'd been no mention of the morgue. Or dental records, in the event a skeletonized body turned up in the desert . . .

She pressed the remote and the door locks snapped shut with a chirp.

"Back in a jiffy, Innocence Lost," she said, testing the sound of sapphire blue Jag's new Goth name on her lips. By the time she found Synthetic Darkness, everyone she'd ever known would have their own Goth identity. Kinda fun.

Dakota took quick strides, entering through the glass doors as if she'd not only glided into a posh, Beverly Hills boutique, but actually owned it.

The receptionist's plastic nameplate read "Ursula Fielder" and she assumed this mousy girl with the big eyeglasses, and a magazine flattened-open to the latest *How to Get a Man . . . and Keep Him,* article was Ursula.

"Is Gus in?"

"We're closed to the public on weekends."

"I understand. Only I'm not the public."

"Do you have an appointment with Dr. Stone?"

"Actually, no." Dakota tried on the *Shy Di* expression that had made the late Princess Diana such a hit with the press. When Ursula furrowed her brow in confusion, Dakota said, "Gus and I are old friends." Then she winked.

Ursula dog-eared one corner of the magazine and pushed back from the desk. "I'll see if he's available."

"Don't trouble yourself." Dakota's eyes cut to the Employees Only door. "I'll see myself in."

"I'm sorry—what'd you say your name was?"

"I didn't. Gus prefers to keep me a secret."

Ursula blinked. She raised a limp hand and pointed. "He's in the back."

Dakota showed herself in. She glanced around to vector her location and spied Dr. Gus Stone's name stenciled on one of the doors.

A light knuckle-tap earned her a hearty, "Come in."

She opened the door and came face to face with Kris and Hamilton Stark, standing behind two client chairs as if they were about to leave. Dakota recognized Dr. Gus Stone, a portly man in his sixties, with a sprig of a comb-over, from photographs in the Trib. He stood next to a massive desk, stubbing out the last of his cigar with one hand while clutching a steaming mug of coffee in the other.

"Nasty habit," he said. "Don't tell anybody. My girl Ursula thinks I quit. If she comes in here and sniffs the air, I remind her I can't do anything about it—that the odor's seeped into the walls."

Kris's jaw went slack. Her eyes bulged. "What're *you* doing here?"

"I was about to ask you the same thing." Dakota glanced past Kris, to her partner. "Hello, Hamilton, we've never formally met but I feel like I know you." This felt like being introduced to the devil.

It didn't seem sporting to demonize someone she'd never spoken to before, but she was pretty sure he was giving off sulphur emissions, and that it wasn't her imagination running hog wild. "I'm Dakota Jones. Kris and I are . . ." She looked to Kris to finish her sentence.

"Acquaintances," blurted the detective. Slitted eyes flung darts. "We've worked on some kid cases together. Ms. Jones owns Runaway Investigations."

Inwardly, Dakota seethed. The muffin she'd eaten at Jitterjava lay trapped in her colon like spackle.

She turned to Dr. Stone, who wore the stupefied look of a cow at a rendering plant. She reached out, and his meaty hand went reflexively to hers. "And you're the hunky and distinguished Dr. Stone."

Done with the brusque handshake, she laid it on thick. "I recognize you from your pictures in the Trib. And let me just say how much I revere you. You're the smartest, most knowledgeable, and possibly one of the handsomest—" never mind the few eyebrow hairs that broke rank with the others "—forensic pathologists I've ever had the pleasure to meet. And believe me—" her eyes slewed over to Kris, and not in a good way "—I've had plenty of dealings with you fellows."

Dr. Stone set the coffee cup on his blotter and stared through a stub of gray eyelashes. If the ME appeared zombiefied by the intrusion, Hamilton Stark acted snake-bit.

Kris squared her shoulders. Assumed a dignified posture and addressed Dakota in an authoritative voice. "Pardon me, could I see you for a moment?" She jutted her chin toward the door.

"Certainly," Dakota said with put-on sweetness. "But I sure don't remember us working any kid cases." She wagged her finger in a no-motion. "But, I have to admit, there's something vaguely familiar about you." She bounced the heel of her palm against her forehead in mock realization. "Now I remember. We were at the same café." Her eyes sliced over to Hamilton. "You were there, too."

Kris's demeanor went frosty. She took two strides and gripped her arm. "Excuse us," she announced to the room at large, then turned Dakota into her own personal puppet by putting her in a "come along"—a police "persuader" technique normally reserved for budging uncooperative arrestees by attacking a nerve pressure point and eliminating the appearance of using excessive force. The surface pressure control tactic Kris picked got Dakota out of the room in a hurry.

"Ow, ow, ow—did anybody ever tell you your fingers are like C-clamps?

Kris took the developing argument into the ladies restroom, trotting Dakota across the marble floor with her shoes echoing like friendly fire. "What do you think you're doing?"

The odor of disinfectant stung Dakota's nostrils. She considered Kris through the bathroom mirror while re-applying lipstick to her full, provocative lips. "I've had a chance to observe you and there are a couple of things—" she was being polite "—you need to work on."

Kris's mouth opened and closed like a catfish. Her voice pitched to incredulity. "*Me*? Things *I* need to work on? Have you taken leave of your senses?"

"This is a very unbecoming side of you. Why all the fuss? Why so hostile?"

"Hostile?" Desperation resonated in Kris's tone and pitch. Her face turned as pink as the threads in her Tartan plaid shirt. "You don't know the first thing about hostile. Try hostile work environment. The word's out about us being lovers and I'm catching flack at the PD."

"What kind of flack?"

Kris's eyes welled. "I walked in at shift change and overheard some of the guys talking about me. Apparently, I'm a lesbian, devil worshipper, and alcoholic. I didn't know my life was all that fascinating. Then it dawned on me that the peculiar, outlandish and ignorant hick family my co-workers always joke about is my family."

"Wait—when did you become a devil worshipper?"

"Focus, will you? I'm trying to get you to understand the kind of problems I have to deal with at work. One of the guys was talking about some senile old biddy who kept calling the police to report seeing a man in the neighbor's yard staring at her through the bedroom window. She insisted it was the person who killed Celia St. Claire. Ten minutes later, he was still there. She freaked out and called the police again. The creeper turned out to be the neighbor's new marble David statue. The old biddy turned out to be my granny.

Kris looked at Dakota, slitty-eyed. "Then, my lieutenant's trying to cram Jesus down my throat—"

"Wait—you never mentioned you had a grandmother?"

"Would you just put a lid on it 'til I finish, for crying out loud?" Tears jeweled her eyes. "Some smartass sent me a subscription to *Spunk Choad*, one of those degrading men's magazines. You know the kind with crotch shots and demeaning, off-color jokes that debase women? The first issue arrived in this morning's mail. It's no longer delivered in a brown paper wrapper, so everyone from the mail clerk to the Chief saw it."

"*Spunk Choad?*" Dakota knew the magazine well. She flashed back on an ugly visual. The first trick she ever turned picked her up at the corner of North Twenty-third and West Northern near the golf club. The john, who had to be at least fifty, paid ten bucks to jerk off on her breasts and have her smear it all over her skin . . . just like the photo in *Spunk Choad*, creased-open and stained, on the front seat of the car. A shudder rippled up her ribcage. "That's pretty rank, gawking at a bunch of navel glazers, spluff-spewing a bunch of snatches . . ."

Kris's eyelids fluttered in astonishment.

Dakota grinned. "It's a Goth immersion thing. I figure if I have to go undercover to find Laura Ann Spencer, I might as well learn the lingo."

"You're getting weird."

"Just doing my homework. When in Rome . . ."

"It's changing your personality."

"Not as bizarre as you've been acting ever since you set foot in Celia's place."

Kris cut her eyes to the wall, and back. "What's a *navel glazer?*" She scrunched her nose. "Like I can't believe I'm asking that question because I'm not sure I really want to know." Revulsion dulled her brown eyes. "And what the hell's *spluff?*"

"Navel glazing's when you, oh, say . . . take matters into your own hands. Don't look at me that way; I'm trying to be delicate here. Spluff's what the spank monkey roars out."

"Aren't you taking this Goth thing a bit too far?"

"Just educating myself, that's all." Dakota turned pensive. "I like the glamorously sexy men's magazines. I think you should tell the guys to buy you a subscription to one of those. Then you could bring it home and we could read the sex letters in bed." She wiggled her brows to break the tension.

"It isn't funny, Dakota. I have to work with these people." But Kris had to fight the smile tipping up at the corners of her mouth. "Remember when I told you about the convict who asked me if he could have my personal phone number and use it as his one phone call? I told you I was booking-in a suspect, and you didn't even bother to ask me what that was all about."

"Fine. Why were you booking in a suspect? You got a lead on who might've murdered Celia?"

"No. The best kind of day in homicide is uneventful. And this was looking like it might turn out to be a completely normal work-day, other than some guy ran out of a vacuum cleaner store dressed in a gorilla suit while I was plunking quarters down the chute of a soda machine outside a grocery store, and hit me with a foam sword at random."

"Yeah, whaddaya gonna do? Put that monkey in the cage. Is a foam sword a prohibited weapon?"

For a moment, Kris looked at her blank-faced. "It's an assault. You can't go around attacking people with foam swords, or foam fingers, or Nerf bats, or . . . wait—why am I explaining this to you? I had a bad fucking day, and now I'm having another bad fucking day."

Dakota shook her head and cleared the thought away like a feather duster. "What's the old man's take on the harassment?" she asked in a mellifluous voice.

"Hamilton? He thought the *Spunk Choad* subscription was in bad taste. But he's another one who tried the Jesus angle on me."

"You're afraid he won't want to partner with you anymore, aren't you?" Dakota said knowingly.

"No. We're cool with that."

She placed her hands on Kris's shoulders. "Imagine, babe—me and you with a brand new, sexy men's magazine, fresh out of the spa tub, licking bubbles off . . ."

"Stop it. I'm pissed." But words betrayed her when she cupped her hands around Dakota's waist.

Dakota gave her a light peck on the lips. "... writing around on those new black silk sheets, reading naughty stories in the letter section . . ."

"Have you lost your mind? This isn't the time or the place."

"Fine." Which meant not so fine. "You can kiss me now. Guess where?" Caustic humor always made Dakota feel better. She'd never seen Kris so high-strung. The girl was cool, calm, and collected. A veritable robot most of the time when it came to her job.

For no good reason, the detective drew in a sharp intake of air. Shock and surprise lined her face.

"Oh. Good. God." She unhanded Dakota. Took a backward step, as if she'd stepped in something vile, and the stench finally rose to her nostrils. "You're nosing around in Celia St. Claire's case, aren't you?" Hand to mouth. "I should've known I couldn't trust you not to come down here, all gussied up, in some lame attempt to charm information about Celia out of Dr. Stone." Disgust resonated in her tone. "Look at you—those stilettos you've got on could open a can of Spam."

Now it was Dakota's turn to be confused.

"Is that what you think? For your information, I'm here to see if they have any Jane Does that could be the Spencer's daughter. You're jaded and suspicious. And paranoid. Seek help."

"Oh. Well, let that be a lesson—I'm on to you." Kris said somewhat dangerously, in a pathetic attempt to reclaim her dignity. "Don't go messing around in police business."

The damage was done. "You really are screwed up."

Kris focused on something behind Dakota and her expression changed. The door to the ladies room cracked open a sliver, revealing one of Hamilton Stark's eyeballs and half of his face. "What's going on? You're not doing the big nasty in here, are you?"

Dakota felt an enormous temperature spike. She jutted her chin in defiance. "I was just telling her about a gift I bought yesterday. I'm wearing it. Not that it's any of your business."

Kris went pale. "This is the ladies room, Hamilton. Can we have some privacy please?" She turned to Dakota with a pointed look. "Anyway, she was just leaving."

Dakota saw movement beyond the door. "Actually, I'm staying." Wounded, she craned her neck enough to peer beyond Stark's shoulder. Dr. Stone stood directly behind him and to the right, so she gave him a little finger wave. With her hips swaying in a way that made Hamilton Stark do a double-take, she trip-trapped back into Stone's office on a "See you around," to Hamilton Stark; and to Kris, who looked madder than a blow-dried wolverine, she departed with a chipper but insincere, "Take two time capsules and call me in the future."

Chapter Seven

The two Jane Does at the Maricopa County morgue were a Native American, estimated to be in her mid-fifties, and a black woman discovered by hikers in the desert. So if Laura Ann Spencer was dead she didn't end up in this particular cooler.

Gus Stone picked lint off his baby blue sweater vest and studied Dakota through thick-lens wire rims. "You can leave your card at the front desk, Ms. Jones. If we get anyone in who resembles your missing person, we'll call."

"Dr. Stone, you've been around a long time—"

"Not sure I like the sound of that. Makes me feel old." A crooked grin took shape beneath his bushy, gray mustache.

"—Celia St. Claire was an acquaintance of mine." Guilt washed over her and she amended her words. "I misspoke. She was a good friend. A long time ago, I was a runaway; Celia helped me out."

"Understood." He held up a hand, effectively halting her. "If you want to know anything about the case, you'll have to read tomorrow's paper."

"Look." Dakota inched closer to Dr. Stone's desk, a massive mahogany rectangle that looked big enough to bury him in. She fingered a small plaque that doubled as a paperweight and measured her request with great care. If she could see the tattoos on Celia St. Claire, she might be able to tell whether they resembled Laura Ann Spencer's work. "I think we can help each other."

One caterpillar brow shot up in an inverted "V."

"My girl did henna tattoos at fairs and malls. Celtic designs and other weird stuff. I know Celia St. Clair had henna tattoos on her body. Maybe I could help you identify the artist if I could see them."

Dr. Stone's shrewd eyes narrowed. "What good would that do?"

He reached for his mug and headed for the coffee pot. "Want a cup?" She shook her head and watched him pour. "It's one of the few vices I still enjoy. This is Kona-Coconut, my favorite. When I die, I want to be cremated and have my ashes scattered over a Hawaiian coffee plantation."

"I don't think about dying. It's the last thing I want to do."

From his place next to the credenza, the ME studied her like smear on a slide.

"Ms. Jones, you're a smart cookie. You know better than to ask for a peek at Celia St. Claire's file."

But she didn't want the file. She only wanted pictures of the tattoos.

"I've got good people working under me. If there's a message in those tattoos, they'll crack the code." Gus Stone showed her the door.

Dakota rose. Placed her business card prominently on his blotter. "And if they don't, I'll take your call."

As the ME swept her out of his office and into the hall, she discreetly eyed him up. Fixed him with a doe-eyed look, and shamelessly appealed to his vanity. "You know . . . if I may say so, Dr. Stone . . . those pictures in the Trib don't do you justice. You still look like you're forty-five."

Not even fifty-five.

Startled by flattery, the ME flirted back. "Okay, I don't care what they say, you're going to Heaven no matter what you did." He straightened his shoulders. Discreetly smoothed the front of his shirt at the same time he sucked-in his paunch. "I *have* been told I have the body of a forty-five year old . . ."

"Well, don't you worry. I know of a desolate back road where you can drop it off . . ." she teased, and playfully gave the cleft in his chin a gentle finger tap.

Behind the wheel of the Jag, Dakota checked her watch. The memorial service for Celia St. Claire would convene at two o'clock that afternoon, and she saw no reason not to attend. No matter how Kris portrayed her, Celia'd been more than an employer; she'd taken her in. Rescued her from the streets, and groomed her as a high-class escort and fantasy provider. Then came the name change thing. She'd even insisted that Dakota enroll in the University of

Arizona, and paid her tuition. Had Celia St. Claire not intervened when she did, Dakota might've ended up in drug rehab, prison, or dead in a ditch at the hands of a john.

Celia'd been the first to congratulate her on winning the lotto, imparting wisdom that'd changed her life for the better: "You have a chance to get out of the business, Dee. Take it and never look back. And if you see me on the street, walk with your head held high—no need to acknowledge me. It's enough that I know you made it."

She hadn't ignored Celia in life, and she wasn't about to ignore her in death no matter what Kris said.

Besides, Kris wouldn't be home until after five. The service would be long over by then. She made a quick detour to Heaven's Urn and changed out of the olive skirt and sweater, into a tasteful black dress.

There must've been a hundred vehicles at Celia's memorial service. Each opened car door reminded her of Shriners exiting a clown car, since there had to be at least five hundred people who'd shown up to pay their respects. Mostly businessmen dressed in dark suits, subdued ties, sunshades, and hats with the brims adjusted low over their foreheads. But reporters lined up outside the funeral parlor, too, accompanied by photographers with camcorders and zoom lenses trained on the massive wooden doors.

Breezing into the foyer, Dakota did a double-take.

Hamilton Stark.

With a grim set to his jaw.

She came so close their fragrances almost collided. She stood perfectly still and unblinking, as if by doing so, the shape looming near the entrance, next to a guest book, could be voided.

Didn't work. Her stomach gave a nasty flip.

"If it isn't Pussy Galore." Kris's partner growled out of one side of his mouth. He moved closer and lowered his voice. Stubborn eyes gleamed. "What are you doing here?"

"I'm probably here for the same reason you are. We're here because *we're not all there.*"

He chuckled without humor. "Looks like the whole cathouse turned out."

Shocked into silence, she felt her blood rise. "No need to go out of your way to pick a fight, detective—I'm right here. What's your problem? I never did anything to you."

The detective braced his arms. "You can wallow in money, you can put on airs and wear designer clothes; but when push comes to shove you're still nothing but a gutter slut."

A sharp pain that started in Dakota's head settled above her right eye. Each time the double doors swung open, organ music from *Phantom of the Opera* blared out, adding to the carnival-like atmosphere.

Kris's angry voice came from behind and to the left. "I don't believe this." A strange, non-verbal exchange took place between the two homicide investigators, as if they possessed the ability to communicate in an unspoken language. His eyes executed orders from afar. She turned to Dakota. "What're *you* doing here?"

"Well, let's see . . . someone died . . . I'm wearing black . . ." Dakota pretended to meditate on the thought. "The obvious answer is 'I'm at a memorial service,' so I'm going to go with . . . 'shopping.' "

Hamilton Stark gave a derisive grunt.

Raw with humiliation, Dakota tried to ignore him. The dead air around her grew thick, compressed by the intensity of the two detectives flanking her.

"I'm paying my respects," she said to Kris. "What're *you* doing here?"

"Excuse us a moment." Kris steered her down the hall, beyond the crowd and out of the flow of foot traffic. They ended up in a bathroom for the second time that day. When the door sucked shut behind them, Kris pulled a small camera out of her pocket and wagged it.

"We're surveilling the mourners, Dee." Neck veins throbbed. Anger mounted. "Celia St. Claire's killer could be mingling with the crowd. Only I can't do my job without having to worry about you pulling shit."

"I don't know why you're so angry. Have you noticed that problems between us only crop up when Hamilton's around? Why can't you get a new partner? Then we wouldn't have all this drama."

"Hamilton's a good cop and we work well together."

"You don't control me, Kris. Neither does Hamilton."

"*You* showing up *here* is just going to land you under the cold, hard scrutiny of my partner."

If Kris was trying to discourage her from attending Celia's funeral, yelling at her in the ladies room had the opposite effect. She loved that old woman.

Then it hit her. She felt an unpleasant lurch in her stomach. "You people think I killed Celia?"

"Not me." Kris glanced up at the ceiling. "Hamilton."

Little hairs on her arms stood straight up. "Why would he think that?"

Kris stared off into space. "I might've mentioned I thought you were trying to squeeze information about the investigation out of Dr. Stone . . ." The words carried a bit of hang time.

A lance of fear speared Dakota's heart. She pressed her lips together until they went numb. "You know the parable of the frozen rattlesnake? No? You take pity on the snake because it's freezing, so you take it home and warm it in front of the hearth. Then it bites you. It has no remorse because you knew what it was when you picked it up." The silence stretched a couple of beats.

"What're you saying? That I'm a snake?"

"I'm saying it's your fault."

"Just remember, Dee. Everyone's a suspect until they're not a suspect. Including you."

"I'm offended. You know damned well I was with you."

"Not all of the time."

"Well, then, I guess that makes you a suspect, too." *So, ha!*

"I have two words for you, Dakota: Go. Home."

Dakota reached for the door handle. Halfway to flouncing out, she returned a parting shot. "I have two words, too, Kristina-hyena: Screw. You."

Chapter Eight

Sunday morning, Dakota trudged to the kitchen with her Turkish house slippers slapping the floor, and a knee-length, silk kimono cinched tight at the waist. She retrieved a glass-bottle of Mexican Coca-Cola from the refrigerator, pried off the bottle cap with an opener, and padded to the couch. It tasted better than regular cola because the Mexicans used cane sugar, not high-fructose corn syrup. She picked up the remote and turned on the plasma TV. It was still tuned to the weather channel. She joined a discussion of the day's forecast, which turned lively when the female anchor turned to the weatherman and said, "Where are the eight inches you promised me last night?" The anchor meant snow, but it didn't come out that way.

Dakota surfed the networks until she landed on the home and garden channel. The featured homeowners wanted to fill-in their swimming pool, and cameramen had filmed the crew laying the prep work.

Dakota considered her own pool from her place on the sofa. Kris loved to swim laps before bedtime. Said the exercise helped her sleep better. In the mornings, they didn't even need to step outside when they could gauge the velocity of a breeze by checking out the ripples on the surface, or watch the plastic blowup shark banging itself against the tiled edge.

The pool demanded upkeep. And even though they paid a pool service, it was still high maintenance. For a person who started out poor and ended up with tons of money, a hectoring voice in the back of her head still nagged: *Do you need it? Can you live without it?*

She didn't need it. Should've opted for a yard landscaped with bonsai. A Japanese garden where she could sculpt potted trees, rake colored sand and arrange rocks to look like streams.

She needed calm in her life. And Kris was high maintenance because she came with Hamilton Stark. Realization dawned. She replayed the test questions in her head: *Do I need her? Like I need air*, she thought. *Can I live without her?* She didn't even want to think about that one.

Prone on the couch, feeling every ache and pain, Dakota switched channels. Even her fingers hurt. The arts and entertainment broadcast featured a cold case about a serial killer. She didn't want to think about Kris and changed channels. The channel she settled on was running a car commercial. She put the remote on the coffee table, a rustic number with crescent legs made of Longhorn horns bolted to an onyx surface. The commercial ended and a martial arts program resumed. Images of Kris and her Jiu-jitsu classes popped into mind. Dakota tightened her jaw. Mind-blowing discovery, however—she learned she could properly operate the remote with her feet. Then she realized that was pretty much her only talent.

Scrolling through the options, she selected the movie channel and joined a re-run of "Tootsie" that was already in progress. She decided to make breakfast.

She removed a frying pan from the cabinet and buttered it, then pulled the egg carton from the refrigerator. A noise from outside made her suddenly alert and she backed against the countertop with a spatula in hand. At the scratching of metal, she riveted her eyes to the front door. The lock made a dull click and the handle clicked open with an audible snap. The door swung inward, and Kris—bent over at the waist, and out of breath—kneed it open the rest of the way. She lugged-in a case of bottled water beneath one arm, and carried a leather gym bag and her keys in the opposite hand.

Dakota thought her heart would beat right through her chest. Kris had come home.

How 'bout that? Sometimes, when you're happy and you know it, you don't have to clap your hands.

"Hey, Dee." Said guiltily. "Whatcha watching?"

"Tootsie."

"What a drag." A hint of laughter flickered behind her eyes.

"Why are you out of breath? Was somebody chasing you?"

"No, I was chasing a Coors truck . . . why do you think?" Kris darted a look at the things she'd carried in, and then got a sour, accusatory look on her face.

Two could play the sarcasm game. Dakota said, "Help a girl when she's in trouble, and she'll remember you when she's in trouble again," and cracked an egg into the sizzling skillet.

The case of water shifted in Kris's grip, and the heft of the gym bag whitened her fingertips. She paused to re-adjust her load, and dropped the gym bag. It thudded to the floor as she hoisted the bottled water onto the kitchen countertop. "What's for breakfast?"

"I'm not cooking for you," Dakota said, flipping the only egg in the frying pan. She gave the detective a pointed look. "Give a man a fish, he'll eat for a day. Teach a man to fish, he'll eat for the rest of his life."

Kris managed a thoughtful head bob. "Give a smartass a match, she'll be warm for a minute. Set her on fire, she'll be warm the rest of her life." She unpacked the water as she spoke. "Need a light?"

Dakota's eyes thinned into slits. "That's funny," she deadpanned.

"I thought so." Kris's mouth curled into a polite smirk.

"I'm still not cooking for you."

"That's okay, I'm totally wasted. I don't feel much like eating." Kris pulled the stopper out of a half-empty bottle of wine and poured herself a glass.

"Kind of early for that, isn't it?"

"Don't pick on me. It's been an awful night. And this morning hasn't exactly gotten off to what I'd call a good start." She wandered over to one of the overstuffed leather club chairs facing the fireplace and took long gulps. "What'd you do last night?"

"Stayed home. Watched TV. Took phone calls. " Dakota barely restrained a sigh. "It appears the two Goths I gave my private number to, gave the cell phone number to their creepiest, most obnoxious friend, who drunk-dialed me five times during the night. What'd *you* do?" But what Dakota really wanted to know was where her girlfriend slept—and with whom.

Instead of answering, Kris left the room.

Could've been an honest mistake. Maybe she didn't hear the question. Or maybe—just maybe—she had a guilty conscience. Dakota finished her egg and decided to face her fear.

Her cell phone chimed with an instant message from Kris.

It read: "I'm fixing to lie down. Don't be alarmed by the color of my lips should you walk into the bedroom. I'm not dead. I just ate a bag of Cheetos."

Fury fueled her next move. Dakota headed down the hall. Her heart thudded like horse hooves on a dirt track as she opened the bedroom door to confront Kris, knowing, full well that this masochistic, need-to-know, mentality could do them in. "What'd you do last night?"

Kris had already crawled between the sheets. The lights were turned off, and, she was lying in the gloom. Tucked into bed, she looked like a pen poking out of a pocket protector. Eyes squinted in calculation. "What'd I *do*?"

She knew Kris so well that her defensive tone told Dakota precisely what she already suspected—*that she'd spent the night with Hamilton.* She swallowed the tennis ball lodged in her throat.

"What I *did* was go over evidence with Hamilton on Celia St. Claire's case. By the way, your friend Cyn Evans won't be calling here again."

She'd never seen Kris so serious.

The revelation scalded her. Kris had no right to badger her friends. Not that she and Cyn Evans were that close . . . still, having Kris inflict herself on poor Cyn, just because Cyn had asked for her help, was out of line.

"How dare you? You can't tell my friends not to contact me. What'd you say to her?"

"I didn't *say* anything. Didn't have to. Even if I did, she wouldn't have heard it. Cyn's dead."

Dakota's mouth gaped. Her nose prickled. Tears blistered behind her eyeballs. "Cyn?" Her voice broke upon sounding the name. Lightheaded and shell-shocked, Dakota leaned against the door frame. She had the disturbing feeling that, when it was all over, she'd need a memory recovery program to unblock the experience. "Please tell me this is a sick joke."

"I wish. Look, I'm not here for long. I only came home for a twenty-minute power nap, and then I have to shower and meet Hamilton at the crime scene."

"Cyn Evans? Dead?" Dakota shook her head in disbelief. "Who called in the body?"

"My partner." Kris possessed a laser-stare made up of one part clairvoyant and two parts lie detector. At the moment, she focused it on Dakota. "Your friend Cyn made a couple of hysterical phone calls to the station, so they dispatched a couple of uniforms to check out the complaints. The calls were determined to be baseless—" she rolled her eyes "—which we now know were *not* baseless . . . so when the last one came in, Hamilton stopped by to check on her as a courtesy." Kris unexpectedly stiffened. Her eyes narrowed. "What'd you watch on TV?"

Dee did a one-shoulder shrug. She was still trying to process the terrible news about Catwoman. "I fell asleep halfway through one of those schlocky, made-for-TV movies."

"Who starred in it?"

"I dunno. The usual suspects . . . who knows? They're all a bunch of washed up has-beens, used-to-bes or never wases." Realization dawned. "Wait—why are you asking me this?"

"You heard from Celia St. Claire, and she died. Then you heard from Cyn Evans, and she died."

"What're you saying? Are you accusing me? " Dakota's heart thudded. "You're *accusing* me . . ." A tear sluiced down one cheek.

Kris sat up. "I'm making an observation. Don't you find it just a little uncanny? A bit ironic? Maybe a tad too coincidental?"

"What's uncanny? That I knew the two victims?" Dakota shifted from one foot to the other like a dancing Rottweiler, slobbering frothy drool. "You know me better than anybody. I can't believe you even asked me that. Can *you* account for all of your time?"

Kris squared her shoulders, a sure sign she wouldn't back down. "I already told you—I was at Hamilton's."

Dakota sucked air. "At his house?" She clutched a hand to her breasts and emitted a pitiful, high-pitched wail. "You didn't say you went to his house; you said you were going over evidence with him."

"And that's exactly what we did."

Dakota experienced a polar shift. Until that moment, she had no idea Kris could be that devious, or even remotely capable of such cruelty. "Well, aren't you the little wordsmith?" Said nastily. "You wanted me to think y'all were at the PD. You lied by omission. How many times has that happened before?"

Kris bristled. "You know, Dee, our entire relationship has gotten off track."

"It takes more than one log to make a fire burn," Dakota shot back.

Kris gave her a brittle smile, and used the "it's not you, it's me," speech with a slight variation. "It's not me, it's you. And yes, I meant to say it that way."

Dakota's voice trembled with the effort of speech. "Did you sleep with him?"

By way of an answer, Kris flung off the bed covers. She stormed into the bathroom looking like she'd been kidnapped in a flash ransom by a drug cartel out of Nogales, Mexico and was hoping to escape dismemberment. The door slammed and the lock snicked shut.

"Don't walk away from me." In a voice fractured with urgency, Dakota trailed her to the bathroom. The shower came on, followed by loud music. The idea that Kris thought she could drown her out ignited Dakota's fury. "Tell me the truth." Kris belted out tunes to her latest investment—a compilation CD of heavy metal covers of ABBA classics. "Don't give me the silent treatment." Kris boosted the volume.

"How could you do that to me?" Dakota whimpered. She slumped to the floor, imagining Hamilton's mouth on Kris's firm breasts . . . his lips exploring every contour of her taut body . . . his engorged penis . . . Kris, polishing his Oscar—an unbearable thought.

An anguished wail roared out. Dakota buried her face in her hands. She was all cried out by the time Kris came out of the bathroom, cocooned in a towel.

Punctured and deflated, Dakota stared up from her place on the floor. Distress puckered her lips. "How could you sleep with him?" she asked in a raw voice.

"I didn't."

"Then why didn't you say so? You didn't deny it."

Kris gave the ceiling a look of resignation. "I guess I wanted you to know how it felt." She was talking about life at Fantasy Escorts Unlimited.

"If I could take back what I used to do, I would. But I can't. But I promise you—I don't want anybody else. Just you."

Kris dropped to one knee. "And I don't want anyone but you."

They fell into each other's embrace.

"I don't want to do this anymore." Dakota inhaled the fragrance of Kris's shampoo. "I don't want to fight. I don't want anything coming between us."

"Then don't ever mention me and Hamilton being lovers again."

"I deserve the same consideration. You have to stop using my past against me. I quit that lifestyle. I chose you."

They struck a deal—no more melodrama over each other's past.

Kris smiled. "You know, somebody should've warned me he kisses like a stroke victim. Oh, he thinks he's a real ladies man." She grinned as if she knew the embarrassing truth—a secret she shouldn't be telling. "I suppose he is . . . if the lady needs her plumbing snaked out."

Chapter Nine

After Kris headed to Cyn Evans's crime scene, Dakota figured a trip to SinisterSisters would keep her mind off Cyn's murder. But when she scampered out the front door dressed in skinny jeans and layered tops, and plunged down the steps into the sun-dappled morning with thoughts of Laura Ann Spencer orbiting her head, she hauled up short. Travis Creeley had her in the trajectory of his bullet-like stare.

Furious, she stormed across the street to his car, geared for a hellacious confrontation.

"Stop stalking me." Bent at the waist, she kept her distance beyond the passenger door. With sunglasses lowered, she fixed him with a death glare.

"I need your help. To find Annie."

"If you don't leave me alone, I'll go to the police."

His lip curled up his craggy face. "Looks like the police come straight to you."

He must've seen Kris leave in the unmarked patrol car. God only knew how long he'd been watching the house.

"I mean it." Even with the passenger seat buffering them, Creeley needed to check the expiration date on his breath.

"Help me find Annie." He measured her through hard eyes, looking every bit as dangerous as he had during their first encounter.

"I'm done with you." She spun away, thumbing the beep-remote on her way to the Jag. Her heart drummed as she fired up the engine. In her rearview mirror, a coil of exhaust belched out of Creeley's old clunker. She backed out of the driveway, adhering to the posted speed limit. The luxury car slumped heavily down the street, but once she passed the unmanned kiosk at the gates of Heaven's Urn, she made a hard right and floored the accelerator. Tires droned on the asphalt.

Travis Creeley receded in her side mirror.

She flirted with the idea that she'd ditched him when she came to a red light and didn't see him anywhere in sight. The driver behind her tapped the horn. The light had turned green, and she continued along her route to Sinister Sisters, hoping Creeley'd gotten the message, knowing he might've received it a little better if she'd pointed her .38 caliber Smith at him. The next time she checked her mirror, he'd come within five car lengths behind her.

"Sonofabitch. Who the hell *are* you?" She spoke to the rearview mirror and hoped he could lip-read.

They played a dangerous game of chicken; her, careening through the yellow lights; him, blowing through the red ones. She'd been racing through the streets like she was auditioning for NASCAR, now she let her speed drop back to the posted limit. She felt pretty sure she'd lost him near an industrial area, and ten minutes after leaving Heaven's Urn, she whipped into the parking lot in front of SinisterSisters—or as she liked to think of it, *alternative-lifestyle Hell, located in the colostomy bag section of Phoenix.*

The company had leased a non-descript, one-story building adjacent to a strip mall filled with odd shops that routinely suffered from turnover. Peeling white paint curled down stucco walls; the only cars ferrying patrons to this derelict section of town seemed to be vehicles that couldn't pass inspection—junkers like Creeley's.

Dakota shuddered.

Stared at the place as if it actually was a huge colostomy bag that needed to be emptied.

Considered leaving, then decided against it.

She activated the remote and the door locks to the Jaguar snapped shut. As she headed for the glass doorway, she felt the disturbing sensation of watchful eyes on her. When she reached the entrance, she scanned the eaves for pin cameras. Sure enough, she detected a couple recessed in the mitered corners. She pressed a buzzer mounted in the doorjamb and heard an audible click.

When she opened the door, the aroma of scented candles mixed with burned incense greeted her. After entering the room, a strange audio and visual assault began.

Druidic strains from an Enya CD filtered into the room from a location farther back in the building, but still not loud enough to drown out the swish of fabric rustling toward her. A tall, willowy woman in mime-loud makeup floated into the room wearing layers of sheer, black chiffon. Black lipstick glossed her mouth; piercing blue eyes jumped from the darkened hollows beneath her brows. White veneers capped her teeth. And a silver bolt pierced her tongue.

"May I help you?"

"I'd like to ask a few questions." Dakota pulled the snapshot of Laura Ann Spencer from her bag.

"Are you a cop?"

"Private Investigator. I was hired by this girl's parents to find her. Do you know her?"

"No. But good luck."

Dakota sensed the Goth chick didn't care—that she only looked like she cared because she was doing a math equation in her head to make herself look interested.

"Look, she's not in trouble. We just want to know that she's safe. The family's worried sick."

"Sorry." Sinister Sister stared through heavily-lined, viperous eyes.

"But you haven't even looked at the picture." Dakota's voice pitched to incredulity.

"Don't need to."

"You're not going to help me, are you?"

Sinister Sister mimed a smile.

Building on her irritation, Dakota inventoried the room in a glance. The interior had all of the characteristics of the Mad Hatter's tea party. She returned Laura Ann's snapshot to her purse, pulled out a business card, and handed it over. "Her name's Laura Ann Spencer. You probably know her as Synthetic Darkness. I'd appreciate it if you'd give me a call if you hear from her."

"You know the way out. Have a nice day." Cordial but detached, Sinister Sister dropped the card into the nearest wastebasket and went scurrying back down the corridor like a roach when the lights flicked on.

Dakota was in the process of flopping into the driver's seat when a young girl in her late teens slipped out a side door and came around the building. With furtive looks, she hurried to the passenger side of the Jag and tapped on the window. Dakota unlocked the door and the girl slid into the seat.

"Liquid Fantasy," said the girl by way of introduction. Huge brown eyes blinked. She wore no makeup on her unblemished, anemic-looking face, and her steel-toed boots, heavy silver crosses and enormous belt buckle contributed to at least half of her weight. She extended a fragile hand and gave a dead fish handshake.

"Homicidal Maniac," Dakota said, lightly pinching the girl's fingers. "Do you have a real name?"

"Let it go." Silence filled their shared space. The teenager flipped down the visor and slumped down in the seat. "Can I see the picture?" Dakota obliged. "Yeah, that's Synthetic Darkness. She came by a few weeks ago."

Laura Ann Spencer had been reported missing almost two months before. Dakota took it as a good sign.

"Was she alone?"

Liquid Fantasy shook her head. "She came with a big biker dude. Must've been twice her age."

"Does Laura Ann do her own tattoos?"

"Nope. She goes to Diamond Dogs Tattoos." The girl's eyes widened. "Don't get me wrong—Synthetic Darkness does great tattoo work, but it's difficult for her to do them on herself. Especially the back of the neck. So she goes to Diamond Dogs."

Dakota twisted in her seat. "How come you're helping me when the other lady wouldn't?"

"You mean Morbid Mistress? She's always like that." By way of explanation, Liquid Fantasy said, "You know, Goths aren't bad people. But you might get better results if you tried to fit in . . . or, at least attempted to look like one of us."

Point taken. Perhaps while at Diamond Dogs, she'd get her own henna tattoo.

"You didn't say why you're willing to help me," Dakota prompted.

"Because I feel sorry for you." The girl giggled.

Dakota left Liquid Fantasy to skulk back into the side door of SinisterSisters and met Kris at Tía Mía's for Mexican food.

They commandeered a corner booth so Kris could keep an eye

on the door. It was a cop thing. If anybody busted in with a tommy-gun, she could whip out her pea-shooter and open fire.

The waitress brought two waters, a basket of blue corn chips and salsa, and scrawled their orders on a guest check pad. While they waited for their *chiles rellenos*, Chief Forster sauntered in, back-slapping the Mayor Elect.

Kris saw them first. "Oh, hell."

Dakota twisted in her seat, saw the reason for Kris's strife, and thought, *Tweedle-Dumb, and Tweedle-Dumber.* Deflated, she reached for her purse. "I'll leave."

"No."

Slack-jawed, Dakota blinked. "Really?" But she was thinking, *Could we get the waitress to take our picture together?*

Her lover nodded. "Screw them."

They shared a giggle. Chief Forster and David Wilson took a nearby table, shook out their napkins and ordered a couple of drinks. When the waitress returned with a Bloody Mary and Scotch rocks, and placed them on cardboard coasters, Kris all but salivated.

"I could use one of those," she said, lustily eyeing the hooch. "The crime scene was awful, Dee." She kept her voice low and avoided eye contact; as if this seemingly insignificant gesture might depersonalize the grisly experience. "Hamilton and I were discussing possible motives and we hit a dead end. This killer leaves clues—Cyn had henna tattoos—but we haven't figured out what they mean." She stopped talking with such abruptness that a tortilla chip could've lodged in her throat. Kris waved the waitress over. "Bring me a Vodka tonic—double—and put it in a water glass."

"Don't push your luck." Dakota'd dined out with the detective often enough to know departmental policy prohibited drinking on duty.

Kris kept a watchful eye on the two men, shrinking deeper into the booth until she'd practically embedded herself in the shiny crimson vinyl.

Holy cow—she's trying to lip read.

"Those jerks are talking about our victims like it's a joke. Treating it like it's a scene out of an electronic game, where evil women are vanquished by righteous men. Game over. A thousand points per corpse. The world is safe. The virtuous ones win." Her eyes took on a speculative gleam. "I don't approve of what Celia and Cyn did for a living, but they didn't deserve to die. No one deserves to have their life cut short by someone playing God—except for death penalty cases. It's okay if the state kills you."

Dakota blinked. She'd never heard Kris talk this way.

Kris's jaw had a strange set to it. She leaned in and whispered, "Hamilton says the clues are in the tattoos. Only I can't see it."

"Does he know what they mean?"

Big headshake. "We've hit a brick wall. Hamilton hates to admit defeat. He doesn't want us to look stupid in the newspaper, so we're not talking it up." Without warning, Kris alerted like a crime dog. "Did you hear that?"

The detective definitely had a gift. Hands down, Kris was the only person Dee knew who could hone-in on gossip whispered from half a room away and still carry on a conversation without compromising her white-hot surveillance.

The waitress returned with Kris's drink; the detective drained the glass like a two-humped dromedary on a trek across the desert.

"Let's leave," Dee whispered, "I don't want you to get in trouble."

"No. You want us to be able to be seen in public?" Said in a double-dog-dare-you tone. "Well, this is about as public as it gets."

"You're scaring me."

"Hell, I'm scaring *me*." Kris stiffened. "Did you hear what Wilson just said? He hates gays and lesbians."

"Let it go."

"Hot plates, ladies," said the waitress, and slid an entrée in front of each of them. "Anything else?"

Kris tapped the empty Vodka glass. "I could use a refill."

"Cancel the drink. She's too plastered to know what she's saying."

They ate in relative silence, with occasional outbursts of indignation coming from Kris. Dakota could hardly wait to snatch up the tab. She dropped two twenties on the guest tray when the waitress dropped off the ticket, then gathered her bag and hoisted the strap over her shoulder.

"Want me to leave first? Or I could slip into the ladies room and give you a five-minute head start to get out of Dodge."

"We're leaving together," Kris gamely informed her.

"You must really want to come back home . . ." Dakota said through a smile.

The detective acknowledged the Chief and Mayor-Elect on her way out. Dakota walked past as if they were invisible, and waited in the Jaguar with the window powered down.

"I'm going back to the crime scene to give Hamilton a chance to grab a bite to eat." Kris said when she came out of Tía Mía's.

"That's just weird working a murder investigation and wanting to break for lunch. How could anyone have an appetite after witnessing all that gore?"

Kris did a one-shoulder shrug. "You get used to it." She shot a furtive glance toward the restaurant door, then touched a lock of Dakota's hair. "So, what're you doing the rest of the afternoon?"

"I haven't decided yet. If the weather holds out, I may swim with the shark." She flashed an enigmatic smile to mask this fib, and powered the window up. Kris tapped on the glass. Dakota looked up expectantly. When she powered the window halfway down, Kris leaned in and gave her a peck on the cheek.

Holy cow. Hell froze.

"Be careful." Kris squinted fiercely and shielded her eyes against the sun.

"You, too."

"I love you, Dee."

"Me, too."

Once Kris pulled the unmarked patrol car out of the parking lot, Dakota took off in the opposite direction. She programmed Mayor Jane's address into the Jaguar's navigation system and pointed the snout of the Jag in the direction of Rio Vista. The most fascinating thing on the drive out occurred when she looked over into the next lane and saw a three hundred pound woman giving birth to a motorcycle, and the tires flattened beneath the strain. It was a ghastly sight. People that big should avoid wearing wild colors, large prints, and getting on motorcycles.

The mayor's adobe mansion sat on a half-acre of landscaped terraces with imported trees and tropical foliage. A prominent sign put passers-by on notice that well-water kept the lawn green—a good thing, since a sprinkler system misted the grass while neighbors' yards had burned to a crisp. Dakota parked at the curb.

She climbed a series of terra cotta steps with glazed Majolica tile risers, and pressed the doorbell. Strains of Westminster chimes leaked out through massive carved doors. An intercom, recessed in a side wall, suddenly crackled to life, and sounds of an indoor scramble leaked out of the speaker. The voice of Jane Roman filtered out. Dee announced her presence, and the door swung open. Mayor Jane flung-out her arms and gathered her in an embrace.

It'd been like this from the beginning—probably because of Dakota's potential to fund a campaign—but over time, the friendship seemed genuine.

The mayor gave her a tour of the downstairs, where they ended up in an opulent living room seated near the baby grand piano. They spoke of Mayor-Elect Wilson's shady past and the winter sale at one of the high-end department stores. When Dakota rose to leave, she hadn't forgotten how Mayor Jane came to her rescue at the shopping mall's grand opening.

"Thanks for being kind to me."

Jane Roman gave her a no-nonsense look. "You have a good heart, Dee. We've all made mistakes we'd like to undo. Me—I wish I'd campaigned my heart out against Wilson. I wish I hadn't assumed voters were smart enough to see through him. As for you—you're weaving the future out of threads from your past. And I think when you're done you'll have a beautiful tapestry to hang for all to see."

They lingered in the foyer, where Dakota did a final eye scan in an effort to burn a lasting image of the mayor's beautiful home into her memory.

"How'd you get to be such a nice lady?"

Lively eyes sparkled. Jane smiled. "You're sweet to say it, but I'm not all that nice. If I do anything well it's having impeccable manners and observing protocol. My forte is knowing how to behave in public." She waved her off with wiggled fingers. "Take care, Dee. Let's meet at my office tomorrow. Right now, there's a gentleman in my bed who needs a little TLC."

Chapter Ten

Sunday night dissolved into Monday morning. Dakota kept her ten o'clock appointment with the Mayor, where, upon arrival, she got a decidedly unpleasant surprise. A couple of suits frisked her at the door. Mayor Jane glided out from an interior office in a pink Chanel ensemble, and motioned her inside once the men finished running the metal-detecting wand over her.

This was new. Appalled, Dee wasn't at all certain she cared to stay.

Mayor Jane motioned her into a leather chair—cowhide stenciled to look like zebra skin. She took her place behind the oversized mahogany desk.

"I'm sorry about the boys, Dee." She thumbed at the door. "Just because I *think* we're on the same side doesn't *mean* we are. What you're wanting to talk about . . . well . . . I can't afford to find out you're wearing a wire."

Dakota's jaw went slack. "Why would I do that? I thought we were friends."

"Look around you when you leave here. All these people who work for me? I thought we were friends, too, but they're already ingratiating themselves with Wilson and his people. I'm learning the bonds of loyalty are fleeting and fragile."

They spoke of a rigged election, David Wilson's guerilla campaign tactics and the possibility that he could've committed the murders of Celia St. Claire and Cyn Evans.

"I wouldn't put it past him." Mayor Jane gave an aristocratic sniff. "There's a time gap in his Curriculum Vitae. I wouldn't be at all surprised to find he did time in a Maryland prison."

"What could he possibly gain by killing Celia and Cyn?"

"You want to know his motive," Jane said, talking like a cop—or someone who watched too many episodes of *Forensic Files* on late night TV. "I've considered that. What I'd really give my eyeteeth to know is whether he was ever a customer. If he felt he had to silence them to keep the word from leaking out." Huge eyes shaded in frosty pink shadow seemed to be making a telepathic plea: *You're a private investigator. Maybe you could find out for me?*

Dakota left the meeting with a sick feeling in her gut. In the sanctuary of her car, she programmed the address for Diamond Dogs Tattoos into the Jag's navigation system. After driving through a couple of intersections, she noticed a car trailing her. As the next traffic light turned amber, Dakota punched the accelerator. When she glanced into the rearview mirror, the suspect car's chrome grill-work grinned back at her. Had Travis Creeley switched vehicles?

Son-of-a-bitch was stalking her.

Probably gave him the best head, ever, and he'd fixated on her. And that so-called missing daughter of his—Annie? Well, that was nothing but a trumped-up story to make her feel sorry for him.

She slowed at the red light, looked both ways and saw that the traffic on either side hadn't budged, and floored the accelerator. When Creeley tried to go through, the traffic started flowing, cutting him off in his pursuit.

It seemed Travis Creeley planned to dog her to the Gates of Hell. But when he closed the gap between them, a motor jock fell in behind and flipped on his red-and-blues. If the curbed driver really was Travis Creeley, he was in for a big surprise. The motorcycle officer standing beside the car had shrunk to the size of a tiny ant with a ticket book.

So, *ha!* Served him right.

Dakota checked her speed. Soon, she angled the Jag into one of the fish-boned parking spaces near the storefront of Diamond Dogs Tattoos. The place had a creepy feel with loud speakers mounted beneath the outside awning, blasting hard rock music into the street. Through the plate glass windows, neon signs glowed against dark walls papered with designs of tattoo art and airbrush stencil transfers. Like Princess Beatrice's hat-buying expedition for the Royal Wedding, Laura Ann Spencer's first tattoo probably started with the classic phrase, *"Here . . . hold my beer."*

As soon as Dakota opened the door, a buzzer went off and her hackles rose. As in slasher films—*"Wait, don't go out to the shed!"* or *down in the basement,* or wherever the hell the killer happened to be hiding—this was definitely the moment she should back out slowly and hope no one noticed. Because this whole deal felt a lot like strolling into a convenience store after midnight to shop the snack aisle, when—*no shit!*—you realize the cashier who was missing from the counter when you first walked inside isn't really in the back, restocking; and everyone who was in the store three minutes before you be-bopped in without a care in the world is dead in the back cooler.

She stepped into the din of reverberating sound. A drill-like hum in the background stopped. Seconds later, a slim man with a trim goatee and long, shiny dark hair ambled in from the back. The wife-beater T-shirt he had on didn't completely cover the full complement of tattoos on his chest, but he had a crooked smile, and looked harmless enough.

"Help you?" he asked, in a roughly textured voice.

Dakota thrust the photo of Laura Ann Spencer at him. "Have you seen her?"

"Laura Ann? Yeah. I do her tattoos."

Finally, a stroke of good luck.

"When's the last time you saw her?"

"It's been awhile." He seemed to be taking in her presence, starting with the heart-shaped locket with Kris's picture inside that hung around her neck, to the layer of pullover tops and the pink and black flannel shirt she'd decided to substitute for a jacket.

"Was she alone?"

He shook his head. "She brought in some biker dude. A loner type. Goes by the name Velvet Tears. I know him as Shawn O'Neil. He's an independent artist who does a lot of tattoo work locally. A mean dude. He'd just as soon rip off your head as look at you."

"What else can you tell me about Laura Ann?"

"Nothing, until you tell me why you're looking for her." He motioned her over to a beat up sofa with the stuffing oozing out, then cupped his hands to his mouth and hollered toward the back, "Take five minutes and don't rub it, don't wash it, don't touch it. Matter of fact, treat it like a syphilitic dick and don't fuck with it."

To Dakota, he said, "She owe you money?"

She started to use the Chase, Hsu, Fleesim and Settle story, but his bullshit radar emitted a low-level hum. When she opened her mouth, the truth spilled out.

"The Spencers are worried sick. I don't think they're trying to get her to come home so much as I think they just want to know she's safe. If you could help me—"

"Why would I want to do that?"

"—I'd appreciate it." She thought fast. "I'd let you do a couple of henna tattoos on me."

"Where?"

Her eyes darted over the surroundings. "Here."

"No, I mean where do you want the tattoos?"

"How long do they last?" It mattered because she'd received invitations to a handful of holiday parties, and didn't want to look trashy in her bugle bead ball gown at the children's hospital's charity event.

"Up to seven days if you take care of 'em."

"How do you take care of them?"

"Like I said, *Don't fuck with 'em.* So where'd you want the tattoos?"

She found an airbrush stencil transfer that might mesh with the Goth sub-culture: a skull biting down on a long-stemmed red rose. And a barcode.

"You can put the skull on my neck. And the barcode on my bikini line."

"Cool."

He went to an old typesetter's case, pulled out a drawer, and thumbed through the inventory until he located the proper stencils. The tattoo artist—who introduced himself as Ike—said he thought Laura Ann had paired up with Shawn O'Neil.

"It's an unholy alliance, dudette. He's built like a brick shithouse, he's mean as a two-step and he's dumb as dirt. Laura Ann's brilliant. I don't know if her parents told you. Her IQ's off the charts." He sighed almost wistfully. As he led Dakota down the hallway, to a room with a chair, a tattoo machine and a bottle of Virucide sitting prominently on a side table, he recited Laura Ann's virtues to the air. "She's an amazing artist. So talented. And pretty. Why him?"

But Dakota had her own question. "If she's so great, how come she doesn't do her own tattoos?"

"Ever go into a barber shop?" When she shook her head, Ike said, "Next time you pass by one, take a look inside. They all cut each other's hair, so you want to pick the dude whose hair looks like it was cut with a hacksaw. That way, you avoid the guy who did the dog-assed chop job. You married?"

"No." She knew what was coming and didn't like to see where this was headed, so she nipped things in the bud. "I'm in a relationship, though."

"All the good ones are. Is he a good-looking guy?"

"Nah," she said airily. "I only like the ugly ones. The last time I had a date with a really cute guy, I was about to invite him back to my place for a drink when he pulled out a catalog of Russian mail-order brides and asked me to help him pick out the best one."

"Bummer," Ike said, then realized she was kidding.

The whir of a tattoo machine came from the next room. Dakota winced at the idea of defacing her skin. Scrubbable tattoos were just fine. Kris might even get a kick out of helping her wash them off. After Ike finished, he rubbed down the chair and instrument tray with alcohol while Dakota rifled through her purse for her wallet.

"You mind paying me in guns?"

The corners of his mouth tipped and she realized he was teasing. She paid for the rose-biting skull and the barcode, and left him her business card, along with a nice tip. They'd gotten along well, and she'd gotten information out of him. Hopefully, he'd keep her in the loop.

Head down, on the way out the door, an incoming customer bumped into her. He brushed against her shoulder, obliging her to take a side step. She looked at him, blank-faced, before recognition kicked in. A serpent of nausea coiled in her gut. Blood pounded in her ears. She might've shrieked.

The apology that'd formed on her tongue hardened into a warning. "Quit following me."

"I want to talk to you."

The sound of Travis Creeley's voice was a cruelty to her ears.

Her muscles had somehow short-circuited the signals coming from her brain and she stood, petrified, instead of running for the car. "Leave me alone or I'm calling the police."

"You think I care?" Eyes squinted in calculation. Ruthlessness simmered just below the surface.

He was loving every minute of this. Any sign of fear would excite him. Dakota knew the type. The man had crocodile genes.

Ike must've heard the door buzzer go off because he sauntered out brandishing his tattoo machine. It emitted a low-level hum in his hand, its needle pulsating a gazillion times per second.

"What's going on, sugar? Want me to take care of this guy for you?"

Creeley struck with reptilian agility. Delivered a one-two punch that hurled the tattoo artist across the room. Ike ended up prone on the floor with a nose shaped like a geometry problem, and the tattoo machine vibrating against the floor.

Filled with a homicidal rage she didn't realize she was capable of, Dakota dipped a hand into her purse. She pulled out the Smith. Creeley's seedy grin died on his blue lips.

"You ever come near me again and I'll kill you."

Creeley backed out the door and lumbered off.

Eyelids fluttering, Ike pushed himself up on one elbow. "Did somebody get the license number of that truck?" He touched his nose and his fingertips came away bloody. His eyes flickered to Dakota. "Friend of yours?"

"I don't know him. He's stalking me."

"Want me to take care of him for you?"

They shared a simultaneous chuckle. Ike couldn't even take care of himself.

"I think we should call the cops." If Creeley didn't table this Annie thing, there'd be a detective down at the jail waiting to interview him behind bars. Or an M.D. in the morgue tagging his big toe.

"No cops." Ike shut off the tattoo machine. "This is a respectable business."

Shadows flickered past Dakota's rolling eyes. Then everything went to hell in a handcart.

In walked Kris and Hamilton, flashing a couple of photographs of their own. At the sight of their serious, reproachful faces, Dakota knew her presence would set off fireworks.

"Hey, Dee. What're you doing?" Kris stared up at her with a

degree of censure. "He make a pass at you?" Her gaze cut to Ike, picking himself up off the floor.

"No." Dakota took a walk on the blunt side. "As for what I'm doing here, I could ask you the same thing." Inwardly cringing under the weight of Hamilton's glare, she considered Kris's partner, and the dangerous expression on his face. "How's it going? Nice tie."

Like to see you hanging from the rafters by it.

"You look good," Hamilton said with put-on sweetness. His jaw flexed beneath his plastered-on smile. "You a working girl today?"

Dakota wanted to take a sharp instrument to his gonads.

Kris elbowed him into silence. "We're following-up a lead."

"And I'm looking for Laura Ann."

"Then we're all hounds on the same blood trail, because your girl just turned into a suspect."

Around nine o'clock that evening, Kris let herself inside Dakota's house. Wearing a ploughed-under look that could only result from poor eating habits, and too many hours at the neighborhood police pub, she entered in a cloud of whiskey vapors, and second-hand cigarette smoke.

Dakota was all for blinders when the need arose. With the remote control in one hand and a melted cheddar nacho in the other, she drew a deep, bracing breath and kept her eyes glued to a dinner train documentary. She finished the chip and took a paper napkin off the Longhorn coffee table. With her fingers free from grease, she smoothed the tails of the oversized silk shirt bunched at her thighs.

"Are you staying the night?"

Kris eased her shoulder holster onto the marble and left it near the door. "I just stopped in to pick up a change of clothes."

A lump formed in Dakota's throat. "Where are you staying?"

The effects of a weary workday played out in Kris's voice. "Don't worry about it."

"I got something for you today."

"Stop buying me stuff."

"You're not mad at me for beating you to Diamond Dogs. You *want* to be mad but you're not." She pushed aside her thick curls, hoping Kris noticed the rose-biting skull on her neck.

"That's what you got for me?" Kris scrunched her face. "That's disgusting. You know how I feel about tattoos."

"This is the one I got for when I go undercover as a Goth." Dakota lifted the silk pajama top and inched down her bikinis until the henna barcode stenciled above her pubic bone was clearly visible. She used her sultry voice. "And this is the one I got for you."

"What is it?" Slightly dazzled, but uncomprehending, Kris moved closer. She dropped to one knee for a closer examination of the temporary tattoo. "It's a barcode."

"Uh-huh."

Kris had moved close enough for Dakota to launch herself at her. She wrapped her arms around Kris's neck, planted a light kiss askew of her mouth, and instantly felt the tension drain from her lover's shoulders.

"Let me get this straight, Dee. Instead of having a red heart with my name tattooed on your snatch, you get this? What's with the barcode?"

"I was hoping you'd scan me with your tongue."

Chapter Eleven

The next morning, Dakota tiptoed out of the bedroom and pulled the door closed behind her. Kris needed sleep, and breakfast in bed might make a nice surprise.

She padded to the kitchen in scuffy slippers, removed several eggs from the refrigerator and broke them into a bowl. Thoughts of *juevos rancheros* made her mouth water. After grating a handful of Monterrey jack cheese into a small bowl, she took the leftover salsa from Thanksgiving and set it within reach of the skillet. Then she changed her mind and added a handful of crushed corn chips, and used up the last of the grilled chicken.

The phone rang.

She dusted off the corn-chip crumbs and caught it on the second shrill. The frightened voice of Heather Lisle, who went by the name of Daphne Blake, another of Celia's girls who took her fantasy alias from the comic strip character from *Scooby Doo*, pealed down the line.

"Heather, slow down. I can't understand you." An unwelcome premonition chilled Dakota's apprehension into an even colder fear.

"You have to help us, Dakota. We're scared to death."

"Heather, I told y'all I'm not that kind of private detective. I investigate runaways. You should contact the police. They're equipped to help you." She turned toward the stove and lowered the burner, then grabbed the spatula, and swirled the eggs until they hardened into clots.

On the brink of tears, Heather continued to plead. "We're afraid. Who's to say I'm not next? A couple of us are thinking of leaving town."

Dakota removed the frying pan from the burner. With the phone wedged between her jaw and shoulder, she whipped around, stopping short of plating the food.

Kris stared from the archway between the dining room and kitchen. She wore silk boxers, a knit camisole, and a look of accusation written all over her face.

"I'm getting another call. Call you back. Ta-ta for now." Dakota didn't have another call but Heather Lisle didn't know that. "I made us a plate of *migas,* " she said. "I was going for *juevos rancheros* but changed my mind because I know you like *migas* better. Here, taste." She lifted the spatula, balancing a sample on the edge of it.

Kris set her jaw. Brown eyes flung daggers beneath a fringe of dark lashes. "One of your prostitute friends?" The detective trip-trapped across the terrazzo tile floor in velour flip-flops, and sat heavily into a chair at the breakfast nook.

"Escorts."

"A hooker's a hooker." Kris skewered her with a look.

The words hit Dakota full force. She pretty much just stared. "That was Heather Lisle, the one from Celia's who uses Daphne Blake as her fantasy escort persona. She's afraid. So are the rest of Celia's girls."

"I don't want you getting involved with those people, Dee. I'm sorry somebody wants them dead, but you're not going near them. Understand?"

Unfazed, Dakota served up breakfast and ferried two glasses of orange juice to the table.

Kris disappeared from the room. She returned with an unopened bottle of Russian vodka from the liquor cabinet. After breaking the seal on the vodka, she took a couple of heady gulps and put the cap back on. The lines in her forehead relaxed.

Dakota gave her a cool stare. Kris's boozing was starting to get out of hand.

"Tell me your plans, Dee. Maybe we can hook up for lunch."

"I suppose I'll spend the day looking for Laura Ann Spencer."

"Isn't that interesting? Her name kept coming up while Hamilton and I scoured the tattoo parlors. Don't you think it's more than a little coincidental that she does these henna tattoos and our victims have henna tattoos on them?"

"That's a pretty big leap, babe, even for you. There are a lots of henna tattoo artists in this city, including the guy who did mine... doesn't mean she was involved in those killings."

"No," Kris drawled out the word, "but the tattoos are damned near perfect. And your little runaway has a reputation for perfection."

After breakfast, Kris left for work in a filthy mood. Dakota searched the Internet in an effort to learn more about Velvet Tears. She told herself things couldn't get any worse—until the phone rang around nine o'clock proved her wrong.

Mayor-Elect David Wilson wanted to meet with her.

He didn't drop any hints, just set the eleven o'clock appointment with the strong suggestion that she keep it. As soon as she hung up, she redialed Mayor Jane. One of the mayoral flunkies offered to take a message, but Dakota declined.

Parked in front of Wilson's office, an adobe ranch-style building on the fringe of Phoenix's red light district, Dakota's uneasiness grew. She should call Kris. Should let her know about the interesting turn of events. She pulled her cell phone out of her bag and punched in the number. But the door to Wilson's office abruptly swung open, and he stepped out into the cold, gray morning and beckoned her inside. She thumbed off the phone before the connection went through.

Inside Wilson's office, she got a big surprise. At the credenza, Chief Forster poured coffee into a Styrofoam cup.

He acknowledged her entry with a jiggle of the coffee pot. "Want some?"

"Already reached my limit, but thanks." Dakota moved to a leather client chair and slid into the seat. Things could get interesting.

Wilson took his place behind a large oak desk. It was totally bare, except for a fresh legal pad, a few sheets of copy paper, a pen, and a banker's lamp with a shade that glowed bright blue above the incandescent bulb. Chief Forster seated himself in the adjacent chair.

Dakota's gaze flitted over the room. American flag on a pole in one corner; Arizona flag in the other. Looked like the guy might be trying to get a head start on the Mayor's office. As a matter of fact, it didn't look much like an office at all. More like a pretend office. A movie set of an office in a fake ghost town made up of plywood storefronts and a painted sky. He had no books. No clutter. No trashcan filled with first drafts. She took-in a deep, dizzying breath. Wilson's tête a tête had all the earmarks of stumbling into a reverse police sting operation where cops fenced stolen goods—only without the inventory.

"You're probably wondering why you're here," Wilson said, picking up the pen and drawing doodles on the legal pad.

Dakota gave a non-committal shrug. She wished she'd thought to purchase a micro-cassette recorder. Too late, she remembered her cell phone had recording capability.

The Chief cleared his throat. She glanced his way, and caught him giving her the visual once-over. Her leather skirt had ridden a few inches above her thigh. She gave it a discreet tug as Wilson slid one of the desk drawers halfway open. He stuck in a hand and came out with a cigar. While unwrapping the cellophane, and whetting it between his lips, Chief Forster spoke.

"It appears you're friends with Jane Roman."

Giving another shoulder-shrug seemed to be the best course of action, considering she happened to be on their turf, stuck in a state of hurling confusion.

"Good enough friends to visit in her home," he went on.

You had me followed.

She'd never even noticed anyone, which called into question her ability to dodge a tail.

Wilson boomed out an observation. "I'm a little concerned about what may or may not be appropriate for you to investigate."

"I'm sure I don't know what you mean."

"Your so-called *friend*—" Forster put air quotes around the word "—Kristina Carson, is a good officer. It'd be a shame if she lost her job because you poked your nose into stuff that doesn't concern you. Might look like the two of you teamed up to cause trouble. And of course, there's the personal relationship between you two that I seriously doubt would hold up under closer scrutiny . . ."

"I have no idea what you're getting at. I'm a private investigator. I look for runaways."

Wilson belted out a laugh. "Whatever you say, Ms. Jones. But let's keep it that way. Understand?"

"I look for runaways," she repeated with polite insistence, and pulled a business card from an 18K gold cardholder with her initials engraved on the top. "You need me to find a kid, I'm your PI. Are we done?" Poise deserted her, and she'd started to perspire. She toyed with her collar to disguise the erratic pulse in her neck.

"You're free to leave. I trust we have an understanding? Good," Wilson said.

Upon rising, her eyes cut to the papers pushed off to one side of the desk. Sheet music. It appeared to be handwritten.

Wilson caught her trying to read upside-down. "I play the harpsichord," he said, straining the conversation through his cigar. Often, I awaken with tunes in my head. Did you learn to play an instrument, Ms. Jones?"

She wanted to tell him she'd tried the skin flute, but had her fill of that. But she didn't see how that would improve the situation. "I tried the guitar but I didn't like the callouses caused by the strings."

She turned to leave, fully prepared—and actually looking forward—to spending the next five minutes dry-heaving into the hedges. Whatever this had been about—whatever scare they'd intended to put into her—made no sense at all. The only thing she felt a modicum of certainty about was this: With hands the size of catchers' mitts, the Mayor-Elect's fingers didn't appear nimble enough to tickle the ivories.

Tuesday afternoon, Dakota was in her study still researching Velvet Tears, when a horn honk pulled her attention away from the computer screen. She recognized the bleat of Kris's BMW and hustled to the door. When she poked her head out, Kris lowered the passenger window and called out.

"Come on, goldbricker, we've got work to do."

Dakota affected a lisp, and used her best Igor-the-hunchback imitation. "Yes, master."

She grabbed her shoulder bag and locked the door behind her. Kris pressed a button and the electric door locks clicked open. Dakota scooted in beside her.

"What's up?"

Kris picked up a handful of papers that had been rolled into a cylinder and rattled them at her. "Celtic designs. Hamilton and I copied them from the victims' tattoos. You and I are going to the library."

It took several hours before either dredged up anything helpful. Then, Dakota saw it.

Upon closer inspection, letters seemed intertwined with the Celtic designs found on the bodies. When she pointed out the anomaly, Kris snatched the pictures away.

Her eyes drifted over the page. At once, they widened. "Wow." She pointed. "I see it."

"What do you suppose this means?"

Neither felt they'd unraveled a killer's message, but both agreed the discovery would advance the detectives one step closer.

Back at Heaven's Urn, as Kris coasted to a stop inches from the garage, Dakota made a tantalizing offer. "I have a couple of filet mignons marinating in the fridge if you want to stay for dinner."

"I think I'll just shove off."

Kris's nonchalance surprised her. Steaks cooked on the gas grill ranked near the top of the detective's *Things to gorge on before I die* list.

Kris snapped the door locks. "Okay, well, maybe I'll see you tomorrow."

With a stunned expression numbing her face, Dakota tried a different tactic. "Sounds good to me. I'm so exhausted I'm ready to drop in my tracks." Flashing a smile, she leaned in and gave Kris's knee a friendly squeeze. She popped open the door and slung out a leg. "Maybe you can earmark a little time for me around lunch, and I'll give you a blow-by-blow account of my afternoon with David Wilson and Chief Forster." With a little finger wave, she alighted the Beamer and pushed the door shut.

Window gears engaged—the window powered down. Dakota walked away with a triumphant smile. She took several steps across the grass, feeling Kris's magnetic pull.

Keep walking; don't look back.

"Dakota, wait."

She turned around and cupped a hand to her ear in an exaggerated, *Sorry I didn't hear you* gesture.

"You talked to the Chief?" Kris seemed to be strangling the steering wheel in white-knuckled effigy.

"Yeah. But it'll keep 'til tomorrow." She cocked her head to the right and listened. "Sorry, gotta catch the phone. See-ya, babe."

"The hell you say." Kris jammed the BMW into *park* and killed the engine. The brake lights went off and the door flew open. Kris hustled to her side.

"So you'll be staying for dinner?"

"Yes, wench. And you'd better not overcook my meat."

"Don't worry, babe, I know just how you like it. Hot, pink and twitching."

Somewhere between the entrée and dessert, Kris's third glass of wine went to her head, and what began as an evening filled with promise degenerated into a verbal bloodbath. The disclosure about visiting Mayor Roman's home put the cherry on the milkshake. The detective went all *Dog Day Afternoon* on her, effectively squelching whatever romance Dakota dreamed up for the evening.

Alone in their bed, Dakota stared out the window at the blow-up shark bumping against the side of the pool. Vile visions of Kris beneath Hamilton Stark's sweaty body filled her head. She drifted into restless sleep, unable to shake the torment of emotions.

The shrill of the telephone jolted her awake.

Dakota grabbed Kris's pillow and crushed it to her ear.

She didn't even bother to check Caller ID. Whatever the caller wanted could wait until morning.

Chapter Twelve

Wednesday dawned with a blood-orange sunrise, and Dakota slit-open one eye. Coffee. *Robust* coffee. Something strong enough to strip the paint off a truck. She lopped a leg over the edge of the bed, sat up, and blinked her surroundings into focus.

A blinking LED on the kitchen answering machine drew her in. She checked the digital call counter, and saw that the log-in time on the first missed-call came from Kris; received during Dakota's experiment in the spa with a new aromatherapy bubble bath. The second came from Heather Lisle. After the earlier conversation degenerated into weeping, sniveling hysterics, it rather surprised Dakota that Heather'd bother to call back. If she said it once, she said it ten times: She only investigated runaway kids. Heather should've gotten it through her head.

Dakota poured a pyramid of Kona-grind into a filter without measuring, and started a fresh pot before retrieving Heather's message. When the coffeemaker sputtered to a stop, she poured herself a cup, lightened it with cream, and let the steamy aroma moisten her face as she whiffed it.

She pushed the *play* button and took her first sip.

"Oh, please, God, help me—pick up the phone, Dakota. He's here. I know he is."

Coffee spewed out of her nose.

Heather went silent with an abruptness so chilling it electrified every nerve in Dakota's body. Breaths of terror rushed down the line. "Dakota, I think I'm next," she whispered. "Please help me." Then a huge suck of air dissolved into the pitiful mewlings of a kitten. "Please don't hurt me."

Dee's heart beat like a savage fist. She could sense Heather's horror at the other end of the line. Her stomach went hollow. She stood perfectly still, rooted in her own fear, feeling her skin crawl up her ribcage.

This was real. It may be over, but to Dakota, it was happening at that very moment.

"What're you doing here? Oh, God, it's you, isn't it? You're the one. I'm begging you, don't hurt me. I'll do anything you want—" Heather Lisle let out a guts-out scream.

For a few eternal minutes, the chaos and violence erupting at the other end of the phone sounded like a couple trying their luck at a home birth. As Heather encountered the malignant side of human nature, Dakota whimpered. Her throat tightened; her eyes burned. Screams curdled her blood. A chunk of ice formed where her heart had been. Helpless to do more than soak up each grisly noise, she stood ramrod straight, listening to a murder in progress.

Silence loomed.

Followed by a ghoulish gasp . . . labored breathing . . . and a gurgle of finality.

A cat screamed in the background.

Then someone depressed the telephone switch, and the line went dead.

Dakota dashed to the bedroom with pyramids of flesh prickling her arms. She shouldn't have washed her hands of Celia's girl. Should've offered her a place to stay. She had plenty of room at Heaven's Urn. What kind of person would turn a friend away? Who'd do that?

Dakota shrieked.

She grabbed her address book from a bedside table. Her fingers shook as she leafed through the pages in search of Heather's telephone information—*found it*. She stabbed out the number with such force a lance of pain shot past her fingertip. Voicemail intervened. The sound of Heather's pixie-like greeting might as well have been a dagger plunged through Dakota's chest.

"Heather, it's Dakota." She felt like she was on the verge of a coronary as the words got stuck in her throat. "Call me as soon as you get this message."

She tried a second number and endured a series of shrill tones, followed by the automated recording of a bored operator announcing a disconnected number.

Dakota double-checked Heather's address. She'd only visited the townhouse once—as a guest at a surprise party for one of Celia's girls who adopted the working persona of *Wonder Woman*—Diana Kyle to her friends. The once-upscale neighborhood had slipped into decline, and while the rest of the area seemed to be enjoying a Renaissance, Heather's street hadn't quite made the cut. Sure, the brick garden home had seemed beautiful at the time, but that grisly phone call proved it'd turned into one big death trap.

Call the police? Don't call the police? Check out the house, then call the police?

If she did call the police, what would she say? *Hi, I'm pretty sure one of my friends just got murdered. How do I know? Because I heard it. Was I there? No, she called me. What's my name? Why, so you can have an officer swing by to make an arrest?*

She wiggled into a long-sleeve knit pullover, pulled sausage-casing tights over her legs, and slipped into a pair of blue jeans and Bally loafers. Grabbing her black leather jacket off a hanger, she headed out the door with her cell phone in hand. On the way to the car, the speed-dialed call she made to Kris's wireless cycled to a recording. On the road to Heather Lisle's, she tried the homicide office and got the third degree from Kris's lieutenant. When she tried to convince him to raise Kris by radio, he taunted her with, "Just what kind of so-called *friend* of Carson's are you?" She hung up on him.

At Heather Lisle's town home, a two-story brick flat in a converted furniture store that went belly-up ten years before, Dakota wrapped the edge of her jacket around her hand before giving the front door knob a twist. It gave way to a gruesome scene that had her stumbling back from the threshold in revulsion.

She'd located the trap door to Hell.

A demonic scream boiled up from the throat of an angry feral cat. Every hair haloed around its scrawny gray body, making it appear twice as large. Green eyes glittered like toxic waste. Before Dakota could jump out of the way, it rushed her. She lost her footing and spun backward, toppling a three-foot barrel cactus in a clay pot next to the door.

As she plucked out thorns, she thought of the ugly tomcat from

Celia's crime scene. This wasn't a mere coincidence. Heather'd been right—there had to be a connection with Celia.

Dakota didn't need a closer look to realize the naked woman was dead. Her skirt was on cockeyed, and bunched up around her hips, as if she'd dressed in a hurry or in the dark. She didn't have on panties, and her legs were splayed. Her face screamed unspeakable terror. On the way over, try as she might to convince herself Heather could still be alive, on some level, she'd known the outcome as soon as the door handle gave way beneath her grip.

Blood pooled around the escort's head. Death froze her ghastly expression. The glint of metal jutting out of her neck caught the light with such vividness each of Dakota's senses came alive. She projectile vomited into a rock garden that substituted for Heather's lawn.

She steadied herself against the doorjamb, punching out Kris's number with a trembling finger. When Kris answered, she panted into the phone. Every spoken word sounded like a sucking chest wound.

"I'm at Heather Lisle's."

"Who?"

"Heather Lisle. She's one of Celia's girls." Tears blurred her vision. "Correction: Used to be one of Celia's girls. Heather's dead."

As dead as the silence that stretched between.

"Can you hear me?" Dakota's voice crescendoed. "I said she's dead."

Kris kept her tone even and metered. "Are you all right?"

"Better than *her*."

"You didn't touch anything, did you?"

Dizzy with the promise of incriminating evidence, Dakota ripped her hand from the doorway and buffed the sleeve of her leather jacket against the molding she'd been leaning against. "No, I didn't touch anything."

"Good. Stay put. I'll call it in. And don't let anyone go inside. We're on the way."

Kris and Hamilton arrived at the same time marked units skidded to a stop in front of Heather's townhouse—"Code-Three"—in a flash of emergency lights, and a peal of sirens. Hamilton slammed the gearshift into park and alighted the vehicle before Kris unbuckled her seatbelt and bailed out. Seated on the stoop with her elbows on her knees and her hands cradling her head, Dakota tracked him striding her way in his tweed jacket, tropical wool slacks and pin-point oxford shirt.

When he came within arm's length, he produced a spiral note-book. "What're you doing here?"

"*Veni, vidi, Velcro.* I came, I saw, I stuck around." The comment slipped out unedited. She darted a look at Kris for support. None came.

"I have a few questions for you." As it turned out, he had a lot of questions. Not to mention a few snide remarks.

"Is that blood on your shoe?" He peered through accusing eyes.

The cat must've tracked blood out, and she told him so. After a blistering exchange, he made no bones about considering her a sus-pect. "Remove your jacket. Hand it over."

Dakota reluctantly obliged. He handed it off to Kris, who retrieved a paper evidence bag, tucked the jacket inside, sealed it with red evidence tape, and tagged it.

"Turn around and put your hands behind your back," he snarled.

"You're not cuffing me."

He pretended to meditate over this comment, then said with unmistakable sarcasm, "Oh, but I am."

She did *not* want to be cuffed. "There's no need for that. I'll go willingly."

"If you ride in my car, you ride in handcuffs." He held a pair of Peerless, stainless steel, hinged-cuffs, and twirled her around so fast her cheek grazed the brick exterior of Heather's house. He ratcheted the cuffs on tight. When she protested, he paid no attention to her objections.

"Ah, the ties that bind . . ." He snipped off his words like nail clip-pers. "Relax. The handcuffs are tight because they're new. They'll stretch after you wear them awhile."

He conducted a brisk pat-down for weapons, then steered her toward one of the marked patrol cars. "Swallow your pride, Pussy Galore. It isn't like you haven't taken a ride with us before."

Dakota looked to Kris for help. "What the hell?" she said in a stage whisper.

Apparently, Kris was still on the spine donor transplant list. Without intervening, she stood by like a clove on a ham, watching, wide-eyed, while Hamilton arranged for a uniformed officer to transport Dakota down to the police station. After Hamilton seated her in the cage of a patrolman's marked unit, he took her shoes.

"For blood spatter evidence." His expression hardened.

"You expect me to 'go barefoot'? That's why all the Neanderthals are dead." Head-to-toe, she eyed him up. "Oh, wait . . . I misspoke."

The back seat of the cruiser had a grimy, nasty feel; its trapped air smelled as ripe and noxious as a hollowed-out horse carcass, mostly from the lingering odors of wine and human waste. She loathed the idea of her feet touching the floor, holding them aloft until her legs grew tired, and gravity triumphed.

The transport officer climbed behind the wheel.

"Could you loosen these handcuffs? My hands are going numb. He put them on pretty tight."

"That's Hamilton for you. He operates on a theory: If you don't want to wear those bracelets, then don't give him a reason to put them on you."

"I'll take that as a no." Wrists tingling, and on the brink of tears, she turned her face to the window looking around for spectators. The entire block had turned out to gawk, including a raggedy old dog sitting rigid among the yucca plants, tense and alert and waiting to take somebody's arm off. She studied the facial expressions and emotionless stares of Free World people who'd gathered on the sidewalk to watch. In the distance, an old Indian wrapped in a *serape* gave her the one-fisted, straight-arm power salute.

"I didn't do anything," she mumbled, seeing the need to put an end to this ongoing flirtation with law enforcement, wincing at the sting of Kris's turncoat behavior.

The patrolman made eye contact in the rearview mirror. "You're Pussy Galore, aren't you?" he asked in a way that seemed almost appreciative, as if she'd done porn movies and he'd sat in the dark, watching, with a bottle of gin and a tube of lubricant. For all she knew, Hamilton circulated her picture around the station.

"My name's Dakota Jones. I'm a private investigator." She met his dark stare and locked gazes.

"No, I don't think so. I think you're Pussy Galore."

"You've mistaken me for someone else. Maybe a girl who looks like me." She didn't think it could get much worse. The worst happened after the cop pulled into the flow of traffic and headed for police HQ. Experiencing the debacle play out was like a screening of home movies of her childhood.

"I know you." Then he reminded her how they met. Told her how his frat brothers learned he was a virgin, and brought him in to Celia St. Claire's for his first sexual encounter. Dakota wanted to retch. The rush of shame heated her cheeks. "You were nice to me," he went on. "I couldn't get it up. You said you wouldn't tell them I couldn't perform—and you didn't."

"You've got the wrong person," she insisted. She checked out his reflection in the rearview mirror, but when he looked back at her, the flicker of recognition passed between them. His thick, black lashes hadn't changed, but bittersweet-chocolate eyes had grown hard in the years after college.

"Bugs Atherton—my pledge brother—asked how you'd rate me. You said I got a ten on a five-scale. Best you ever had, you told him. I never forgot that. If you'd ratted me out like I thought you were going to, they would've thought I was queer, beaten me bloody, and driven me out of the fraternity. You saved me. When I finally met my wife, I didn't have any trouble in the sack."

"That's how it should be," she said tightly, keeping up the pretense of mistaken identity. "Glad it worked out for you, but again . . . wrong person."

He went on with his story. "You're still real pretty. I wondered what would make you take a job like that. I thought about that night a lot once I got out of the police academy and watched the ladies on Northern strut their stuff . . ."

Blah, blah, blah, and blah. A sigh shuddered up to the vomit-stained ceiling. She closed her eyes, lulled by the sound of his voice.

". . . I took a lot of assault calls that first year, and thought how easy it would've been for someone to hurt you."

Dakota came out of her slump. "What do you mean?" She sat erect, feeling her muscles tighten like a stringed instrument. "Were you thinking about hurting me that night?"

"Not me. Other guys. You were playing a part—the Bond girl, Pussy Galore—she was tough. But you weren't much older than me, and I saw how vulnerable you were." His eyes cut away from the mirror to the red light. "I wanted to thank you then. I'm thanking you now."

She slumped against the seat back, and curled up like a tortellini. They rode the rest of the way in silence. When the officer pulled into the sally port, he made a casual comment.

"Stark's not a bad guy—"

Now that's a stretch.

The *You're-pulling-my-leg* factor kicked in, triggering eye-rolling on her part.

A smile rode up one side of his mouth. "—He's one of the most conscientious men on the force. Sure, he gets a little carried away every now and then, but he's really just a pushover when it comes to pretty ladies."

"He's a prick." Said with cutting reserve.

"I know he comes off that way to a lot of people, especially women, but he's a dedicated officer and he knows the job."

I'm sure he'll be 'Police Officer of the Year.' Let's hope he'll still keep his secret identity as Hamilton Stark.

He parked the car nearest the entrance. Police-package safety locks built into the squad cars made it necessary to manually unlatch the back door handle from the outside, and as she climbed out, he firmly grasped her upper arm to steady her.

Face-to-face, she remembered him. The memory of that night rose like an apparition: Drunken frat rats; Celia lecturing them after they hectored the escorts from outdoors. They'd called unwanted attention to the place while belting out *Sweet Caroline* or *Barbara Ann* or *Peggy Sue*, even though none of the girls went by those aliases. Poor guy—must be around twenty-five, now. For a second, she almost felt a tug of affection. He'd lost the baby fat in his cheeks, but still seemed boyish in a deadly sort of way.

A light breeze swept through the sally port's tunnel, swirling Dakota's hair around her face. He still had her by the arm, steering her to the back door when she asked—voice trembling—if she could call in a favor.

"Try me."

She darted a glance at the cell phone pouch on his Sam Browne. "I want to make a phone call."

"You can ask to call your attorney once you're booked-in."

Dakota shook her head. "I don't want to call a lawyer. I want to call a friend. If I give you the number will you dial it for me? I'd consider us even-Steven."

He removed the phone and punched out the phone number she recited. Then he held the cellular up to her ear. A series of staccato tones clicked.

"Jane? Is that you? Oh, thank God." Dakota's composure tanked. "It's me—Dakota. I'm down at the police department, in one melluva hess."

Chapter Thirteen

The Mayor came down to the PD and sprung Dakota herself. As a mayor, Jane might be a lame duck, but she wasn't a dead one; clearly, she still had friends at the courthouse and pulled strings with the magistrate. When Dakota heard the click-clack of low-heeled pumps coming down the corridor, as far as she knew, she'd been released on her own recognizance.

"I think you ought to go undercover to find this killer," Jane mumbled discreetly, on the short walk to her black Lincoln. Gunmetal clouds rolled in from the north, dropping the first splatters of rain onto the sidewalk. Jane pointed. "The car's across the street." The two women picked up the pace. "It's clear to me someone's trying to frame you."

"Me? Why would anyone want to frame me for murder?"

"It has to be you, dear, because whoever's doing this is killing people from your past."

Thoughts turned to Kris.

Nah, Kris was safe. The sick-o that the police were looking for killed prostitutes, not her lovers, and she'd never slept with any of Celia's girls. Oh, sure, Fiona McHugh was undeniably a lesbian, but they'd agreed, early on, not to mix business with pleasure. None of the other girls had ever shown any interest in her.

Mayor Jane must've been talking. She gave Dakota's sleeve a hard pull, and said, "So? Will you at least consider it?"

Dakota shook off her thoughts. "Consider what?"

"Going undercover as a prostitute."

Dakota stopped dead in her tracks. "Are you crazy? Kris would kill me."

"Kris doesn't have to know. Now, hurry. C'mon."

"You have no idea what you're asking of me." Dakota walked against the rain with her chin tucked into her chest.

"You're right," Jane said, and thumbed the remote for her Lincoln. Door locks popped open with a chirp. "What do I know? They weren't my friends."

Dakota let herself in on the passenger side. The Lincoln slumped heavily out of the parking lot, and into the lane of traffic.

"Damn it." Dakota couldn't believe she was even considering Jane's suggestion.

"We're being followed." Jane craned her neck to check out the mirrors. Dakota twisted in her seat. Rain glittered against the back windshield as the wipers squeegeed off droplets. "Don't look."

"What kind of car? All I see are headlights."

"How should I know?"

"Old? New? Dark? Light? You should know there's this creepy guy stalking me."

"Well, dear, consider yourself lucky. You're not really anybody until you have your own stalker. I'm thinking of getting one myself." The light at the upcoming intersection turned amber and Jane slowed. At the last second, she punched the accelerator. The Lincoln hydroplaned, then blasted through the intersection like Hell's torpedo.

The chase car skidded to a stop. Jane made a hard left off the main drag. She dog-legged a couple of streets, then pulled into the driveway of a home with the porch lamps off, and killed the headlights.

Dakota lifted an eyebrow. "NASCAR training camp?"

"No. Outrunning the police. There wasn't much else to do my senior year in Tubac."

Dakota sat on a chaise lounge near her pool, bundled in a Navajo blanket. She was watching a handful of floating candles as they bobbed along the surface, when footsteps broke the silence and the glass door swung open.

Kris stepped outside. "I guess you're furious with me." She gave a little chin duck.

Dakota let the silence speak for her.

"Pretty clever, calling Mayor Jane to get your ass out of a crack."

Dakota set her jaw. Her ass wasn't in a crack. She'd done nothing wrong. She'd been a good citizen calling for help. "If this is how you people treat complainants, I'm guessing your treatment of suspects borders on abusive."

Kris took the chaise lounge next to Dakota's. Slumped forward, she rested her elbows on her knees, flicking out a finger enough to graze her lover's wrap.

"I know you didn't do it, Dee."

"Then why didn't you tell that to that hateful cretin . . . sorry—" *For the record, not sorry* "—your partner?"

"Hamilton's just doing his job."

"Did y'all find the cat?"

Kris shook her head. "He left paw prints all over the crime scene, though."

"Lucky break," she deadpanned. "Now all you have to do is run them through FAFIS to crack the case."

Kris stared, stone-faced. A twitch started in her chin. Then her eyes crinkled at the corners. Dakota could tell she got it—the play on AFIS, the Automated Fingerprint Index System used by North American law enforcement agencies across the United States—the F standing for feline, of course.

Kris cracked. "And you accuse me of gallows humor . . ."

"What about a tattoo?"

"Yep. Dr. Stone should have photos for us, any day. Hamilton volunteered to pick them up so we can study them. He wants these murders to stop."

"Screw him."

"I'd rather not." Kris cracked a smile. "Do we have any whipped cream?"

"You hungry?"

"Starved."

"There's pie in the fridge."

"That's not the kind of pie I had in mind."

They held each other's gaze, with Dakota weighing her physical needs against her anger.

She slung her long legs over the side of the chaise lounge and walked toward the door. As she left Kris behind, she called over one shoulder. "If you want me, I'll be in bed."

"I think we should play 'grocery store' now," Dakota said huskily.

Kris nibbled her neck, near the soft spot behind her earlobe. "How do you play? I don't believe I'm familiar with your little game."

Dee moved beneath the weight of her partner's arm, adjusting it so that Kris's hand could caress her right breast. "We got a shipment of fresh melons in today. You're the quality control officer. You should feel them for freshness." She pressed her hand on top of Kris's, forcing a squeeze that sent shockwaves through her body.

"Umm. Nice."

"Tasty, too. Our store gives free samples. You should try them," Dakota used her sultry voice. "Bite into one. I want you to."

The detective nipped one breast. "Like that?"

Dazzled by an inner vision of gold and white fireworks, she answered by way of a long, sensual moan. "Babe . . . that's fabulous. Do the other one."

"I don't like this store. There's no music."

"We have music," Dee said in a rush. "We play whatever kind of music you like."

"Good. Because studies show people shop a lot longer and buy more stuff if they're in a pleasant environment." Kris leaned over and turned on the clock radio. It took a moment to dial into her station of choice, but soon, Counting Crows was finishing up their hit, *Long December*, and Train set the mood with *Drops of Jupiter*.

Soon, the detective seemed totally into shopping at Dee's grocery store.

"Taste the other melon," Dakota prompted.

"I wouldn't want to be a pig about it."

Dakota threaded her fingers through Kris's short hair, and fisted her dampened locks. "Be a pig. You have to buy them now, since you bruised them," she said firmly.

"I didn't bruise them."

"Yes, you did. I manage the produce, and I say you did. And you owe for the pie you ate."

"And just how do I pay for . . . these groceries?" Kris scooted close enough to tongue Dakota's ear.

"We go to the check-out line." She parted her ankles, took Kris's hand and positioned it between her legs.

"Then what do we do?"

On some level, Dakota sensed that Kris enjoyed the game. It seemed to inflate her self-confidence in her new lesbian role, which in turn, made for better sex.

"What we do," Dakota said, "is you have to scan the barcode." She gently pushed Kris's head down.

"I beg to differ with you. I'm buying the produce. *You* scan *my* barcode. I'm the customer. The customer's always right." Kris's words sang with laughter.

"Wrong. This grocery store is self-serve. You touched the melons, you bought them. Now scan the barcode until I say you're paid up."

When they switched roles, the final sale included melons, thighs, wings, cherries, and a banana Kris dug out of the nightstand drawer. For a brand new store, business seemed to be booming.

Moonlight poured into the bedroom, bouncing off sweat-glistened bodies. Against the sheen of silk sheets, sated lovers held each other close enough to feel each other's heart thudding.

"What're you thinking?" Dakota murmured, smiling into Kris's hair. She felt like she'd survived electrocution, yet, Kris appeared almost autistic with detachment. The abrupt change in moods was as overshadowing as a gathering of thunder clouds.

"Just remembering stuff about my daddy."

"Oh," Dakota said. Kris rarely mentioned her family. After a scary silence, she said, "How come you never talk about him?"

"For one thing, he's dead. If I talk about him, it makes me remember."

Dakota pressed for details. "Remember what?"

Partially trapped in bedcovers, with her bare feet and manicured toenails pointing toward the ceiling, Kris traced a fingertip along Dakota's collarbone. "The night his captain and the police chaplain came to our house to tell me and my mom he'd been killed."

"Your daddy was a cop?"

"Uh-huh."

The admission turned into eerie stillness. Sure, Kris had never taken her home to meet the parents, but Dakota had merely thought it was because she wasn't ready to disclose to her folks that they were a couple.

"How'd he die?"

"Bled out on a filthy sidewalk."

"No, I meant under what circumstances?"

Abruptly, Kris wrangled her arm from beneath Dakota's head and flopped onto her side, with her face to the platinum moon. "I'm going to sleep now."

Dakota raised herself up on one elbow. "I think we should talk about this, don't you?"

"Why?" Said dully.

"If it's important to you, then it's important to me." When Kris didn't respond, Dee finger-nudged her. "I want to know what happened to him. I want us to be able to talk about things that bother us. You know about my scumbag father; why can't I know about your dad?"

"Let it alone."

"He was shot, wasn't he? Was he responding to a robbery call?"

A snort of unsuitability traveled through the room. Kris rolled onto her back. Exposed breasts pointed skyward like small, hard pyramids. She answered in a lethal monotone.

"Not shot. His throat was cut."

Dakota sucked air. A grisly visual popped into mind.

"When I got on the PD, the brass made it known that the file was off-limits to me. That whoever showed it to me would be disciplined—direct orders from the Chief." Kris's breaths quickened. Her voice had taken on an airy, almost surreal, quality. "For a long time, I didn't go near it; even after I transferred into Homicide. But one holiday, Hamilton and I were the only ones working. He said he was going out to get us a bite if he could find a restaurant that was open. I thought I was alone . . ."

Dakota hung on every word. This would not be a quick story. "You stole the file?"

Kris took a deep breath, and let it out on a slow exhale. "Stop with the questions, Dee. I know how you think; how the gears in your mind turn. I won't say how I appropriated that file . . . I could probably be filed on for committing a crime . . . and, the statute of limitations hasn't run. Let's just agree that I managed to get a look at it, and be done with it.

"I read the offense report. It took forever. I'd finally psyched myself up enough to look at the crime scene photos, when who should walk in, but—you guessed it—my good buddy, Hamilton Stark. Only we weren't buddies back then. No telling how long he'd been lurking in the doorway, watching. I could've probably gone on like that for hours, if I hadn't smelled the grease wafting out of the hamburger sack. I almost stroked out."

Dakota realized she'd been holding her breath. She let it out in a slow, deliberate stream, feeling like she was floating in the abyss. "What'd the old man say?"

"At first, he didn't say anything. Just stood there, blank-faced. I knew he was thinking he had to make a choice—me, or his career."

Problem solved. They were both still working at the PD. Of course he'd picked Kris over indefinite suspension. Neither got fired because nobody else knew about it. Kris's little burglary caper had turned into their mutual secret.

Looks like the old man might have an honorable bone in his body, after all.

Unless . . .

Realization dawned.

Maybe that's how he conned Kris into sleeping with him.

"Like I said, Dee. I know how your mind works, so just leave it alone. I got the file. I scoured that case from cover to cover. I saw color glossies of my father with his head in a pool of blood. It didn't even look like him. And I swore to God, right then and there . . ."

Her shoulders wracked with sobs. She tuned up in an eerie wail.

For the next few minutes, Dakota held her close. Comforted her with the kind of *There-there* assurances used to calm small children. Told her nothing so tragic would ever happen to her—that God didn't operate like that, and it probably skipped a generation. That things were different these days. Officers had better training, and better equipment. Take body armor, for instance. Cops these days had so much superior technology at their disposal they could hear a mouse fart three miles away.

Kris didn't laugh, but her cries subsided. She rose from the bed and padded, barefooted, to the bathroom where she honked like a goose into a tissue. She returned, composed, and slid, naked, between the sheets.

Dakota spoke softly to the back of her girlfriend's head. "Want to talk some more?"

"No."

"Just so you know, I'm here for you. Did they ever find out who did it?"

Kris snorted in disgust. "*Who*? Or *what*?"

"I don't understand."

"Oh, you, of all people, should understand," she said with a sinister mix of sarcasm and rage.

"What does this have to do with me? I never met your father."

"A hooker slit his throat and stole his wallet. There, you have it. *Now* can I go to sleep?"

Chapter Fourteen

Thursday, around five in the morning, Dakota roused to the panicky ring of the doorbell. She threw back the covers and gave the air a deliberate sniff. So much for the house being on fire. But if the house hadn't caught fire, then what was the reason for the early-morning invasion? She glanced over at Kris, cocooned in the top sheet. After their talk about Kris's dead father, the detective—unable to fall asleep—had downed enough rot-gut to pickle her liver.

The door chime tapered off, replaced by relentless pounding that sounded like the opening salvo at a DEA raid.

Dakota snatched her kimono off the pile of clothes dropped hastily onto the floor, and left her girlfriend snoring like a walrus. She cinched the tie into a half-bow, grabbed her snub-nose off the night stand and headed, barefoot, through the house.

A quick peek through the peephole revealed the silhouette of a female.

The plaintive cry of her name filtered through the thick mission door.

"Da-Ko-Taaaaaaaaa. Pleeeeeeaaaase."

Fiona McHugh.

Dee slid back the chain. Let it grate along its track, and clatter to a standstill. With the gun at her side, she yanked open the door.

Dakota shushed her. "You'll wake up the dead. What're you doing here?" Fiona stood, wide-eyed and scantily clad, on the terrazzo tiles. Instead of inviting her inside, Dakota stepped out on the porch and looked the length of street.

Fiona clutched at her friend's shoulders. "Dee, you've gotta help me. I'm being watched. And that cop—that investigator Stark—he doesn't give a rat's ass. I reported it and he said not to worry."

"What do you expect me to do?"

"Help me."

"You know I don't do private investigation cases like this. I find runaways." Beyond the sidewalk, dewdrops glistened on the pebble garden like beads of water on a hot skillet, galvanized in a silvery sheen from the blue glow of the street lamps. Dakota thought of the compromising photo of Fiona McHugh, taken with Jake and Lorraine Spencer's only child, now accessible on the Internet, for anyone to see. "Speaking of runaways, do you know Laura Ann Spencer?"

Fiona's gaze dipped. "A little." She toed the tile, momentarily, before locking her eyes on Dee. "But I haven't seen her in a couple of months."

"How do you know her?"

"She did henna work for me. Hell—she did all of us."

"That's a nice way of putting it." Said cattily.

"You know about me and her?"

"That you're lovers?"

Fiona slumped to the tiles and seated herself with her back to her friend. She settled her elbows on her knees, and sank her face into her hands. "We're not lovers—not the way you say it. She started out doing my tattoos. One thing led to another. She showed up at my house one day, unannounced, and asked if I wanted my tattoos re-done. I didn't have enough cash on me, and asked if I could pay her later. She suggested there might be a way I could get my tattoos done without exchanging money."

Dakota stared in disgust.

Laura Ann Spencer was underage.

No matter how flat you rolled the tortilla, there was still another side. And the other side had a name for it—statutory rape.

Dakota felt her face contort into revulsion. Fiona must've noticed, because she went into a panic.

"You won't say anything to the cops, will you? She's so confused."

"It's a crime."

"She's lesbian, Dee. She didn't have anywhere else to go. It was better than experimenting with a street whore."

"She has a boyfriend. A biker dude. And, oh—wait—*did I mention she's underage?*"

"She doesn't need that control freak. She digs chicks. Look, Dee, if it means anything, I have feelings for this girl. Our romps weren't just sex on my part. We were in love."

"That sounds an awful lot like the argument pedophiles use to justify their crimes."

"Laura Ann won't say anything that'll get us in trouble."

But Dakota was thinking about the picture . . . Laura Ann didn't have to say squat.

Dakota crept back to her room, careful not to awaken the snoring mummy sharing her bed. With great stealth, she slipped beneath the only portion of fabric Kris hadn't shrouded herself in. She drifted into slumber until she felt the sting of the morning sun toasting her back.

Groggy, she sat up and checked the time. Ten o'clock.

Her eyes slewed to Kris's side of the bed. It had all the makings of a crime scene, minus the *corpus delecti*. Kris must've left for work not long after Fiona showed up on the doorstep.

An hour later, after Dakota showered and dressed, she sauntered into the Phoenix Police Department with her short leather skirt hugging her thighs. She smoothed her hands against the chamois-soft doeskin, took a deep breath and brazened out an entrance worthy of a starlet.

All eyes shifted to her.

She scanned the faces for Kris, who seemed to be mired in the thick of controversy. She didn't expect the Welcome Wagon committee to greet her, but she wasn't prepared for a public beheading, either, especially at the hands of Kris. As soon as the detective caught sight of her, she forged through her colleagues, knocking arms and bumping hips, to head Dakota off at the door.

"Out," growled the detective under her breath. Kris steered her by the arm, into the corridor. She gave a casual head nod to a passing uniform, said, "'Morning . . . howzit going?" and got a noncommittal shrug for her efforts. When the troop walked out of earshot, she fixed Dakota with a hard stare.

"Just what the hell do you think you're doing? It's bad enough I have to come down here and put up with wisecracks and crude jokes about us, without you showing up pouring gasoline on the flames. What do you want? And why couldn't it wait until I got off work?"

"I came to tell you Laura Ann Spencer's been seen with a biker dude."

"Yeah? Well, we'll look into it." Kris turned to leave. She stopped short of re-entering the Homicide Unit with such abruptness Dakota backed up on instinct. "And, by the way, you need to pull your snout out of this investigation."

Snout?

SNOUT?

"Do you get that I'm trying to help you?"

"And, since you've got nothing to do with what's going on down here, I don't guess I have to tell you to stay out of the police station."

Kris's diatribe rendered her speechless. Wordlessly, Dakota spun away. She picked up her pace, and headed for the exit with one thought circling inside her head.

The PD's a public place.

You can't order me out of a public place.

The tiff with Kris didn't land Dakota in a mood to shop, but the department store contacted her to let her know their shipment of satellite radios had arrived, and she could redeem the "rain check" they'd given her a few weeks before. With only three weeks until Christmas, she needed to pick up a gift in the event the two of them could hold it together long enough to celebrate. Besides, Kris loved music. If worse came to worse, the satellite radio would make a nice consolation prize if the relationship continued to unravel.

The new mall bustled with customers, pickpockets, car burglars and shoplifters. Instead of parking at the far end of the lot, and power-walking to get her exercise, Dakota pulled up under the portico where valet parking had been set up. She removed the car key from her ring, keeping the house keys, safe deposit key and the keys to Kris's BMW for herself.

Christmas trees with twinkle lights and bowling ball sized ornaments glittered in the mall's rotunda. A five-car locomotive choo-choo'd along its track. It wound through obstacles and disappeared into a papier mâché cave, only to shoot out the other end and circle the tree near the North Pole. A tired-looking Santa bounced a

crying toddler on his knee, while a couple of elves sneaked a cigarette behind a Styrofoam candy cane. Mrs. Claus looked like she'd
gone on a bender instead of a break. By the time she staggered to
the porch of the Claus Cottage, she was so oiled and lubed that she
practically slid out of her rocking chair.

Dakota breezed into the electronics shop, checked the placards
suspended from the acoustical tile ceiling, and located the satellite
radios. She settled on a system that could easily be docked in Kris's
patrol car.

The cashier pointed out the subscription information for it to be
activated, and referenced the 1-800 number on the box. After paying for the gift Dakota stopped by a trendy boutique and bought a
bottle of perfume, then headed back to the valet to pick up the Jag.
The smell of a new scent, spritzed on her wrist by a sales clerk with
a test atomizer, still hung in her nose. But not so heavy as to dull
her senses. As soon as the valet turned her car back over to her, and
handed her the key, she whiffed the unpleasant body odor of Travis
Creeley.

The parking attendant waited patiently for his tip.

Instead of pressing a few dollars into his hand, Dakota sniffed
him. He didn't smell so hot, but he certainly didn't smell like Travis
Creeley, either.

"Who'd you let inside my car?"

"I dunno what you're talking about, Miss. I just park cars."

"Let's get something straight." Dakota measured his expression
with the pernicious acuity of a hawk. "Christmas is right around
the corner. You probably need this job. Tips ought to be pretty lucra-
tive this time of year."

He kept his eyes firmly averted.

"That man—did you let him inside my car?"

"He only wanted to sit behind the wheel for a minute."

"What'd he give you?"

"Twenty bucks. They pay minimum wage here."

Dakota smiled. "It'll cost at least seventy-five to have this car
detailed." She held out her hand, palm-up.

"Lady, I ain't gonna give you my tip money."

"Oh, I don't want it from you. I'm going to get it from your boss.
Whatever happens after that is strictly between you and him."

The young hustler dug in his pocket. Peeled four twenties off his roll and asked for change.

She snatched the twenties from his hand. "Think of that last five dollars as a tip—for me—for not turning you in."

At Heaven's Urn, she slowed near the kiosk and found it unmanned. The community funded a guard position through residents' quarterly dues to the homeowner's association. She made a mental note to ask the head of the association why Frank, the guard, hadn't covered his post in three days. But when she came even with the guard shack, a sign placed prominently on the glass pocket door cleared that up. Someone had taped a flyer with Frank's smiling face on it. Along with his date of death, and the address for the trust department at a local bank, in case anyone wanted to donate to his family. Poor, decrepit Frank probably died of old age, not foul play, and it suddenly made sense how Creeley was able to get in.

Dakota trashed the packaging for Kris's radio, got out the manual, found the toll-free number, and called the company. When a recorded menu came on, she pressed the correlating number on the keypad for installation. The electronic selection process meant pressing numbers until a live body came on the line.

"Yes, I bought a satellite radio and need to have it activated."

A foreigner spoke in a clipped accent. "You need to speak to the activation."

"Right. I need to have the radio activated."

"Yes. You need the activation."

"Is this activation?"

"You will hold for activation."

Click, click.

Whoever she talked to disappeared from the line. Momentarily, a new voice answered.

"Activation." Different foreigner, different accent.

"Yes, I bought a satellite radio and need to have it activated."

"Activation."

"Hello? Can you hear me?" No response. "Am I getting through to you?" *Déjà vu.* A chilling realization haunted her. These were the words on Celia St. Claire's henna tattoo.

The activation specialist must've said something. A long pause

followed, and the voice of a different troubleshooter of indetermi-
nate sex, age, and nationality said, "Activation. State your business."
The abbreviated conversation turned out to be barely more than a
repeat of the first one. When she mentioned she couldn't understand his accent, he said, "Please do not interrupt."

Dakota reared back in disbelief. "I didn't interrupt you. I need
help activating a satellite radio. Are you going to help me, or not?"

"You have begun to become insulting."

"Where are you based? What's your location?"

"This is not your business. You have reached Activation."

"Are you in the United States?"

"This, Sri Lanka."

"I want to talk to an American."

"You are a capitalist bastard."

The connection went dead. Stunned, she redialed the toll free
number. After fumbling through the electronic menu, her call
routed to Activation. A different foreigner answered her call, most
likely of Pakistani extraction, judging by the way the man trilled
his "R"s.

"I need to get a satellite radio activated."

This time, she got as far as programming the unit.

"It doesn't work."

"Please to wait five minutes for your radio to work."

"You want me to wait on the line?"

For the second time in an hour, Dakota wound up listening to the
buzz of a dead connection. Fifteen minutes went by, but the radio
didn't work. She placed the contents back into the box, and stuffed
it in a hall closet with a blanket tossed over it. She had work to do
on Laura Ann Spencer's case, and Kris's love of music would have
to take a back seat. Not to mention she probably should exchange it
for a portable navigation system, in case Kris ever felt the need to
locate a backbone . . .

Chapter Fifteen

Early Friday morning, Dakota quickly dressed in yoga pants, a tank top, and a long-sleeve thermal knit shirt. The soft glow of light from the Spencer's kitchen still shined in the distance, meaning Jake Spencer probably hadn't yet left for his job at Spen-Soft, and she could catch the couple at home together. She decided to check-in by power-walking the two blocks to their house; maybe they'd derive relief from a *No news is good news* message, and a promise to keep digging.

To be on the safe side, now that Travis Creeley seemed to be able to come and go as he pleased, she tucked her gun into the pocket of her hoodie. With the door keys in the other pocket, she walked through the house, across the tile floor, with her athletic shoes squeaking like field mice.

Moonlight blued the neighborhood. In an unguarded moment, lulled by the distant swish of highway traffic, Dakota relaxed. The crisp, morning air burned her lungs in the most refreshing of ways, and she took deep breaths until she experienced a dizzying rush. Grass and blown leaves were the only movement. Shadows from palm fronds cast lacy patterns in the orange glow of the street lamps.

She looked up from behind her web of spidery black lashes and saw the octogenarian that neighbor women were complaining about, out for an early jog, with his "soldier," dangling at-ease, and his two "duffle bags" swinging back and forth beneath loose running shorts. Music leaked out of the ear buds to his iPod. He'd focused, trancelike, on some distant object, and sneaked onto her radar screen before he noticed her. This allowed enough time for her to cross to the other side of the street, where she tried to slink off, unnoticed.

Didn't work.

As the gap between them closed, he yelled, "Hiya, little cutie-pie," in the high-pitched wheeze of an old man.

She did a little finger wave, and grinned by way of hello, wondering what all the hoopla was about. Poor thing had a face like a dried-up riverbed, he appeared harmless enough, and he couldn't get any traction with her. Let him play sugar-daddy to somebody younger and dumber. Besides, he ran slower. And even if he didn't, it'd be hard to out-sprint a copper-jacketed stinger traveling at 1200 feet per second.

As they came even with each other, he said, "Want a date?"

"No, thanks." Head down, keep moving.

He let loose with a unique tapestry of curses that ended with him raising his hand and rejecting her with anatomical specificity. She finished her trot to the Spencer's with her thoughts free-associating: She and Kris lived in a world where stupid people were needed to populate it. After all, there weren't that many Fulbright Scholarships to go around. Every neighborhood had a senile old geezer—why not theirs? And let's not forget the people in low-level jobs who did all the dirty work. Who'd spear trash along the highway for free, if not the cretins in the work-release program who were locked up in jail for asinine criminal behavior?

Equally disconcerting was the Spencer's reaction to her impromptu visit. They didn't seem particularly overjoyed to see her, but she considered their frosty demeanor may have been the result of her interrupting a spat. Or sex. *Not.* They did offer her a fresh pastry from the bakery box to take with her on her way out, though, and she barely held back a sigh of pleasure at the taste of the bear claw.

On the way back home, the streetlights blinked off. In the gray light of dawn, the same palm fronds she'd passed twenty minutes earlier hung as stationary and limp as whisk brooms. In another few minutes, the horizon would turn into a huge neon jawbreaker freeing itself from a smear of melted Crayolas in various shades of pink and orange; and those same palm fronds would turn into brilliant green fans for the Jolly Green Giant's flamenco-dancing cousins.

Cold pinpricks started at the nape of her neck. Slowing to a cautionary pace, she arrived home to find the house covered in graffiti dicks, the front windows smashed, the front lawn trenched, and a pile of dog droppings on the front porch. She also found a note taped to the front door that said, "Suck on this, Derek."

Derek lived next door.

Beneath the note, a Post-It that appeared to be an afterthought, penned in a completely different hand, read: *Check the mail.*

The un-posted package left inside the mail box didn't tick like a time bomb, and it appeared to be too small and flat to hold a stick of dynamite and an alarm clock. It had no return information on it, only her name—D. Jones—written on the wrapping in jagged, psycho-script. She stuck in a hand and gingerly pulled it out by one corner, inspecting it for tape, or other areas to lift fingerprints. If Kris ever stopped bickering long enough to run a print through AFIS, maybe they could figure out who'd left this strange calling card.

It appeared harmless. With her pulse vibrating in her throat, Dakota opened the box—*Holy Brahma cow.*

She stared at the pair of cotton bikini panties. Small and worn. The underclothing of a child. With elastic that crumbled with age the moment she stretched it to see if she could find a tag attached.

An unwelcome nudge from Travis Creeley?

The crisp, desert breeze carried a familiar scent to her nostrils, a quick impression buried deep inside her brain. Her pulse quickened. Could the underpants belong to Laura Ann Spencer? Did they remind her of something she'd smelled in Laura Ann's room?

She unbolted the door and hurried into the house, but left it wide open for an easy getaway. Once inside, she scanned the room for signs of intruders before taking another next step toward the telephone. The only movement came from a thin whistle of air moving past the broken glass—that, and the inflatable shark, caught in the undertow of the pool's filtration system, bobbing at the other side of the house.

She grabbed the nearest cordless, dashed back out onto the front porch, and dialed 911.

Then she went next door to give Derek a piece of her mind.

A half hour later, when the police showed up, she turned them away. They were no longer needed—*and oh, by the way, thanks for the speedy arrival since there could've been a killer in the house.* Derek agreed to have everything fixed by nightfall, being the suspect's "baby daddy" and all; he didn't want to see his pyromaniac ex-girlfriend, who'd recently stopped by to set fire to his previous house, go to jail. Within the hour, Derek returned from the paint store with paint chip samples to match the exterior latex; by ten o'clock that morning, painters arrived. The glass repair truck pulled up to the curb shortly after the paint crew, and a landscaping service arrived shortly after the glass repair truck left. Derek called in his housekeeper, Consuela, to clean up the mess inside, and by three o'clock that afternoon everyone except Dakota had packed up their gear and scrammed.

Alone in the quiet, Dakota headed straight for the computer. The Spencers had all kinds of weird native plants among the shrubs and groundcover leading up the walkway to their home. Had that been the familiar scent coming from the package in the mail box? She accessed the Internet, seeking to identify plant life able to withstand the harsh Arizona climate.

An email message popped up.

Her breath caught in her throat. For several seconds, she stared at the sender's address.

Velvet Tears.

She moved the cursor and clicked-open the message.

I've seen you around. You're hot.

Word on the street is you're looking for me.

Wanna meet?

Dakota typed "Yes." She hit the reply bar and the message disappeared into cyberspace. She didn't have long to wait for Velvet Tears to send an answer.

Meet me at Club Crimson tomorrow night, nine sharp. I'll be in the Karaoke room on the third level.

Club Crimson? The place had a reputation as the roughest Goth club in town. And what was this bit about seeing her around? Was Velvet Tears watching her every move? If so, why?

Thanks to the E-mail message, the house had a quiet feel that seemed less serene and more disconcerting now that she'd heard back from Velvet Tears. She pushed back from the computer and hurried to the living room to draw the sheers. Her heart picked up its pace.

The front door lock snapped open unexpectedly—had she forgotten to lock it after turning Fiona away? Dakota released the curtain pull. She grabbed the nearest object—a bronze Remington figurine—and prepared to brandish it.

Kris stepped into the foyer. When she saw Dakota with the upraised statue, she halted in her tracks.

"You scared the hell outta me." Dakota lowered the bronze. "I almost brained you. You should call before barging in."

"I live here—"

And thank God for that, Dakota wanted to say, *because I don't know what I'd do without you in my life.*

"—unless you hauled my stuff out into the front yard and torched it."

"Not yet, I haven't."

"What's with the cloak and dagger act?" Kris shrugged out of her blazer and tossed it over the nearest barstool.

Dakota decided not to mention the underwear. "I thought I heard a noise. I came in here to check. Next thing I know, you busted in."

"I didn't bust in. I used my key."

"Whatever. You scared me. I wasn't expecting company."

"I'm not company."

"You got that right. Company implies you're fun to be with. Instead of foreplay, all I've been getting from you lately is multiple sarcasms." *Except for the make-up sex from last night,* Dakota thought, as she returned the figurine to the accent table.

Kris cracked a smile. "You're funny. Do we have anything good to eat?"

"Are you coming on to me . . . because I'm no-shit furious with you. You can't keep treating me like this. You know what? I don't even want to get into it with you. I've got stuff to do."

"I merely thought I'd ask what's for lunch."

Dakota huffed out her displeasure. "If you came home for lunch, we're out of food. If you came home for a fresh helping of afternoon delight, we're out of that, too."

"We need to talk," Kris said. Luminous brown eyes did little to hide a universe of pain. "Let's go out tomorrow night. We'll have dinner at a nice, quiet place with tablecloths and candlelight—maybe that new Italian place Hamilton talks about—and we can catch up."

Hamilton. Always Hamilton. Nothing made the grade unless it came from Hamilton.

"I have plans." As soon as the words toppled out, Dakota flinched. Probably not a good idea to discuss the impending rendezvous with Velvet Tears.

Kris cocked an eyebrow. "What kind of plans?"

"I need to get out more." Dakota took a deep breath. "You hurt me today. Oh, don't look so surprised. The way you acted down at the PD, muscling me out into the hall? You can't just throw me to the wolves, and then expect the status quo to be restored." Her voice climbed. Anger pinched the corners of her mouth. She looked hard at Kris but Phoenix's ace detective didn't seem to get the message. "Listen up. Either accept who you are, or keep hiding it. I really don't care one way or another anymore. But I won't be your dirty little secret."

"Don't talk to me in that tone. You know how hard it is for me."

Tension loomed between them. Then, Kris snatched up her blazer, slung it over one shoulder and stomped out in a huff, slamming the door hard enough to rattle the windows.

Dakota flopped onto the sofa and clutched a throw pillow to her chest. Then her mouth tilted at the corners. Who'd have thought that would actually feel good?

Mid-afternoon, Mayor Jane's voice blared over the answering machine. Dakota sat bolt upright from her imprint on the couch, and swiped drool from one corner of her mouth. She hurried to the kitchen and snatched up the phone before voicemail cycled off.

Mayor Roman got down to business. "Have you given anymore thought about our little talk?"

"About going undercover as a prostitute?"

"I prefer to think of it as surveilling the red-light district."

A true politician.

"Look, Dee—" paper crackled in the background "—I've picked out an area near the strip clubs, massage parlors, dirty book stores, nude model studios, escort services and the triple-X movie houses. Go down there and poke around. Blend in. Ask questions. See what happens."

"I suppose I could."

"Atta-girl. I knew I could count on you." The phone went dead.

Dakota heaved a heavy sigh. Mayor Jane had no idea what she was asking. Still, she might find out whether any of the working girls knew Laura Ann Spencer.

Around eleven o'clock that evening, the self-styled private eye sat behind the wheel of her Jaguar, with the engine idling and the heat turned down low. She watched the high-traffic area through binoculars, taking in the streetwalkers, drumming up business.

A flood of memories—all bad—came rushing back. She could almost lip read the conversations, and smell the testosterone bubbling up from the loins of the johns:

"Hey, baby, wanna date?" Said with the skirt hiked up to a fare-Thee-well. *"I'll show you a good time. Whatcha looking for?"* Breasts hanging past the open passenger window.

"Whatcha got to offer?"

"No, baby, you gotta tell me what you want. Hey . . . you're not a cop, are you?" Said cagily, with a backward step. "You in, or, you out, daddy? What's it gonna be?"

"What'll ten dollars get me?"

"Ten bucks? Baby, ten bucks'll get you a punch in the face. I'll do you for twenty-five."

"Fifteen."

"Twenty."

"Twenty, it is. See that motel over there? Meetcha across the street. Room Three."

And that's how it worked. Like riding a bicycle. Dakota shuddered. Never again. She focused the lenses on the field glasses. Several thugs advanced on one of the hookers. If the woman realized they were there, she strutted ahead with confidence. They surrounded her from behind. One grabbed her arm. Spun her around and shook her. Another took her other arm in a kind of tug-of-war.

Dakota tossed the binoculars onto the passenger seat. Revved up the engine and wrenched the Jag into gear. Roared up from the alleyway, onto the street. She powered-down the passenger window, and came to a skidding stop with all four tires screaming.

Activity faltered.

"Let go of her, you lousy piece of shit."

"Who the hell're you?"

"The Heat."

They took off flying down the street in the opposite direction, receding in her rearview mirror like a swarm of angry hornets.

The prostitute rearranged her tube top. "Thanks a fucking bunch, bitch. Now my kid won't eat tomorrow."

"What?" Dakota's jaw gaped. "I thought you were in trouble."

"Yeah? Nobody asked you for help. Next time you wanna be a Good Samaritan, mind your own business. Stupid bitch." She wobbled off down the street on one broken heel, flipping Dakota a stiff middle finger on the way back to her corner.

Through her side-mirror, Dakota glimpsed the looming silhouettes of the woman's assailants. As they piled into a panel truck, she wrenched the steering wheel, hard left, and did a mid-block U-turn. The Jag bounced over the median and she slipped into the flow of traffic, four cars behind them.

At first, she'd only planned to copy down their license plate and get Kris to run it. She felt for a scrap of paper, and a pen. But they were exceeding the speed limit, and she had a hard time catching up.

They barreled through the amber light, with the tailpipe belching cones of gray exhaust. Dakota braked to a stop, but kept them in view. When she spied a hole in traffic, she floored the accelerator and brazened through the red light.

She'd jotted down the first three LP characters when they turned onto a road that led to an industrial area. Chills climbed Dakota's ribcage.

She abandoned the chase when the truck zipped into the Mayor-Elect's parking lot.

A half-block away, sandwiched between two narrow buildings, Dakota curbed the Jag and killed the lights. Picked up the binoculars and watched the van's headlights go out. Several occupants fanned out from the truck. Made their way up to David Wilson's office. Let themselves in with a key and disappeared from sight.

She sat, rigid, waiting for lights to come on inside the building. They didn't.

She focused the field glasses and noticed a shadowy specter, still inside the van.

Lost in concentration, she never heard any movement outside

her car until a tap on the window jolted every hair, straight-up, on her arms.

She barked out a scream.

The man at the window twirled his finger in the universal roll-down-the-glass hand motion.

Dakota fumbled for the electric button and lowered the window a couple of inches, then smoothly gripped the gun butt tucked beneath her thigh.

With the weapon firmly in her grip, she challenged him. "What?"

"You got no business following people around."

"This is a public place. I'm the public."

"Yeah? Well, maybe you need to move along before somebody gets hurt." He moved his jacket aside enough for her to glimpse the butt of an automatic weapon protruding from his waistband.

"By 'somebody,' do you mean me, or David Wilson?"

The fake grin on his face melted into a sneer. "Maybe you don't get the message. Maybe you're brain damaged. Maybe you're the kind who only learns when they get taught a lesson."

"Oh. I see. You mean me, don't you?" Dakota oozed sarcasm. Having your finger on the trigger of a .38 apparently did that—made a person feel bullet proof. With the trip wire to her common sense fully restored, she said, "Okay, well it's getting late. I'll be going now."

She crammed the car into gear and stomped the accelerator, spewing up dust and gravel in the getaway.

Yep, I'll be on my way, she thought. *But you haven't seen the last of me.*

Chapter Sixteen

By the time eight o'clock rolled around Saturday night, Dakota had dolled herself up like a Grade-A, biker babe. As she paced past the window overlooking the illuminated swimming pool, a shark fin skimmed past on a breeze. Water glimmered aqua-blue, as lovely as the Caribbean. But the sight did little to soothe her frayed nerves. Not all man-eaters lurked in Heaven's Urn. Some trolled Club Crimson.

When she moved into the incandescent light of a table lamp, the faint reflection of her silhouette came into sharp focus in the glass. The black, cashmere sweater caressed her skin, accentuating her breasts and elongating her neck. Matte black lipstick filled in her penciled-on lip liner, while smoky mascara outlined her eyes. She even managed to draw-on a few "Twiggy" lashes, angled down from the rim in short, clean spikes. In this current look, she anticipated the men at the Goth club would find her quite "killer"—perhaps, in more ways than one.

To raise her comfort level, she patted the waistband of her black, leather skirt. The tiny North American Arms five-shot, loaded with hollow point stingers, rested inconspicuously against the flat of her belly. A guy she knew had made a hard plastic cover to Velcro on top of it so that the little .22 caliber resembled a pager. Dropping her hand to her thigh, Dakota grazed the hard casing of a butterfly knife taped to her skin. She really wasn't a knife kind of girl. But if someone happened to get the jump on her, she had another way to save herself. With the .38 caliber snub nose nestled against the small of her back, and a set of brass knuckles duct-taped to the inside of one wrist, she pronounced herself good to go.

Small wonder she didn't rattle when she walked.

Club Crimson didn't have valet parking. Matter of fact, it didn't have much of anything going for it except its remoteness. Parking under the only street lamp for blocks held no allure. In a no-man's-land like Club Crimson, it'd only serve as a beacon to guide those ruthless enough to key the door, or kick in a fender with a steel-toed boot. Better to stow the Jag up the street a few blocks and walk, than to tempt fate.

In the heart of Phoenix's industrial area, the proprietors didn't have to worry about cops shutting them down on a noise complaint, or rousting the ghouls who patronized the smattering of small businesses that stayed open after dark: the Goth club, a 24-hour mechanic shop that Dakota suspected might actually be a chop shop, and an all-night liquor store with a side line of religious artifacts unique to Satanism, Santeria, and Voodoo.

In this rough section of town, any upstanding, working-class citizen had long departed by the time Club Crimson cranked up the volume loud enough to rattle the fillings in your teeth.

The outside of the building showed the patina of neglect. Inside, the club was divided into three levels. The first floor invited boozing and schmoozing, rubbing and grubbing—with a full bar that ran the length of one wall, and mattresses on the floor instead of bistro tables. The second tier took on all the characteristics of a mosh pit, with the crowd furiously shoving, pushing and body-slamming each other to the beat of the music—the way tomatoes in a blender ended up.

Strains of heavy metal shrieked through the warehouse—a black-painted, seemingly endless void, without acoustical tiles on the ceiling—leaving caustic tones to hang in the ear long after the notes had been played. Beneath strobe lights, the crowd moshed to the mind-numbing screams of the lead guitarist, who apparently had a second career as the king of piercings.

Welcome to Satan's playpen. Grab a pitchfork and skewer a date.

Dakota wormed her way through the crowd of Goths. Halfway to the third level—the floor with Karaoke and an open mic set up—a crowd-surfing girl wearing nothing but a black bustier and thong under a trench coat, clipped her in the back of the head with a boot tip.

Dakota cursed.

Can't believe I wore my favorite pullover. This thing will have cigarette burns, camel spit and God-knows-what on it by the time I get home.

A couple of loudmouthed Goths body slammed her. She bit the inside of her mouth and tasted blood. Already, the crowd-surfing girl had been stripped of her clothing. Darkly clothed, unidentifiable hands groped her, but her screams drowned in the chaos of the music and scary chanting coming from the far side of the room.

"Do it. Do it. Do it . . ." became "Do her, do her, do her . . ."

I don't belong. What if I get seriously hurt?

What am I saying? It's not a matter of if. It's when.

What the hell's wrong with me? Oh, now isn't this fun—watching some cretin jack-off on the back of that chick's shroud? God Almighty. These people are like monkeys: What they don't tear up, they shit on.

Must've had a screw loose to tell that reprobate I'd meet him here.

I can always wear my injuries like badges of honor . . . point out to the paramedics on the way to the hospital, how I got each one . . .

Unexpectedly, the idiot directly in front of her did a stage dive, and a hole opened up. Dakota rushed past and broke from the crowd. She staggered to the steps leading to the third level and made her way into the Karaoke room. A passing waitress took her order—a canned soda, unopened. The girl, who'd dressed like a galley wench, gave Dakota a real *Whiskey-Tango-Foxtrot* look of the arched-eyebrow, snarling-lip variety, followed by a dramatic eye roll. Dakota couldn't care less. She wouldn't risk someone slipping GHB, or worse, into her beverage. Drinking the local moonshine in sketchy places like this could potentially lead to unpredictable drunkenness, bad gastric reactions, and temporary motor paralysis. But Club Crimson had a reputation for serving a concoction called a Pink Oboe, known for producing an aphrodisiac effect in women and temporary impotence in men, making for interestingly confused social situations. *No thanks,* she thought, *I've had my fill of that.*

Onstage, a beefy Goth male belted out "White Rabbit." He sang off-key, but he performed with heart, and when he finished, onlookers gave him a standing ovation. Dakota kept her seat. When the fans sat down, only the performer stood in front of her.

"You looking for me?" he said.

Canine teeth protruded beyond his bottom lips. Probably veneers, sharpened into points. Dressed in black, with a floor-length cape flowing over his massive shoulders, he took on all of the characteristics of a vampire in search of a neck.

A golf-ball lump rose to her throat. "What makes you think I'm looking for anybody?"

"You don't fit in. Oh, I'm not saying you didn't give it a good try." He did the finger tap to nose gesture. "You're just not one of us. I've seen you around. You know how hot you are?"

Shrouded in mystery, it was all very *Deep Throat*, and yet she recognized phrases from the email. The guy had snake eyes.

She swallowed hard. "You're Velvet Tears?"

A nod.

A heavyset Goth chick the spitting image of Mama Cass, with piercings the size of hubcaps dangling off her eyebrows, took the mic. She'd picked out a Jimi Hendrix tune and raped it for all it was worth.

Dakota cupped a hand to her ear. "Is there someplace quieter we can go?"

"How 'bout we go downstairs and do a little *Gorilla-ing and Godzilla-ing?*"

She thought of those spunk-stained mattresses, and didn't even need to ask what the slang term meant; answer . . . *No, absolutely not.* "How 'bout the bar?"

She wasn't looking forward to traversing the mosh pit again, but she figured if she all but Super-Glued herself to Velvet Tears, he could easily plough through the crowd.

Then it hit her.

No wonder they called it Club Crimson; half of the moshers, stage divers, and crowd surfers left bloodied and battered at the end of the night. But then what'd she expect from people whose brains had been strip-mined by the local moonshine, and illegal drugs.

A disembodied female voice rose above the noise. "Hey *you*— private-eye. You found the guy that knows Laura Ann." She said this as she disappeared from sight, and then reappeared directly in front of them.

Dakota stared into the glazed eyes of the girl from Sinister Sisters. What was her name? Liquid Fantasy. Yeah, that was it. Her stomach gave a nervous flip while her head screamed, *Are you trying to get me killed?* Frustration blurred her anger—Velvet Tears had taken off through the crowd.

When she tried to burrow into the mosh pit, the mob seemed to instinctively peg her for an interloper. They moved in for a tight seal, effectively preventing her from following.

"Get out of my way before I kick your biker butt." The words popped out before she realized she'd been thinking them. Now, her sassy mouth had issued an invitation.

The fight was on.

The first opportunity Dakota had to tell her side of the story took place in Club Crimson's security office—after losing a shoe and involuntarily crowd surfing into the burly arms of a uniformed Phoenix police officer.

And not just any officer.

Oh, no. That'd be too easy.

She found herself in the unenviable position of explaining what happened to the same smart-mouthed cop who gave her hell at the mall's grand opening.

Exhausted, bruised, and reeking like putrid refuse in a restaurant dumpster, she ran down the evening's events in quick, abbreviated strokes. Not to mention shredded cashmere. Minus a glass slipper. With an ice pack pressed to the back of her head, Dakota blinked back tears. She didn't fall apart until she returned to the sanctuary of her own home.

In the safety of her empty digs, she reflected on the night's events, flopped on the leather sofa, with an uncorked bottle of her lover's merlot steadied between her legs.

Kris should've been home with her.

Simple as that.

Chapter Seventeen

Sunday morning, Dakota dragged her aching body into the kitchen. The sight of Kris, standing at the counter, making a pot of coffee, stopped her in her tracks. The coffee maker gurgled to life, dripping a rich-smelling stream of chocolate-raspberry into the glass carafe.

Dakota forced a smile. "Where've you been?" From the unblinking stare on Kris's face, it wasn't hard to tell. "Well," she said through a sigh, "I'm glad you decided to come home. I missed you last night."

"I'm not here to stay. This is a business call."

"Monkey business? Did that cow who spray-painted graffiti on my house come back?"

"No."

"Oh, good. Because I thought for a minute she might've gotten the wrong place again."

"I'm here on official police business," Kris said, with a trace of danger in her voice. "Your friend, Fiona McHugh? You do remember her, right?"

"She's not my friend. We used to work together, that's all."

"She's dead."

Air rushed out of Dakota's lungs. Her blood pressure dipped.

"That's right, Dee. The landlord found her body early this morning. Went over to collect the rent, which, by the way, lucky for us she was late on her payment—otherwise, it could've been days before she stank up the place and the neighbors called in—when, *Voilà* . . . what does he find? A dead female on the floor."

Dakota closed her eyes, weary from the callous delivery of another death notice. "Was there a cat?"

"I can only guess. The landlord left the door open when he ran out to call nine-one-one."

"Tattoo?"

"You know she did."

Dakota threw back her head until the dizziness from a combination of last night's brawl, and today's sleep deprivation, subsided. "We have a problem," she said dully. She moved, zombie-like, to a cowhide club chair, and sank into the seat cushion. She dreaded the inevitable conversation with her partner. "Fiona called me on Thursday." Forget that she came by.

Kris's eyes sparked. "Why didn't you tell me?"

"I tried to. But you were so nasty to me. I decided it'd be best not to bring it up."

The detective braced herself against the countertop. She gave the coffeemaker a slow headshake, then reached for a mug and poured herself a half-cup. Then she moved to the pantry and filled it with Irish whiskey.

"What're you thinking, Kris? That I had something to do with this?"

"I'm thinking Fiona's death is quite a problem—*for you.*"

"I barely knew her."

"Yeah? Where were you last night?"

Dakota stiffened. "I can't believe you'd think I had anything to do with this."

"Why would I think you're involved?" Kris asked in a controlled, dispassionate voice. "Just because you said you were going out last night, and wouldn't say where, or tell me who you were going with doesn't mean I suspect you of anything having to do with this Fiona thing." She was being sarcastic, of course.

"You cops are all alike."

"I don't think you had anything to do with Fiona McHugh's death, Dee. Sad to say, however, my partner doesn't share my opinion. Unfortunately for you, I happened to bitch about you taking off for God-knows-where last night; and because you either can't or won't come up with an alibi, Hamilton's going to be even more convinced you're mixed up in this."

"Why're you even talking to him about me? What I do is none of his business."

"We're friends, Dee. If I don't have you to talk to, I confide in him. Simple as that."

Trying to get Hamilton Stark off her butt was like trying to blend into the kelp at the shark aquarium with a bucket of chum guts in each hand.

Dakota gave a heady sigh. "I went to Club Crimson to hook up with Shawn O'Neil."

Kris spewed coffee through her nose "You what?" She swiped her face with the back of her hand. Deposited her cup in the sink and grabbed a cup towel to blot her hand. "Are you just trying to piss me off—"

Oops. Probably not a good time to discuss the episode with the Mayor-Elect, either.

"—or, maybe you're suffering from insanity?"

"I wouldn't use the term suffering. I'm enjoying every minute of it."

"Don't get smart with me. I may be the only friend you have down at the PD."

"I have an alibi. Should be fairly easy to check out since I kind of started a fight in a mosh pit, and the cops showed up. I'm pretty sure there's a lengthy paper trail."

"*Kind of* started a fight?" Kris's face reddened.

"It's not like Princess Kate lost her sapphire. Are you at all aware that the veins in your neck are popping out? They're as big as PVC pipe. That just can't be healthy."

"Exactly how does one *kind of* start a fight?"

"Well, one might talk smack. That might kind of piss off the Goths."

Kris stared in stunned silence.

"Anyway," Dakota's lips parted into a tentative smile, "I got crowd-surfed into the arms of one of your brother officers. Remember that jerk from the mall who ticked off Mayor Jane? Yes, him." She nodded knowingly, "He can alibi me."

Kris stared at the vaulted ceiling for what seemed like an eternity.

Dakota attempted to draw her out. "Aren't you going to say anything?" No response. "You're mad at me, aren't you?"

"No, I need to finish processing this ugly visual of you, surrounded by angry Goths."

Tension invaded their shared space, as heavy and acrid as a room filled with black smoke.

"I lost a shoe," Dakota said softly.

"Thanks for providing that great evidentiary nugget, Cinderella." Kris continued to stare off into space.

"I think I might've seen a Goth chick get raped." Dakota watched Kris's eyes close tight. "Well, I didn't exactly see it. Heard it." No reaction. "Maybe it wasn't anything after all," she added hopefully. "Could've been an act."

"Let me get this straight. You went to Club Crimson; found Shawn O'Neil; started a fight; witnessed a rape; lost a shoe in the mosh pit, and got arrested. Did I leave anything out?"

"Not necessarily in that order. And I didn't say I got arrested. I was merely detained."

"*Detained.* Well, that's ever so much better, isn't it?" Kris drenched her words in syrup. Sickening, sugary-sweet syrup, with a jar of five-alarm, jalapeño peppers thrown in.

Dakota bobbed her head, triumphant. "Yes, I happen to agree with you one hundred percent. Now that you can establish my whereabouts last night, that should clear me of any wrongdoing. Tell the old man to put that in his pipe and smoke it." Her eyes thinned. "You're trying not to smile, aren't you? Yes, I believe you are. I can see how hard it is for you. Sadly, your face is starting to crack. You can't control it. As soon as it gets away from you, I'll know you're not mad anymore. *Hup!* There it goes . . ."

Kris laughed. "What am I going to do with you, Dee?"

Make love?

As Dakota unbuttoned the top button on her silk pajamas, Kris's cell phone rang. Once again, Hamilton Stark ruined the day.

Night fell, and the working girls came out of the woodwork. Dakota loathed being obligated to people, but Mayor Jane had pulled strings to spring her from jail, and accepting Jane's suggestion to go undercover as a hooker—well, face it; it wasn't so much a suggestion as it was an order—seemed like a way to return the favor. Honoring their agreement, Dakota located a string of hot-sheet motels, and positioned the Jaguar near a dumpster, in one of the parking lots.

She checked out the evening activity through field glasses. Dressed in a skimpy skirt and tube top, with the arms of her sweater tied around her waist, Dakota expected to fit right in. She was glad she'd gotten a flu shot; the mercury had dropped, and prancing around in flimsy clothing would only make the evening more miserable. While waiting for an opportune moment to exit the vehicle, wander over and blend-in with the prostitutes, she wondered what the night would hold for her.

Without warning, a john stepped out from between two parked cars and approached one of the prostitutes. Dakota focused the lenses on the binoculars for a better view.

No—it couldn't be.

Travis Creeley.

So much for blending in.

She studied his every move. Tried to read lips from the safety of her car. He didn't appear to want sex. Whatever he wanted was taking way too long for that. She powered down the window enough to catch snippets of conversation. The persistent bastard was still stalking her.

Creeley touched the street whore's hair. It was most likely a wig, since the girl appeared to have darker skin; and beneath the glow of the street lights, the coppery red frizz billowing down past her shoulders didn't seem to go with her complexion.

Creeley's words drifted over on a breeze. "I kept locks of my little angel's hair."

Chills danced over Dakota's skin. A distant memory presented itself, bringing forth a new dimension of terror from her past.

Her father used to clip locks of her hair every year on her birthday.

She shuddered as much from the memory as from the cold, squeezing her eyes tight enough to banish these barbershop weirdnesses from her mind.

That's it, she thought, *My work here is done. No way am I doing this. No damned way.*

At home in Heaven's Urn, in the sanctuary of her office, Dakota winnowed through her email, checking for new cases, and responding to pleas from parents trying to find their runaway kids. She stumbled upon an anonymous account, typed in Ransom font. The message cried out for automatic deletion, despite its intriguing sub-ject heading: *Final warning.*

Wary, she clicked open the email and read the contents: *You got no cause following people around. Mind your own business before some-body gets hurt. Consider this your last warning.*

She printed out the email. Weighing her options, she telephoned Kris.

No answer.

Even worse . . . would Kris believe her when she dropped the bombshell? After all, these were the same words Mayor-Elect Wilson used on her, at his office.

Chapter Eighteen

Monday morning, Dakota surfed cyberspace with a fury, hunting down leads that might pinpoint the anonymous email's origin.

When the phone chirped, she snatched it up on the first ring. The sound of Kris's voice brought instant relief.

"Thank God it's you." Dakota said.

"What's wrong?"

"Do you know how to trace an email back to its real owner?"

"No, but I think Hamilton does."

Dakota set her jaw.

Of course Hamilton does. How silly of me. Hamilton knows how to do everything . . . guess that makes him a jerk of all trades.

Dakota infused cheer into the conversation. "Oh, okay, well could you ask him the steps to take? I got a weird email and I'd like to identify the sender."

"What do you mean, weird? How weird? Weird like I'm gonna pop out your eyeballs and stuff them in your cheeks, weird? Weird like I wanna skull fuck you in the cargo area of a hearse, weird? What, exactly, is weird in your book, Dee?"

Way to put someone on the defensive.

"Are you insinuating that, because of my past, weirdness knows no boundaries for me?"

Kris backpedaled. "What's weird for me may not be weird for you. It's subjective."

"Never mind." Dakota shifted gears. "Listen carefully. I need to know about those crime scenes. And I know what you're going to say."

"You know I can't discuss that with you."

"But I may've hit on something that can help you."

"Oh?" The upward lilt of Kris's voice, albeit guarded, convinced Dakota to go on.

"Were any of the victims missing a lock of hair?"

"I don't know. Why?"

"Meet me at the ME's office. I need to see Celia's body."

"I'm not going to sponsor your visit to the ME. If you want to see Celia's body you'll have to clear it through them."

"I understand completely," Dakota said, injecting sweetness into her words. If Kris wanted guerilla tactics, so be it. "Say . . . what's that reporter's name that's always looking for a big scoop? You remember, don't you? The guy with the curly brown hair, who's always dogging you for information every time y'all get a nasty case? Because I thought maybe I'd relay some information I came across . . . maybe run this killer idea I have about these unsolved homicides past him . . . maybe see if he thinks the same person I think might be our serial murderer?"

Kris let out a string of profanity. "Do not use the term serial killer, Dakota. He's a pattern killer. There's a difference."

"What makes it different when they're all still dead?"

Kris launched into a fresh new diatribe, starting with, "Do not go to the press," and ending with salty epithets Dakota hadn't heard since days on the elementary school playground. When she ran out of steam, Dakota made another run at her.

"So, you'll meet me at the ME's office in twenty minutes?"

At the ME's Office, Dakota took one look at Kris, pressed against Hamilton Stark like a conjoined twin, and gave a disquieting sniff. Was there anything those two didn't do together? The ugly bathroom visual from the last visit made her wince. Ironically, he'd followed her in there, too.

Clearly exasperated with her, the duo located Dr. Stone behind his desk, and swept her inside with them. Celia's body remained unclaimed, and unless they could find a relative to take responsibility for the corpse, she'd end up in a pauper's grave, or become another cadaver donation for the medical school.

Kris did the talking. "We need to view the remains of Celia St. Claire."

Dr. Stone was his old blustery self. He braced his arms across his chest and looked them over. "Reason?"

"To be blunt, you may have overlooked something."

Although Kris could benefit from charm school, at least she didn't say, *Ms. Jones thinks you screwed up.* This might be the closest thing to an apology Dakota could expect.

Dr. Stone thumbed a sausage-like digit at Dakota, but his words were meant for Kris. "She's working with you now?"

Hamilton said, "Not with me."

Kris shot him a look meant to cut him dead. Then she turned to Dr. Stone. "You might say she's 'of counsel' to us. At the moment. Subject to change."

Dr. Stone invited them into the cooler, angling over to one of the metal drawers with his paper surgeon's booties skimming the tile. In the distance, doctors performed autopsies to classical music as the whir of Stryker saws cut through bone. Thanks to the influx of illegal aliens crossing the border, as well as the number of deaths bleeding over from the drug cartels, Stone and his employees had plenty to do as more bodies were wheeled into the pungent, form-aldehyde-infused morgue.

The jarring sound of rollers, running along their tracks, sent an icy shiver snaking up Dakota's torso. Celia St. Claire's skin had a blue cast to it. Reflexively, Dee averted her eyes. Celia wouldn't have wanted to be seen this way.

Dr. Stone did an exaggerated waist bow. He seemed more amused than angry at being second-guessed, and slipped into a British accent. "Pray tell, Your Majesty, what have I overlooked?"

"Can you tell us whether a lock of hair's been removed from the corpse?"

"From Celia," Dakota insisted with passion.

The detectives looked at her, dagger-eyed. Then Kris said, "Yes, doctor, can you tell us whether the vic—Celia's—missing a lock of hair?"

"How am I supposed to be able to divine that information? People come in here all the time with bad haircuts."

Dakota flashed a smile and touched her fingertips to Stone's sleeve. "Something that's seemingly insignificant could be relevant if all the girls are missing locks of hair, right?"

Dr. Stone shifted his attention to Stark. "Rather unusual, don't you think, for an amateur to come up with such a suggestion?"

Hamilton and Kris traded guarded looks. The doctor had paid her a compliment.

As Stone examined Celia's scalp, Dakota pressed her lips tightly together to keep her smile in check. While the others stared at Celia's head, Dakota studied the henna tattoo with cold scrutiny. It seemed Kris's field notes contained only a crude sketch. Not the detailed intricacies Dakota could see.

A series of questions posed within the tattoo began with a *Hello*, and asked if the artist could be heard, and whether he was getting through. He wanted to know if it was late there, and whether there was laughter on the line. He wanted to know if the object of his interest was alone.

It was a pretty big message crammed into a small amount of space, Dakota mused. But no one asked her. No one paid much attention to her, at all, except for the erectile-dysfunction king, who kept sliding her sidelong glances. Her thoughts drifted back to the faintly painted message on Laura Ann Spencer's bedroom ceiling.

Dr. Stone confirmed the missing lock of hair. Then he agreed to check the other bodies, and get back with the detectives.

"Well, Ms. Jones," Hamilton said cheerily, "you must've known Celia *very* well to know how much hair she had." Cheer turned to mockery. "Anything else you'd like to tell us about your relationship with her, or the other dead girls?"

Kris elbowed him into silence. But like in a courtroom, when a judge instructs the jury to disregard a witness' testimony, the damage had already been done: Hamilton not only planted a vicious seed, he fertilized it.

Kris excused herself from the room, pulling Dakota with her. Outside the door, beyond Hamilton's earshot, she began her own interrogation.

"He's right. How well *did* you know Celia?" she asked in a church voice.

"Your partner may be a few oars shy of a boat race, but I didn't think it was contagious."

"Hey—Nancy Drew—I have a better question: How'd you think of this?"

"Just a hunch."

"Bullshit."

"Hey—Your Majesty—just so you know, cops don't own the franchise on hunches."

"I don't think you're telling us everything you know."

"Are you kidding me? What's wrong with y'all? I feel like I'm picking low-hanging fruit here. Don't you see it?"

Kris stared, bewildered.

"It's textbook. Serial killers usually take some kind of trophy, but you never mentioned anything. Then I remembered reading somewhere that sometimes they take something that smells like the victim. Hair often has a fragrance, if nothing else, from the shampoo a woman uses. I don't think coming up with the idea is such a cavernous leap. Matter of fact, I think your partner's just pissed because his brain's so narrow-minded he couldn't make the leap if he was riding a stuntman's motorcycle with a JADO rocket strapped to his ass."

The detective laughed. Not one of her sarcastic chuckles, either, but a big ol', guts-out, belly laugh. "Come on, you big goofball." Kris clamped a hand around Dakota's arm.

"Admit I'm right. Hey—where're we going? You're not arresting me are you?"

"Not yet." Kris steered her back into the company of two bewildered men.

"I think she's onto something, Hamilton. You shouldn't be so hard on her. None of us caught it."

"I read a lot," said Dakota with fake modesty.

What she wanted to do was shout, *Kris took up for me. Stick that down the front of your pants and set fire to it, you big jerk.*

"You read a lot?" Hamilton gave her one of his trademark, insincere smiles. "So what do you make of the tattoos?"

A remote and disturbing memory sneaked in, catching Dakota unaware.

Her father played the piano.

Routinely struck up little waltzes on the ivories.

One-two-three. One-two-three.

"Dance for me, girl. Take off your night gown and dance for your old man."

"Stop looking at me that way."

One-two-three. One-two-three.

She wore bikini underpants. The ones she suspected Creeley left in the mailbox the morning the next-door neighbor's "baby mama" fueled her psychosis with a can of spray paint and a blunt object could've belonged to Dakota.

"Dee." Kris shook her by the shoulder. "What'd you do? Go on vacation?"

Travis Creeley.

Travis Creeley, serial killer?

My father?

Dakota shook off the memory. "I'm sorry . . . what?"

"The tattoos." Hamilton, again, back to his condescending old self. "What's your take on the tattoos?"

Dakota dropped her gaze. Studied the toe of one shoe and measured her words carefully before looking back up at her adversary. "I have no idea. But there's this man . . . Travis Creeley. He's been hanging around. It probably wouldn't hurt to keep an eye open for him."

When Dakota returned from the ME's Office that afternoon, she telephoned another one of Celia's girls—Fiona's friend, Diana Kyle—to set up a meeting. Only the Fantasy Escorts resident Wonder Woman didn't answer the phone. The call routed to voicemail, and a robotic message invited the caller to leave a message.

Dee tried to keep her voice airy and light. She didn't want to alarm Diana, and she had no plans to take on any bodyguard cases if Diana pressed her for help, but they definitely needed to talk.

"Diana, it's Dakota Jones." An unexplainable chill rippled up her back. "Look, I think we should meet. Exchange information. I can come to your place, or you're welcome to come to mi—" she bit off the word. Inviting an escort to Heaven's Urn would put Kris on the warpath. "Change of plans, Di. I can come to your place or we could meet at the diner down the street from Celia's. Remember the one with the fresh sweet rolls? Do they still make those? Call me back with a time."

She left Diana all of her numbers. But the minute she hung up the phone, the dread that began when the answering machine clicked on refused to let up. When an hour passed, and she felt no better about the unanswered call, she decided to drive to Diana's condominium.

On some level, she knew better than to take a time-stamp ticket and park in the garage.

On some level, she knew that parking a few blocks away would provide more anonymity, should something go terribly wrong.

Like if Diana should die in the night.

She checked the numbers on the escort's residence against the one in her address book, and pressed the doorbell several times. No one answered.

Could be broken.

She lifted the brass doorknocker and banged it against its strike plate.

Again, no response from inside.

It would've been perfectly proper to call the police on a welfare concern. On some level, she knew better. She didn't want to be ostrich-headed about it, but other than the nagging voice in her head, she had no concrete evidence anything nefarious had happened to Diana Kyle.

Her mind played with several scenarios, most of them involving property damage by the police department, the fire department, and the invasion of privacy at the hands of a locksmith.

Before leaving, she removed a tissue from her handbag, and wiped down the doorknocker for prints.

Chapter Nineteen

The morning paper broke a gruesome story in thirty-six point type, the kind reserved for assassinated Presidents, deployed nuclear bombs, and the death of the newspaper owner.

FOUR PROSTITUTES DEAD—SERIAL KILLER SUSPECTED—
POLICE STYMIED

Dakota closed her eyes in a tight, child-like squeeze, all the while knowing that when she opened them, the headline and story would still be there.

She read on.

Mayor-Elect David Wilson shifted his mouth into overdrive on two fronts. First, he made the Chief of Police look like the next super-hero. Second, he assured the city that prostitution and violent crime would "be given a full court press" by the Mayor's Office once he occupied his new post. She wasn't familiar with the phrase, and looked it up on the Internet before leafing through other articles. It turned out to be a basketball term.

A smaller story, buried on page three, quoted Mayor Roman suggesting the crime rate would be lower if Chief Forster would pull his head out and let Wilson check his own hemorrhoids for a change. She'd probably been drinking when the reporter called, but such political gaffes sold newspapers, and, face it, a lot of people who'd been asleep at the wheel on Election Day were beginning to echo Mayor Jane's sentiments.

Dakota barked out a laugh. Ah, the perks of being a lame duck.

She finished reading the metro section, and picked up her file on the Spencer case. Even though the investigation had become disjointed, undeniable links between Laura Ann, the tattoos, the fantasy escorts, and Shawn "Velvet Tears" O'Neil convinced her to dig deeper. This was no ordinary, run-of-the-mill runaway case.

Maybe the chick who "outed" her at Club Crimson had news on Velvet Tears.

Dakota headed back to the Sinister Sisters in an effort to connect the dots through Liquid Fantasy. When she walked inside, she didn't immediately recognize the girl. A purple moose to the orbital bone and a puffy lip with a split in it tended to do that to a person.

Hand-to-mouth, Dakota said, "What happened to you?"

"Like you don't know."

"Did you follow me into the mosh pit? Because I didn't go in there to start trouble. By the way, I know a good surgeon if you need one."

"I didn't follow you into the mosh pit. Velvet Tears beat the crap outta me."

"Two words: Press charges."

"Like I want another ass-whipping? No, thanks. Maybe you should leave now."

"Maybe we can help each other."

Dakota sensed the Sinister Sisters weren't big fans of hers, but she quickly discovered they liked Velvet Tears even less. The possibility of evening the score intrigued them, so they gathered in the front parlor over cups of herbal tea and heard her out.

"What if I could catch him? Maybe bring him here all trussed up like a Christmas turkey?" Dakota joked.

"You'd do that?" Liquid Fantasy.

"Maybe. But first I have to find him."

According to the Sinister Sisters, they hadn't seen Laura Ann, and didn't know where Shawn O'Neil lived. But they had a photo taken by the Sinister Sisters security camera the night Velvet Tears punched out Liquid Fantasy, and they knew someone who knew him.

An employer of sorts.

Dakota whipped out a pen and scratch paper. "Does this employer have a name?"

"You know. The guy who's going to be the next Mayor. David Wilson."

The last place Dakota wanted to go after leaving Sinister Sisters was the first place she struck out for. This time, she'd try charm rather than impudence.

The chill inside Wilson's office had less to do with the temperature than the political climate. From her place in one of Wilson's guest chairs, his crisp, cornflower blue, pinpoint oxford shirt had enough starch in it to stand on its own as he settled uneasily into his big chair. From his place behind the big desk, he reminded her of a sidewinder on a flat rock, coiled in surprise by the unexpected, unwelcome visit.

"I'm sorry to bother you, but I'm looking for someone and I thought you could help me."

"Thought you were a private investigator. Don't they find people?"

"I understand he's an employee of yours."

Already shaking his head, he chuckled without humor. "A lot of people are on my payroll. You'll have to do better than that."

"Shawn O'Neil."

Wilson's eyes narrowed. He gave a predictable answer. "Never heard of him."

Formidable opponents didn't back down. Dakota slid the surveillance photo from her purse, stretching forward enough to hand it across the blotter. "Really? Take a look."

Wilson gave her a half-smile. Without even bothering to glance at the picture, he handed it back with a dismissive flick of the wrist. "Never saw him before."

"That's not the word on the street."

Wilson's hand momentarily dipped below the desk. In seconds, the side door swung open, and two of his thugs entered the office.

"Ms. Jones was just leaving. See to it that she makes it safely to her car. It's a rough neighborhood," he said dryly. "Wouldn't want anything to happen to her."

Dakota simmered all the way back to Heaven's Urn.

How dare David Wilson's goons put their mitts on her? Mayor Jane may be a lame duck, but she had a team of lawyers who were locked and loaded, and if Wilson thought he could intimidate *this* private investigator, he had another think coming. Mayor Jane would just *love* for one of her attorneys to file a civil suit. See how Wilson liked being embroiled in controversy before he ever took office . . .

She wheeled the Jag into the driveway, surprised to find an unmarked police car taking up her usual space. When she let herself into the house, she found Kris and Hamilton sitting on the sofa skimming knees with each other. Anger blurred Dakota's vision. Kris had a lot of nerve bringing the old man into the home they shared. Unless he was coming to help move her stuff out, he had no place in Heaven's Urn.

Instead of a guilty expression, Kris sprang to her feet. "Where've you been, Dee?"

"Winning friends and influencing people." She kept her voice light and cheerful, but inside her head, she was constructing a voodoo doll out of corn husks, and setting it ablaze.

Hamilton stood. He moved, panther-like, around the coffee table with a natural grace that prickled the hair at the nape of Dakota's neck. These people hadn't shown up for tea and scones.

"Diana Kyle is dead." Kris delivered the news with all the unemotional bluntness of a news commentator. "You were the last person to leave a message on her machine."

Chills ravaged Dakota's skin. "Means nothing."

Hamilton's jaw flexed. "When's the last time you saw her?"

"It's been years."

"But you went to her house." His eyes narrowed into cold slits.

Instinct told her to deny, deny, deny. No way they could know that. She'd wiped-down the doorknocker to a spit shine. But Hamilton's expression told her he knew a secret. And if they caught her in a lie, they'd never stop dogging her. She gave him a blank stare.

Hamilton's lips twisted into a smirk. "We lifted a fingerprint off the doorbell. Then we ran it through AFIS. Whaddaya know? It matched the right index finger they have on file for you. You lied to us."

"I told you the truth. I haven't seen Diana in years." Dakota's eyes flickered to Kris. In a secret communion only lovers could share, they exchanged awkward looks.

"Don't just stand there, help me."

But Kris's expression said, *Sorry, Dee, it's outta my hands.*

"You've worn out your welcome." Dakota glided to the front door. Her cheeks burned. Her breath quickened. "It's time for you to leave."

The detectives rose from the sofa and moved easily to the door under her intent regard. When they reached the entrance, Hamilton said, "Aw . . . I was really hoping you wouldn't say that . . ." and moved with lightning speed. He grabbed one arm and spun her around, clicking on handcuffs before Dakota's survival skills had a chance to kick in.

"You're under arrest." He hauled her out the front door on tip-toes, with Kris looking on in stunned silence.

An eerie calm settled over Dakota on the ride to the station. Kris should know she'd never hurt a working girl. Prostitution wasn't a career little girls grew up wanting. They wanted to become ballerinas and brides, movie stars and mothers. Desperate girls turned into hookers only when they reached a dead-end on the highway of broken dreams.

Dakota snorted in disgust. She could hardly look at Kris, mute and staring straight out the windshield. Kris, who'd sworn she'd always love her, even if Dakota had an ass like a forty-dollar mule, couldn't even muster a tender glance, or an "Are you okay, Dee?" Hamilton Stark, she expected this from. Hamilton Stark owed her nothing. Kris, on the other hand, had betrayed her.

She plotted to use her one phone call to contact Mayor Jane.

God forbid she should spend the night in lockdown.

And when she returned home, Kris could pack her shit and slip happily back into the walk-in closet of gender confusion.

Chapter Twenty

"*Oy, vey.*"

Dakota's startle-reflex kicked in, and she opened her eyes.

The drunken Jewish woman jailers placed in her cell around two-thirty that morning, sat on the adjacent cot, making barnyard noises and rubbing her feet. The private eye lifted her head and blinked the metal bars into focus.

"*Oy, vey*—you look like a *vilde chaya.*"

"Who's Vilde Chaya?" Dakota rolled herself upright, wondering what to make of the elfin woman with her champagne-colored hair, still lacquered in a perfect coif.

"Not who, *bubbula*. What. A vilde chaya's a wild animal. You look like a witch with that awful hair."

"Yeah?" Dakota glanced around. "In case you haven't noticed, we're in the Crossbar Motel. Nobody here looks particularly fetching."

"You should get with my hairdresser, David. What a mensch. Salt of the earth, even if he's not Jewish. He's still good people, but *faygala*. He calls me his fairy godmother. I call him my fairy god-son." She swatted her chubby knee, threw back her head and belted out a hysterical laugh. When she finished cackling at her own joke, she wiped away tears, massaging the loose skin near her crow's feet. "What can I say? I love him."

Weary, Dakota lowered her head and mashed her temples until red comets streaked across her field of vision.

"My lawyer, Mikey Rosenstein—you've heard of Mikey Rosenstein, haven't you, *bubbula*?—he's only the best of the best. A partner at Epstein, Cohen, Rosenstein and Weinberg." She cut her eyes to the ceiling. "That's the late Lon Cohen, God bless his soul, may he rest in peace.

"Anyway . . . Mikey tells me, 'Don't worry, Pascha. The Rolls will dry out and run good as new.'" She swatted her manicured hand through the air and expelled a breath of air that made her sound like an emphysema patient. "Who wants to drive a car that smells like three-day-old goat guts? Not me. They'll never get that brackish odor out of the leather. They should put up more lights around the waste plant. And a sturdier gate."

"You drove into the sewer?"

"Not the sewer, *bubbala*. The place where they clean the water. What's it called?" She snapped her fingers in an attempt to jog her memory.

Dakota ventured a guess. "Reclamation plant?"

"Right. Anyway, I told Mikey Rosenstein—God love him—to zip his *shmekele* back into his trousers and get me outta this germ-infested jail. God forbid he should put the squeeze on those blood-suckers to give me a new Rolls. That's why we buy insurance, right? Only Mikey Rosenstein tells me, 'They only have to dry it out, Pascha, they don't have to furnish you with a new Rolls.' What's that all about, I asked him? I want a blue one this time. Screw the insurance company." She ran her fingers along the bed's metal frame. "I'd sooner have a pap smear with a rake than spend another hour on such an uncomfortable cot. And did you see the dust balls? Big as tumbleweeds."

The door clanged open and Kris stepped into the cell.

"*Oy, gevalt.* Another vilde chaya. What happened to you? You look like you survived electrocution. I'll leave my hairdresser's card for you at the front desk. David can fix that mess, you know. I'm talking about the hair, not your drinking problem."

"What?" Kris's eyes bulged.

"Two things you've gotta remember when you hit the sauce, *bub-bula*. One, never drink alone. Two, make Everclear your drink of choice."

"I'll remember that." Kris shifted her gaze. "We ran a check on Shawn O'Neil. He's got a criminal record as long as a giraffe's neck."

Dakota eyed her up. Kris was no longer beneath her contempt.

"Anyway, there's nothing to directly tie you to the murders so you're free to leave."

Translation: Before Mayor Jane files a lawsuit.

"*Mazel tov*. If you see Mikey Rosenstein on your way out, you tell him Pascha says *meesha masheena*—that Pascha wishes him a horrible death—if I'm not sprung before they bring in green baloney and moldy bread to *nosh* on. I might as well visit my sister-in-law—now there's a vilde chaya."

Dakota stood, wiped her palms against the jail coveralls and brushed past her girlfriend with the confidence of a super-model.

Gus Stone was striding up the walkway to the ME's office, sharing a laugh with colleagues and patting a full belly, when Dakota alighted the Jaguar a few minutes after one o'clock that afternoon.

All cleaned up in powder blue, tropical wool slacks and matching cashmere pullover, Dakota felt the pull of their attention on her cleavage.

"Dr. Stone, could I see you a moment?"

He fanned off his pals and waited for her to catch up. After a finger-crimping handshake, they fell into step. When the ME placed his hand against the small of her back as he opened the door to let her pass, he swept her inside like a VIP.

"That was pretty impressive, yesterday. How'd you know that woman was missing a chunk of hair?"

"It was a hunch. And it got me thrown in the clink, thanks to Hamilton Stark."

"Stark's 'good people.' A fine investigator. Phoenix is lucky to have him."

"Let's agree to disagree." They reached Stone's office and he beckoned her into a guest chair. "Can I see the bodies?"

"You're quite the little ghoul, aren't you? No you may not. You get certain privileges extended to you when the detectives are here to vouch for you." He glanced around for effect. "I don't see them, do you?"

"Please? The paper reported a serial killer on the loose. Tourism's big here. Can you imagine what that'll do to the economy if this string of murders goes unsolved for very long? I can help you."

Stone straddled one corner of his desk. Folded his arms across his wool sweater vest, and viewed her through a keen eye. "What makes you think you can help?"

"I'm not sure yet. If you could just let me see the bodies, maybe something will come to me." She leaned in and played her trump card. "Look, Doc. I did a little research. The county didn't give you a raise this year. They claimed there's no money in the coffer. But the sheriff got a nice chunk of change after that big TV special came out on CNN about the tent jail. He got a lot of notoriety out of Tent City. And you know how that works . . . you have to pay celebrities what they're worth. They nicknamed him the toughest sheriff in the west. So why not you? If you solved this case . . ."

"Don't play with me, Ms. Jones."

But Dakota rambled on, unbridled in her argument. "Don't you see, Dr. Stone? The sheriff had a chance to save the county *money*. You have a chance to save *lives*."

With a stern warning not to touch anything, Stone escorted her into the morgue. A lifeless body lay on a gurney, and he whipped back a sheet to reveal Diana Kyle. The corpse of the young lady who pretended to be Wonder Woman appeared blue under the light.

"I'm posting the body today. She's missing a lock of hair, just like you said." Stone pointed to the tattoos.

Dakota squinted for a better look. "What do you make of the musical notations?"

The doctor shook his head. "I can't figure it out. It makes no sense. Your nemesis, Detective Stark, says the music would be gibberish when played together."

She eased a notebook out of her purse. "You mind? I'd like to jot this down."

"Young lady, you're a guest. If you so much as leak one scintilla of information to the press . . ."

She didn't let him finish. The consequences carried an unpleasant penalty, possibly one with a lengthy jail term. "You have my word." She lifted her little finger into a pinkie-swear. "I want to help just as much as you want to get a killer off the streets. Celia was my friend. I knew all these girls. I feel like I have a vested interest in helping to solve their murders."

She wrote her observations down on paper. Under the forensic pathologist's watchful eye, she scrawled a crude facsimile of the tattoo, and the words intertwined within the decorative swirls.

These comments referenced Venus, and whether it blew the

mind, or was Venus everything the artist's subject wanted to find? And did she miss him while she was trying to find herself?

Puzzled, Dakota wondered if Venus was supposed to be a planet, a tennis player, or a marble statue in Italy? Or the goddess . . .

She said, "Were the other girls missing locks of hair?"

"Yes."

"I *knew* it! Listen, you're a smart man . . . maybe you can come up with a theory for what I'm about to say. While I was locked up in the slammer, it occurred to me that each of these women died three days apart."

"So?"

"It's a three-day cycle."

"Meaning?"

"I thought you'd know. It's like one day, Celia's killed. Day two goes by, day three goes by. Then it starts all over again. One, two, three. One, two, three."

Dr. Stone angled over to a box of latex gloves and slipped on a pair. He returned to Diana Kyle and lifted her arm, scrutinizing the tattoo. After a moment, he gently repositioned the arm at her side, snapped off the gloves, dropped them in a toe-operated waste receptacle lined with a red bio-hazardous plastic bag, and fixed Dakota in his stare.

"Like to dance?"

She scanned the room in a furtive glance, looking up, looking down, but not looking directly at the ME. Surely this wasn't a come on. "You're asking me to dance?"

"No. I only mention it because that's a waltz."

"Beg your pardon?"

"One-two-three, one-two-three. It's the beat of a waltz."

"Please don't think I'm being too forward," Dakota said, "but would you mind giving me your home phone number?"

"Reason?"

"Don't you want to be the first one I call when I figure this out?"

"Not the first one." He fingered past the vest to his pocket for a business card to write on. "The only one."

Back home, Dakota sat at the dining table, pouring over her notes. The large piece of drawing paper she'd torn from the packet gave her plenty of room to map out each victim's tattoos, in the scant hope of deciphering the musical notations.

A breathy phone call from Mayor Jane skewered her concentration.

"Oh, Dee, you poor dear. I'm so sorry I wasn't home when you called. It must've been terrible for you, spending the night in jail. But now you're out, so it's all better, right?"

"It sucked."

"I understand they released you this morning. I couldn't wait to find out—how's your case going?"

"I still don't have a good lead on Laura Ann Spencer—"

"Who?"

"Laura Ann Spencer. The runaway I'm trying to find."

"Not that case, dear. The prostitutes. Have you given anymore thought to going undercover?"

"I'm weighing the pros and cons." The cons: She could get hurt or killed. The pros . . . well, so far she hadn't come up with any pros.

"Did you dig up any dirt on Wilson? Do you need anything? Money? What can I do to help? Want my boys to file a lawsuit? They'll get Chief Forster by the ying-yang and twist so hard he'll think his pecker's a rubber band . . ."

No, she didn't need anything at the moment.

Yes, she'd phone if she unearthed anything useful.

And thanks ever so much for the call, and let's do lunch. Ta-ta for now.

Dakota went back to her task. No need for resentment. It wasn't Mayor Jane's fault she happened to be a day late and a dollar short. Everybody had a life. It wasn't the Mayor's job to sit around waiting for a bail-out call from a rehabilitated hooker.

Plus, she reminded herself, Jane had high-level connections. She could pull strings. Or cut them, if they happened to be wrapped around the scrawny neck of a private investigator.

Near midnight, after her bitterness dissolved into irritation, Dakota climbed onto the couch. Snuggling up with a blanket, she settled back and watched the moon turn the pool's surface into glitter. She watched the inflatable shark bob across the swimming pool until her eyelids felt as if they had lead weights attached to them.

Musical notes swirled in her head.

A waltz.

One-two-three, one-two-three.

Bits of a familiar tune lingered in her conscious mind, but since her days at the university, she'd become more of a talk-radio girl. Music was Kris's thing.

She fell asleep, unable to identify the song . . . and awoke with a start.

"Oh, my God. I think I've got it."

She pulled herself upright and stumbled to the table. Turned the paper where she could see the notes and words from Celia's tattoo.

The opening bars to a Billie Myers song revealed themselves to her.

She hurried to the study and logged onto the computer. In minutes, she ran the Billie Myers hit, *Kiss the Rain*, through a search engine and got a match. Then she checked the words on Diana Kyle's tattoo against the Internet. The lyrics were attributed to *Drops of Jupiter*, by the multi-platinum group, Train.

Now if she could only convince Kris to disclose the words found in the tattoos on Cyn Evans, Heather Lisle and Fiona McHugh . . .

When she finally migrated back to her bedroom, she drifted off to sleep wondering, *Why would the killer go to such lengths?*

Chapter Twenty-One

Thursday's sunrays sneaked beneath Dakota's black satin sleep mask. She pulled off her blinders and checked the time, threw back the covers and dashed for the bathroom. If she hurried, she could make it to the Spencer's before Jake left for work and Lorraine headed off to her activities at the country club. Laura Ann's computer history might reveal useful information, and if the Spencers allowed her the run of their house, who knew what she'd find?

A quick phone call settled the matter. Jake would wait at the house until nine. Japanese businessmen didn't tolerate tardiness, and if Spen-Soft, Inc. wanted that revolutionary new software contract, he'd better be present to show them around. The software magnate was standing on the front terrace, checking his watch, when Dakota jogged up in a colorful track suit.

"You're almost late."

"That must make me on-time," she said, infusing cheer into her tone. After all, he didn't have to let her snoop around. For all he knew, she could've made her millions working as the famous cat burglar that cleaned out a number of Phoenix's upscale homes a few years back.

"If you leave, be sure to activate the alarm. The code's on the table. When you program in the number, you have less than thirty seconds to get out the front door. Dawdle, and the security company will show up with the police in tow."

She was halfway to thinking, *Wow, the Spencers must really trust me,* when the Spen-Soft's CEO added, "We'll change the code tonight."

"Listen, Mr. Spencer, I really do appreciate—"

"Save it." He picked up his briefcase and pulled his key remote from his pocket. The BMW barked to life as Spencer headed out to the driveway. "Lorraine said you can finish the tamale casserole in the refrigerator if you get hungry. She said you cannot cut into the homemade coconut pie she made for her bridge club."

As the software mogul backed onto the street, Dakota disappeared into the Spencer's home. For several minutes, she surveyed the contents of Laura Ann's room from her place in the doorway. A new detail caught her eye. An important twist she hadn't noticed before.

The hair on all Laura Ann's dolls had been butchered in Goth fashion. She moved to the display and examined each one. Mohawk. Buzzcut. Bed head. Twiggy. The Beatles on PCP. Appalachia-meets-garden shears. And one that met all the criteria to be a vilde chaya.

Dakota took out her digital camera and photographed each "do," then settled in at the girl's computer hoping to dig up an address on Velvet Tears. The missing teen's email address bank had a few names, none of them tracing back to Shawn O'Neil. Dead-end there, but her calendar had an interesting entry for the upcoming Saturday. It read: Renaissance Fair, and it was circled in red.

Count me in, Dakota thought.

After she went as far as she could with the computer, she helped herself to a banana and a bowl of fresh-cut pineapple. She left the Spencer's, stuffed to the gills, and plotted the evening's itinerary with each step home. She needed to make one phone call; and that call would determine whether or not she sat in front of the TV all night watching old Kathryn Hepburn re-runs.

The die was cast when Selina Price, who took her escort identity as Princess Leia from the popular *Star Wars* flicks, answered on the second ring.

Dakota said, "I realize we haven't talked in a while, and I blame myself. But I'm trying to figure out the connection with Celia and the other girls, so tag, you're it." She wondered if Selina still straightened her long, dark-blonde mane. Or whether she'd opted for a trendier cut, and used honey-bun hair pieces during work nights at Celia's.

"I haven't made much of an effort, either," admitted the escort, "but I don't have time to visit now. I'm going on vacation until this horrible mess is solved. I may even move back home."

"Where's home?"

"Buena Vista, Colorado," Selina said through a sigh. "The stereo-typical 'nice place to be from, but you wouldn't want to live there.' Only I've decided maybe I do want to live there. My high school sweetheart's getting a divorce, so maybe we'll pick up where we left off, before I got too big for my britches and left town. Not to mention the low crime rate. I'm scared, Dakota."

"How about getting together tonight? I'll buy dinner. We can talk over a glass of wine. I'm in the mood for the *chicken cordon bleu* entrée at Bistro Marie's."

With the cordless phone scrunched between her cheek and shoulder, Dakota rummaged through an array of juice boxes and settled on mineral water.

"No can do. I'm supposed to attend a party."

"Business or pleasure?"

"Not sure. You know how it is. It can start out as one thing and end up another. All the invitation says is that it's a costume party. I decided to go as myself."

"As Princess Leia, or as your real self? Now, that I'd like to see." They'd once run into each other at the supermarket; with Selina looking plain but pretty in her Daisy Dukes and pullover, while Dakota, wore jeans and a stretchy silk-knit tank, with a Prada handbag dangling from her grip. It was an awkward meeting. Outside of their jobs, they had little in common.

"I wouldn't show up as anyone but Princess Leia. My real self would fade into the wallpaper. Besides, I've been doing this so long I've almost forgotten who I used to be. Sad, isn't it? I pretend to be someone I'm not, so men I bring pleasure to can pretend they're someone they're not."

"Mind if I tag along? Safety in numbers. And it'll give us a chance to talk."

Selina agreed.

And around seven o'clock that evening, Dakota dressed in full, Pussy Galore regalia, like an action figure straight out of "Goldfinger," She squeezed into a spandex unitard two sizes too small. She dug her blonde wig out of a box in the bottom of her closet, and wrangled her feet into a pair of platinum lamé boots that fit her shins like sausage casings, and choked off her circulation with the vengeance of a tourniquet.

She met Selina in front of the diner down the street near Fantasy Escorts Unlimited, and they rode together to the private address in a ritzy Phoenix neighborhood that reeked of old money. The place was nothing short of a mansion. On an estate. With botanical gardens and fountains. And carriage houses, and a cabana. Dakota blinked-in the wealth. Heaven's Urn had million dollar homes, but this place . . . well, she'd never seen anything comparable in Phoenix.

They stepped into a marble rotunda, abuzz with activity, where matching Baccarat chandeliers, dripping with rock crystal pendalogues brightened the room. To one side, a wing painted in Wedgwood blue opened up. And opposite, in another wing painted in Wedgwood sage, a staff of uniformed waitpersons bustled in and out with food trays. Ahead, two crescent-shaped staircases came together in an arc at the second floor. Huge gilt picture frames with ancestral canvases of stuffy-looking people with dour facial expressions hung on the walls. A massive arrangement of fresh flowers spilled over a remarkable walnut breakfront that had intricate carvings of majestic creatures; a string quartet played in the great room. There must've been a hundred guests milling about, but Dakota honed-in on only one.

She halted in her tracks.

"Is that the Mayor-Elect?" She clutched Selina's arm and pulled her close as Selina presented the invitation to the doorman. "I can't go in. People know me. There's the Chief of Police."

Leia's forehead wrinkled. "Of course David Wilson's here. The party's for him."

"Whose house is this?"

"A major contributor to his campaign. What's the problem?"

Dakota's eyes slewed around to a side door. "Good Lord. There's Kris. And Hamilton Stark. Is that Dr. Stone? It is, isn't it? I can't go inside."

"It's a big house, Dee. Just avoid them. Besides, I feel safer having you around, and if anybody says anything, you're my guest."

Just what I wanted.

To spend an entire evening ducking people I know.

With a scornful grunt, the butler made it known they were hold-ing up the line.

"Are you in, or out, Dee?"

She took a deep breath, vectoring her enemies' locations in a glance. "I'm in."

Heaven help me.

She found herself caught in a human shell game, dodging any-one with a familiar look, slipping off into parts unknown, and tak-ing great care to surface wherever Wilson, Kris, the old man, and Chief Forster were not. When a kindly old gentleman brought her a glass of champagne, she found herself cutting the conversation short, and ducking into the powder room. Once she'd regrouped, she returned to glimpse Selina Price, dangling off the arm of one of Phoenix's top real estate brokers, on the way upstairs.

Jostled by party guests descending the same steps, Dakota fol-lowed in Selina's wake. A party-goer dressed as Marie Antoinette gripped the banister, but her frilly ball gown arced out so far that anyone passing her had to flatten against the wall. A man engulfed by a papier mâché wedding cake, followed close behind, pinching the cloth on Marie's sleeve to steady himself. At the top of the stairs, a couple dressed as hot dogs, along with a person wearing a zebra head, stood out from the sea of costumes. The buzz of conversation all but eclipsed the stringed quartet in the foyer, but it was the noisy argument taking place at the mansion's front door that filtered up to the landing, and caused Dakota to turn and give a mental shriek.

An uninvited party-crasher didn't take kindly to being turned away.

Travis Creeley.

Panic closed her throat. Had he followed her here? If not, why on earth would he want to attend a shindig for David Wilson?

She crouched low, burrowing her way to the top of the land-ing. Checking the length of hallway, she hurried down the corridor, beyond his view. A cluster of businessmen imitating penguins in their tuxes and yellow, cone-shaped beaks, swilled highballs and traded stories about the future of Phoenix's economy.

Dakota opened the first of many doors, peeking inside dark rooms where beds were piled with expensive wraps and ladies' eve-ning bags. The last door she tried brought an unpleasant surprise.

Selina Price and the real estate tycoon were centered in the king-sized bed, going at it like a couple of high-stakes contenders at a pie-eating contest.

She pulled at the door until it clicked shut. As she turned to leave, she came face-to-face with Kris.

The detective's eyes flicked daggers. "What the hell are you doing?"

"A job."

"You're *hooking*?" What began as an angry whisper spiraled to a shrill. "All you need is a lamp post and a public defender."

"Keep your voice down." Dakota's eyes darted the length of the corridor. "No. And thanks for your vote of confidence. You're lucky I'd rather not call attention to myself, just now, or I'd slap the fire out of you for insulting me."

"*Ha.* Don't pretend you don't enjoy calling attention to yourself when you're standing here decked out as Pussy Galore in a silver, spandex body suit that shows Carlsbad Cavern *and* the Grand Canyon."

"And what'd you and the old man come as?"

"A pair of homicide aces." Quick-witted Kris.

"Sure you didn't come as the front and back halves of a donkey—without the costume?"

"You have no business here, Dakota."

"Wrong, again, Kristina-hyena. Y'all may be working security, but I'm an invited guest."

"Who invited you? David Wilson?"

"Princess Leia."

Kris's eyes bulged as if they'd been inflated to ten PSI. "You showed up here with one of Celia's hookers?"

"Escort." Dakota reached out and clamped her fingers around Kris's face, shaping her lips into a fish mouth, as if she'd come across a plastic egg of warm Silly Putty. "Say it with me. Ess-cooort. Escort. There. That's not too hard, is it?"

Kris slapped her hand away. "Whatever. Let's hope she doesn't turn up dead."

Dakota kept her voice low and controlled. "And just what do you mean by that?"

"You're such a disappointment, Dee." Kris stormed down the

hall and disappeared in the crush of guests who were mingling around at the top of the landing. The next time Dee saw her, she'd reached the first floor.

Selina Price came out of the bedroom, rumpled and mussed, and reeking of alcohol. The tryst had left her coils of cinnamon-bun hair as unflattering as a Rastafarian beachcomber. She tucked a business card into the bosom of her gauzy dress and said, "Let's blow this pop stand."

Dakota didn't put up a fuss.

She talked Selina into leaving her car at the restaurant where they'd met earlier that evening since "friends don't let friends drive drunk," and dropped Selina off at her adobe tract home in a respectable part of town. Sure, Selina'd invited her inside, but no thanks. Dakota'd had her fill of that—not that she expected Selina to end up dead, but she certainly didn't want fingerprints pointing in her direction if the unthinkable happened.

Upon returning to Heaven's Urn, Dakota slipped into a silk nightie, lit the fireplace, and settled in for the remainder of the evening, studying song lyric clues left behind on the bodies of her friends.

At two-thirty in the morning, she decided to put the day out of its misery. To ensure a fitful sleep, she guzzled a glass of wine before turning off the lights and donning the Lone Ranger sleep mask.

Chapter Twenty-Two

The last thing Dakota expected when she awakened was the first thing she got.

Kris showed up, unannounced, with bagels and begging.

"I behaved terribly last night. Can you ever forgive me, Dee?"

"I'll have to meditate on it. That certainly wasn't one of your more stellar moments."

"You have no idea what you mean to me. If I lost you, I'd . . ."

"Die?"

"I'd have to find somebody else to piss me off," Kris said through a grin. "You're really gifted in that way. I could search the world over and still not find anyone as annoying as you."

"That's supposed to make me feel better? You practically accused me of murder."

"Humor me, babe. I'm not very good at apologies."

"I disagree. You're not at all good with apologies. You're like the cavewoman of apologies. Why don't you just club me over the head and write it on my forehead in Magic Marker? That's how bad you are at this."

"I'm trying. Want a bagel?"

"Maybe after."

"After what?"

"For an ace detective, you're really dumb," Dakota said, taking Kris's free hand and cupping it to her breast.

The make-up sex turned out to be a four-point-five on the Richter scale. Afterward, Dakota and Kris reclined at opposite ends of the spa tub; they studied each other through a froth of bubbles. Dakota ran a toe along the detective's thigh, hoping when she got close enough to Kris's hand, she'd take a hint and rub her feet.

Rub them, hell. Kris ought to be kissing them after all the mean things she'd done.

"Suck my toes."

"No. You suck mine." The detective lifted her foot inches from Dee's face, only to get her ankle batted away. "It appears we've reached a standoff."

One thing for certain, Kris prided herself in being an expert negotiator. But even expert negotiators could be held hostage.

"Suck my toes and I'll let you help me with your investigation," Dakota said smugly.

It took a few seconds for Kris to crack the code. She took a sharp intake of air. "What do you know?"

"Hmm, let's see . . . *what* do I know?" Dee spoke to the soap using her playful voice. "What *do* I know?" she asked the towels. She shot her partner a look of intrigue, and noticed the beginnings of feverish excitement settling over her cop-face.

"We could work together."

"We *could*." Dakota weighed the possibility. "I'm just not sure we *should*."

Kris came up from a slump, breathless at the possibilities. "Do you know something?"

"Do *you* know something?" Dee arched an eyebrow.

"I asked you first."

"Suck my toes."

"Later."

"How do I know you'll follow through?"

"Have I ever withheld sex from you?"

Dakota felt her leverage slipping away. "Tell me what you know."

"It's obvious to me, someone's trying to set you up for these murders," Kris said in earnest. "And it's obvious to me that you're not backing off, so I figure we might as well work together on this."

Dakota pulled her foot away as if she'd been burned. Sat erect and stared, wide-eyed, at her lover. "Really?"

"This is bigger than the both of us. It just makes good sense."

Dakota narrowed her gaze in shrewd observation. "This isn't a trap?"

"I'm a cop. If it was, I wouldn't tell you."

"I dunno, Kris. You can be pretty stupid at times. Like taking Hamilton's side over mine. I'm still pissed off y'all arrested me."

"I didn't arrest you, Dee. Hamilton did."

"You should've un-arrested me."

She got a vehement headshake for the suggestion.

"I couldn't. You were his prisoner. I couldn't interfere. The unwritten rule is: 'You catch 'em, you clean 'em.' "

"Thanks for all your help."

"Please. Let's not argue." Kris stroked Dakota's knee. "I'm offering you a chance to work with me."

"And where does Hamilton fit in?"

"You're not dealing with him. As a matter of fact, he doesn't know anything about this, so I'd just as soon keep it that way." Kris laid out the plan. "I want to trade information. You figured it out about the locks of hair. You must know more stuff you're not telling us."

"Say it." Dakota made a pouty face.

"What?"

"That you need my help to solve these cases."

"Fine. Consider it said."

"No. Say the words."

Kris raised her hands in surrender. "Dee, I need your help to solve these cases."

"Because Hamilton's too stupid to figure it out. Say it."

"Okay . . . Hamilton can't figure it out."

"No. You have to use the word 'stupid.' I need to hear you call him stupid."

"You win. Hamilton's stupid."

"And because I'm prettier."

"That's true."

"Say it."

"You're prettier than Hamilton."

"And you like me better."

"That's the understatement of the year. I love you."

Dee stood. She reached for a spa towel, patting bubbles dry and watching Kris's eyes smolder. She tried out her sultry voice. "What are you waiting for?"

"I'm still soaking." Like a water-logged Sphinx, Kris relaxed with her arms along the sides of the spa tub, and an eternal smile playing across her lips.

"You'd rather shrivel up like a California raisin than join me in the boudoir of iniquity?" Dakota grazed her fingers over her nipples. "Suit yourself."

After an exhausting sexual marathon, Kris and Dakota sat on the bed, eating bagels smeared with strawberry cream cheese, and pooling information.

"As a token of good faith, I'll go first," Kris said, holding up a finger in the universal, *Wait a second* gesture, long enough to swallow the last bite. "Shawn O'Neil's criminal record shows multiple assaults. He has several aggravated assaults from a few other states, but no convictions."

"What do you make of that?"

"I'm thinking maybe somebody pulled strings. Got the charges dismissed."

"David Wilson." Dakota infused conviction in her tone.

"Mayor-Elect David Wilson? Are you hallucinating?"

"If you'd been nicer to me, you could've weaseled this information out of me days ago. Shawn O'Neil works for Wilson. Wilson has several goons on his payroll. I should know, seeing how we've met."

"Now it's your turn," Kris said, "tit-for-tat."

"I just exchanged information on Wilson."

"Yeah? Well, my information was better than yours."

"No, it wasn't."

"It was. I could've found out Shawn O'Neil was Wilson's employee."

"Only you didn't. I had to tell you."

"In the great hierarchy of things, who Shawn O'Neil works for just isn't that important."

Dakota braced her arms across her chest. In her best *All bets are off* voice, she said, "I figured you might pull something like this. You don't get to say what's good information and what's not. Maybe I know something that'll crack this case wide open."

"Fine. To prove I intend to play fair—and you can't say anything to anyone about this, Dee, and you have to swear it, because I could lose my job—I'll show you the close-up photos Dr. Stone took of the tattoos."

"Really?" Dakota pulled her legs under her, Yoga-style. "This is big." Dee measured her outstretched arms to illustrate not just big. *Really big*. Huge, even. "Because if you let me see those pictures, I'll tell you what the tattoos mean."

Each scrambled to clear the food off the bed. When Dakota returned from taking the plates to the kitchen, Kris had already set her briefcase on the bed, and was arranging the eight-by-ten glossies of the victims in chronological order.

"They're song lyrics," Dakota said, "The words and notes on Celia's body were taken from a Billie Myers tune."

"How do you know?"

"Because I used to take piano lessons when I was little. And because I looked the words up on the Internet to make sure." As an aside, Dakota added, "I'm surprised you didn't snap to that. It's your kind of music."

Then she told her about Diana Kyle. "Those are lyrics from *Drops of Jupiter*, by Train."

Kris sucked air. "What's it supposed to mean?"

"I'll let you figure that out. Now wait 'til you hear this next part."

Dakota discussed the strange dichotomy between the waltz pattern and the tattoos, but Kris's nonchalant flip of the wrist indicated she didn't put much stock in the idea.

"Lots of killers do patterns of three. It's probably nothing. The real clue's in the music on the tattoos."

This was so like Kris to rebuff her. Just because she wasn't part of the law enforcement brotherhood . . . just because she didn't have the same training background . . . well, that didn't make her too stupid to figure things out. Kris probably couldn't wait to run to Hamilton and share; a stupid move since that know-it-all, glory hog would try to claim credit for her hard work.

As Dakota wrote down the words hidden in the tattoos of Cyn Evans, Heather Lisle, and Fiona McHugh, she filled Kris in on last night's party—including Travis Creeley's attempt to crash it. Then she mentioned her plan to attend the Renaissance Fair.

"Isn't that tomorrow?" Kris said. "I'll go with you. I'm not up to visiting the hospital while you're laid up in traction, or worse, all because you stumbled upon Shawn O'Neil."

"I can fend for myself."

"I'm going, and that's that." Brown eyes gleamed stubbornly.

"Fine." No use arguing. "Let's recap. We know I'm being framed for these murders. We know Laura Ann's into Goth, and is hooked up with Velvet Tears, who's hooked up with Wilson. We know her dolls are missing locks of hair—"

"What? When did you find that out?"

"Yesterday. Quit butting in."

Kris launched into a charade. She not only zipped her lip; she put in the invisible key, turned the lock, and tossed the key over her shoulder and into the air.

Dakota went on, ticking off each point on her fingers. "Laura Ann's dolls had their hair butchered. Is it a coincidence, or is she somehow tied into these killings? David Wilson's bankrolling Shawn O'Neil, AKA Velvet Tears. The unfortunate mosh pit incident happened because the owner of Sinister Sisters ratted me out to O'Neil. Later, he went to her office and beat her to smithereens, so that kind of explains why I got tossed out of David Wilson's office by two goons."

Kris's face contorted in confusion. "You confronted the Mayor-Elect? I heard you earlier when you implied you'd met him, only I thought you meant you met him at the party. Are you crazy? He controls the Chief of Police. Chief Forster controls me. I'm already walking on eggshells at work, and *you go confront the Mayor-Elect*? Did I say that right?"

"That's fairly accurate."

Kris's frustration came out in a huff. "You're going to end up supporting me. I hope you know that."

"I can hardly wait. Then you'll have to mind me or I won't feed you."

"I hate you."

"Babe, if you'll promise to continue to hate me this much twice a day, every day, then hate me 'til your tongue falls off." She fanned out Dr. Stone's pictures and pointed to Cyn Evans's tattoo.

This one asked if a rival was pretty, and if she loved him, and suggested that the writer didn't really want to know the answer.

Dakota looked over expectantly. "So what's it mean?"

Kris mouthed words without sound. Then she broke into a melody, using the lyrics. "It's *Silver Springs*, by Fleetwood Mac."

"What's it supposed to mean?"

Slow headshake. "I have no idea."

"Here's Heather's tattoo." Dakota read off the words. Clearly the writer was a tortured soul, hearing his lover's name in every breath, and every word.

Kris snapped her fingers. "Santana. The song's called *Smooth*." Her eyes strayed to the ceiling. "Oh, man, I should've figured this out a long time ago."

"What are we supposed to do with this information? Are these songs the killer shared with each victim?"

"You mean like back when I was in high school, and my crush and I had our own special song?"

It sounded plausible. "Do Fiona McHugh's," Dakota said.

Kris pulled the photo closer and read the words aloud. "I'm such a loser. This one, I should've known. So should you. It's my favorite."

"How would I know that? I never even saw these until now."

"Evanescence," Kris said. And when Dakota arched an eyebrow, she cleared up the confusion. "That's the group. The song is *My Immortal*." Kris sang a few stanzas. "Now do you recognize it?"

"So what should we do?" Dakota asked. "String these all together like it's one message? Or does each song represent his message to the dead person?"

The doorbell bleated out an annoying series of rings.

They exchanged guarded looks.

The chime went on, relentless; as if an angry neighbor arrived to complain about dog droppings on the lawn; or the repo man showed up foaming at the mouth because he couldn't crowbar open the garage and reclaim the Lamborghini.

Dakota said, "I'm not expecting anyone. You?"

"That's gotta be Hamilton. I recognize the irritation in his finger." Kris rolled out of bed and made a mad dash to throw on clothes. "I should see what he wants."

"Hey—I have an idea." Said sarcastically. "How 'bout we just don't answer the door?"

"Must be important if he drove all the way over here, Dee."

"Hamilton Stark," Dakota muttered, shrugging into her robe and cinching it at the waist, "makes me want to vomit."

"What?"

"I said the man's as bright as a comet." She padded, barefoot, to the front door, forcing a smile onto her face.

He was looking toward the street when the lock clicked. By the time she opened the door, he'd turned and leveled his sights on her like a double-barrel shotgun. "I want to talk to you."

"Great, let's chat." Dakota greeted him with syrupy sweetness. "How've you been? There's crow in the fridge, if you dropped by to eat. We're out of coffee and donuts."

"Don't get smart with me." He eased the flap of his jacket aside, exposing a wicked .45. "Can you account for your whereabouts last night?"

She'd hardly been an invited guest at the Mayor-Elect's party. Piggybacking on Selina's invitation didn't count unless Selina was willing to swear they were together. Burying herself in work all night didn't exactly make a decent alibi. And what business was it, of his, anyway, where she was and what she was doing?

She asked, point blank.

"It is my damned business because I'm investigating a series of murders where . . . now, try not to be alarmed—" sarcasm thickened his tone "—but you happen to be my main suspect."

"Uh, well . . ." She glanced down the hallway anticipating Kris.

"'Uh, well . . .' is hardly an impressive answer, given the fact we have another murder victim on our hands."

Kris had somehow slipped into the kitchen, fully dressed, without Dakota knowing it. With her chin tilted in defiance, she sauntered over and answered for Dakota. "She was with me."

"Kris?" Her presence—and her disclosure—left him momentarily speechless. Then he went rabid. "Bullshit. You're covering."

"No." Kris kept her face carefully blank. "We were together all night. Until I stepped out for bagels this morning. I don't think she could've gotten dressed and slipped out to kill somebody in the time it took me to get back home."

"She even put a hickey on my left boob," Dakota chimed in helpfully. "I can prove it, if you'd like."

Kris shot her a wicked glare. She drawled out, "Dee," in the low, throaty growl of a junkyard dog.

Hamilton squinted against the morning sun. His eyes glinted with fury.

Dakota swallowed hard under his intent regard. Dr. Stone hit the nail on the head. Hamilton Stark was a good detective. He'd developed some sort of internal loran for fish tales. Having his partner tell him a bold-face lie had to be a bitter pill to swallow, especially since there wasn't a damned thing he could do about it.

He directed the final salvo at Kris. "I hope you know what you're doing, because we've got another dead girl on our hands. Dispatch received an anonymous tip phoned in. I'm on my way to the crime scene. Looks like our man—or woman, as the case may be—killed that escort who dressed up like Princess Leia."

Chapter Twenty-Three

Saturday morning held considerably more promise. Dakota sniffed the air and looked down her street. No sign of Travis Creeley anywhere. Even better, no sign of Hamilton.

Cranky, Kris climbed into the Jaguar. "I don't know why I have to wear this old granny dress."

"So we'll blend in."

"Save it, Dee. We're not going to blend in. I look like a fool, and you don't look much better." She lifted a handful of fabric from the skirt and let it drop back into place. "We couldn't run away in this get-up if turtles were chasing us."

"Quit grousing. I thought it'd be fun to primp like medieval ladies and strut our stuff."

"It's not cute, I'm telling you. We stand a better chance of blending in with the *touristas* than we do with the players."

"I've got an idea." Dakota smacked the steering wheel with the heel of her hand. "If you don't want to go to Renaissance Fair dressed like that, I could doll you up in Goth-gear. We could put you in leather. Whiten your face and blacken your eyes and lips . . . just thinking about it makes me hot. Maybe we could stay here, put on some heavy metal and I'll let you do me like the Demented Whore you were meant to be."

"What the hell are you talking about? Where do you get off calling me a demented whore?"

"That's your Goth name, babe. I looked it up on the Goth translator."

"Don't tell Hamilton," Kris said, half-kidding, half-serious. "He'd be on my ass, for sure."

Like he's not already.

The squabbles on the drive out were playful attempts at reconciling, Dakota knew, but did Hamilton Stark's name have to come up every day? Having him around, either in person, or in conversation, was like having a malignant tumor growing out of your forehead—you realize your friends think you look like a unicorn, but nobody'll tell you to your face.

After browsing the crafts offered for sale at Renaissance Fair, Kris and Dakota wandered toward the food concessionaires.

Kris's eyes glazed over at the sight of roasted turkey drumsticks. "I'm so hungry I could eat a whole one."

"Can you believe they have *gelatto* here? That's what I want. A triple dip of—*Holy smoke, don't move.* It's Laura Ann Spencer. With Velvet Tears."

"Where?" Kris craned her neck.

"Check nine o'clock, next to that booth. Stand in front of me. He doesn't know you." She grabbed the detective and forced her to move to one side. Her breath came in gulps. "We should sneak over and find out what they're doing."

"Are you nuts? We might as well have twinkle lights around us in these clothes."

"I say we do it." Dakota shielded her eyes against the glare. "I see bruises on her. Look at her arms. He's controlling her. Just look at her, following him around like a puppy. Frickin' recidivist might as well have her on a leash."

Kris let her fingers linger on Dakota's arm. "Since they don't know me, I could walk up to them and snoop around. Maybe pretend I work here. Or ask how they're enjoying the fair."

"That's a dumb idea."

"Why's it dumb? He knows you, so that lets you out."

"It's dumb because . . . okay, go-go-go . . . they're walking away."

Kris gathered her skirt and hurried across the grounds. The flower tiara fell off her head and rolled away in the dust. Some do-gooder shouted, "You dropped this, m'lady," snagging Velvet Tears' attention.

His eyes slewed around to the wild woman sprinting toward him, but made contact with Dakota's. He grabbed Laura Ann's wrist and gave it a harsh tug. A strange, unspoken communion passed between them, then the two raced toward the strip of vendor tents.

Kris trotted off in the opposite direction, presumably to head them off. Dakota grabbed the hem of her gauzy skirt, pulled it up to her knees and followed their dust. As she neared the vendor tents, a bearded man with a tray of hand-made rings stepped into her path. She skirted him with the precision of a cutting horse, narrowly ruining his day. Her eyes flickered over the area. O'Neil and the girl hadn't stopped at the tents, so she continued to run. She advanced on a cordoned-off perimeter where the jousting competitions were in full swing. As two knights lowered their lances and spurred their mounts, Dakota stared past what would become the point of impact. Shawn O'Neil and Laura Ann Spencer looked over their shoulders, locking gazes with her.

Dakota ducked under the rope, to the collective gasps of onlookers. Festival employees yelled, "Stop," but their cries fell on deaf ears as she ran past the horsemen to the other side.

She stumbled into a similar arena, sectioned off for bare-knuckle fighting. Contestants in leather loin cloths, their bodies greased to a sinewy sheen, took swings at each other while the crowd cheered-on their favorites.

Goths' heads bobbed in the distance, jostling the crush of people as they forced their way through the crowd. The place had all the allure of a mosh pit.

Dakota entered the ring.

The bigger of two contestants halted in mid-surprise, allowing the underdog to clock him in the jaw. Eyeballs rolled past fluttering lids. Goliath crumpled to the canvas mat. The crowd roared with delight.

Dakota made it to the other side, cleared the fight ring and rushed ahead. She should've known she'd lose sight of them. They had plenty of room to hide behind thousands of vehicles, parked clear to the horizon. Winded, she got her bearings and headed back the way she came. When she arrived at the food concessionaires', she stopped in her tracks.

Kris was still standing there, never having followed in the first place, having a lively conversation with a man in a blazer and khakis.

Hamilton.

Furious, Dakota sauntered over with purpose in her step.

"You're keeping me out of the loop," Hamilton ranted. "You're protecting her for personal reasons."

"That's not true. If I thought she was guilty, I'd put her away."

"As I recall, you *did* think she was guilty, and you *did* want to arrest her. What the hell did she do that made you change your mind? Is the sex that good? Damn it, Kris, it's like you've fallen under her spell. Like you've discovered the golden vagina, so to hell with your career."

"That's crazy talk."

"Is it? Well, one of us needs to be able to think clear-headed, and according to what I've seen the past few days, it sure as hell won't be you."

Wearing layers of sweat and grime like a Miss America sash, Dakota interrupted the conversation. "There you are, wench," she said with a chipper lilt. To Hamilton, she said, "Well, well, well. If it isn't our knight in rusty armor. Fancy meeting you here."

The detective scowled. "I was just leaving."

"Oh, do stay, m'lord. I can't imagine what my life would be like without you in it." Dakota bent her knees in an affected curtsy.

"Fuck you." He walked away with Dakota calling out in all her glory.

"Aw, please stay. Was it something I said? Can't we all just get along?" Without a backward glance, he flipped her the universal finger-gesture of contempt, leaving her no choice but to shout, "Next time, you should ask those transsexuals if they have AIDS *before* you sleep with them." Then she felt bad for demeaning transsexuals for sleeping with Hamilton, since it'd been Hamilton she'd meant to demean.

Chapter Twenty-Four

Sunday's headlines were as tall as skyscrapers, with typeset in a size that hadn't been used since the assassination of John Fitzgerald Kennedy.

SIX WOMEN DEAD—SERIAL KILLER STILL AT LARGE

The lead story contained an interview with Mayor-Elect Wilson. His knee-jerk solution seemed Victorian in its extreme. It entailed women dressing in long sleeves and high necklines in public, while barricading themselves behind closed doors after sunset.

Dakota finished her coffee, slipped into the bathroom for a final grooming check, then jogged down to the Spencers to give them the great news.

"Congratulations, your daughter's alive. I saw her at Renaissance Fair yesterday."

Lorraine Spencer clutched a hand to her chest. She let out a wounded animal gasp and blinked back tears. "Did you talk to her? Is she coming home? How'd she look? Are you *sure* it was her? Is she eating properly?"

Jake Spencer, in his golf shorts and knit top, waited, stoically looked on.

"I didn't get to talk to her. She was with this biker guy . . . Shawn O'Neil. Goes by the name Velvet Tears. She looked . . . honestly? It looked like she'd been roughed up. The main thing is she's alive. And I have to believe in a crowd that big, that if she really wanted to get away from the guy, she could've screamed bloody murder and attracted all kinds of attention."

Before walking away, Dakota exchanged handshakes and promised to keep them updated.

"Speaking of creepy people," the software CEO called out after her, "do you know anything about the creepy guy lurking around the neighborhood?"

Dakota cupped her hands to her mouth. "Don't worry, I'll take care of him. Next time you spot him, call me."

Dakota arrived home from the Spencers to the smell of fresh-brewed coffee, and the sight of Kris pouring herself a tall orange juice. Only it wasn't strictly OJ. She'd left the vodka bottle out on the counter.

"How'd it go with the Spencers?"

"They're glad to know their daughter's alive, but I got the idea they thought I could've done more. Jake Spencer rubs me the wrong way. He doesn't come out and directly accuse me of goldbricking, but he has this eye-squint that gives me a bug-under-a-microscope kind of feeling."

"Did you tell them she's under the mind-control of a cretin? And that when they do get her back, they'll have to debrief her like a Moonie?"

"I should've mentioned it might not hurt to buff up on the Patty Hearst case; on what happened after her parents got her back from the Symbionese Liberation Army."

"You should prepare them for the fallout." Kris took a long drink, then sliced the tumbler through the air with an unsteady hand. "Don't you feel any duty to warn them?"

"Let me answer you this way: Do you feel any compulsion to warn the rest of Celia's girls?"

The sarcasm wasn't lost on Kris, no matter what the ratio of vodka to orange juice happened to be. "What? You don't think the PD's doing enough?"

"Maybe you and I ought to have a powwow with the remaining fantasy escorts." Dakota took a seat at the dining table and waited for the coffeemaker to end with a sputter. "They might be able to help us piece our pattern together."

For once, Kris seemed to agree with her. She patted her pockets looking for car keys.

"I'll drive." Dakota dangled the key fob to the Jaguar. She hadn't expected the detective to put up a protest, but she dropped in a gentle reminder, anyway. "You've had a drink this morning. It's better if I'm the one behind the wheel."

"You think I'm a boozer, don't you?"

"I'm merely offering to chauffeur you."

"If you think I've got a drinking problem, say so."

"I'm worried about you." With Kris suddenly in her face, Dakota's jaw muscles went tight.

"Don't waste your time. It's only a problem if I can't handle it."

Yeah, right.

Essence of hooch was starting to ooze from Kris's pores, and the natural color in her pink English cheeks had taken on the look of freshly-ground sirloin sprinkled with dried oatmeal.

The coffee maker gave a final hiss. Dakota made her way to the counter, and poured two steaming cups of French Vanilla. She offered one to Kris. "I'd appreciate it if you'd have coffee with me," she said, and the dejected investigator sat down at the table.

"How many interviews are we talking about?"

"There's Brie Munroe, who dresses up as Sabrina Duncan . . ."

"That's lame, taking a character from a TV show. I'll admit 'Charlie's Angels' used to be popular with brain-deads. I'll even admit I caught snippets of reruns while channel surfing."

"Whatever. I didn't decide what to name her. There's Hannah Lee, who dresses up as Holly Goodhead—"

"What's with all these Bond girls? Doesn't anybody daydream about plain old Betty Lou Neighbor, the girl from next door?"

"Hey, it's not my fantasy," Dakota reminded her. "Then there's Abigail Addison, who dresses up as Barbarella for Fantasy Escorts Unlimited. Unless Celia hired more girls, that's all I can remember."

"Who do we drop-in on first?"

Dakota took a quick sip, and picked up the address book by the telephone. "Brie and Hannah live the closest. I say we start with them."

Twenty minutes later, Dakota and Kris pulled up in front of a cluster of garden homes. Unlike Heaven's Urn, Brie Munroe and Hannah Lee didn't live in a gated community, but in some ways, getting in and out proved to be a good deal more complicated. For one thing, the streets were arranged like two horseshoes, one above the other. For another, the houses were almost indistinguishable from one another, and the road signs had to be a police officer's nightmare: Mary Ann Lane, Marian Street, Marion Avenue, Mary

Ann Court, Merry Anna East, and Merry Anna West. Not to mention the continuous wrought-iron fence in back that joined each property to the next. For a burglar looking for an easy escape, it'd be best to choose locations near the entrance, and pole vault over the railings.

Brie Munroe hadn't been crying when Dakota talked to her—*what? Ten minutes ago?*—but, when she opened the door, she clutched a tissue in one hand while daubing at red-rimmed, misty eyes. Whatever just happened was not an allergy flare-up.

Dakota said, "Did we come at a bad time?"

"It's nothing, really. I just got off the phone with my mom. I asked if I could come home for a while, just until the police catch this animal. She was screaming at me, telling me what a disappointment I am, and said, 'I'm sorry I ever adopted you.' I guess I'm adopted then."

"I'm so sorry." Dakota.

"You don't look like one of Charlie's angels." Kris.

Brie motioned them inside. "You look exactly like a cop. Or, a gymnast, maybe?"

Dakota gored Kris's ribs with an elbow, *Knock it off.* She inventoried Brie's house, memorizing details of French furnishings, and locating exits the lady could beef up.

Brie softened. "This is my day off. I don't have to dress up like anybody. Most days I just want to be plain Brie." When Kris cocked an eyebrow, Brie said, "That's my name. When I'm on my own time, I'm just plain Brie. If I'm out on a date with someone who's not a paying customer, I'm just plain Brie."

Kris asked to call her Sabrina instead of Brie. By way of explanation, she said the name had already stuck in her mind, like one of those songs you heard first thing in the morning that you couldn't get out of your head for the rest of the day. Brie understood.

"So you actually date regular people? You have a boyfriend? And yet you work as a hook—" Kris caught herself "—fantasy escort?"

Brie cut her eyes to Dakota. "Didn't you explain how this works?" With a backhanded flip of the hair, her blonde tresses sailed over her shoulder and cascaded down her back like thick Palomino mane. She motioned them over to a couch positioned in front of multi-paned windows. When they sat, rays of sunshine penetrated the glass and warmed their shoulders. Brie padded silently to the kitchen in her pink satin house slippers. "I just made a pitcher of Bloody Marys."

"Fantastic," Kris enthused.

"None for us," Dakota said on a strained voice. "I'm on the wagon . . ." *Not true.* ". . . and Kris doesn't like to drink if I'm not having one." *Also not true.* "She says it'd be like teasing the pet dog with food. *It just isn't nice.*"

Brie brought two ginger ales and placed them on silver coasters atop a daintily carved coffee table that could've been an heirloom. She slid onto a chaise lounge with down cushions, and relaxed against the chair back.

"Celia didn't have any enemies," Brie said. "You asked me that when you called, and I've put a bit of thought into it. The answer's no. Hannah might know more. She often helped Celia with the books."

Kris piped up. "Hannah's the bookkeeper?" She whipped out a small spiral notebook from her shoulder bag, and grappled for a pen.

"Not exactly." Brie exchanged a guarded look with Dakota. "Is it okay to talk around her?"

"Kris and I are working together. You can tell her anything you'd be willing to tell me."

"Yes, but you know what I'm about to say," Brie said with an implied warning in her tone. "And I need to know whether to tell her, or not."

Kris scowled. "Hello, I'm sitting right here."

Dakota rested her hand on Kris's knee. "Celia did a cash business. Fantasy Escorts is hardly the type of business a patron would want showing up on the family's credit card. I don't know what sort of setup Celia had, or if she had a second set of books for the IRS . . ."

Brie chimed in with additional details. "Hannah would straighten out the books. I didn't care, long as I got paid. The rest of us figured Celia was grooming Hannah to take over the business when she retired. Fine by us. Nobody got bent out of shape over it."

Kris, jaw muscles tightened like banjo strings.

Oh, hell. She's thinking money laundering.

Back outside, on the way next door to the garden home where Hannah Lee lived, Kris said, "That's just great. Maybe we've got an even bigger problem. And you knew this. But you didn't tell me."

"I didn't think it was important." Dakota raised up her hands in frustration. "It's not like you make it easy to talk about Celia. Whenever the subject pops up, you bite my head off."

"Maybe we're looking at this all wrong. Now I'm wondering whether this investigation might be rooted in money. In organized crime. Stranger things have happened. I'll run it by Hamilton."

Hamilton again.

Hannah Lee, Celia's Holly Goodhead escort, greeted them at the door looking harried and distraught. As she invited them inside, she announced that her day hadn't started out well, and she'd seriously considered going back to bed. "My five year old clown fish died. As I was flushing him, he started swimming again."

Hannah's home resembled Brie's on the outside, but her furnishings leaned toward English antiques, Chinoiserie accent pieces and coconut-scented candles. The walls in her living room were painted a muted shade of peach that complemented her auburn-tinged hair and made her complexion radiant. As Dakota and Kris settled in for a chat, Hannah mentioned that she and Brie had planned to open an antique store someday when they retired. Now that Celia was gone, retirement looked like it might take place sooner than later.

"No, Celia didn't have enemies," she told Kris when the detective began asking questions. "Neither did the other girls."

"And yet they're dead," Kris offered with characteristic bluntness.

"Oh, sure, Fiona pissed off that weird Goth chick, but the little outcast must've gotten over it because she hasn't been back."

"Tell me about cooking the books." Kris, again.

Hannah Lee lowered her tortoiseshell glasses and peered over the rims. "I don't know what you're talking about."

"Sure you do." It was as if Kris whiffed the air and her bloodhound traits caught a scent.

Hannah checked her Rolex, and suddenly remembered she had a prior appointment.

Kris coolly eyed her up "We can get a subpoena."

"Do that." Hannah turned to Dakota. "Good to see you again, Dee. Don't be a stranger." She adjusted her glasses and cut her eyes back to Kris. "You, I never want to see again."

The girlfriends quit bickering about getting the bum's rush from Hannah as soon as Dakota wheeled the Jaguar into a parking space in front of Abigail's apartment.

The door to Abigail's apartment was ajar.

Dakota felt a shiver run up her back. She breathed out a scary, "Oh, no."

"Six hookers dead and this Barbarella wannabe twit leaves her house unsecured? That's beyond stupid."

"Maybe it's trash day," Dakota mumbled, her radar suddenly up and tracking. "Maybe she's hauling out her garbage, and she'll be right back. I used to do that. Pets," she added with conviction. "Leave the door open a few minutes and let the pet out to do his business."

It took the two of them leading with their shoulders to force their way inside. The tawny-skinned, dark-haired beauty had apparently tried to crawl to safety, but only made it to the threshold before passing out in a crumpled heap.

"Who'd do such a thing?" Dakota wailed. She averted her eyes from the fist-sized bruises on Abigail's face and breasts, and the bloody lip and loose teeth. "We need an ambulance."

But Kris was already on her cell phone with an ambulance *en route*.

Abigail, barely breathing, cracked one eye open. The other had swollen shut. Her voice came out weak and raspy. "Dee. The others said you wouldn't help . . . but I knew . . . you'd come."

Dakota and Kris exchanged wary looks.

"What happened?" Dee asked. "Who did this to you?"

"Old . . . man. Asked about . . . you." She coughed up blood and a tooth fell out.

Travis Creeley.

A tear leaked out of Abigail's unopened eye. It turned pink near a gash, and trickled down one purple cheek. "I . . . didn't tell . . . him. Honest. Am . . . I . . . gonna die?"

"Not today, sweetie." To Kris, she said, "Let's get her to the car. The hospital's not that far. No sense wasting time waiting for paramedics." She gripped Abigail's arm and waited for Kris to help hoist the girl to her feet.

"They're on the way. They have equipment we don't have. Miracle drugs. Oxygen. Expertise. They're professionals."

Dakota grimaced. "If this were you, would you want to wait?"

"Well, what are you waiting for?" Kris seized Abigail's free arm and they carried her, limp and moaning, to the Jaguar.

Chapter Twenty-Five

Once hospital personnel transferred Abigail Addison to a gurney in ER, and then wheeled her down a corridor, out of sight, Kris clutched Dakota's wrist.

"Let's go."

Standing, saucer-eyed, in the emergency room, Dakota protested. "The doctor told us to wait here."

Calm, yet, insistent, Kris spoke with great urgency. "He told us to wait because there's an officer assigned to the ER. The PD stations them here to take reports of gunshot or knife wounds, rapes, and what not, when they'd otherwise go unreported. It's how we catch burglars who get shot by homeowners. If we piddle around long enough, we'll get sucked into the investigation. Besides, whatever happens, it's out of our hands. We'll do a lot more good going after Travis Creeley."

"We can't leave her here. What if he comes back and finishes the job?"

"Dee, you're the only one who can recognize the perp on sight. Now let's go."

Dakota wasn't conscious of having crossed the room but when they reached the exit, the emergency room lay behind them.

"Can't we arrange for protection? Call Hamilton. Tell him to get down here and stay with her."

Kris's eyes practically bungee-jumped out of their sockets. "*You* want *me* to call *Hamilton*?"

"You're going to anyway. Might as well bring him in on the ground floor and put him to work."

"That's very mature of you, Dee."

"I have an internal compass. I can be a grown-up."

Ten minutes before, they'd abandoned the Jaguar at the ambulance entrance with the motor still running; now, it was like having a getaway car. Belted into the passenger seat, Kris stabbed out a number on her cell phone. "Hamilton? Kris. We've got a problem."

She filled him in on Travis Creeley, then listened without speaking. While driving toward the highway, Dakota feigned disinterest, as if taking in the scenery and the smear of passing cars; in truth, she took in every word of the one-sided conversation.

Finally, irritation did her in. "Ask him to send protection. A bodyguard."

"Can you get the captain to authorize a uniform to guard Abigail?" After a few seconds, Kris gave Dakota a vigorous thumbs-up. "Yeah. Okay. Fine. No problem. Five o'clock? Dinner's a bad idea. Because I have plans. Yes, with Dakota." Long pause. "Okay, we'll be there." Kris pulled the phone from her ear and thumbed the key pad's off-button. "He wants the three of us to get together and compare notes to narrow down whether Travis Creeley's the guy we're looking for."

Dakota huffed. That was a lie. He wanted Kris but got her, too. Package deal. "Is he at all uncertain? Creeley beat the crap outta Abigail. She's an eye-witness. She told us. What more proof does he need?"

"Eye-witnesses have been wrong before. Innocent people have ended up being convicted for crimes they didn't commit. He wants to make sure."

"Oh. Right. Hamilton's fair that way, isn't he? An equal opportunity detective."

Kris flashed the first smile of the day. "You're just mad because you have to share me for dinner."

"Maybe so." Dakota bridled her anger. "But I guarantee one thing: I may have to share the main course, but when it comes to dessert, it's just you and me, babe."

Early Monday morning all hell broke loose.

Hamilton Stark steadily hammered Dakota's front door, until both sleepy-eyed women came to see what all the ruckus was about. One of the sleepy-eyed women brought a gun, and put it on the entry table only after peering through the peephole to make sure it was him.

"I told you it was him," said Kris as Dakota looked longingly at the .38. "I recognized the knock. Let him in before he wakes up the neighborhood."

Dakota opened the door. Measured him in a glance, and rejected him. "I can't tell you what a nice time I had last night." Really, she couldn't. It'd be a lie, and lying was wrong.

He stood on the porch, stone-faced, but he got it. She knew he got it because he was biting the inside of his lip, trying to vanquish a smile.

Then he silently counted on his fingers, and said, "Statistics bear out that one in twenty-five people are sociopaths; but only one in two hundred thousand people are schizophrenics. Fascinating, right? So I counted all the people I see on a regular basis, and sure enough, you're the twenty-fifth person."

"Good one," Dakota said, and let him inside. "Just so you know, you're no longer beneath my contempt." He wasn't even worth her contempt. "I'm going back to bed."

"Want coffee?" Without waiting for an answer, Kris slip-slapped to the kitchen in her velour slippers, still going "commando" beneath the blue cashmere robe.

"I'm sure he's not staying," Dakota snapped. "You're not staying, are you? Because I bet you'd rather get an early start solving cases, wouldn't you?" She thought back to last night's dinner at Tío Luís, and grimly accepted that it wasn't the platter of chiles rellenos giving her heartburn. Picking up the tab had been the only gentlemanly thing Hamilton had done that evening.

"Don't be so eager to run me off." He bypassed Dakota, tailing Kris to the coffeemaker. "I posted a guard at Abigail Addison's door. I even dropped by to make sure everything was copasetic. I told the officer, no one goes in or out except doctors and nursing staff."

"Sounds good to me." Kris emptied a couple of scoops of dark roast into the paper filter.

"You'd think, wouldn't you?" he said with a twinge of irony, then braced his khaki-covered haunches against the countertop as if he'd plunked coins down the chute of a parking meter and wasn't going to leave until he used up every last minute. "During the night, our perp came through the window and did her just like the others, minus the sex. When the nurse returned to check her vitals, a mangy black cat shot out."

"She's dead?" Kris steadied herself against the pantry. "How can that be?"

"I guess somebody should've told them not to put her in a room on the ground floor, you think?" he said dripping sarcasm.

"Don't blame me," Kris said, still dumbfounded and practically speechless.

"You're the one who took her to the hospital. You were the one in charge. You could've arranged for her to be on an upper floor, where an intruder couldn't break in and help himself."

"You're the lead investigator. Why didn't you do it? You arranged for an officer to be posted at the door to her room."

"Stop it, both of you." Dakota joined them in the kitchen. She clinked three mugs together removing them from the cabinet. "How do you take your coffee, Hamilton?"

"Black."

"And how are you drinking yours this morning, Kris?" Her eyes strayed lazily to the liquor cabinet. "Irish?"

"Black. *Like always.*" Kris returned her attention to Hamilton. "Fill us in."

The detectives swapped information. Kris reviewed the leads Dakota had come up with.

"Seems like you gals are working a maverick investigation." Hamilton held out an empty mug.

"Around here, people get their own coffee." Kris jutted her chin in the direction of the pot.

Dakota intervened. With a mock smile, she took his cup. "Nonsense. You're a *guest* in my home, Hamilton. Let me get that for you." She poured him a splash, returned his cup, and settled in to monitor the detectives' conversation. Idiot. Let him think he had her waiting on him.

Later, in the privacy of her study, Dakota decided the only really good thing to come from Hamilton's visit was when he allowed her to download the digital pictures he took of the henna tattoo found on Abigail Addison. After he left, she printed them out on high-grade photo paper and showed them to Kris.

The message was about falling to Earth with dripping wings, because heavy things wouldn't fly, and the sky might catch fire.

This reminded Dakota of the mythological story of Daedalus and Icarus, and how the wax wings Daedalus made for Icarus melted when Icarus flew too close to the sun.

Kris recognized the lyrics instantly. "Nina Gordon recorded that song. *Tonight and the Rest of My Life* is the name of it."

"Did Hamilton recognize it?"

Kris barked out a laugh. "Are you kidding? He doesn't listen to my music. He has his own. If it isn't on the classical station, he tunes it out. Or throws a tantrum 'til I let him change the dial."

"Do us a favor and don't tell him about it."

"Why not? He's part of this investigation."

"He's a glory hog." Dakota held up a finger, and corrected herself. "Make that a *pig*. A big *boar* in snappy clothes."

She didn't expect Kris to get it. But saying it made her feel ever so much better.

Bore.

Early Monday afternoon, Chief Forster's secretary called the house with an order from the PD's commander. Kris was to show up at his office at three o'clock sharp.

And she was to bring Dakota Jones with her. No exceptions. No excuses.

Seated near the secretary's desk, just outside the Chief's office, Kris scooted to the edge of her chair and leaned in close.

"Why does he want to see us?"

"I have no idea." But the dread in the woman's face told them otherwise.

"Give me a hint," Kris said. The Chief's assistant slumped miserably at her desk. "Please?"

"I can't. He'd fire me. You'll have to enter the lion's den on your own."

"He's late. He said three o'clock sharp, and he's late. Is he even in there?" Kris's attention strayed to the closed door leading into Forster's office.

"He's with someone. It's taking a bit longer than he thought." The secretary went back to the computer keyboard, pecking at it in a way that led Dakota to believe the woman must have other skills that impressed the Chief enough to hire her.

A nasty uproar erupted from the inner office, shattering the calm and quickening the pulse of all three women.

The booming voice of Mayor-Elect Wilson vibrated through the walls. "Maybe you should be handling this better. We've discussed this."

"Don't threaten me. You're nothing but a Baltimore transplant. I know your secrets. Without me, you'd have come away with a standard twenty-percent of the vote, and Jane Roman would be trimming off your balls with manicure scissors."

"Fix this before things get ugly."

Visibly shaken, the secretary reached across the desk and turned on the Bose radio. Strains of Chopin filtered through the speakers. "It's safer," she said knowingly. "My motto for job security is *Wear blinders and use earplugs.*"

The door banged open and Chief Forster poked his head out. "Carson, you're late. Get in here. And bring Ms. Jones with you."

He gestured them into leather guest chairs. Dakota scanned the room. David Wilson must be hiding in the Chief's private bathroom. Either that or he'd used the escape hatch and slithered off, unnoticed, through the side door.

"It's come to my attention you girls are working this case on your own."

They traded looks of betrayal. Dakota's said: *Told you he was a cutthroat.* Kris's said: *Just kill me now.*

"Since you seem to be doing so well on your own, Carson, maybe you don't need the Phoenix Police."

"Sir, I can explain . . ."

"I've made my decision. You're off the case." He stood with his feet slightly apart, like a gunslinger ready to draw down. "Turn over your service weapon."

The flush of fear drained from Kris's cheeks. She sat, barely breathing, ashen-faced, and slipping into the kind of shock generally associated with death messages.

"Your gun." Chief Forster snapped his fingers, *Let's have it.* "Until further notice, you're on suspension."

Kris stood on wobbly knees. Blinked back tears and reached inside her jacket. Removed the gun from her shoulder holster, popped out the magazine, and pulled back the slide to clear the chamber. A shiny round hit the carpet and landed near the leg of Dakota's chair.

Kris handed the empty weapon, butt-first, to her commander.

"Leave your badge and ID on the desk." Once Kris complied, Forster scraped everything into a drawer.

Unable, or unwilling to move, Kris waited with the confounded expression of someone who'd been chased through the neighborhood by thugs, only to reach the safety of her front door in time to be shot by a burglar.

"It's time to go, Kris." Dakota gave the de-frocked detective a gentle wrist-pull.

"Best of luck, Ms. Carson." The Chief punctuated the blessing with a nod. "Ms. Jones, see that she makes it safely off the premises, will you?"

Still stunned, Dakota asked, "Did Hamilton Stark have anything to do with this?"

Can we just go? Kris pleaded with her eyes. When Dakota didn't budge, she said it.

"Ms. Carson has the right idea. A pro always knows when to fold."

Dakota mustered a tone filled with bravado. "We'll find out soon enough. Mayor Roman will—"

"Mayor Roman's about as effective as a wet firecracker. Don't count on her to fight your battles. And by the way, best of luck with your leads. I don't suppose I have to tell you we have long-term accommodations for you, in the event you interfere with this investigation in any way."

Outside in the parking lot, Dakota scanned the horizon. For such a beautiful day, things sure turned out badly. "Well, at least he didn't fire you."

Kris still wore the look of someone who'd been pole-axed. "What the hell do you think an indefinite suspension is?"

"He didn't say you were on indefinite suspension."

"No, he said I was suspended until further notice. He fleeced me of my badge, my ID, and my gun. I don't know how else you expect me to interpret that. Those are the tools of my trade. He neutered me. Then he lifted his hind leg on me."

Dakota stuck her hand in Kris's pocket and pulled out the cell phone. With Kris still trembling in mind-numbing despair, Dakota scrolled through the digital address book until she found an entry for Hamilton.

She hit the talk button. The detective answered on the second ring.

"Where I come from, people like you are called stool pigeons. You ratted out my girlfriend to the Chief of Police, you cowardly son-of-a-bitch."

"You don't know what you're talking about," said Hamilton, silver-tongued and covering his tracks.

"Don't try to weasel out of it. She's been suspended, thanks to you."

"When did this happen?"

"Like you don't know. That's the bad news . . . the good news is that you're out of our lives, and I don't have to put up with your arrogant ass anymore."

"You've made a mistake."

She paused long enough to take a quick breath, to dish out more rapid-fire insults, interrupting his feeble explanations.

"*Bup-bup-bup*—don't even try to cover your tracks. Dr. Stone was wrong about you. You're not an ace detective; you're evil. How could you do this to her? She looks up to you—although I can't for the life of me understand why—you untrustworthy, spineless fool."

She searched her brain dictionary for more adjectives.

"Hang up," Kris said softly. "That's enough."

"Is that her? Is she with you? Put her on the phone."

"I will not. If you have something to say to her, you'll have to filter it through me, Benedict Arnold."

Kris did an eye-cross, sighing like a blow-up doll with a slow leak.

"Tell her I promise to keep her in the loop. And that I'll do my best to get her reinstated."

"Listen, alligator mouth, you might be able to sucker her in, but I'm wise to you. Leave us alone and stay out of our lives."

Tension didn't subside once they got home. As the two women outlined a contingency plan to hunt down Laura Ann, Velvet Tears, and Travis Creeley, the telephone rang.

Dakota found herself fielding a phone call from Mayor Jane.

"Have you gone undercover? Seven girls are dead."

"We're doing our best. And we have a solid lead," she said, no longer thinking of Creeley as a person of interest, but as the prime suspect.

"Who's 'we'?"

"Kris." Dakota shot a quick look at her lover, seated at the table, slumped forward with her head on her arm, and her shoulders heaving. The sight of Kris, sobbing, tore at her heart. What Hamilton did was indecent. But Jane had said something, and Dakota needed to answer. "Kris and I have thrown in together. It just made sense, you know, since we were stepping on each other's toes."

"Good show. Now get back to work and find us a killer. If you can do it before David Wilson takes office, I'll totally make it worth your while. Whatever you want, name your price."

Dakota turned her back to Kris. She cupped a hand to the phone, and said in a low whisper, "Can you get Kris her job back?"

Chapter Twenty-Six

Tuesday morning, Dakota made an unpleasant discovery.

Prior to her bed partner's suspension, she'd assumed the biggest worry she had to contend with was Kris's partnership with good-looking, golden-throated Hamilton Stark. Wrong. Seeing Kris confident, self-assured, and constantly in the company of a man she'd engaged in a one-night-stand with paled in comparison to having her home drunk, weepy and underfoot.

Since the indefinite suspension, she'd gone through the pantry like she had a full-blown marijuana addiction, which wouldn't have been as bad if she hadn't littered the house with empty wrappers, cookie crumbs, and plates with dried-on macaroni and cheese. And she'd taken to dressing like a Wal-Martian, wearing clothes and shoes that didn't match, and then stepping out in the yard to get the newspaper, or worse, venturing out in public when her ass, tits and stomach should've been covered.

Her attire of choice on this particular morning, as she walked back inside the house with a copy of The Trib in the crook of her arm, well—*Holy cow. This was just plain wrong, wrong, wrong.*

Dressed in the bottom half of a lace teddy, she looked like a slab of pork packaged in a doily. Making Dakota want to yell, *C'mon, if you're going to strut your stuff in public, at least give it your best effort. I mean, you obviously took the time to select your ensemble, but then— bam!—you ruin it with those beat up old deck shoes. I never thought I'd say this, but girl, go put on a pair of stilettos.*

"Okay—one question—did you know my great-grandmother?"

Kris scowled. "What's that supposed to mean?"

"She's the one who had a house to rent in a small town in Southwest Missouri. She put an ad in the paper for it saying 'No niggers, drunks, or whores.' What's sad is that this happened in the late eighties. Not the 1880s, the *1980s*. What's worse is the paper printed it. She got a renter out of it, though. She also broke my *Speak & Spell*, come to think of it. Didn't like 'plastic things that talked to her.' We found out later that she had dementia. Go figure."

Kris slitted her eyes.

"You kidding me? I mean, honestly, are you kidding me? You couldn't find lace gloves to go with your lace outfit?" Dakota hectored. "Huh. Well. The lack of effort's duly noted."

"What's your point?"

"When did a 65-year-old Jewish woman from Long Island get trapped in your body? You've turned into a vilde chaya."

Dakota needed to take decisive action, and quickly.

The best strategy entailed splitting up job duties, so she talked Kris into going after Laura Ann. After all, Velvet Tears didn't know who Kris was, or what she looked like. It stood to reason she might actually get close enough to trail him to Laura Ann's location, and the Sinister Sisters made a good starting point. While Kris dogged the Goths, Dakota would be confronting David Wilson, point-blank, about his involvement with Shawn O'Neil.

After a timely lecture on superstore sub-cultures—when at Target, *pants required*; when at Wal-Mart, *pants optional*—the women struck out in different directions.

Dakota barely cleared Wilson's front door, when two of his goons flanked her.

"Nobody lays a hand on me," she said with passion, then whipped around and jammed a finger inches from Wilson's chin. "I overheard you talking to the Chief of Police. If you have nothing to do with the deaths of these women, then you need to come clean about Velvet Tears. I want to know where to find him."

Wilson played dumb. "You're crazy. Get out of my office."

"I'm not going anywhere until you level with me." Bodyguards stepped toward her with malice in their eyes. "I wouldn't throw me out, if I were you, unless you're dying to be the lead-off story on the six o'clock news." She fanned her hand through the air as if to read a skywritten message. "'Tonight's top story . . . what does Mayor-Elect David Wilson have to hide about six dead girls?' Think about it. Could get nasty."

"What do you want from me?"

"Hey, I just want to know where I can find Shawn O'Neil," she said innocently.

"I don't have anything to do with these deaths, or these freaks. Whatever you're poking your nose into, leave me out of it."

Dakota played a hunch. "You know Shawn O'Neil. You've known him for quite some time. He has a criminal history as long as your arm, and guess what? One particularly nasty police encounter occurred in—*get this*—Baltimore. Only nothing ever came of it." Her pulse drummed in her throat. She took a deep breath and pressed on. "I'm thinking maybe somebody with connections got the charges dropped. Now seeing as you're from Baltimore, we can do this the easy way, or we can do it the hard way. Easy means you talk to me. Hard means you'll see a TV reporter in your face."

"I hired O'Neil as a poll watcher on election day."

"There's a big difference between poll watching and voter intimidation. Do you really think when the media has a nutcracker around his filberts Shawn O'Neil won't turn into a big ol' crybaby? You'd be wise to talk to me while you've got the chance, Mr. Wilson."

"Have a seat in my office." Wilson waved off his thugs.

By the time Dakota left, Wilson had exacted a promise from her to leave him out of the investigation in exchange for providing her with a way to get in touch with his former employee.

"Once you find him, what you do with him is up to you. But don't ever come back here, understand?"

"Deal."

He wrote down an email address on a scrap of paper and handed it over. "You can reach him through this website. He'll answer you because he'll think it's from me."

Dakota examined the notation.

Sinister Sisters again.

"Thanks for the assistance." She rose to her feet and left him to wonder whether this would really be the last time she'd bother him.

Dakota lounged by the pool, taking advantage of a mild winter afternoon with nothing but a cashmere blanket from Scotland thrown over her legs. By the time Kris returned home around three, she'd re-stocked the pantry with comfort food, and made a fresh pitcher of margaritas.

"So, what happened at Sinister Sisters?" Dakota poured her a drink. A ripple of guilt went through her as Kris sucked the first one down, but it seemed like a fair trade considering Celia's girls were still dropping like raindrops.

"They weren't exactly forthcoming. They know Velvet Tears, but they only admit to having contact with him through email."

Dakota thought of the beating Liquid Fantasy took. "It goes way beyond that. But hey, I had a hard time getting anything out of them the first time I talked to them, too."

Kris nodded. "After that, I went to the tattoo parlor. Looks like they were on the up-and-up with you." Keen eyes brightened.

Dakota waved a scrap of paper. "David Wilson gave me an email for Shawn O'Neil. I think we should set him up. If you and I brainstorm, we can figure out a way to trick him into meeting us. He'll think he's supposed to hook up with the Mayor-Elect, only it'll be us." Her arms sliced the air in a guillotine motion. "Not much he can do once he's cornered. Then, we just have to hatch a plan to make him talk."

Fisting sleep from her eyes, Dakota opened the front door bright and early Wednesday morning. The last thing she expected was to see Hamilton Stark, popped-up on the porch like a demented jack-in-the-box, surly with suspicion, and loaded for bear.

Without invitation, he pushed his way inside, ranting as he shrugged out of his overcoat.

"Everything about Travis Creeley leads right back to you, Puss—Jones."

"That's because he's stalking me."

"He's been asking every hooker in Phoenix about you, so do yourself a favor and come clean. Was he a client? Are you doing him now?"

"You can't speak to me that way in my own house."

"Like it or not, you've got a serious connection to this guy. And everything about him circles right back to you." Musket-ball eyes suggested he knew more than he'd let on.

Did Hamilton Stark suspect Travis Creeley might be her father?

She hadn't even allowed herself to believe it until now. She'd fled their home to escape the abuse. Was Creeley killing girls in retaliation, trying to force a confrontation? Was she next on his list?

"Are you cold?" Hamilton asked without concern. "Or are you shaking because I struck a nerve?"

"You need to leave." She moved to open the door, but he blocked her path.

"Where's Kris?"

"She doesn't want to see you, Benedict Arnold."

"I'd rather hear it directly from her."

"Like Helen Keller, you're not hearing anything." She motioned him out the entrance, slamming the door behind him.

Kris shuffled in, groggy, and squinty-eyed. "What kind of moron shows up at a person's house at six in the morning?"

"Hamilton. He accused me of being involved with Travis Creeley. He accused me of doing the guy. I asked him to leave."

Kris stiffened. "Did he ask about me?"

"I'm sure he's doing everything he can to get you reinstated, babe." *Not doing squat.*

Kris flopped onto the sofa. With her feet curled beneath her, she stared past the pool, to some distant point beyond the back fence. After a lengthy silence, her brown eyes jumped, settling on Dakota's face like a human lie detector. "Have you told me everything?"

"There's one thing I left out." All out of fight, Dakota joined her on the couch. "I'm pretty sure Travis Creeley is my father."

"Don't mess with me, Dee. That's not funny."

"No, really."

"You told me your father was a therapist. You lied?"

"I didn't lie. That was a long time ago. Back when he worked in a Denver hospital. Back when people thought my family was . . . respectable."

"What happened?" Kris said on a long, drawn-out breath.

"What the hell didn't happen? He kept a journal of all the stuff he did to me when my mother was out of the house. She found it after I ran away. I'm sure he blames me for her death."

They talked into the morning, through pots of Kahlua-laced coffee, about the miserable childhood that finally ended once Dakota landed on the streets of Phoenix to fend for herself.

A destructive sense of tension that had become almost palpable filled their shared space. It ended with the ring of the telephone.

Dakota grudgingly answered. "Runaway Investigations."

Brie Munroe's words tumbled out so fast it took a few beats to catch up.

"Hannah's moving into my house. I have more deadbolts. Besides, there's safety in numbers, right? And we're not budging until this is over. So if you want to talk to either of us, we'll be here, barricaded in my house. I have Caller ID, but if you call from a different number, we're not answering unless we know it's you."

"Sounds good."

"We need a code, so we'll know if you call. Hannah says to let the phone ring twice and hang up. Then call right back. Got that?"

"Got it. Two rings and call right back."

"In a few minutes, we're going out to stock up on groceries. Who knows how long this'll last? I feel like we're under siege, and I, for one, don't plan on ending up like the Donner party."

"Good plan."

"You wanna know something else, Dee? Hannah walked out of the room, so I'll be quick about it," Brie whispered into the mouthpiece. "The bitch gets on my nerves. I never realized what a slob she is. This morning, she squeezed the toothpaste tube in the middle. I mean, who does that? And she didn't rinse the soap scum out of the sink after she washed her face."

Dakota's eyes strayed to Kris. "You can put up with it for the time being."

"The bathroom sinks are black, Dakota. That means every speck of dust shows."

"Be nice. Remember, she's your houseguest."

"*Ha.* Hannah's no guest. She's a second set of eyes. And she's coming back now." Brief pause. "Hannah, you're dripping coffee on the carpet." Said frantically. "Dee, I've gotta go."

Dakota hung up the telephone and rejoined Kris on the sofa.

Weary and a bit tipsy, Kris sighed. She slid out a hand and intertwined fingers with Dakota.

"I'm sorry for what happened to you when you were little, Dee . . . before you took to the streets. It's a wonder you didn't turn out like Sybil." Kris's eyes darkened. "Hell, I'm sorry for all the bad shit that happened to me, too. But I don't want us to be together because we're emotional cripples who can't be with anyone normal."

"The main reason I'm still with you is because of that thing you do," Dakota said, suddenly playful. "That finger thing." She pulled Kris's hand close, and ran it up her thigh.

"Not now, Dee. This is a meaningful conversation. We're having an emotional breakthrough."

She released Kris's hand. "So how come you're with me? I find your choice in music annoying—"

"You sound just like Hamilton."

"—I hate your job . . . wait, God forbid I have anything in common with Hamilton, so don't compare me to him . . . I can't stand the midnight disruptions where you get up and leave me to go investigate the next dead body . . . tell the truth, it's the money, isn't it?"

"I make a good living." Kris caught her mistake. "Correction. Made a good living."

"Why'd you choose me?"

"I honestly don't know. What I do know is that you make me want to be a better person. I like who I am when I'm with you. I like me. I like you. I like us."

"You do realize if it turns out Travis Creeley's my father, we'll have to move."

"I'd live under a bridge abutment with nothing but a bedroll to be with you, if I had to. Only that won't be necessary. We'll get the Court to issue a Protective Order."

"You know better than anyone those things don't work. Since when is paper strong enough to keep a crazy person from harming you? Paper won't deflect a tire iron. Or a bullet."

"We'll stockpile an arsenal of weapons. If we so much as hear him skulking around in the bushes, I'll cap him and you can help me drag him inside," Kris said through a grin. "We'll stick his hand in your jewelry box and call it a home invasion. Justifiable homicide."

"Don't say that, not even as a joke."

Kris downed the last of the Kahlua-laced coffee. Eyes glimmered with conviction. "Don't worry, Dee. I won't let anybody get you." They spoke of Velvet Tears, and Kris advanced a theory. "Maybe Travis Creeley and Shawn O'Neil are tied in with each other."

"Seems farfetched. What's the obvious connection?"

Kris lifted her shoulder in a non-committal shrug. "Nothing, I suppose, other than coincidence." Her face brightened. "Unless we connect-the-dots to David Wilson."

"Aren't you putting the cart before the horse? We don't even know whether they're acquainted with each other."

"Let's find out." She rose and pulled Dakota along with her. The investigator part of Kris's personality came out, and she led her not to the bedroom but to the study. Kris headed for the computer and slid into the chair. "Wherever you see a rat, there are a hundred you don't see. Believe me, the trap we set for Velvet Tears will flush out other rats." With her face bathed in the glow of the screen, she held out her hand, palm-up, for the email address, and let her fingertips fly over the keyboard. For the first time in days, Kris's eyes danced. "We'll make the message from David Wilson. Let's disguise it as an invitation. We'll tell O'Neil that Wilson has more work for him; that our man should meet at the vacant shoe warehouse behind the tattoo parlor late tonight, or early in the morning."

"It's awful dark back there. Nobody would see or hear anything if Velvet Tears stuck a shiv between our ribs. I don't want to die in some desolate alley with feral cats eating my face."

"Believe me, dying's the last thing I want to do," Kris deadpanned. "This'll accomplish two things: if Travis Creeley's with O'Neil, and Creeley committed the murders, it'll break the pattern of three. You said yourself, the murders are being committed to the cadence of a waltz. Did your father like waltzes?"

Did he ever.

Chills snaked up Dakota's legs.

"If O'Neil comes alone," Kris talked on, "we'll lean on him until he coughs up Laura Ann's whereabouts."

"And, by *'lean on him,'* you mean resorting to brute force?"

"Honestly, Dee, you're so naïve. It's the only thing a dirt-bag criminal truly understands."

"If we wind up in a gun battle, you won't get reinstated. You'll lose your job, for real."

Kris snorted. "Do you really think I'll have a job to go back to when this is all over?"

Chapter Twenty-Seven

A sick feeling started in the pit of Dakota's stomach long before the designated meeting time with Velvet Tears.

For one thing, the street lights behind the tattoo parlor were out, and the alley next to the warehouse was pitch black when they stepped out into the soupy night air.

"I don't like it," Dakota whispered. "I want to go."

"Try to look at it this way," Kris whispered. "If you can't see them, they can't see you."

"Who's *them*?"

"Whoever's out there."

"Think we have to worry about more than one?

"I wasn't thinking that. Not until you brought it up. Thanks a bunch."

"So you *do* think there's more than one?"

"No. Quit worrying, Dee. Instead of obsessing over Shawn O'Neil, why don't you come up with a peace plan for the Gaza strip?"

"You don't have to get huffy about it." Wishing she'd snagged a warmer jacket from the closet, Dakota stomped her feet to warm them, and got a cutting glance for the effort. "What if he's wearing night goggles?"

"O'Neil's a punk. He won't be wearing night goggles."

"Remember '*The Silence of the Lambs*'? The villain had night vision goggles."

"It was a movie, Dee. O'Neil thinks he's meeting Wilson. Now put a lid on it."

"I hear you breathing," Dakota said softly.

"Let that be a comfort to you. Imagine how you'd feel if I wasn't."

"Don't even say that."

"And *you* don't say *anything*. I mean it. Stop talking. I need to be able to hear a rat fart."

"You're good at hearing stuff. You're like a dog. You hear things other people can't."

"Smell. Dogs can smell things people can't."

"Can you smell him? Can you smell Velvet Tears?"

"Stop talking, Dee. I mean it."

"Would've been better if you'd let me keep on thinking you could hear him. I don't remember what he smells like."

"*Shut up.*" Said through clenched teeth.

Deadly calm settled over the industrial part of the town. Between the unexpected dip in mercury and the rash of killings, the hookers had stayed inside tonight, leaving only strays of the four-legged kind, and an occasional homeless person to wander the streets.

In time, their eyes adjusted to the dark. During brief moments when the cloud cover tore away to expose snippets of moonlight, they got their bearings. A man's silhouette turned out to be nothing more than a lamp post. A shadowy specter turned out to be a dog on the prowl. And a frightful noise that began as an eerie scream, turned out to be a couple of tomcats teaching each other who was boss.

Huddled behind a dumpster, with shared bodily warmth on her mind, Dakota lifted the binoculars. She dialed the lenses until the intersection came into sharp focus.

"What if he doesn't show?"

Kris shivered. "Too early to tell."

Eye-stinging winds whipped at Dakota's clothes. She let the field glasses hang by their strap, and retreated behind the waste receptacle. "I'm turning into a Popsicle. Can't we go home now?"

"Thought you descended from hearty, pioneer stock."

"Not me. My people were lily-livered. They had pasty white skin, stayed out of the sun, and died of consumption and measles. I come from a long line of pansies."

Lulled by the whistle of wind shear coming off nearby buildings, she let Kris's miserable Indian-warming-dance momentarily distract her. Her eyes searched the sidewalk behind them. Dakota had the skin-crawling feeling they weren't alone. She jumped at a noise. For no reason other than instinct, she shifted her attention to the alley.

The snick of a switchblade changed everything.

Her heart went dead in her chest.

The ghost ring of a flashlight distorted the silhouette of the person who carried it. When she saw Velvet Tears, her stomach lurched. The Goth didn't come alone. In less time than it took to bat an eye, Dakota realized they were outmatched. Three of Wilson's thugs followed like geese in an inverted "V."

Dakota grabbed Kris's wrist. "Dial nine-one-one. Hurry."

"Already tried. No service. Apparently there's no WiFi at 'www-dot-Gates-of-Hell-dot-com.' "

"Come out from behind there," bellowed the biker. "You're outnumbered. Come out on your own, and you won't get hurt."

"Any ideas?" Kris said under her breath. "Now's the time."

"You think they'll hurt us if we come out?" Dakota carefully modulated her voice to conceal the terror building inside.

"I think we're done for, either way. If we come out, they'll just hurt us quicker. Think you can scale a twelve-foot, chain length fence?" Kris thumbed at the obstacle behind them.

"I said come out," O'Neil yelled. "You wanted to talk, so let's talk."

"Maybe he means it," Dakota said hopefully.

Kris grabbed her arm. "On the count of three. I'll head straight for them. You veer off to one side and make a break for it."

"Why move toward them?"

"You have a better chance to get away. Your legs are longer. When you're in the clear, call nine-one-one. Then drive the Jag around, pile me in the back seat and head for the hospital."

"Last chance," hollered O'Neil.

"I'm sorry I got you into this," Dakota whispered, knowing this desperate apology might be her last. "I love you."

"Me, too. I love me, too."

They stepped out from behind the dumpster, and got the shock of their lives.

David Wilson arrived, suited and certain. He gave them a knife-like look meant to cut them dead.

"We've been double-crossed," Dakota hissed through her teeth.

"You think?" Kris.

"You brought a cop with you, Ms. Jones? You were supposed to come alone." He tutted at her mistake, *tut-tut-tut*. His expression turned dark and forbidding. "Haven't you heard? Snitches get stitches and end up in ditches."

"What are you doing here?" Cold air exaggerated the warble in Dakota's voice.

"Your investigation's over. Do you understand?"

"You can't tell me what to do."

Wilson let out a diabolical laugh.

Kris drove a finger into her ribs. "Shut up, Dee. Let's just see what they want."

"Obviously, you're the type who has to learn by experience." Wilson did a quick hand-move the envy of dog handlers, and his thugs slowly advanced. "Like I said, your investigation's over. Should you choose to continue, the next lesson will be even more severe. O'Neil, let's go. We've got work to do."

Oh, great. There's room for a "next lesson." Guess they're not planning to kill us.

Velvet Tears grinned big. In the dark, his vampire teeth phosphoresced in an eerie shade of chartreuse. He shot them the finger, and calmly walked off with Wilson, leaving them to deal with three hoodlums. The men fanned out, effectively cutting off their escape.

"Fence. Run," Kris said, and peeled off like the lost man in the Blue Angels formation.

With the vivid image of junkyard dogs, shredding them to bits, hanging in Dakota's head, she stayed hot on Kris's heels. The cyclone fence closed in, twenty feet away. Kris reached it first. Her foot clattered against metal mesh, rattling beneath her weight as she jammed in the toe of her shoe to scale it.

Stampeding feet thundered in their ears.

Dakota lunged. She got a good grip and hoisted herself off the ground, well on her way to freedom. Then a meaty hand came down like an anvil and plucked her off. She fell backward, to the sight of a dark, swooping blur, and saw Kris peeled off the top with the ease of a Velcro strip. The sound of ripping fabric hung in her ears.

A blow to the chin sent Dakota reeling. Her mouth filled with the taste of liquid metal. Her head spun like a teacup ride. In a moment of disorientation, she crumpled to the asphalt and took a kick in the gut. The impact knocked the air from her lungs. Curled into a fetal position, she felt the excruciating pain of a steel-toed boot planted in her ribs.

Her surroundings blurred. Vulgar insults debasing the entire female gender faded to a thin, high pitch. Then everything went black.

She woke up to the sound of her name being called. With her head lying on her out-stretched arm, seeing Kris from the chest up from this lopsided angle, Dakota realized they'd cheated death. After several dedicated eye blinks, the smear of an adjacent building came into focus. Bricks.

"Thank God, you're alive, Dee. I thought we were goners."

"Did you get to shoot any of them?" she said weakly, hopefully.

"I managed to pull my piece. One of them wrestled it away, and pistol-whipped me like a play toy. That's all I remember." Kris made a slow head turn. "Maybe they were nice enough to leave it behind. We should at least have a look around before we go." She helped Dakota to an upright position. "Think you can walk?" Then she rocked onto all fours, stood, and gently pulled Dakota to her feet. "I learned a valuable lesson here. *Shoot first, ask questions later.*"

"I hurt all over. Where are those stupid mall kids with their stupid phone cameras when you need them?" Dakota stood on shaky legs and tested her ability to walk. She moved with the speed of a slug on a cold December morning. Then she inspected her bloody hands in the ambient light. "I learned action movies don't exaggerate the pain of having your nails ripped from your fingers, or getting your ribs kicked in. And I'm pretty sure the only way I'm going to be able to brush my teeth is by laying the toothbrush on the counter and moving my mouth back and forth over it."

"You still have teeth? Well, hey, that's great. Let's get outta here."

They stumbled toward the car, clearing the alley like a couple of drunks.

"You've got a knot on your head the size of a grapefruit," Dakota said.

"Not surprised. It's throbbing like a hard dick."

They limped the rest of the way in silence. At the Jaguar, Kris made an announcement. "Next time, we'll get the jump on them instead of the other way around. I got a good look at their faces."

"So you can describe them to the PD's sketch artist?" Dakota said expectantly.

"No. If I ever see them again, I've decided to kill them. Wilson, too. He's the son-of-a-bitch behind all this."

"The way you get back at people like Wilson is to publicly disgrace them. Let it drop."

"They whipped us like rented mules. Why should we let it drop?"

Dakota sighed. "Think of it this way . . .taking a beating's a lot like having a baby. You don't want another go 'round until you've forgotten how bad it was."

Chapter Twenty-Eight

Dakota awakened Thursday morning, vaguely aware of Kris's muffled voice. She gingerly rolled onto her back, feeling every ache and raw nerve in her body. Idly counting the seconds until Kris got off the phone with Hamilton Stark, she stared at the ceiling and wondered what defective genetic component had compelled her do such a stupid thing.

"Yes, we'll meet you in a half hour. G'bye." Kris thumbed the off-button. Her eyes slewed to the other side of the bed. "That was Hamilton."

Dakota cocked an eyebrow, the only part of her body she couldn't feel. "It's always Hamilton."

"It's not always Hamilton."

"Yes, it is. Doesn't he have other friends? You're not even his partner anymore. What's wrong with that guy?"

"Actually, he's doing us a favor."

"I'll bet." Dakota avoided Kris's stare. "He probably bought us a bottle of expensive champagne so we can toast to a brighter future before we're shot by a firing squad."

"Hamilton wants us to meet him at the ME's Office." She got up and disappeared from the room. When she returned, she'd dressed and put on sunglasses to hide a swollen eye. "Do these glasses make me look smart?"

"No, and they don't hide how stupid you look in that shirt."

"I'm not wearing good clothes down to the morgue. You can't get the smell out. There's no other way to say this, Dee. Your friend, the Charlie's angel—what's her name—the blonde?"

Dee's breath caught in her throat. "Brie."

"Right. Brie Munroe. She's dead."

Hamilton Stark was standing in front of the ME's Office when Kris angled the BMW into a parking space. It took extra seconds to unfold like Origami giraffes and extricate themselves from the car, moves that gave Hamilton the unique opportunity to say, "Excuse me, are you here to collect donations for Easter Seals?"

Kris took a couple of cautionary steps using the handrail to steady herself.

Hamilton's taut face softened. "Kris? Are you hurt?" He hurried to her side and took her gently by the elbow. "What can I do to help?"

"What about me?" It galled Dakota to watch him assist Kris to the front door; him, with an arm around her waist; her, leaning her head against his shoulder. "Hey, I'm hurt, too."

"You're doing great," Hamilton called out, with over-the-shoulder, pep-rally enthusiasm. "Work through the pain. You can do it."

They disappeared through the door, turning into a haze of colors behind the glass.

Moping the rest of the way up the steps, Dakota joined them inside the foyer. They were nose to nose, talking in the low tones of an undertaker.

Hamilton gave her a head-to-toe glance. "You sweat like you're running from the police." When she gave him an uninvitingly blank stare, he added, "Oh, wait. You are. Let's have it. You're not telling me everything."

Kris opened her shoulder bag. She pulled out a manila folder with the music lyrics from the earlier crime scenes, and handed them over to Hamilton.

Dakota stood speechless. She'd done all the work, only to have it gifted to Benedict Arnold by the very person he'd betrayed.

He slipped a couple of photographs to Kris. "These are copies of Brie Munroe's tattoos. What do you make of them?"

Dakota moved closer. Peered over Kris's shoulder and whiffed the lingering scent of back-alley grime in her hair. She tried to make out the words while fighting off a steel-toed flashback.

This time, words told of an emptiness since she'd left him, and about trying to find a way to carry on. Of searching himself and everyone else to see where he'd gone wrong, but there wasn't anyone to blame.

Kris cracked the code. "This comes from Sarah McLachlan's song, *Adia*." She turned to Hamilton. "What's this guy trying to tell us?"

"Or woman." Hamilton slid Dakota a sideways glance.

"It's not a woman." Entranced, Kris continued to study the pictures.

"How can you rule that out?" Hamilton visibly stiffened.

"I don't know any women—even lesbians—who'd get a thrill out of gawking at the body of a dead woman. But a man would. He'd take the time to study the female form because it's so different from his own. More intriguing," Kris said, with the detachment of a clinician.

"You do it." Hamilton challenged. "You stare at bodies of dead women."

"Not because I want to. Examining crime scenes is my job," Kris said. "Or, used to be."

"Contemporary music isn't my bailiwick. What do *you* think the killer's trying to say?"

"Beats me." Kris again, still hiding behind sunglasses.

"Interesting word choice." Dakota massaged her aching arm.

Hamilton turned his full attention on her. His eyes went dark, and his stern jaw, tight. "You say you're innocent, but obviously this is all directed at you. So what does it mean?"

"I don't know. I'm a talk-radio kind of girl," she said without guile, but she was meditating on the idea that these might be messages from her father.

"At the moment, I have several 'persons of interest.' Travis Creeley's one of them."

"What about Shawn O'Neil? You haven't ruled him out, have you? Because he definitely has the killer instinct." Kris shot Dakota a knowing glance.

"He's still a 'possible,' though not as possible as Creeley." Hamilton took Kris's hand and fixed her with a fawning gaze. "Do you have a copy of your notes? I'd like to keep these."

"The notes are mine." Fist to hip, Dakota immediately felt the sting of the one good lick she'd managed to connect with her assailant. Her hand still smarted. "I'm the one who figured out the musical references. Well," she added with a quick cut of the eyes to Dr.

Stone's office, "me and the good doctor." A random idea entered Dakota's thoughts. "What's with all the cats? Was there a cat in the house with Brie?"

"Cat . . . cathouse. Slang for whores." He smirked. "Just a thought."

"I don't find that the least bit funny," Dakota said with a sniff. "You're avoiding the cat question. What gives? You said you'd keep us in the loop."

"Hannah Lee found the body. According to Hannah, she came inside Brie's house, turned on the light, and saw red. The cat got spooked when she started screaming. It ran out the open door, tracking bloody paw prints all through the crime scene."

"But they were staying together so nobody could hurt them," Dakota mumbled. "That's what Brie told me." The words spilled out before she could stop them. Hamilton's eyes thinned into slits. She knew they were thinking simultaneous thoughts—that she'd talked to Brie before she died.

Dakota inwardly winced. "They moved in together so they'd be safe. Where the hell was Hannah?"

"She admitted she went out to meet a client," Hamilton answered with sarcastic superiority. "The john no-showed her. How do you like that? I guess we can chalk it up to a character flaw with hookers. If there's a buck to be made, they'll be out pounding the pavement."

"Was Brie's hair cut?"

"I'll find that out when Dr. Stone finishes posting the body."

In the sanctuary of Kris's BMW, the faint lettering of the side mirror warned, *Objects in the mirror are closer than they appear*, serving as a bitter reminder while Dakota watched Hamilton Stark's receding presence.

"My father used to cut off locks of my hair," Dakota said flatly.

"What? Why?"

"He did it on each birthday. Stuck them in that journal I told you about. I asked him, once, why he had to go and do that. He said he didn't want his little angel's hair to get dark. And that cutting a piece off every year would help him tell a difference."

"Weird." Kris took a deep breath and gave a slow exhale. "But I've heard weirder stuff."

"And you're about to, again. When I turned twelve, he wanted pubic hair clippings."

"Sick. You didn't give them to him, did you?" Kris asked on a sidelong glance.

"He handed me the scissors. He said I could do it, or he'd do it. To tell you the truth, I thought he'd stab my genitals, or cut something off if he got close enough with those things. I told him I'd do it, and I did. Went into the bathroom . . . locked the door behind me . . . snip, snip . . . here you go." She played charades with her fingers molded into scissors, then snipped the air, to show how she tossed invisible hairs at him. Then, what started as a whimper, turned into a cry.

Kris kept driving. "I'm sorry, Dee. I'm so sorry. But we don't know for sure, this guy Creeley is your father. It could be just another kook, obsessing. The world's full of them."

"We need DNA," Dakota mumbled. She dried her eyes against the backs of her hands. "I'd like to take a pair of scissors and cut off his pubic hair. And while I'm down there, lop off his kid-diddler. We could take it to Dr. Stone and let him send it out for analysis."

"You have a violent side to you, Dee. I'd try to keep that under wraps, if I were you."

A light bulb idea went off in Dakota's head. She instantly brightened. "Hey, listen to this." She twisted in the seat with great care. "Travis Creeley called me. It should be on the phone records."

"No, it'll just be listed as *Incoming*."

"Not if you tell the phone company you need the records for an investigation."

"Right now, I'm operating on the assumption I'm on a temporary suspension." Kris favored her neck, moving her head in a slow revolution. "Hamilton's going to help me get reinstated." Kris floored the BMW and sailed through the amber light. "I don't want to screw things up."

Hamilton may've promised to get Kris reinstated, but he'd made no mention of his progress during their meeting. Now he had their notes. It was beginning to look as if he planned to solve the serial murders himself, without crediting his ex-partner for her stellar contributions.

"I don't use my cell phone much," Dee said with sudden excitement. She fished it out of her purse and popped the phone open like she'd just reeled in the catch-of-the-day. "I'll check my 'received calls' to see if Creeley's phone is still logged in." Seconds later, she showed Kris the highlighted number. "Should we call him?"

Kris answered by way of whipping the BMW onto the shoulder. She made a hard right into a thrift store parking lot, jammed the car into park, killed the engine, and twisted carefully in her seat.

"Call him."

Dakota pushed the talk button. "It's ringing. What should I say?"

Instead of hello, Creeley greeted her with a demonic chuckle. "Knew you'd get in touch sooner or later. What's on your mind?"

Dakota and Kris sat locked in each other's gazes, and barely breathing. "I'll take the case. Just stop hurting girls."

"Wouldn't have happened if you'd worked with me to begin with."

Dakota closed her eyes, sick at her stomach, certain Creeley murdered her friends. Her eyes snapped open. Several seconds of dead air had elapsed. Creeley must've said something.

"What? I didn't hear you."

"I'll meet you tomorrow."

"Where?" Dakota held the phone aloft so Kris could hear.

"I'll call you later with the address. You're not gonna set me up with the cops. Just be ready to move tomorrow night at eight o'clock."

Kris sliced a finger across her own throat.

Dakota understood. She put the phone back to her ear. "I won't meet you at night. If you expect me to meet you, then pick a public place during the daytime."

He rasped out a sigh. "Call you tomorrow. Be ready at ten in the morning."

The line went dead.

"I want protection. I think he killed Celia and the girls. He said if I'd cooperated, it wouldn't have happened to begin with."

Kris pulled out her own cell phone and punched one of the numbers on speed-dial.

Hamilton.

Had to be. If scientists ever developed a brain chip to install in peoples' heads so they could communicate without speech, Kris and Hamilton Stark would be the first volunteers.

Kris ran down the situation with the detective. "So you'll set up surveillance so she doesn't get hurt? Great." When she signed off, she gave Dakota the low down. "Good news, bad news."

"Give me the good news."

"He doesn't think you have anything to do with the murders anymore."

"And the bad news?"

"He called you a crazy bitch. But he also called you a junkyard dog. He said he wasn't sure a junkyard dog like you needed any help. For Hamilton, that's huge."

"So I have to meet Creeley by myself?"

"No, Hamilton agreed to wire you, and to furnish a couple of back-up officers."

"That sounds like good news."

"He's still calling you names."

After Kris drank herself to sleep, Dakota slipped the satellite radio out of the closet and headed for the study. She closed the door, picked up the telephone and dialed the toll free number.

Despite navigating the electronic phone menu, she still ended up talking to three different people before being connected to Activation.

"I need to have a satellite radio activated."

"Please to recite serial number," said the foreigner, a man who may've been of East Indian extraction.

Dakota read the serial number off the box.

"Already, the radio has been connected many days."

"No, no, no. You don't understand. They were supposed to connect it, but they didn't."

"Please to turn it on."

Dakota followed instructions. "Okay, it's on. Now what?"

"Enjoy music. Have most happy musical holiday. We are here to help you. Good day."

"Don't hang up. The radio isn't turned on."

"Please to turn it on."

"No, I mean it's on, but it's not working."

"I do not understand. You have already the connection many days."

"I know it's supposed to work. But it doesn't."

"No music when such radio on?"

"No. No music. It just reverts to the preview channel."

"Me pervert? You are bastard."

The connection went dead in her ear.

Chapter Twenty-Nine

When Dakota retrieved Friday morning's paper, a hand-written note fell out.

It read:

Meet me by miniature golf course at Castles + Coasters at 10 a.m.
No cops or you'll wish you + that dyke you live with were stillborn.

Dakota's hands trembled. Creeley's psychotic scrawl bore out his demented personality. Three times, her eyes drifted over his handiwork. With a racing heart and throb in her throat, she dashed inside the house looking for Kris, and found her lathering her hair in the shower.

Words tumbled out in a hyperventilating rush. "Creeley picked the kiddie park. When's Hamilton getting here? I'm not going in without a wire. What if Creeley has a knife? He could gut me in two seconds flat." She took a deep breath, then wilted to the bathroom floor with her back to the spa tub. "What am I doing? He wants me dead. I'm next."

"Calm down." Kris snatched a towel off the bar and whisked away beads of water. "You don't have to do this if you don't want to. What happened to those women isn't your fault. And you're not law enforcement, so it's not like you have a duty to do anything."

"He's my father. He's killing my friends." She broke from the thousand-yard stare, and turned her head toward her naked lover. What should've evoked a twitch in the groin brought a gruesome image to mind . . . Kris, prone dead on the floor. Dakota fisted her eyes until yellow comets flashed behind closed lids. "Of course I have to fix this."

When she pulled her hands away, the crumpled note floated to the floor. Kris, already in a terry cloth robe, wrapped a fresh towel, turban-like, around her head.

"I'll go in your place. Creeley won't be expecting that."

"Oh," Dakota said faintly, "that's a good idea. Why don't you show up and really piss him off—" her voice spiraled up in an eerie crescendo "—then we'll both be dead."

"Stay calm. Let me get Hamilton on the line."

"Wait." Dakota's mind conjured up several random scenarios. "Maybe we can get Creeley to kill Hamilton. Or David Wilson."

"You're raving."

"Yes, but those are good ideas."

"Like it or not, Hamilton's my friend. Would you really want to see me unhappy over the death of a friend?"

"You'd get over it. We could set up a little shrine next to your side of the bed, with his picture and some candles, and whatever else he likes. We'll memorialize him, right down to the Bally loafers and the food he eats. What does he like?"

"He loves classical music."

"Music, it is," Dakota said excitedly. "We'll line the night stand with old sheet music to protect it from the candle wax. You can keep a bottle of wine by the bed to get you through it."

"Stop it, Dee." Kris stomped out of the bathroom, and headed for the telephone.

Within the hour, Hamilton Stark arrived with a couple of cop cronies, and wired Dakota up like a cheap stereo.

"You shouldn't have any misgivings about this. This equipment's state-of-the-art. This baby's so sensitive it can pick up people lip-syncing at five hundred yards." Hamilton's eyes danced as Kris helped Dakota slip into a second shirt.

"Where will y'all be while I'm walking around like a moving target?"

Hamilton thumbed at the two plainclothes officers. "Mark will be recording in the van. Joe will be helping pass out clubs and balls in the miniature golf hut, or wherever else you might end up. I'll hang back and keep you in view."

Kris piped up. "What about me?"

"You stay put," Hamilton said with unmistakable protectiveness.

"No point in both of you getting hurt."

"I'm going to get hurt?" Dakota's voice shot up into shriek.

"Of course not. Bad choice of words. Everything will be fine." Hamilton took her by the elbow and steered her, zombiefied, toward the door.

Dakota looked over her shoulder. "Remember what we talked about earlier? I'm going to cut a deal with that psycho son-of-a-bitch."

Kris grabbed her coat and keys. "Hamilton, wait. You can't drop her off at the amusement park. If Creeley sees the van, he'll know it's a set-up. I'll drive her."

Dakota seconded the notion.

Hamilton's jaw torqued. "Fine. But then you turn around and get back home. I'll call when we're done."

In the BMW, Kris came up with a contingency plan. She assured Dakota that she had no intention to abandon her. "When I drop you off at the gate, I'll circle around and park at the far end of the lot. You go on ahead, and I'll go straight to the miniature golf course. Wherever Hamilton is, I'll hang back a good fifty feet. You'll be covered, don't give it another thought."

"Miniature golf. That's pretty tame, right?" she asked with child-like expectance. Her smile slipped away. "Unless he shoves me into the windmill and clubs me to death."

"You'll be fine. Just don't go into the castle with him."

Dakota slumped against the seat back and stared through the windshield. "If anything happens to me—"

"It'll be all right, Dee. If he wasn't afraid to kill you in a public place, it would've already happened. If it's really bothering you, I'll go in your place."

Dakota's heart warmed. She reached across the seat and rested her hand on Kris's thigh. Nice to know, that in a cold, callous world, there was someone out there willing to take a bullet for her.

As soon as Dakota paid the admission and stepped inside the kiddie park, the sinking feeling in her gut gnawed at her like a parasite. Each step toward the golf course eroded her confidence. Her eyes darted around, scoping out nooks and crannies for signs of Travis Creeley. Hamilton had been so sure Creeley would fleece her of any weapons that he insisted she rendezvous with the chief suspect without her gun.

But Hamilton underestimated her will to live. When she faked one last trip to the bathroom to throw up her toenails before leaving the house, nobody bothered to frisk her. If they had, they would've found the .38 stashed in the waistband of her jeans. It was her life on the line, not his.

She lifted a hand to her brow and squinted against the sun. Spotting Officer Joe behind the counter of the golf hut shored up her confidence.

Okay, maybe Hamilton knew what he was doing. Maybe he wasn't such a bad guy. Possibly even likeable, on some level. He loved Kris, and wanted her safe. They had that in common.

She walked up to the miniature golf counter, scanning the horizon for Hamilton and Officer Mark.

"Playing nine holes or eighteen this morning, ma'am?" Joe asked. He abruptly cut his eyes to the left, then back to Dakota. She tracked his gaze and saw Hamilton bending over a water fountain, pretending to drink. She breathed a sigh of relief.

"I'm not sure. I'm waiting for a friend," she said.

Joe touched a finger to his ear. For a moment, he appeared distracted.

He had radio contact with the guy in the van. Was her mic not working? Other than a quick check back at the house, nobody thought to double-check before she entered the park.

The officer evidently knew panic when he saw it. He said, "Lovely day, isn't it? Great weather, we're surrounded by friendly people. *Everything's perfect.* So . . . tell you what I'll do. If you want to pay for nine holes, I'll throw in another nine on the house. Whaddaya say?"

His eyes flickered past Dakota's shoulder. She sensed Creeley was close when Joe visibly stiffened.

"Come with me."

She recognized the gravelly voice without turning to look.

Creeley had appeared out of nowhere, clean shaven and wearing a sun hat, with thick make-up troweled-on to mask the burn scars. He sank his fingers into her upper arm and applied great force.

"Whaddaya say, ma'am? You and your fellow want nine holes or eighteen?"

Dakota's voice warbled. With every hair standing on end, she glanced over her shoulder and called out to the officer, "We decided to play a different game," and hoped he received the telepathic message she was sending him.

Creeley spoke in a low growl. "You trying to pick up that guy?"

"What's wrong with you? It was your idea to meet by the golf course."

The path forked ahead of them. She assumed they were headed in the direction of the roller coaster for a private, stomach-churning adventure; but at the last second, Creeley gave her arm a hard yank, and they merged with a group of Japanese sightseers.

"Where are we going? I thought you said miniature golf?" Dakota scanned the faces in the crowd but saw no sign of Hamilton.

Her heart thundered.

Her world came into sharp focus. The aroma of buttered popcorn filled the air. Pink and blue cotton candy, wrapped around paper cones, attracted children like honey bees with its sweet, sugary smell. The scent of magnolia blossoms from a grandmother's cologne wafted over on a breeze.

Dakota's surroundings momentarily blurred.

They came even with the arcade. Without warning, Creeley pushed her inside. Dakota's gut sank. It was filled with teens and game machines, and a deafening din that made her ears pulse to the beat of the background music. It'd be hard for the police to hear if she cried out. Beneath the arcade's low-lights, neon colors from nearby pinball machines flickered across the man's face, shading his jaw in slashes of primary colors.

"Why'd you pick those women?" she yelled.

"I'm looking for my little girl. You know where I can find her?" Creeley's eyes burned with a hate so strong it whipped her breath away.

"How could I? I don't know anything about her."

"She'd be about your age."

"That makes her an adult. Maybe she doesn't want to be found."

"She does. She wants her daddy. She misses her daddy. She loves her daddy."

Creeley's words made her skin crawl. "Why'd you hurt my friends?"

"I've missed my little Annie." He steered Dakota to a corner machine, pinning her between the machine and wall, effectively blocking her escape.

"You didn't have to kill them."

"Has little Annie missed me?" Creeley lunged at her. Ground himself against her as he shoved his hand beneath her shirt. Dakota's scream got lost in the rumble of bells and whistles.

"Get off me, you pervert." She struggled to push him away, and ended, face-up, on the floor. If he located the wire, it'd be all over.

A couple of boys at the next machine reacted with horrified looks, but instead of trying to help her, they abandoned their scores, mid-play, and backed away.

"You killed my friends."

Creeley groped her breasts. "Yeah, I might've roughed her up a little," he panted. "Bitch wouldn't tell me anything. You should be proud to have such a stand-up friend."

Creeley straddled her. Sweat dotted his forehead, dripping onto her neck as he ripped open her shirt. She tried to cover herself, but Creeley easily pulled her hands away. Had he seen the wire? Every move he made to disrobe her, forced the oxygen from her lungs. She tried to scream, but the noise that came out sounded more like the noise of a lobster hitting boiling water.

"She probably doesn't think much of you, now that she got her face rearranged," he said, breathless and enraged, and pulsating with testosterone, "What happened is as much your fault as mine."

Frothy slobber whitened the corners of Creeley's mouth.

As quickly as he'd pounced, he peeled away from her like a bad horror flick in reverse.

Hamilton had one of Creeley's arms; Kris had the other. Like a well-choreographed fake-out with the showmanship of professional wrestlers, they slammed him, head-first, into a pinball machine. Creeley went limp. He slid to the floor with all the bravado of a wet noodle.

While Hamilton handcuffed him, Kris moved to Dakota's side.

"Told you I wouldn't let anything happen to you."

"You need to work on your timing."

"Hey, I'm here for you, aren't I?" Kris sheepishly ducked her chin. "I'll always be here for you, Dee."

"Then help me to my feet and kiss me like you mean it."

Kris glanced around nervously. "My colleagues . . ."

"You don't work at the PD anymore."

Without another word, Kris gave Dakota a hand up. Steady on her feet, she settled a tongue kiss on Dakota's lips that left no interpretation necessary.

Travis Creeley looked on in shock.

Officer Mark looked on, pleasantly surprised.

Officer Joe looked on, possibly titillated by the sudden display of girl-on-girl action.

But Hamilton Stark flinched in revulsion.

A mini-celebration took place at Grape Balls of Fire, a piano and wine bar near police headquarters. After Creeley was booked into the Maricopa County jail, Hamilton, Kris, Dakota, and the officers from the surveillance team met for back-slapping and merlot-guzzling. Hamilton was especially congratulatory. He even offered to pick up the tab, and when no one balked, he graciously paid for drinks and appetizers, and left the waiter a generous tip.

As the cops went home to their wives and girlfriends, Hamilton waited at the bar entrance until Kris and Dakota came out of the ladies room. As much as Hamilton irked her, it was hard for Dakota to stay angry when he helped get Creeley off the street.

He slung his arm around Kris's shoulders and hugged her to him. "Guess this is as good a time as any to tell you, *partner* . . ." He enunciated the word, then balled up a fist and chucked Kris's chin with a gentle right cross.

It took a few seconds for the comment to soak in.

Kris clutched the sleeve of his pinpoint oxford. "What are you saying? Am I back?"

"Back in the fold, kid. The Chief said to tell you to report to work Monday morning."

Dakota's enthusiasm stalled, leaving her to wonder why the Chief hadn't called Kris himself.

Hamilton must've read her thoughts. "Forster doesn't like eating crow. He sends his minions to do his dirty work." He turned his attention back to Kris. "Anyway, I'm glad things worked out. It just wasn't the same. I'd rather fly solo than break in a new partner. So . . . forgive me?" He held out his arms and Kris flung herself into them. Hugged him tight and blinked back tears.

"I just want things to be the way they used to be." Kris said.

He rocked his cheek against the top of her head as Dakota gave them a dedicated eye blink. Had he just sniffed her hair? She'd reached her level of tolerance for Hamilton Stark's schoolboy charm when he unexpectedly asked Kris to excuse herself.

"I'd like a word with her, if you don't mind." He thumbed at Dakota. "It'll be all right, Kris." But instead of leaving, Kris hesitated. Her eyes darted from one to the other. "Run along," he said. "I'm not good at public apologies."

Kris's brows shot up, incredulous.

They had to be thinking the same thing: *Hamilton Stark, delivering an apology?*

"I'll wait outside." She pushed open the massive doors, and stood a few yards beyond the entrance, watching them through panes of leaded glass.

Hamilton turned to Dakota. "You did good out there today."

"Coming from you I guess that's high praise." Unmoved by his brutally handsome features, she cracked a grin that would've sent most men into a tailspin.

"Never let it be said that Hamilton Stark doesn't apologize for his mistakes."

Dakota's jaw dropped open. She took a quick breath and held it.

"Bottom-line, I apologize for accusing you."

"Okay."

"Creeley's obviously a loon. That was a brave thing you did today. You've got brass balls and Freon nerves. I admire that." He gave her arm a fraternal squeeze. "Well, I have to return that equipment to the station. It belongs to the tactical team. So . . . we're cool?

"Sure."

The air around them thickened with a lingering discomfort; with him looking very GQ in casual preppie clothes and the faint application of a mysterious scent; and her, draped in a little black dress that accentuated all her curves.

"See you around." He brushed past her, leaving her to marinate in the lingering disbelief.

Well, hell. I reckon he's not the devil in a suit, after all.

"Why'd you have to be nice, all of a sudden?" she muttered aloud to Hamilton's departing shadow. "Now you're going want us all to be friends, aren't you?"

Chapter Thirty

Saturday morning's headlines raised the city's comfort level:
                    SERIAL KILLER ARRESTED
The front-page news went on to mention how private investigator Dakota Jones, philanthropist and owner of Runaway Investigations, teamed up with Detective Hamilton Stark to catch the man who'd been murdering women. While Dakota suspected Hamilton planted the vague reference to her past connection with Celia and her girls, she had no proof. And even if she did, what the paper printed wasn't libelous.

Kris was still nursing a hangover when Mayor Roman showed up at the house, decked out in a gold lamé sailor suit with corded epaulets on each shoulder. As the keynote speaker at a fundraiser for the new resort, she wanted to underscore the theme of the proposed man-made lake by getting dolled up in regatta attire. Her zest for the new tourist attraction even bled over into her greeting.

"Ahoy, skipper."

"Nice to see you, Admiral." Dakota stepped aside, enough to let Mayor Jane slip in.

"What a delightful home. I saw pictures of it in that issue of that decorator magazine, so I feel like I've been here before."

Dakota offered the Mayor coffee.

"I can't stay. You were on my way, so I thought I'd stop by to congratulate you and Kris for getting that man, Creeley, off the street." Jane's smile contorted into a grimace. "But what about David Wilson? Is Chief Forster covering up for him?"

"I don't know. Kris has been reinstated, but she's not officially back until Monday, so we're not in the pipeline."

The Mayor dismissed the room with a glance. Headed for the

front door with her heels clicking against the floor tiles. "Don't put this on the back burner, Dee. You know me—I help my friends. Finish what you started and get me something on Wilson before I'm history."

Dakota watched her leave, her pert walk creating a peppy sway all the way to the big black limo the city rented for dignitaries. She closed the door, effectively shutting out everyone but Kris.

The bleating telephone scattered her thoughts.

A female voice said, "I know where to find Velvet Tears."

"Who is this?" Dakota grabbed a pen and pad from the kitchen drawer.

"I'm the owner of Sinister Sisters. Remember the night you were at Club Crimson? The night Velvet Tears beat me up?" she said. "Look, I figure I owe you one for ratting you off that night, so consider this payback. I don't want to meet with you, and I don't want to be the go-between, setting up a meeting between you and that freakazoid, Shawn O'Neil. Meaning if I give you this information, no one better know I'm involved. Got that?"

"We can have that agreement."

"He's staying at a fleabag motel out on the highway. I think it's called the Peppermint Patty. Indians run it. That Goth psycho drives a dark, metallic green truck. It looks almost black. Only way you can tell it's green is if he parks it in the sun."

Dakota scrunched the phone between her jaw and shoulder as she flipped through the telephone directory. She found the address for Peppermint Patty's.

With hesitation, she asked, "Why are you doing this?"

"I think Synthetic Darkness might be in real trouble. I don't want to see her get seriously hurt, okay?"

Dakota tried to keep her on the line. "Do you have a license number for O'Neil's truck?"

"Sure." The woman dripped sarcasm. "Like I wrote it down just for you."

The line went dead in Dakota's hand.

Kris and Dakota had a devil of a time getting the motel clerk at Peppermint Patty's to give them a master key. Without a badge to flash and credentials to give her legitimacy, Kris couldn't very well claim to be one of Phoenix's finest, so Dakota tried another angle.

"I'm a private investigator." She flashed her credentials. "This woman hired me to find her husband."

Kris twisted her head in Dakota's direction, à la Exorcist.

"We think he's shacked up in room two-twelve with a hooker, and I'm supposed to take pictures of them together so the judge will give her the kids." The clerk gave her a slow blink. "Three kids. Little kids. There's little Randy, and little Jody, and little Tammy." She ad libbed a quick background history to cement the deal. "Her husband kicked them out of the house so they've been living on the streets. The truant officer gave her two days to get those children back in school, or go to jail. If we can show the judge pictures of that creep with another woman, he'll let her have the house back and little Tammy and Joey."

"Jody." Kris said, practically crossing her eyes trying to keep up with the lie.

"That's what I said. Little Jody and—what's your other kid's name?"

"Randy."

"Right. Little Randy and the rest of the kids can go back home. Live in their own rooms and have their mama cook them their first hot meal in two weeks." For effect, she mentally conjured up the recollection of a dead pet funeral from childhood, until her eyes misted. "What do you say? Are you with us? For little Tammy?"

"Don't forget Randy and Josie," said Kris.

Her wooden performance as a concerned mother had gotten annoying.

Dakota stuck her hand out. "Do we get the key, or not?"

The door to two-twelve swung away, revealing a swill pit of open pizza boxes with crusty remnants of uneaten pepperoni, fast food wrappers, and a case of empties. Tattoo equipment had been set up near the bathroom sink, and Laura Ann Spencer's Goth habit had been draped over a chair. Newspaper articles about the dead girls were strewn over the unmade bed.

Dakota swallowed hard. Gooseflesh crept across her forearms.

Travis Creeley. Did we get the right guy?

Kris dug through the rubble while the motel manager looked on.

"Look at this." She waved a paper with a phone number on it at Dakota. "It's obviously a cell phone. What do you think?"

"Call it."

Kris punched in the numbers and hit the talk button. Then she tapped-on the speaker button so they both could listen.

Mayor-Elect David Wilson answered.

They exchanged awkward looks. Kris handed the phone to the desk clerk. She coached him to say, "Hey, Wilson."

The Navajo grunted into the mouthpiece. Kris jerked the phone away, holding it aloft so Dakota could hear.

"O'Neil, is that you? Is everything set for tonight? I want this finished before Christmas, understand?"

Kris mouthed, "What do we do?"

Dakota did the universal, guillotine chop, hand-slice to the palm. Kris hung up.

The Navajo's eyes narrowed into slits. "What'd you say the names of those kids are?"

Chapter Thirty-One

In her adult lifetime, Dakota had compiled a mental list of things to be wary of: certified mail, cops on the doorstep, a team of SWAT sharpshooters near her bank, and middle-of-the-night phone calls.

So when Kris's telephone shrilled at three in the morning, Dakota's eyes snapped open like electric door locks. Kris must not have heard the annoying tone. This drinking thing had definitely gotten out of hand.

Dakota flopped over her enough to reach the bedside table. She answered Kris's cell before it went to voicemail.

Chief Forster identified himself. "Congratulations. You're back on the force. I'm sure Stark filled you in."

"You called in the dead of night to tell me that?"

"No. I'm calling to tell you to get your ass down here. We've got another dead prostitute. She goes by the name Hannah Lee – she's the one that dresses up like Holly Goodhead from the Bond movie."

Dakota sucked air.

"Same MO. So nice work, but Creeley's not our guy because he's in jail."

She grabbed Kris by the shoulder and gave her a violent shake. She got a hangover groan for her efforts.

"The good news is we've got a witness. Since she's refusing to talk to a male investigator, tag, you're it. So . . . you coming down or not?"

"I'm on the way."

"Good girl."

"What's her name?"

"Hannah Lee."

"Not the victim. The witness."

"Hold on." Paper rattled in the background. "Spencer. Laura Spencer."

"You have to let me talk to her," Dakota pleaded.

Kris looked like hell in a tow sack. Her short, bed-head hair-do complemented her short fuse, and the bags under her eyes had taken on all the characteristics of old luggage.

"Leave me alone. You're lucky I let you tag along." The detective touched her temples, mildly massaging them with her fingers. "I don't feel so hot."

Dakota wanted to say she didn't look so hot, either, considering she was starting to resemble one of those hard-drinking, hard-hitting, florid-faced hookers propping up the chain link fences around the rat-infested motels out on Northern Boulevard.

"You reek like a still."

"Gimme a breath mint. Or a stick of gum."

"A silo full of Altoids couldn't help you this morning. I say keep your distance. And don't let her light up a smoke. The fumes could blow up the building."

Kris scowled. "Your cellmate said to drink Everclear."

"You're taking advice from a drunk driver? You'd get better advice posing questions to a child's plastic eight-ball. Now hurry up and shower, while I put on a pot of hot coffee."

They encountered Laura Ann, seated in the interrogation room, looking like yesterday's dog food.

Black, spiky hair porcupined out from her head. Dark circles hung beneath the girl's huge blue eyes like partial eclipses.

Kris pointed to the newly reclaimed badge at her waistband and introduced herself. "You can call me Kris. This is Dakota Jones. She'll be sitting in on this interview, if that's okay with you."

Laura Ann Spencer ignored Kris's outstretched hand. She studied Dakota and recognition kicked in. The Goth wagged her finger. "You're the chick who chased me at Ren Fair."

Not wanting to intimidate the girl by towering over her, Dakota slid into a chair. "I wasn't trying to hurt you. I own Runaway Investigations. I was hired by your parents to find you. They've been out of their minds with worry."

"Jake and Lorraine?" Laura Ann snorted in disgust. "They don't care about me. They're only worried about the corporate image."

"They cared enough to send me to look for you. When we learned you'd taken up with Shawn O'Neil, your mother was beside herself with worry."

Laura Ann's tough exterior cracked. When she squeezed her eyes shut, tears leaked out the corners.

"Velvet Tears is a really bad dude. He held me prisoner. Raped me. Tortured me. He works for David Wilson. God knows what they're plotting while I'm in here shooting the shit with you."

Dakota assured her she'd be safe. That they'd take her back to Heaven's Urn. But first, they had to talk about the killings.

Kris took the chair opposite Laura Ann. Before she could pull out her pen and notepad, Dakota blurted out the question everyone wanted the answer to.

"Did you murder those girls?"

Laura Ann recoiled. "I didn't kill anyone. What would make you think I had anything to do with that? I loved Fiona. She was good to me. Then she broke my heart. Said I was too young and to come back in about ten years."

Kris steered the interview back on track. "What were you doing at Hannah Lee's place?"

"Fiona and I did the bar scene a couple of times a week with Hannah and Selina. When I escaped from that ratty hotel, I went to the only place I knew where people wouldn't judge me." She leaned forward and rested her elbows on the table. Then she sank her head in her palms. Her shoulders bounced with heavy sobs.

"I used the key under the back flower pot. When I let myself inside, this horrible hiss came out of nowhere. The door was still open and this big, scary-ass cat ran out. Hannah doesn't own a cat. Next thing I knew, I was on the floor."

Kris nodded understanding. "The killer. I understand you caught a glimpse of him. I need you to tell me all you can. What he looked like, if he said anything, if you recognized his voice. We can put you with a sketch artist if you think that'll help. Anything."

Laura Ann fidgeted in her seat. She drummed her black-lac-quered fingernails against the tabletop, then swiped her hands across her eyes, streaking her cheek with mascara. She settled against the chair back and stared, raccoon-eyed.

"It could've been Velvet Tears. I don't know for sure. He was a big guy. Taller than me. He knocked the stuffing out of me when he went by." She pointed to two purple circles on her knees. They stuck out from behind black fishnet tights like a couple of jellyfish. "I went down on all fours." She showed them the abrasions on the heels of her palms.

Hours of questioning didn't help Laura Ann provide a better description. When the wall clock lined up with five o'clock, Kris called it quits.

"Take her home to her parents, Dee. I'll finish up the paperwork and hitch a ride home."

Meaning with Hamilton.

Kris and Dakota walked out of the police station with Laura Ann Spencer sandwiched between them. When they reached the BMW, Kris gave Dakota her keys and glanced past her shoulder.

Brown eyes twinkled. "It's Hamilton. Gotta go." She trotted up to meet him.

Even though the detectives were out of earshot, it didn't take a directional mic and a video camera to understand what they were saying.

Chief Forster called me in early. See that girl over there? She saw the killer.

"They did what?" Dakota shrieked.

It occurred to her she was still holding a butcher knife, slicing avocados to garnish the tortilla soup simmering on the stove; and that a knife-wielding woman striking a pose as demented as this might appear mentally disturbed.

Kris shrugged off her jacket and tossed it over the dining chair.

"They let him go. His court-appointed attorney got a Writ of Habeas Corpus."

"Speak English."

"It's a command to bring him before the Court and justify why he's being held prisoner. There's no way to detain him any longer. It's clear he didn't kill Hannah, since the MO's the same as the other deaths."

"But he assaulted Abigail Addison."

"Who, by the way, is also dead. No complainant, no crime."

"What about me? He assaulted me."

"You didn't press charges for the amusement park melee. I hate to say *Told you so*, but I told you so."

"What about him stalking me?"

"Did you file on him? No, you did not. You can't expect the police to help you if you're not willing to meet them halfway."

Dakota laid the knife on the countertop. Walked straight to the refrigerator and unscrewed the cap off a wine cooler. Chugged half of it down to take the edge off, and said, "I think the PD needs to form a justice squad. Assign two or three linebacker-sized men to go out and bludgeon pukes like Travis Creeley into an oily blot on the asphalt. I'd pay taxes for that."

"Did you get Laura Ann home to her parents?"

Dakota nodded. "First time I ever saw any emotion out of Jake Spencer. Big crybaby. You ask me, there's something weird about that guy. Maybe that girl had good reason to run away. Want a bowl of tortilla soup? Made it from scratch."

"I can think of something I'd like better." Kris unbuttoned her shirt. "How'd you feel about having Naked-Lunchtime in the spa tub?"

Chapter Thirty-Two

Early Monday morning, Dakota was lying, face-up, in bed, staring at the ceiling. Beside her, Kris stirred. While anticipating the alarm to go off, a question kept lolling around in her head: *Who are the PD's suspects now?*

Can't be Creeley.

Or Laura Ann, if you believe her story that she saw the killer.

That narrows the field to Velvet Tears and David Wilson. Or any one of a million other people. Including Kris and me.

Hamilton's suggestion that the killer could be a woman no longer seemed that farfetched. Laura Ann specialized in henna tattoos. The dead women had henna tattoos. Henna tattoos filled with musical notes and song lyrics. The song lyrics on Celia's body had appeared on Laura Ann's ceiling . . . lyrics Kris knew by heart. And—

A shiver traveled the length of her arms.

—Kris had an ingrained hatred for working girls.

Dakota squirmed under the weight of her analysis. No wonder Hamilton pointed the finger at her. Had Kris discussed Dr. Stone's theory on the pattern of a waltz? Had she unwittingly told Hamilton how Dakota's father played piano? How he made her practice? How she knew the mechanics of musical notes?

She shook off a childhood image of her and her father playing a duet.

Then there was the Chief of Police, a man under Wilson's thumb, who didn't think twice about cutting Kris's ropes and kicking her off the force. And what about other members of the PD, men who muscled Celia into providing the escorts for sexual favors, in order to stay in business?

The list of potential suspects was endless.

So why hadn't any of them been offered polygraph examina-tions? After all, that's what cops did. Oh, sure, the polygraph couldn't be used against you in court, but it gave the cops a tool to determine whether they needed to continue their focus on a par-ticular person of interest. Or, they gave people lie detector tests to eliminate them as suspects. Then again, Hamilton Sparks wouldn't let a little thing like non-deceptive polygraph results stop him from bird-dogging his prime suspect if he'd gotten it in his head they'd killed somebody.

Kris twitched to life. With her back to Dakota, she whispered, "Dee. You awake?"

"What's wrong?"

"I've been thinking." She rolled over, face-to-face, and itching to brainstorm. "The Chief hates me, and David Wilson has too many ties to this murder investigation. There's something hinkey about this whole situation. There's no way Chief Forster will help me get a warrant to search Wilson's home and business. I'm thinking we should meet with Jane Roman."

Dakota seconded the idea. Within the hour, they were carrying their morning coffee to the Jaguar in go-cups.

Mayor Jane hardly rejoiced at the sight of them, especially since it was seven-thirty in the morning and she'd answered the door with that just-laid look. When Dakota noticed a shadowy figure receding deeper into the parlor, she was even more certain they'd torpedoed the politician's early morning tryst.

But the Mayor instantly warmed at the prospect of making trou-ble for Wilson.

"The thread connecting him to the murders is pretty thin," Kris admitted. "The only way the Chief would help me get that search warrant is if Wilson paraded in front of the courthouse with his hand on a Bible, wearing a sandwich sign with *Jail me, I'm the serial killer*, printed on it."

"I think you may have enough to take it to a judge I know. I'll put a bug in his ear. Let him know you'll be in shortly."

Dakota cracked a smile.

That was him—the judge—lurking in the living room. Had to be. The irony of the situation cemented a basic contention about advancing in the world of Phoenix politics: *It's not who you know, it's who you blow.*

Back at Heaven's Urn, Kris got out of the Jag and walked to the BMW with purpose in her step. "This is where we part company. I'll call you after we serve that search warrant."

Instead of hurt feelings for being cut out of the loop, Dakota decided to make another run at activating the satellite radio she bought Kris for Christmas.

She dialed the toll free number and settled in for another rough time. Eventually, she keyed the number for the Activation department, and waited for a live voice.

"Melly Clistmas."

"What is this? Singapore? I demand to speak to an American."

Click. Buzz.

She started over from scratch, vowing to call as many times as it took, in order to speak to someone whose native language was English.

"Merry Christmas from satellite radio."

"Oh, thank goodness. You don't know how happy I am to be able to talk to an American. Is this Activation?"

" 'Sup?"

Great. An American 'hood rat. "Is this Activation? I need to activate a new radio." When he gave an unintelligible answer, she said, "Are you eating something? Because I can't understand you."

"Don't getchoo neither, boo. So whatchoo want, de activation?"

"I don't want it deactivated. I want it activated."

"Thas what I said. You want de activation?"

This time, Dakota severed the connection.

When Kris hadn't returned by five o'clock that afternoon, Dakota turned on the TV and flipped through the news channels, hoping to see a breaking story on the Mayor-Elect. In this instance, no news was not good news.

By six o'clock, she called Kris's cell, hoping to get her estimated return time. Would she be home for dinner? Should Dakota eat without her? Did she want to meet at Tío Luís' for *chiles rellenos* instead?

She reached her voicemail and left a message.

It wasn't like Kris not to keep her posted.

By seven, Dakota decided to go downtown and grab a bite on

her own. Maybe swing by the PD and orbit the parking lot to see if Kris's car was still there. She retreated to the bathroom for a quick shower. The most important topic cycling through her brain revolved around what to eat for dinner. She stepped into the warm spray with lasagna on her mind.

Mama Elena's it is, she thought.

She took her time sudsing her hair, shaving her legs, and trying out the new body gel Kris brought home the previous week, before the cow patty hit the fan and she took off for Hamilton's.

Come to think of it, Kris never actually admitted to spending the entire night with Hamilton; regardless, it seemed like a dicey topic to bring up now, especially since their relationship was back on track.

She'd turned the bathroom into a sauna, creating a kind of zero-visibility fog that could've used its own light house. Feeling along the counter in front of the mirror, she located her cell phone and concentrated on punching out a text to Kris:

"Starving. Mama Elena's? I could use a—"

The door slowly opened. A gust of cool air rushed in, chilling her skin. Foundation issues already? In a new home?

"—steamy bowl of—"

The phone went off in her hand. A text message popped up on the screen.

It said, "Turn around."

Travis Creeley.

Dakota sucked air. Grabbed a spa towel and made a feeble attempt to shield herself.

He moved through vapors, overpowering her in two strides. Dakota writhed to break free as he took her to the floor. Snarls of profanity spewed from his mouth. He pinned her at the shoulders. When she continued to resist, he banged her head against the unforgiving travertine marble.

Her head smarted. She lay perfectly still and barely breathing. Travis Creeley was studying her breasts. His groin throbbed against her hips. Dread filled Dakota's every pore.

Déjà vu.

Childhood memories exploded in her head. A couple of bars of Beethoven played on the piano, and then *Annie, where are you? Come in here, princess, I've got a big surprise for you.*

"Get off me, you sick pervert." She tried to gash him with her fingernails. To roll out from under him and grab the nearest blunt object and cave his head in.

But the nearest blunt object was the Remington bronze. She'd never make it to the living room before he caught up to her. Or to the bedroom, to the .38 on top of the night stand.

Creeley gave a low growl. "You know who I am. I can't believe you'd let other people get involved in our relationship this way."

Dakota spit in his face. "We have no relationship."

"Your mother died because of you."

"That wasn't my fault."

"It wasn't mine, either. But you still got to take her place, didn't you, Annie?"

Unmitigated fury swelled her lungs. What started out as a healthy fear turned to outrage. If she got the chance, she'd kill him.

Creeley went for his zipper.

"Remember this?" He let out a diabolical chuckle and wriggled up her torso.

The crack of a hammer clicking back on a monster firearm, echoed off the tile.

"Get off her." Kris's voice brought tears of relief to her eyes. "I have four-and-a-half pounds of pressure on a five-pound trigger pull," she said with eerie calm. "I'd have no qualms killing you after what you put her through."

It was over.

Creeley froze. He should've remained motionless. Should've raised his hands in surrender and given up.

With his back to Kris, Travis Creeley climbed off of her. But as she rolled away and got to her feet, he grabbed her hand and jerked her back to him. Locked in a stranglehold, she had nowhere to go. Creeley used her as a shield as he backed toward the bathroom door, then violently knocked Dakota into Kris on his way out.

The two hit the floor. Shoes pounded against terrazzo tiles.

Kris scrambled to her feet. With her gun leveled, waist-high, she followed. Dakota pulled herself upright, then carefully walked across the slippery floor. The sickening snap of a tree limb echoed through the house.

The front door opened, but only one set of footfalls thundered off into the night.

Travis Creeley's.

Every time Dakota moved the ice pack within arm's-length of the big grapefruit puffing up on Kris's head, the detective screamed, "Ow, ow, ow," and drew back.

"C'mon, you big baby," Dakota said, only to have Kris flinch again. "I give up. Do it yourself."

"If you'd pressed charges on that dirtball, none of this would've happened," Kris snapped, taking the cup towel Dakota wrapped around a handful of ice cubes. When she came within inches of her head wound, she grimaced. "Ow. Unlike you, I do plan to file charges."

"That's right, blame me." Dakota's ears pricked to the sound of a car. "The police are here. I'll go throw on some clothes."

"Don't you want to know what happened at Wilson's today?" Kris called out in a pouty voice.

"Sure." Still wrapped in a bath robe, Dakota halted. "Did you get anything?"

The doorbell rang.

Kris eased off the sofa and headed for the door. "He wasn't home, but we found plenty of stuff, including a solid link to Velvet Tears and Sinister Sisters. Talk about cooking the books. The Chief's playing dumb about it all, but he's not happy, especially since his name showed up on a couple of interesting documents. Mayor Roman's ecstatic because the media will have a field day with this." She gripped the doorknob and shooed Dakota away with a flick of the wrist. "Somehow the press knew what was about to happen, and showed up while we were serving the warrant. I don't suppose you had anything to do with tipping them off, did you?"

The doorbell rang again.

"Not at all."

Kris's expression said, *Like hell you didn't.* She opened the door. Two officers stood beneath the glow of the porch lights. She invited them inside, as Dakota hurried to her bedroom closet.

Leaving her to wonder, *If I didn't make that call, who did?*

Chapter Thirty-Three

Tuesday morning, the Trib's headlines proclaimed:
ELECTION SCANDAL POINTS TO MAYOR-ELECT
. . . with a stock photo of David Wilson, and a caption that read:
Have you seen this man?

The front page had more dirt than a cotton patch. Allegations tying Wilson and Shawn O'Neil to criminal activity in Baltimore sizzled on the page.

Kris and Dakota were sharing a section of paper, reading over each other's shoulders when Hamilton Stark stopped by, starched, pressed, and unusually chipper. As the ladies sipped coffee, he chattered like a magpie and wagged his own copy of the Trib.

"Did you see it?" He looked directly at Dakota. "How 'bout a cup of coffee, princess? A little something to soothe the parched pipes of a hard-working man?" He dismissed her with grin, and a cool eye shift to Kris.

Dakota inwardly seethed.

Sure, they'd made peace. But they weren't friends. If the look on Kris's face hadn't said, *Play nice*, she would've told him to get his own damned coffee, preferably at a donut shop down the road. Instead, she headed to the kitchen and poured him a cup of double-chocolate fine grind.

Recalling Hamilton's grueling apology after such a fractious history between them, she was no longer convinced this was a "Hamilton" issue; it could've been a "Dakota" issue. While loitering by the coffee maker, she thought it only fitting to be the bigger person and do the same. Besides, burying the hatchet with Hamilton would make Kris happy. And since the way to a man's heart was through his stomach—unless you were talking about a knife—she pulled an individually wrapped biscotti out of her personal cookie stash, and offered it to him.

He considered her for a second, his spectacular eyes dazzling beneath a fringe of dark lashes, and said, "No, but thank you."

Lacking an appetite, she ate it herself.

Hamilton was still talking about the election scandal, rambling on about the Chief of Police doing everything short of shrouding himself in an asbestos suit to cover his ass, when Dakota handed off the mug.

"Around here, we fetch for ourselves. If you're going to become part of the landscape, you'll have to fit in." To keep from coming off bitter and surly, she flashed him a bright smile. "*Mi casa es su casa,*" she added, while enjoying a simultaneous thought, *Only, I'd just as soon you stayed away from my casa.*

Apparently, Hamilton had become inoculated to sound-bites of sarcasm during his years on the force. A stint in homicide could do that to a person. Even Kris fell for the pleasantries. Which seemed surprising since Kris could be a contender for the world record-holder for most jaded viewpoint.

It was probably the main reason she drank to excess.

Then Hamilton did something bizarre. "I want you to have my cell phone number, just in case."

Dakota and Kris exchanged looks of the *Did you hear what I just heard?* variety. Puzzled, Dakota got her cell phone out and entered his number in her contact list. She wasn't sure what'd gotten into him, but it was a friendly gesture. And she could always delete it.

Hamilton refolded his news copy and slapped it onto the coffee table. "The station's going nuts over this latest shakeup. Forster's admirers hope he'll come away unscathed by the taint. His detractors think he's about to get his comeuppance."

"And which category do you fall into?"

"Dee," Kris called out sharply. "There's no love-lost between Forster and the homicide unit."

Hamilton brushed off the exchange. "I just left Dr. Stone's office."

So that's what that smell is, thought Dakota.

He unfolded a piece of paper. Dakota moved behind his place on the couch next to Kris, and peeked over his shoulder. "I made a drawing of the tattoos on Hannah Lee. Not a very good drawing," he admitted, giving Dakota an over-the-shoulder glance. "On an artistic scale, it's more Picasso than Rembrandt."

"Or, Salvadore Dali," Dakota said, then flaunted a cheesy grin to show she didn't mean it. Except she did.

This was actually starting to seem rather fun, she thought, having Hamilton pretend to want to include her in their conversation; while she pretended to accept him as a visitor in her home. Kind of reminded her of all those improv acting classes she never got to take . . .

She and Hamilton would never create the kind of bond where she could trust him to come by and water the plants while she and Kris flew off on a Hawaiian vacation. One didn't expect much out of a guy whose only houseplant was a Chia pet.

For no good reason, she got an uncharitable visual of the dashing Hamilton Stark, a man who possessed the bright empty beauty of a Ken doll, kicked back on the cowhide sofa in his Fruit-of-the-Looms, with his bare feet on the coffee table, eating a bag of Doritos and bean dip . . . or dashing through the house wearing their underwear on top of his head . . . or sliding between their silk sheets, just to get a sensation of what it'd be like to sleep in their bed.

As quickly as it formed, the image vanished.

Once again, Dakota was back in on the conversation about Hannah's tattoo.

Kris snatched the drawing away from Hamilton and studied the handiwork. For a few seconds, she went quiet and sunk into her own thoughts. "That's Ten-thousand Maniacs. *Because the Night*. I love that song." She handed him back his artwork and sang a few bars off-key. He passed the picture to Dakota without making eye contact.

Dakota scanned the page. Same Celtic overtones. Similar curlicues and musical notes. Her eyes drifted over the words.

This message had something to do with acceptance. About taking him as he was, holding him close and trying to understand that desire is hunger; and something about fire and a banquet.

Dakota offered her take on the lyrics. "This guy's a serious whacko. It's almost like he's begging for forgiveness. Or acceptance."

"I don't see it that way," Kris said. "I'm not willing to read anything into this other than the fact that he's just plain crazy."

"He's sending a message," Dakota challenged. "Otherwise, why go to all the trouble?"

"You know, Dee," Kris, again, jaded and suspicious, "it's like the dreams you're all the time asking me to help you interpret. Sometimes, two girlfriends sitting around eating hot dogs is just that—*two girlfriends sitting around eating hot dogs.*"

She lifted her bare feet to the edge of the coffee table and crossed them at the ankles. Her eyes slewed to Hamilton. "Any ideas on where to dredge up David Wilson?"

He retrieved his copy of the newspaper and gave Kris a playful swat on the leg. "What about that girl? The witness. Maybe it wouldn't hurt to show her Wilson's picture. Ask her if this was the guy who ran roughshod over her the night Hannah Lee died."

"Outstanding idea." Kris took another look at Wilson's photo. "I doubt she reads the newspaper. Seeing this may jar her memory."

Dakota didn't think so, but diplomacy triumphed, and she kept her thoughts to herself.

Laura Ann Spencer didn't add anything to the equation. After checking out the picture of Wilson, she couldn't be sure. It was dark. Maybe it could've been him; then again, maybe not. Since they'd never formally met, she wouldn't swear on a Bible.

Jake Spencer flung open the door to his daughter's room. Kris and Dakota kept their seats on the bed, but Laura Ann rocketed to her feet with a look of shame flushing her face.

"Come on, lollypop. I promised you a big surprise."

It wasn't Spencer's words, as much as his tone, that Dakota picked up on. It was almost as if he was talking in code, using a greeting that contained a hidden meaning. Even Kris alerted, and she'd had no previous contact with Laura Ann's father.

Laura Ann dropped her gaze. She toed the rug . . . gnawed her bottom lip. Dejected, she murmured, "I have to go now. Sorry I couldn't help."

She moved to her dresser and took a brush to her hair.

Her father stepped aside to allow Kris room to pass. But Dakota didn't take getting evicted lightly. She joined Laura Ann at the mirror.

"You should let it grow out. Go back to your natural color. It's really pretty in those old pictures your parents showed me. *You're really pretty.*" She rested her hand on Laura Ann's shoulder.

Their eyes met in locked reflection. An unspoken moment cemented the bond.

She pressed her fingertips against the girl's skin and made a final appeal. "If you ever want to just talk . . ."

Jake Spencer spoke a little too loudly. "I'm sure that won't be necessary. She already told you all she could. Now, I'm sorry, but we really won't be needing your services anymore, Ms. Jones. If you won't take money, just leave Lorraine the name of your favorite charity on your way out, and we'll cut them a nice check for your trouble."

"I'll do that. So long, Laura Ann. Remember . . . I'm just up the street if you need me."

Dakota's thoughts slipped back to Travis Creeley, and how he'd stolen her childhood and terrorized her into obedience.

They had a lot in common, she and this pitiful Goth child.

Kindred spirits in the most bitter way.

Come in here princess, I've got a big surprise for you.

Late that night, Lorraine Spencer telephoned Dakota's house in hysterics.

"Laura Ann's gone missing again. Jake went in to check her room and she was gone. I don't understand it. Why would she leave? She's safe here."

"I'll get right on it." Dakota bridled her thoughts—*You wouldn't let a Doberman guard a spiral ham, would you?*

An argument broke out in the background. Obviously, the software CEO had entered the room, and caught his wife on the phone making arrangements.

"I told you I'd go look for her. We don't need that woman's help. Hang up."

Lorraine Spencer muffled the mouthpiece and grew a backbone. Her words came through loud and clear. "We're taking whatever help she's willing to offer, Jake, and that's that. And if you don't happen to like it, you can grab everything you can carry with two hands and move the fuck out."

Chapter Thirty-Four

Dakota and Kris put Tuesday to bed without finding a trace of Laura Ann. Early Wednesday morning, after Kris left for work, Dakota went back on the hunt for the missing teen.

Around noon, she swung by the PD and found a throng of media gathered on the steps of the station. Soon, Kris exited the front door with Hamilton in tow, noticed the Jaguar and gave a big wave, and the pair met her in the parking lot. Dakota jabbed her finger against the electronic windows, and the glass hummed down.

She lifted her sunglasses and pushed them back over her forehead. "What's going on? I haven't seen this much furor since the last jailbreak."

Hamilton grinned big. "Guess who just showed up with two attorneys and turned himself in?"

"David Wilson?" Dakota's jaw went slack. "Is this a joke?"

"Nope."

Apparently, all hell broke loose when the DA showed up to offer the Mayor-Elect immunity. According to the rumor mill, if Wilson would admit to election tampering, hiring Velvet Tears to intimidate voters, and implicate the Chief of Police in the scandal, the DA would go light on him.

No wonder Kris loved her job. Cops were always the first to know.

Hamilton flashed a pleasant smile. "Kris and I were about to celebrate. Care to join us? I'm buying lunch. We'd love to have you. Only we can't wile away the afternoon. We'll be heading out on a full stomach to find Velvet Tears."

Conversations with Hamilton, no matter how brief, were starting to feel like the first five minutes of a bad movie. You knew it was going to suck, but you already paid your money and felt a mis-guided compulsion to see it through.

Dakota begged off. "I'm working a case."

"The Spencer girl? Kris told me." He gave a slow headshake. The droopy-eyed basset hound expression he'd come to perfect seemed out of character with his precision fashion sense and steel-trap mind. "Bummer . . . as you kids say." He raised a fist and gently cuffed Kris's arm. "Off we go, partner. See you later, Dee."

Dee?

In the way of old friends?

Kris shot Dakota her best *He's trying* look, which seemed to be a hybrid of her *Can't we all just get along?* look and her *I wouldn't pick at that scab if I were you* look. The media erupted with a loud clamor. The front doors to the PD burst open and David Wilson came down the steps at a full trot, flanked by a couple of silk-suited lawyers. Behind them, the DA walked out sporting an ear-to-ear grin.

Never in a million years had Dakota expected anything heroic out of Hamilton Stark, despite Dr. Stone's favorable opinion of the man. And, yet a noble gesture unfolded before her eyes, right in the middle of the parking lot, with a dozen mics to pick up the sound-bites.

Clearly a man on a mission, Hamilton Stark strutted toward the Mayor-Elect. "Hey, Wilson, where were you between the night of December twenty-first and the morning of December twenty-second, when Brie Munroe was killed? You know Brie Munroe, right?"

Wilson came to a dead stop. His attorneys each curled their fingers into a sleeve and pulled.

Kris and Dakota exchanged mortified looks.

"Too chicken to answer?" Hamilton hectored. "Hiding behind your lawyers?"

Wilson's neck veins plumped to the size of garden hoses. "I never hid behind anybody, detective."

"It's not a rhetorical question. Where were you?"

Kris hurried to Dakota's side. Braced her hand against the open window of the driver's door and said, "Has he lost his mind?"

Hamilton worked himself into a snit. "Can't account for your whereabouts? You killed that girl, didn't you? *Or, had her killed.*"

Kris paled. "Hamilton's off his leash. I wish he hadn't said that. I already have enough horror shows going on in my head." Her eyes darted around uncomfortably. Her hands fidgeted at her sides. She looked skyward as if expecting a Cessna to fly by and skywrite how to deal with an out-of-control partner. "I just got reinstated. I wanted to keep a low profile, but no. Spotlight on Kris. Lord Almighty, why can't somebody else take turns watching him?"

"Pay attention." Dakota stared in disbelief, taking in the unfolding drama.

Hamilton fell into step with Wilson and his attorneys. "If you didn't kill Brie Munroe, then how come you won't tell us where you were that night?"

Wilson spotted Kris and Dakota. He grabbed a mic from a nearby reporter who'd strayed too close, and locked the two women in the trajectory of his smoldering glare. "I can account for my time. If you must know, I was out beating up two women. Tell them." He jutted his chin in their direction. Like hot lava changing its course, the herd of reporters turned toward the Jag. "I may be guilty of assault, but I'm no killer. Tell them."

"They're headed this way." Kris went breathless at the sight of rolling cameras and outstretched mics. She gave Dakota a quick lesson in protocol. "Whatever they ask, just say 'No comment.' "

Dakota slid her sunglasses back over her eyes, and covered her hair with a Hermes scarf. If she had to be on the six and ten, she might as well strike an elegant post.

Microphones tilted into their faces. Reporters alternated questions like a machine pitching baseballs.

"Is it true what he said?"

"Did he beat you up?"

"Did you know Brie Munroe? Do you believe he killed her?"

"Tell us your names."

"Can you alibi him?"

Dakota reached out and wiggled her fingers, *gimme, gimme.* Someone shoved a mic into her hand.

Kris swooned. "I'm going to get fired," she airily said, with her lids at half-mast. With nowhere to go, she leaned against the Jag.

"Dakota Jones, private investigator. And this is Kris Carson, one of the best detectives this town ever saw."

The redheaded reporter who'd loaned Dakota her mic, snatched one from the hand of a competitor. "Can you alibi David Wilson? Did he really assault you the night Brie Munroe was killed?"

Wilson yelled, "Tell them. Tell them the truth. That I had you beat up."

Dakota gave them her best doe-eyed look. She turned her good side to the cameras, and fluttered heavily-mascaraed lashes.

"I have no idea what he's talking about."

Dakota and Kris went their separate ways, with Dakota striking out to find Laura Ann, and the two homicide detectives heading off in search of Velvet Tears.

Dakota started at the tattoo parlor.

Ike claimed he hadn't seen her, so she aimed the leaping cat on the front of her hood toward Sinister Sisters. The proprietor denied seeing Laura Ann, too, but Dakota wasn't so certain. Lies seemed to come as easily for these people as the truth, and she'd been burned by them before.

Outside the front door of Sinister Sisters, Dakota paused in the shade of an ornamental palm tree long enough to fumble through her handbag and retrieve her car keys. As she plotted her next stop— the Peppermint Patty; maybe Laura Ann went back to the fleabag motel?—the strong smell of vile fumes penetrated her nostrils. She took a quick breath and held it.

A huge hand clapped over her mouth. The parking lot instantly tilted. Cars turned into a smear of colors. Her eyes stung.

Pepper spray?

Chloroform?

"You won't play with me anymore, Annie?"

Travis Creeley.

She did a panicky review of her options.

Kill or be killed.

She stomped his instep with the heel of her shoe. He shrieked and let go, as she came around with a right hook. Creeley tackled her, knocking her to the gravel. He banged her head, hard, against the asphalt.

"Do you know who I am?" he yelled in a rat-like screech.

"You're the devil." She gasped for breath. "How could I forget you? You look different, but you haven't changed a bit."

"You shouldn't have left me, Annie. Remember the good times?"

He had his fingers laced around her neck, squeezing, choking the living daylights out of her. One hand clawed him in a frantic attempt to break the chokehold. The other floundered for her handbag, groping, searching, hoping to find a way out before her surroundings turned brown.

She grazed the butt of the .38. Wrapped her palm around the grips, and slotted her finger through the trigger. Creeley raved on, oblivious to her desperation.

Fire exploded from the barrel of the Smith.

Travis Creeley's face froze in a ghastly expression. Shock gave way to betrayal. His eyes crossed, floating upward into his head. The maroon hole to the right of his brow looked like a third eye, locking its accusatory glare on her for ruining his life.

Without Creeley's hands choking off her air supply, Dakota's senses came into sharp focus. A distant scream pierced the air. Travis Creeley slumped to one side and keeled over.

Dakota rolled away.

On some level, she knew he was dead. But she propped herself up on both elbows with the gun still in hand, just in case. Confrontations with Creeley had progressed like a B-grade horror flick. Each time she'd thought she was safe, the proverbial hand shot up out of the grave and curled around her ankle, in another attempt to drag her, kicking and screaming, to the gates of Hell.

Footfalls stampeded toward her, then braked to a stop. Realization dawned. Cops arriving on-scene to a "shots fired" call might think a woman with a gun would use it to keep them at bay. She didn't need any nervous Nellies drawing down on her. With great care, she slowly placed the snub-nose on the ground.

Sirens screamed in the distance. The air felt thick and unbreathable.

I'm free.

I'm finally free.

The first officers at the scene cordoned off the area with crime scene tape. With that done, one went to the trunk of his patrol car for a disposable blanket to throw over Creeley, while the other performed a paraffin test on her hands for gunshot residue. By the time a third officer showed up to photograph the crime scene, as well as the red fingerprints Creeley gouged into Dakota's neck, perspiration ringed the armpits of her shirt sleeves.

She wasn't aware how much time had passed as she sat, wordlessly staring off into space, but by the time Hamilton and Kris curbed the unmarked cruiser in the Sinister Sisters parking lot, twenty minutes had gone by.

Kris bailed out, and barreled toward her. "Are you all right?"

"Yeah." Everything was fine except for the pesky little problem of breathing. "But he's not." She gestured to Creeley, still on the ground where she dropped him with a jacketed hollow-point.

"Sheesh. What happened?"

"Aren't you supposed to read me my Miranda rights?"

"You're right. Don't answer that. Hamilton's here to interview witnesses. They're sending another detective out to talk to you. Conflict of interest, you know."

The officer taking pictures asked Dakota to pull her hair up and remain still, while he took a close-up shot of the back of her neck.

"There's no conflict of interest, Kris. You're a detective; I'm a victim."

Kris's eyes cut to the uniform, snapping away with the camera. She took a deep breath and let it out slowly.

"No, Dee, you're not just a victim. You're the love of my life."

Hamilton returned to the police station after the ME arrived in the Black Mariah and picked up Creeley's lifeless body. After the homicide lieutenant took Dakota's sworn statement, and the sworn statements of countless other witnesses who supported her version of what happened, Kris drove her home, in the Jag.

Wrung out and exhausted, Dakota headed for the spa tub, stripping off layers of clothes and discarding them like bread crumbs. She went from a zombie state, to a talking doll with a pull chain around its neck. Only nobody had to pull the chain. It was as if the talk mechanism had stuck in the on-position, and would only stop when the battery ran down. For almost a half hour, Dakota went on a continuous rant.

"I keep replaying it in my mind," she said to the bathroom ceiling, "but I can't think of anything I could've done to make it turn out different. Maybe if I'd taken my keys out before I left Sinister Sisters instead of fishing them out on the front porch.

"I should've gone to the tattoo parlor last. Then I would've missed him completely." She glimpsed herself in the mirror, naked and bruised, with red welts where he'd sat on her thighs, and grape-sized purple ovals on her neck where he'd tried to turn her into a corpse. "I'm glad he's dead. I hated him."

Kris appeared in the doorway. "Don't say that. Don't say anything else until the grand jury no-bills you."

"I'm telling the truth. If you tell the truth, you don't get in trouble."

"Wrong. If you tell a lie, you get in trouble. If you tell the truth, you get in more trouble."

"He just sat there with this stupefied look on his face. Like he wanted to ask me what just happened. And when I realized what I'd done, I was glad."

"Stop talking."

"I even prayed, 'Die, you sick son-of-a-bitch.' He keeled over like I had magic powers."

"Stop talking, damn it, I don't want that on my radar screen." Kris appeared beside her in the mirror in a blue work shirt, looking a bit puckish, her mouth pinched. "We're not married. I could be called to testify. Until this is over, stow it."

Dakota stared in stunned silence.

"I think you should get cleaned up and go straight to bed."

"I'm not sure I can sleep." She looked at Kris through pleading eyes. "Are you staying with me?"

"I can't. That's what I came in here to tell you. Hamilton called a few minutes ago. He got a lead on Velvet Tears and we're going out to find him."

"What about me?"

"Once I'm gone, you can chatter like a parakeet. Get it out of your system. Only make sure you're not telling this stuff to real people. Sit by the pool and discuss it with the shark."

"You told that cop we were lovers," Dakota said flatly. "Aren't you scared you'll get in trouble?

"Guess we'll have to wait and see, won't we?"

On the Darwinian scale of gender issues, it seemed that while no one was looking, Kris had miraculously evolved.

Chapter Thirty-five

The first thing Dakota noticed when she awakened Thursday morning was that Kris's side of the bed hadn't been slept in. Had the detectives found Velvet Tears, she would've called. So where were they? Probably still out looking for him.

Must've been some lead Hamilton got.

But hey, good news. At least she'd have firepower.

Kris had left behind her back-up revolver, a nickel-plated Smith & Wesson similar to the stainless steel model the PD seized as evidence, until the Grand Jury cleared her of wrongdoing in Creeley's death.

Even with the prosecutor's "Don't leave town" warning hanging over her head, she and Kris could still have a decent Christmas, still two days away. The un-activated satellite radio hidden in the closet nagged her. She made another attempt to get it set up, and after going through the usual menu gyrations, she reached a foreigner in Activation.

"Do not say anything to me until I finish telling my story. I need a satellite radio activated. I know there's a preview channel. I punched the right buttons and waited. You people say this damned thing has been activated, but it has not. It reverts back to the preview channel when I make my selection. So I don't want to know what's wrong with it; I don't want to know how it works. I just want you to fix it. Do you understand me?" She rolled the radio over, prepared to supply the serial number.

"Howdy, ma'am."

"Did you just say *howdy*?"

"Aren't you American?"

"Yes. What are you?"

"Indian."

"Like American Indian, Eskimo, East Indian . . . what?"

"I am from New Delhi."

"Are you mocking me?"

He reverted back to his native dialect. "When I get foreign customer, I speak to them in the way of their people. You are American. I believe from Texas?"

"I'm in Arizona."

"Where is this Arizona?"

"Next to New Mexico."

"I am most sorry to tell you, we do not serve Mexico. Thank you for your call."

Two seconds later, she was listening to dead air.

Instead of repacking the radio, she dumped it back into its box and tossed the whole shebang into the closet without even bothering to throw a blanket over it.

Since she still needed to look for the Spencers' kid, Dakota put the Peppermint Patty motel at the top of her list. After a quick shower, and a change into blue jeans, a purple pullover shell, ankle boots and a Prada bag, she tried Kris's cell. No answer.

On the long drive out to the Peppermint Patty motel, she tried calling again. Nothing.

It wasn't as if the motel was a total rat's nest. In fact, there were a few cars in the parking lot, mostly vehicles bearing out-of-state plates, whose owners remained happily ignorant of the Patty's reputation; and only one eighteen-wheeler, idling in the far corner with its heat system purring above the cabin.

She contacted the desk clerk, a surly woman who didn't buy the *Looking for my trifling husband* routine. It took considerable time and effort to talk the hatchet-nosed crone out of a master key, but when the old battleax showed interest in Dakota's wristwatch, dangling the Rolex in front of her caused the key to room two-seventeen to drop into her hand.

"You don't stay long." The clerk attempted to fit the watch around her pudgy wrist. "And don't shoot him. This is a nice place."

Yeah, right. A nice place to visit, but I wouldn't want to . . . die here.

Dakota slotted the key into door lock to room two-seventeen.

Instead of hearing an audible click, or meeting with resistance from an inside deadbolt, the door swung open under the pressure of her fingertips. She clapped a hand to her mouth. Her heart raced and her breath went shallow. Laura Ann Spencer lay on the floor, with her skin the color of flour.

She was stone cold dead.

"Who did this to you?" Dakota mouthed through splayed fingers.

The throaty growl of an angry cat tuned up near the bathroom. Patches of orange fur haloed around its body. Yellow eyes glittered. When it bared its fangs, Dakota jumped out of the way, and flung the door open wide. The frightened animal ricocheted off the door, and shot, bullet-like, down the steps, where it disappeared beneath the balcony.

With her heart pounding furiously, Dakota took in the damage within the trashed-out room. Such destruction could've been the result of Laura Ann, in a desperate fight for her life.

Uncharitable thoughts turned to Velvet Tears.

She dug for her wireless and stabbed out the number to Kris's cell phone. It went directly to voicemail.

"Call me. Where are you? The most awful thing happened. Laura Ann Spencer's dead."

She resisted the urge to barge into the crime scene. Instead of giving in to the temptation, she tried Hamilton's cell number. But Hamilton didn't pick up, either. When the system rerouted to voicemail, she tried to keep the panic out of her voice.

"Something terrible has happened. I need to talk to Kris immediately. If you know where she is, tell her to call me." She added, "Please? It's crucial."

Dakota hung up and tried their work number. Even the office phone routed to an answering machine. It wasn't as if death took a holiday, but it seemed the homicide unit was locked up tighter than a drum. Heart pounding, she gave up trying to find the detectives, and called the police emergency line.

"Nine-one one." The dispatcher quizzed her. "What's your emergency?"

"I want to report a murder."

"What's your name?"

"Dakota Jones."

The dispatcher gave her a no-joke chuckle. "What's the location?"

"I'm at the Peppermint Patty motel."

"Is anyone there with you?"

"No. I'm by myself."

"Did you kill her?"

"*What?* I didn't kill anyone." Clever trick, establishing that she was the only one at the crime scene. "Hey, wait a minute. I didn't say the victim was a female."

"Honey, you didn't have to. You've been in the newspaper all week." The edge in her voice served as a bitter reminder. It meant, *You found one of the dead girls. You became a person of interest to the police. Then you killed the PD's prime suspect. Only the girls keep dropping like flies. And now you've found another dead girl. Coincidence?* "Don't bite my head off for doing my job," the dispatcher went on in her calm, capable monotone. "Do you know the victim?"

"Her name's Laura Ann Spencer." Dakota shivered. She wanted to get out of the cold, but didn't dare share a room with a corpse. From her place at the door, she could survey the parking lot and wait for the police to arrive. "She's just a kid. I own Runaway Investigations, and I came here looking for her."

"Sure you did. Do you need an ambulance?"

"Didn't you hear me say she's dead?"

"How was she killed?" The dispatcher remained detached. It was like talking to someone with autism.

"I don't know."

"Knife? Bullet-wound? Blunt-force trauma?"

"Since I didn't do it, and since I haven't gone inside the room— *for obvious reasons*—I don't really feel qualified to answer that."

"What does that mean, *'obvious reasons'*?

"I didn't want to taint the crime scene, and get accused of murder. Do I have to spell it out for you?"

"Calm down. Did you rent the room?"

"Of course not." Dakota had to give her credit; the woman was good at her job. She'd probably already typed out a confession for her to sign.

"Ma'am, how'd you get inside the room?"

"First of all, I did not get *inside* the room. I only made it as far as the *outside* of the door, where I happen to still be standing, like an upstanding citizen, waiting for the cops to come and do their job. I got the passkey from the desk clerk, and when I opened the door, I saw she was dead. Not hurt. Dead. So I didn't go inside."

"Did you feel her pulse?"

"I already told you I didn't go inside."

"Then how do you know she's not still breathing?"

"Because she's not moving. And because the bottom half of her neck is purple."

"I'll get an ambulance rolling, just in case."

Dakota barked out a laugh. Not that this was the least bit funny. "What? So they can whip out the shock paddles and shock her back to life? Are you serious?"

"Calm down, Ms. Jones."

"Lady, the only way I'll calm down is if the boys in the meat wagon have tranquilizer darts."

"So you *do* want an ambulance dispatched to your location?"

Dakota pulled the phone from her ear and stared at it. Then she put it back up to her ear. "What we need here is the Black Mariah."

"I beg your pardon?"

"The hearse. The body snatchers from the ME's Office. That's what we need. And cops. Send lots of flatfoots."

"I've dispatched a couple of units to your location. Remain on the line with me until the police arrive."

It was all so clinical, the way the police operated. They'd become jaded from years of seeing things no normal person would want to see, much less become a part of.

Dakota overlooked the corpse in the way of a grieving animal that'd lost its mate. She stared in numb horror at the tattoos on Laura Ann's body, and wondered if she should notify Jake and Lorraine Spencer that their only child was dead, and quickly decided the police should do it.

A cold, nagging feeling chilled her to the bone. She narrowed her eyes into a squint. Tried to make out the information in the tattoo. The dispatcher was still asking questions, but Dakota no longer cared. There was something wrong about the notes. They differed from those found on the other girls. She tried to fix the tune in her head and got a childhood memory, instead.

We were sitting on the piano bench. My father played 'Moonlight Sonata.'

"Ms. Jones, are you still there? Ms. Jones? What's going on?"

What an odd change for a killer to make.

The other musical bars had been excised from contemporary pieces.

She took a stab at humming the notes. This was from a minor key . . . like a creepy Rachmaninoff tune; or the intro to a grade-B horror movie. Her flesh crawled. Why the abrupt switch? And why kill Laura Ann? She wasn't a prostitute. She wasn't anything. Just another missing teenager. Was this the work of a copycat killer? Wouldn't that be a coincidence?

"You didn't move anything, did you?" asked the dispatcher.

"No. I already told you I didn't go inside. But I can see the place is a wreck."

"Don't touch anything."

She wanted to say this wasn't her first rodeo. Only with her miserable luck, she'd turn into the PD's lead suspect again. And sarcasm didn't bode well when replayed on a nine-one one tape to a jury of one's peers.

Sirens shrilled in the distance like witches screaming.

"I hear them. They're close."

"Stay on the line. You can hang up after you read me the unit numbers on the patrol cars."

Red and blue emergency strobe lights flashed in the distance. The first patrol car rounded the corner and bounced into the parking lot. The motel manager burst through the office door as the second unit slid to a stop.

"I have to go now." Dakota thumbed off the cell phone, pulled the door to, and went to the edge of the balcony to wave the patrolmen upstairs.

Chapter Thirty-six

Dakota stood by, helpless, as Jake and Lorraine Spencer arrived at the morgue; him, distraught; her, white as a sheet, and rickety in her stance.

"I'm so sorry." What else could she say?

The CEO regained his composure. "I want to see her."

"No, you don't. You really don't. I made the identification so you wouldn't have to."

"I need to tell her something."

What? That you're sorry?

Dakota gave the air an aristocratic sniff and stepped out beneath the portico and looked out over the parking lot. A motorcycle roared up, and a heavy-set man wearing acid-washed denims, biker leather and a racing helmet, pulled into the parking space reserved for Dr. Stone. With clunky biker boots on, the rider had a devil of a time dismounting the Harley Davidson. As Dakota moved through the parking lot at a fast clip, he pulled off the helmet and spoke.

"Good evening, Ms. Jones."

"Dr. Stone?"

"Gus." He approached her, standing by the driver's door of the Jaguar with her keys dangling, and shifted the helmet to make it easier to shake hands. "The law says you have to wear it," he said. "I'm pretty sure all the medical examiners in the state got together and lobbied for them awhile back. Not because it saves lives. It's a brain bucket. It won't keep you from getting killed, but it'll sure keep your brains, eyes and teeth together in one place. Convenience, that's what these are for. You know how forensic pathologists are; we try to harvest as many organs as we can. You called this one in?"

"Remember when I first came to see you about the Jane Doe? This is the girl I was looking for. Only she has a name. Laura Ann Spencer. Her parents are waiting inside."

"No rest for the wicked. It was good to see you, Ms. Jones." He turned to leave but she called him back.

"Dr. Stone?"

"Gus."

"Is that a tattoo on the side of your neck?" She moved in to get a better look, all the while thinking, *Until the police have the killer in custody, isn't everyone a suspect?*

"You caught me." He glanced toward the doors, embarrassed. "Like it?"

"I'm not sure. What's it supposed to be?"

"Skull and crossbones. Can't you tell?"

"It's pretty dark out here. Is it real?"

"Nah. It washes off," he said almost sheepishly. "I just wanted to try something new."

"And the bike? That's a pretty scary looking hog."

"Borrowed." He avoided direct eye contact. "I must seem like an old fool to you."

Dakota cracked a smile. "You look hot, Dr. Stone. Bike or no bike, you're a real hottie." But what she was thinking was, *Really, those eyebrows are starting to resemble the ones on Afghani peasants.* "Can I talk to you for a second about Celia?"

"Celia St. Claire? What about her?"

"Did y'all ever find any of her relatives? Did anyone ever claim the body?"

"No relatives. Looks as if Mrs. St. Claire might've been the end of her line."

"So what happens now?"

"We'll transfer the body to the medical school. She'll likely end up as a research cadaver."

Dakota blinked back tears. She swallowed a lump so big she almost choked on it.

"I'll do it."

"Do what, Ms. Jones?"

"Claim her. I'll take care of the burial if you can help me sign off on the proper paperwork."

Gus did a slow head bob. "Out of curiosity, Ms. Jones, why would you offer to do that?"

A long silence settled between them. He watched her with morbid curiosity as she looked him over with an analytical bent. Could she trust him? In the end, she decided she couldn't.

"Ms. Jones?" he softly prompted her to answer. "Why would you do such a thing?"

"Because I can, Dr. Stone. Because I can."

She spent the remainder of the evening at Lorraine Spencer's home. It seemed like the right thing to do since the couple had a bit of a knock-down, drag-out in the ME's foyer. Lorraine called her husband a child molester. Jake called his wife a frigid bitch. The police got involved when Dr. Stone's office called them, and somebody had to go to jail.

That was the law in a "domestic."

Lorraine sat quietly at the breakfast table, cradling a dainty teacup between her palms.

"Is there someone you want me to call?" Dakota asked. "A friend who can come stay the night so you won't have to be alone?"

"Not really."

"What about family members?"

"Our parents are dead. Nobody else speaks to us. It's a long story, rooted in jealousy."

"What about the women at the country club? The ladies you play bridge with?"

"Shallow bitches, all of them. I only did it for Jake's business." Lorraine rose, zombie-like, and glided to the liquor cabinet. She removed the lock and pitched it in the trash. "Won't need that anymore," she said wryly, grabbing a bottle by the throat and hauling it to the counter. She took a couple of tumblers out of the cabinet and poured two straight whiskeys.

"Wait. None for me, thanks." Dakota waved her off.

"They're not for you, Dee. They're mine." Puffy-eyed, she chug-a-lugged the first one, then daintily sipped at the second. Her cheeks flushed hot-pink against her immaculately coiffed hair. She gave Dakota a slow blink. "Do you have a gun?"

"Yes."

"May I borrow it? Just for tonight. I'm afraid to stay by myself."

An eerie silence stretched between them.

Dakota returned a wan smile. "No, ma'am." She gave Laura Ann's mother a slow, deliberate headshake. "I won't help you do yourself in, Mrs. Spencer. If you're planning to take your own life, you'll have to do it without me."

Dakota's cell trilled. She grappled for her purse, relieved to hear Kris at the other end of the line.

"Where are you, Dee?"

"At Lorraine Spencer's. Did you get my message?" And then, "Isn't it awful?"

Kris echoed her sentiments. "Yes, just awful. Dee . . ."

"I'll be here a little longer," Dakota said out of her hostess' ear-shot. "I need to find someone to stay the night with Mrs. Spencer. I'm scared she might be suicidal."

"I need you to come home."

"Honestly, Kris, did you just hear what I said?"

"Did *you* just hear what *I* said?" Kris's voice cracked.

Dakota went on point. "What's wrong?"

"Just please come home."

The hair on Dakota's neck prickled. "Are you alone?"

"No."

"Who's there?"

Kris choked on Dakota's name. "Please don't ask me anything else. Just get home as soon as you can. And no police."

The line went dead.

Dakota gave Lorraine Spencer a last look. Between her lover and Laura Ann's mother, she chose Kris.

"I have to leave for a bit. But I'll be back. Don't do anything stupid, Mrs. Spencer. The prosecutor's office is going to need you."

"Should I bail him out?" Looking small and frail, seated at the big table, Laura Ann's mother polished off the second glass of whiskey.

What the hell's wrong with you? Did you just hear yourself?

"It occurred to me I'd have nothing if I left him. He controls the funds. I know this may sound crazy to you, but I don't even know how to write a check."

The stridence in Kris's voice replayed itself in Dakota's head. "I don't mean to be rude, but I have to go. Don't bail him out. Let him sit overnight. You both have a great deal of thinking to do." She rushed to the door and let herself out. Ran, full-bore, to the Jag and threw herself behind the wheel. Except for the faint flicker from the wall sconces on the porch, the lights in the home she shared with Kris had been extinguished.

With her gut sinking and the Smith drawn, she entered the house and slapped-on wall switches as she called out her lover's name. While visually clearing each room for intruders, the clock chimed midnight. When she arrived at their bedroom, she made a horrific discovery.

Kris was gone. But their bed was littered with locks of her hair.

Dakota shrilled at the two indentations in the bed linens. She interrogated the room as if it were a crime scene. "Ohmygod. What've you done to her?"

With her frayed nerves sparking, Dakota moved closer to the bed, to the transparent paper film of a press-on henna tattoo. Air rushed out in a gasp.

Her mind raced with possibilities. She tried to read backwards, but it took too long. Making her way to the bathroom, she removed a pair of tweezers from the drawer, and returned to the bed. She pinched one corner of the used transparency between the tweezers, and flipped it over. Against the ecru background of the Waterford comforter, the words jumped up to meet her gaze.

The message referenced running into her, and revealed that he'd hold his tongue and pretend he'd moved on. That he'd go down with the ship, and not put his hands up in surrender. No white flag. The killer was in love and always would be.

Dakota didn't have to recognize the artist, to get the message. It reverberated, loud and clear. Her scream pierced the quiet, echoed off the bathroom tile, and hung in the air long after the wailing stopped.

With the shrill of despair still lingering between her ears, she cried out, knowingly, to the room, "What have you done to her, you demented son-of-a-bitch?"

Chapter Thirty-seven

Dakota emerged from the bedroom in a sprint. She ran through the living room, past the plate glass window where the now-deflated shark, bobbed just beneath the water's surface. She skidded into the kitchen, to the drawer where they kept a joint address book with emergency contacts and random numbers to contact friends. Work, cell, home, next-of-kin contacts. Friends-of-friends who could be called to help track down other friends. Celia's name was in the book. So were her girls'.

And penciled-in under the "S"s, almost as if it were an after-thought rather than a deliberate entry done in Kris's crazy scrawl, she found Hamilton's name along with his address.

She picked up the telephone and stabbed out the number to his cell phone. When he didn't answer, she repeatedly pressed the redial button until he did.

"Where can I meet you?"

"Why, Dee, what a pleasure." How nice to hear from you," he said in a velvet voice, and she sensed him smiling into the phone. "Wait—you sound upset. Is everything all right?"

"Everything's fine." She doubted he believed her, but she kept her voice flat and calm. "Did you find Velvet Tears?" She squeezed her eyes tight, forcing her own tears past the corners.

"Why, no. I'm sorry to say we didn't. But you know how it is with those Goth types. While the rest of us are following the law, they're out there taking white crosses, black mollies, L.A. turnarounds, you name it. With any luck, he'll end up in the emergency room getting his stomach pumped. We'll get him then. Look, let me catch up with you tomorrow, Dee. Whatever you have going on can wait."

"This can't wait. I have to see you. Where can we meet?"

"Why, Dee . . . don't tell me you finally decided you want some of this?" He teased her with his tone. "Didn't Kris tell you? I'm seeing someone." He gave an Arizona chuckle; half cough, half laugh.

She heard unintelligible noises in the background, like the soft, rhythmic movement of what could've been a mattress gently bumping against the wall. Then his voice sounded different, as if he'd put her on speaker and laid the phone down in a rustle of fabric.

"I have to see you. This can't wait."

"I'm kind of busy right now." Hamilton's breathing patterns had developed an unusual cadence, like a marathon runner sucking in breaths until his lungs burned.

"Cancel your plans."

"I'm out with my girlfriend." Background noises suggested he was *inside* his girlfriend. Faraway feminine moans leaked into the conversation. Telling breaks in his speech left little to the imagination . . . it sounded like Hamilton was plunging a toilet in his passion-rumpled bed. A guttural, spontaneous groan hit her like a punch in the face. She'd unwittingly experienced his climax from five miles away. Then they were suddenly off speaker phone and he was back to his usual, obnoxious self.

"I don't think she'd appreciate getting cast-off to one side for a rendezvous with a lesbian. Can't we do this tomorrow?" He said this in a brandy-smooth voice.

She'd experienced a new low. "We have a problem," she said, and pretended she hadn't just been a reluctant participant in a telephone threesome. Her heart beat triple-time.

"And what is that?"

"I know who the serial killer is."

"You do? Why don't you tell me?"

He still didn't get it. And maybe that was for the best.

Her next plea for help went to nine-one one. She got the same dispatcher she'd spoken to before; the woman came on line, cool, calm and collected. Dakota decided right then and there, that if she lived through the night, she'd bake her a batch of homemade, chocolate chip cookies and deliver them in time for Christmas.

Meantime, she spilled her guts.

"It's Dakota Jones. I need the police. As many units as you can send."

"What is your emergency?"

"I know who's been killing all those girls. He has my girlfriend. I don't know if she's already dead, but we've got to do everything we can to stop him."

She told the woman everything she knew. Asked for a BOLO on Kris, so the uniformed troops and unmarked patrol cars could be on the lookout for her.

Dakota's heart drummed. She copied down Hamilton's home address, then ran to the Internet and looked up the directions on a map. She needed to verify this was the part of town Kris had spoken of, and that he hadn't moved. Before leaving the house, she flipped out the cylinder and checked Kris's borrowed Smith for bullets.

Six rounds. All copper-jacketed hollow-points.

With a true aim, she'd only need one.

Inside the Jaguar, she programmed the coordinates for Hamilton Stark's house into the luxury car's electronic map.

Hamilton's house stood out from other tract homes in the neighborhood because of the paved-brick driveway. It led to a modest stucco-faced adobe structure that had been updated to suit the times. Ornate, wrought-iron burglar bars were set into the windows. Solar lamps, stuck into the ground along the walkway, lit up the house like the Mothership. The scent of his cologne still hung in the air, and she knew she'd only missed him by minutes.

Dakota rang the bell, then rapped out a series of beats on the door using her knuckles.

Three long. Three short.Three long.

S-O-S.

"Answer the door, Romeo," she said through gritted teeth. Her heart pounded so hard she could almost see the fabric of her shirt move. "Answer the door."

The lights inside went off. She heard footfalls beyond the door, and held her breath for a few seconds in order to listen. She had no idea how many minutes he stayed away, only that she continued to work the doorbell every few seconds until it annoyed even her, and until he realized she wouldn't be turned away.

Metal clattered against metal. The door cracked open a slice, and she could see Hamilton dressed in a robe. She pressed her hand, hard, against the wood. The glint of a security chain slid along its track and snapped to a halt. With eyes like the prongs on a stun gun, he stood still and mute as he appraised her through the dark, unlit backdrop of his living room.

"Where's Kris?"

A look of mild surprise settled onto his face. "She's not with you?"

Dakota let the silence speak for her.

"Look, Dee, like I told you, I'm on a date. If you could come back another time . . ." He was listening to the left. His lips curled into a polite smirk.

"Now's the time." Spoken with a firm set to her mouth.

Hamilton torqued his jaw. His smile flat-lined. The chain scraped against metal and dropped, dangling, against the wood molding. The door swung open and the strong smell of urine hit her like a punch in the face. He stood in his bathrobe, a silk paisley number befitting a man about town, in the gelid darkness of his living room.

"Have a seat." He flipped a light switch and the ceiling fixture brightened the room. With a flick of the wrist, he motioned her toward a slip-covered sofa. The door closed with an authoritative clunk.

She hadn't expected him to toggle the lock. Casting furtive glances around the room, she looked past shadows and fixtures and anything else that conspired to block her vision

"What's on your mind?" He thunked his forehead with the heel of his hand. A dramatic gesture she took to be mockery. "Ah, yes. You were going to tell me who the serial killer is." His face went tight.

"I saw Dr. Stone tonight. He has a henna tattoo."

"Is that right?" His voice had turned melodic and taunting. He threw in a *Couldn't-care-less* cock of the eyebrow. "And what does this have to do with me?"

"I've never been inside your house, Hamilton. It's nice. Mind if I take a tour?" Her eyes darted furtively over the room in an attempt to gauge where the exits might be. The idea of escape became an engineering mystery to her.

"What the hell's wrong with you?" Hamilton's pleasant veneer fell away. "I told you I'm busy, yet you come over, disturb me, and you still haven't said who the killer is. My patience is running thin with you, Dakota. Does Kris know you're here?"

"I'm thinking she probably does."

"Then that makes things a little awkward." Expressionless eyes studied her as if he were dealing with a stubborn child with a low IQ.

"Mind if I use your bathroom? I don't feel so good. I ate bad seafood tonight."

"No, you may not." He stared through dark coals, smoldering at her presence, his acid tone turning corrosive. "Go home."

"Really. Bad. Seafood. Then the Spencer girl's mother and I had a few too many, I guess. Now I think I'm going to be sick."

Now or never, Dakota thought, that's how it works.

Chapter Thirty-eight

Without permission, Dakota sprang from the couch and bolted into the hall. Kris's partner lashed out. Strong fingers barely grazed her. He commanded her to stop. She deliberately bypassed the first closed door—scary sounds came from inside, and she wanted no part of it. She sprinted down a long hall of open doors. When she reached one that was closed, she tried the knob.

"Stop where you are," Hamilton shouted.

Dakota ducked inside, simultaneously pulling her gun. She flipped on the light, saw the lump under the covers, and toggled the lock.

Hamilton fisted the door. Screamed profanity and demanded she come out.

"You tricked me, you fucking bitch. You'll be sorry you tricked me." He kicked at a spot near the door knob. "I'll kill you."

She believed him implicitly.

Jarred by the crack of the door almost giving way, she shoved a chest of drawers along the floor, scarring the hardwoods and barricading herself in.

"Kris?" She sidestepped her way to the bed and ripped back the covers. The detective lay unconscious between the sheets, her face pale and her hair butchered. A henna tattoo covered her arm.

Dark bruises circled her neck. Two maroon-colored thumbprints stood out, bright, against her windpipe. Her eyes were stuck, half-open. Evidence of petechial hemorrhaging— broken capillaries—had rimmed them red, but Dakota detected the shallow rise and fall of her chest.

A pile of clothes lay in a heap next to the bed.

"Kris." She jostled her arm. "Kris, wake up."

The demon yowls of a thousand cats filtered through from an adjacent room.

She stabbed out three numbers on her cell phone.

"Nine-one one. What is your emergency?" The same dispatcher she'd spoken to earlier, came online.

"This is Dakota Jones."

"Again? Let me guess . . . you found another body?"

"Yes. Only this one's still alive. I need an ambulance and a shit-slew of cops. Send the SWAT team. I'm not kidding."

"You have a hostage situation?"

"Yes." She recited the street number.

Keystrokes on a keyboard clattered in the background. With mild curiosity, the dispatcher said, "That's Hamilton Stark's address."

In the background, the crazed detective howled like a wounded animal.

Dakota's words came out in a hyperventilating rush. "He killed those women, and he tried to kill Kris Carson. I need the ambulance for Kris, and some backup. Send lots of firepower." She'd seen enough crime shows on TV to know these calls were recorded, and wanted to give police enough information to work with in case things didn't turn out so well.

"Is Detective Stark there with you?"

Dakota thrust the phone in the direction of the door.

"I'll kill you, bitch."

"Did you get that?" She sensed something bad about to take place in the hallway.

"Help's on the way. Stay on the line."

"Lady, I'm not going anywhere. Only way I'll hang up—"

"You ruined everything."

"—is if he gets inside this room."

Footfalls receded.

Dakota's heart pounded.

"Can you go out the window?"

Dakota's stomach clenched. "Burglar bars."

"It's okay. Everything's going to be fine. Just stay with me."

A couple of half-hearted whimpers bubbled up from Dakota's throat. On some level, she knew the dispatcher was making super-ficial conversation to calm her down until the first unit arrived.

They could be dead by then.

"Are they coming?" She lapsed into a panic. "How far away? Tell them to step on it. There's something awful-sounding in the next room."

"What kind of sound?"

"Like the devil threw a party and hired ghouls for the orchestra."

Almost simultaneously, classical music blasted through the house. Footsteps thundered toward the door.

"Ohmygod, he's back." Her eyes darted around for another piece of furniture to barricade the door with. Hamilton Stark lived in Spartan quarters. Then again, why show an interest in furnishings when women were his toys?

"Listen carefully, Ms. Jones. It's difficult to hear you. No matter what happens, stay on the line, and don't hang up."

"If they don't get here quick, we'll die."

"Kris Carson . . . is that *our* Kris Carson?" Fear tinged the dispatcher's tone.

"Yes. She works homicide. She's his work partner. He tried to kill her tonight."

"What's he doing now?"

Dakota screamed a blood-clotting scream of the damned.

"Honey, what's happening? Tell me what's going on."

"Give her to me, bitch."

"Smoke's pouring in under the door. He set fire to the carpet. I have to break the window."

"No." Command resonated in the dispatcher's drill-sergeant tone. "Listen to me, Ms. Jones . . . Dakota, do *not* break out the glass."

Dakota hesitated. "It's filling up the room. He wants us to burn to death," she whimpered. The rustle of papers at the other end of the line meant the dispatcher was probably leafing through some sort of departmental training guideline until she reached the standard operating procedure listing questions to ask a caller during a fire emergency.

"Is there a bathroom?"

Dakota's eyes slewed around. "Yes."

"Run water in the tub. Put the bedspread in it. Get it sopping wet. Then cram it under the door."

Dakota ripped off the down-filled comforter and flung it aside.

She peeled off a wool blanket and headed for the tub.

When she returned, a gauzy gray layer of smoke filled the room.

"We need air. I'm breaking the window."

Dakota's telephone lifeline barked orders. "No. Don't do it. You will *not* do it, do you understand? You don't want to create a backdraft. That's a last resort. FD's got engines on the way. Okay, I've got two units within ten blocks of you."

"We'll be dead by then."

"No, you won't. Did you stuff the wet bedspread under the door like I told you?"

A horrible crash split the sheetrock. Then, another swing, and a twenty-pound maul broke through. Smoke snaked through the opening.

"Ohmygod, he's coming in." She sprinted to the bathroom, opened a cabinet looking for anything of use, and threw the comforter into a tub threatening to overflow.

Wailing sirens paled against the crackle of flames.

"Give her back to me and I'll let you go."

"Where are they?" Dakota pleaded with the dispatcher. Tears sluiced down her cheeks.

"Close. Where's he now?"

"Taking down the wall with a sledgehammer."

"Do you have a weapon?"

As if on cue, Dakota fired two random shots at the broken sheetrock. She heard the deadly ping of bullet-scored metal that coincided with a yelp from Hamilton.

The opening widened against another blow. Smoke billowed in.

"I can't see my hand in front of my face. I wrapped Kris in a wet comforter. I have to break the window. We can't breathe."

"Fight the urge."

But she couldn't.

A commotion ensued outside of the house.

Must be the cops, trying to get in.

They wanted in, she wanted out. The irony was almost laughable.

She abandoned the phone on the bed long enough to ransack Hamilton's closet for a heavy object to smash the panes. As she settled for a couple of wooden shoetrees, she imagined the dispatcher flipping to the section in her emergency notebook titled

What to do if the idiot breaks a window.

She reared back and slammed them against the pane. Glass exploded. One went through to the other side. The other ricocheted off a metal bar and bounced back onto the floor.

She dragged Kris to the window. Looped one limp arm around her own shoulder and hoisted the injured woman to her feet. It took most of her strength to steady Kris against the wall, holding her up where she could breathe in fresh gulps of air.

Dakota took one good breath before a current of brown smoke entered the room. She let Kris crumple to the floor, and left momentarily, crawling along the wall, feeling her way into the bathroom. The water in the tub was still running. Dakota fisted a wet towel to her nose, and crawled back to Kris.

She breathed through the wet towel, but let it drop to the floor. It took both hands to drape the makeshift filter around Kris's face, and secure it so it wouldn't slide off under its own weight. Then she reclaimed her own water-soaked cloth and wrapped it around her face. With the last of her remaining strength, she lifted her partner to her feet and shoved her against the window.

If Hamilton Stark came through the walls, she'd kill him.

A dark, bulky specter appeared in the window.

What the hell?

She'd seen the movie "Ghost" and wondered if this looming black shape had come to claim its share of souls.

"Are you the devil?" she whispered, in awe.

The apparition spoke. "I've been called worse. Hang on, lady, we'll get you out."

She didn't remember slumping to the floor, or how long she'd been immobile with Kris by her side. But the sound of clanging metal a few feet above their heads meant help had arrived, and for now, that's all she needed to know.

A peaceful sleep lulled her into its realm. At first, she went willingly.

It wasn't half bad, this sensation of euphoria.

It was simple.

And deadly.

The last of her reason fought back.

"Don't go to sleep, Kris. We have to stay awake." This was a majorly fucked up way to die . . . on Christmas Eve. With her arms embracing the love of her life, Dakota prayed for a miracle. After a sincere "Amen," she surrendered to the pull of the abyss.

She awakened to a heavenly wonder disguised as the roar of a distant engine.

Followed by the demon shriek of grinding metal.

Then, in the din of reverberating sound, as an acrid black haze shrouded the room, the outer wall to Hamilton's bedroom pulled away, opening up like the great yawn of a sleeping giant.

Chapter Thirty-nine

Invasive red and blue lights flashed, turning Hamilton's front yard into a light show for the neighbors to come out and watch. As firefighters tended to Dakota, and paramedics worked feverishly to revive Kris, at least a dozen shadowy apparitions streaked across the lawn like angry spirits fleeing the inferno.

Cats—infuriated felines in every shape, breed and color.

Water from fire hoses knocked down flames licking at the roof.

Nearby, police surrounded an old man in his pajamas and parted him from his shotgun. As he inclined his head in the direction of Hamilton's garage, Dakota noticed Stark, himself, face-planted on the bricks, with blood pooling around his head like fresh paint.

The man, possibly a next-door-neighbor, was getting his Miranda rights recited to him like a rosary. When the officer finished reading the Constitutional warning off a laminated card, he lifted his chin, and said, "Do you wish to make a statement, sir?"

"He stole Fluffy." The elderly man wagged a finger in the direction of the body.

"What?"

"My Himalayan."

"You shot a man over a cat?"

"He was taking them. He kept them inside his house. You never heard such a ruckus. One day Fluffy didn't come home. I asked him about it." The old man's voice warbled. "He told me to mind my own business."

Dakota listened in. Apparently Hamilton operated with impunity throughout the neighborhood. She felt a tug of affection for the old gentleman. All right, so she only took cases on runaways, and the occasional Alzheimer's patient who wandered off. But she couldn't let the poor fellow do himself in. The cops would arrest and hold him until they sorted out the mess. And the pathetic neighbor, in his addled shape, was no match for Phoenix's finest.

She decided to help, and borrowed a pen and piece of paper from an obliging firefighter. Then she stepped in between the first line officer—the same policeman Mayor Jane had dressed down at the mall—and the old man.

"I'm Dakota Jones," she said by way of introduction. "I own Runaway Investigations. There's a telephone number on this piece of paper that belongs to a good friend of mine. When you get down to the police station, this is the phone call you want to make. Ask for Jane. Tell her Dakota sent you."

Paramedics transported Kris to the hospital.

By the time Dakota left, the only parts of Hamilton's house that weren't covered in soot and water were dusted with a fine layer of extinguishing foam, which most of his neighbors agreed was a visual improvement.

A uniformed officer transported her to the police station to give a sworn statement. This time, she rode in the front seat instead of the cage. As he pulled away from the scene, she gave the site one last look and thought, *Holy smoke, this place is right out of central casting.*

"What's your name?" The transporting officer slid her a side-long glance.

"Dakota Jones."

"Really? Are you kidding me?"

She turned her head and looked through the glass, at the smear of colors from neon lights on the boulevard. She continued to stare out the window, and wondered if the end result of this one-sided conversation would reveal another person with a link to her past. In the end, she decided she didn't give a flip one way or another. As she drifted in and out of the officer's monologue, her thoughts kept turning to Kris. That, and the series of contamination showers she'd need to rid herself of the whole experience, or as she liked to think of it, the Silkwood treatment.

She learned the patrolman's name when he said, "Man, oh man.

I can't wait to tell my wife. You're a real celebrity at *Chez* Johnson. That playground you donated? Every Saturday, we take our kids over there to play. And if the weather's nice, which it almost always is, we take along a picnic."

Chapter Forty

It didn't take long for Dakota to give a written statement. She said what she had to say in brief, abbreviated sentences. It might not have been what they were hoping to get, but she said all she was willing to say until she could get an update on Kris's condition. The officer who carried her downtown gave her a ride back to the Jag, and by the time she arrived at the hospital, she learned Kris had already been treated and released. She found the detective in the spa tub, vigorously scrubbing off the henna tattoo. The contrast of her pink English skin was made even more luscious by the fluff of iridescent bubbles cowling her neck like Queen Victoria's lace collar.

"Hey," Kris said weakly, her raw voice scratchy. "Thanks for showing up when you did."

"Thanks for being alive when I showed up."

"That was the easy part. I just kept thinking of you." She looked away and spoke in measured sound-bites, with an economy of words. "Under the circumstances . . . I think it'd be best . . . to go back in a few weeks for an AIDS follow-up."

It wasn't until after Dakota said, "Sure, whatever you need," that Kris was able to face her again. Dakota saw no point in digging for details when she knew what a hospital rape kit entailed. She'd had several; the first, not long after she ran away; the second, when Celia St. Claire brought her into the fold.

"Well, then," Kris said, all crisp and businesslike, "I'll do just that."

"The crime scene detective's coming by to process the bedroom. They want to recover the tattoo film with the words on it. Which artist recorded that song?"

"It's *White Flag*, by Dido." Kris's calm exterior shattered with the first burst of tears. "He was sending me messages. He killed those women because I spurned him. He blamed you for taking me away. What he didn't realize, is that I was never his to begin with."

"I don't understand. Celia and the girls never did anything to him."

"But they were expendable. You were expendable because you used to be like them. He couldn't get over the fact that I chose you. So he started killing them off and sending me messages using verses from the music I like."

The last thing Dakota wanted to do was bring up the Spencer girl. But Kris would know soon enough when the morning paper hit the porch. "He murdered Laura Ann Spencer."

"I know." Kris refused to make eye contact. "One of the uniforms told me at the ER."

"On some level, I think I knew it was Hamilton when I saw the tattoo on Laura Ann. He only put classical music on that one." Dakota said.

"It was supposed to be you tonight, Dee. After we finished looking for Shawn O'Neil, I told him I couldn't have a drink with him. That I had to get to the new mall before it closed, to pick out your Christmas present.

"The BMW's down the street. Some jerk-wad pulled out in front of me. When I swerved, I hit the curb and blew a tire. I was hoping to borrow your car, only you weren't home. When the doorbell rang, I thought maybe you'd forgotten your house keys. When I looked out the peephole and saw Hamilton, I let him in."

He'd come to Heaven's Urn expecting to find Dakota. By the time Kris figured it out and confronted him, he realized he'd have to kill her, too.

"I was so mad about what happened to the Beemer on the walk back home. I kept wondering, *Why me?* Later, I was glad it happened. Because I would've been at the mall, and he would've killed you, Dee. And if he'd been able to follow through, I wouldn't want to live either." Her composure disintegrated into another crying jag.

"Can I get you anything? A tall glass of bourbon?"

Kris gave her a vehement headshake. "I didn't get a chance to buy you anything for Christmas, Dee," she said through a sniffle. "So I've decided that's my gift to you. I'm not going to drink anymore."

Dakota blinked. Did she hear correctly? This was huge. "You'd do that for me?"

"Well, not just for you. As you know, I'm not much into group activities so I figured I'd spare myself the embarrassment. Nothing screams "pathetic loser" like an alcoholic in denial having a debate with herself out loud in front of strangers." Kris shrugged. "Anyway, I'm cool with it."

"I got something for you," Dakota said. "I'll get it, but I need to explain something before you open it." She dashed out of the room and returned with the satellite radio, hastily wrapped, and stuck together with duct tape. She handed over a pair of scissors.

"That's not going to cut it," Kris deadpanned, and finished soaping off the last remnant of tattoo. That Kris could still find her sense of humor meant there was room to get their relationship back on track. For no good reason, she said, "I hate music." This came out of the blue, spoken with conviction. "I'm not sure you'll turn me into a talk radio girl, Dee, but if I never heard any of these songs again, it wouldn't be a minute too soon."

Dakota glanced down at the unopened present. "You probably need some alone time. I'll come back." But she was thinking, *Screw satellite radio.* "And you'd better hurry and get dressed," she added, backing out the door with the box under her arm. "That detective's going to want to talk to you. We can do the Christmas thing later."

After Kris finished preening and the crime scene detective arrived, Dakota slipped into the guest bedroom. She dialed the toll free number and went through the keypad gymnastics.

"Activation."

"I want Deactivation."

"Serial number, please?"

She gave it.

"Congratulations. You've already got the activation."

"Not *the* activation. *Deactivation.*"

"That's a different number."

"You can't just connect me?"

"Thanks, I'll disconnect you. Have a nice day."

Click.

Dumbfounded, she dug out the instruction booklet and leafed

through until she found a different toll free number tied into Customer Service.

"Merry Christmas, you've reached Deactivation."

"I want to close my account."

"What's the serial number to the unit you're calling about?"

She gave it.

"And, what's the problem?"

"Don't take this personally, but you people suck."

She repacked the satellite radio in its box, along with the receipt, and was locking it in the trunk of her car when the front door opened and the crime scene detective sauntered out. He put his fingerprint kit and camera in the police vehicle and pulled out a charred, soggy feedbag shaped suspiciously like the purse left back in Hamilton's rubble. She'd assumed it'd been destroyed in the fire. Before leaving, the investigator asked her to inventory the contents, and made her sign for it.

About the time Dakota reached the porch steps, she jumped at the roar of a car engine. An old station wagon with one burning headlight shot past the guard kiosk and careened her way, bearing down on the asphalt at a high rate of speed.

The driver bounced over the curb and onto the lawn belonging to a neighbor two doors down. The car screeched to a stop, where it continued to idle and belch out brown exhaust.

A person of androgynous build, dressed in camouflage fatigues and a bandana-covered head, jumped out of the driver's door with an automatic weapon leveled at the house, and yelled in a diabolical voice, "Take that, Derek, you syphilitic, brain dead hump." Dakota flung open the door and dove across the threshold to the slap of bullets chipping mortar.

When the car roared off after trenching the lawn, she ventured outside and saw that the sounds she'd mistaken for automatic gun-fire actually came from a paintball gun. If mansions were dogs, the one on the other side of Derek's would be a colorful Dalmatian.

Well, call me fifteen and send me back to high school.

After taking a picture with her phone-camera, Dakota came back indoors and found Kris sitting outside in a chaise lounge next to the pool. It was almost six o'clock in the morning, but the purple Arizona sky was still dotted with stars. The crime scene detective had bagged and tagged the bed sheets, sealed the locks of hair in small brown envelopes, and had taken the evidence with him. Even though adrenaline still coursed through their veins, neither felt up to re-making the bed. Besides, it'd be a miracle if they could sleep at all.

Kris said, "Mayor Jane just called."

"I gave an old man her phone number. Is she angry?"

"No. She's engaged. She asked us to stop by her house around eleven o'clock, Christmas morning, for a formal breakfast, so she can show off the ring."

"What'd you tell her?"

"I said we'd be there." Kris took a deep breath. "She's a nice lady. And she's your friend. From now on, your friends are my friends."

They adjourned instead to the guest bedroom, where thermal insulated blackout shades had been installed for sleep-days when Kris worked the night shift. For the next few hours, they cuddled in the dark, between 1000-thread-count sheets, gingerly stroking each other's wounds and bruised egos. Beneath down covers, with only the whoosh of acclimatized air to disturb the silence, Dakota turned to Kris.

"Did you really mean it when you said my friends will be your friends?"

"I did," Kris whispered.

"Good. Then you won't be upset with me. I claimed Celia's body. I'm going to pay for her burial."

"It's a nice thing you're doing. And since I've been such a jerk, I'll pitch in and buy her a headstone."

"Really?"

"Yes. I want a fresh start. I love you, Dakota."

"And I love us."

Epilogue

Friday morning, Christmas day, the ladies curbed the Jag in front of Mayor Jane's estate. Icy stalactites had formed on the trees. The Mayor had forgotten to turn off her lawn sprinklers. As for the ground, stalagmite ice shards coated the grass like thousands of angry crystal teeth.

"I'm glad she invited us over to see her engagement ring," Kris said unenthusiastically. She stared through the windshield, seemingly lost in thought. "I'm glad we had someplace to come today."

"It must be huge." Dakota craned her neck to make sure the lid on the Dutch oven in the floorboard behind the passenger seat hadn't vibrated off during the drive over. "Do you think I made enough tamales?"

Kris reflexively touched her neck. She'd probably be reliving the night Hamilton Stark tried to squeeze the life out of her for a long time.

On some level, Dakota felt a pang of sorrow for him. It must've been agonizing to sit next to Kris, day after day, knowing he couldn't have her.

Still, he'd killed all those women.

Kris blinked back tears. "Just because I didn't love him the way he wanted me to, doesn't mean I didn't love him." She smoothed her black velvet slacks, and picked at invisible lint on her white silk tuxedo shirt. "I hope Mayor Jane hired that string quartet, like she did last year."

"Are you going to be all right? We don't have to go in if you don't want to. We can go wherever you say."

"I'll be fine. Besides, she's your friend."

"At least it's not another political fundraiser. Sometimes I feel like I'm less of a contributor, and more of a glorified ATM."

They reached the front door with the wind whipping at their faces. A sensor-activated camera made a noise like the whir of a dentist's drill as it sighted them in. The intercom crackled to life; the voice of a foreigner spoke unintelligible English. It seemed an eternity before the Mayor materialized behind the leaded glass panes.

"I should've bought her a gift," Dakota muttered.

The door swung open. Mayor Jane stood before them, ashen-faced.

"Thanks so much for the invitation." Kris injected a cheery lilt into her voice, an emotion Dakota knew she didn't feel. "Let's see that gorgeous ring."

Without emotion, Jane lifted her hand. The huge diamond sparkled in its platinum setting.

"So who's the lucky guy? And when do we get to meet him?" said Dakota, inwardly wishing Jane would invite them in out of the cold.

"There's been a new development." Jane held a piece of paper in hand that'd been folded into quarters. "This event isn't really a Christmas party. It's supposed to be my wedding day."

Vapor escaped from Dakota's mouth. She stomped her feet to keep warm.

"I'm sorry. I'm not thinking straight. Come in out of the weather." Jane turned on one foot and glided through the marble foyer. A housekeeper intercepted them, halfway, and received the pot of tamales.

They entered Jane's glorious living room. It'd been trimmed in white ribbons and bisque angels. A patinated antique table had been set up with an embroidered runner, with a leather-covered Bible centered next to two wedding bands. A man in a black suit, who could've passed as a minister, hung quietly in the background.

Jane unfolded the note. She placed it, face-up, on the coffee table, and flopped into the nearest Bergere chair. She rested her elbow on the padded arm, and sank her head into her palm.

"Thanks for wearing black and white. You two were supposed to be my bridesmaids." She made a feeble attempt at "jazz hands" and said, "Surprise." The sick grin turned into a grimace. "I figured once you got here, you couldn't say no. And I knew the fewer people I told, the less likely the press would end up on my doorstep for what was supposed to be one of the happiest days of my life."

Dakota's eyes strayed to the note.

"He's gone," Jane said dully. "They forced his car off the road and took him."

"Who's 'they'?"

"Whoever dropped that off." Jane gestured to the paper.

Kris sat quietly, letting the news soak in.

"I'm trying not to think the worst. Part of me wants to believe he's still alive, while the other part knows he's dead." She clutched Dakota's hand. "Please help me, Dee. I know you only look for kids, but I'm begging you. I'll pay you anything you want."

"You need to call the police. And the FBI."

"No police. No FBI. They'll kill him for sure. It says so." Her eyes flickered to the note and back.

Kris asked the million-dollar question. "Who is he?"

"Remember when I told you I had a friend who was a judge, who'd sign your search warrant as a favor to me?"

Kris nodded.

"That's him." Jane's face drained of color. "Judge Bill Tate."

Meet the Authors

Sixth-generation Texan LAURIE MOORE received her B.A. from the University of Texas at Austin and entered a career in law enforcement in 1979. In 1992, she moved to Fort Worth and earned a law degree from Texas Wesleyan University School of Law in 1995. She is currently in private practice in "Cowtown" and lives with her husband and two rude Welsh corgis, and recently retired as a licensed, commissioned peace officer after 34 years in law enforcement. Laurie is the author of *Getting Mama Out of Hell, Dawn of the Deb, Deb on Air—Live at Five, Wanted Deb or Alive, Deb on Arrival—Live at Five, Couple Gunned Down—News at Ten, Woman Strangled—News at Ten, Jury Rigged, The Wild Orchid Society, The Lady Godiva Murder, Constable's Wedding, Constable's Apprehension,* and *Constable's Run.* Contact Laurie through her website at www.LaurieMooreMysteries.com

RUSSELL DAVIS is the Concentration Director of the Genre Fiction program for the MFA program at Western State Colorado University. He has written and sold numerous novels and short stories in virtually every genre of fiction, under at least a half-dozen pseudonyms. His writing has encompassed media tie-in work in the *Transformers* universe to action adventure in *The Executioner* series to original novels and short fiction in anthology titles like *Under Cover of Darkness, Law of the Gun,* and *In the Shadow of Evil.* He has also worked as an editor and book packager, and created original anthology titles ranging from westerns like *Lost Trails* to fantasy like *Courts of the Fey.* He is a regular speaker at conferences and schools, where he teaches writing, editing and the fundamentals of the publishing industry. He is a past president of the Science Fiction & Fantasy Writers of America, and his most recent collection of short fiction and poetry, *The End of All Seasons,* came out in 2013. Contact Russell through his website at www.morningstormbooks.com.

Curious about other Crossroad Press books?
Stop by our site:
http://store.crossroadpress.com
We offer quality writing
in digital, audio, and print formats.

Enter the code FIRSTBOOK
to get 20% off your first order from our store!
Stop by today!

CPSIA information can be obtained
at www.ICGtesting.com
Printed in the USA
LVOW04*2022021216
515530LV00010B/129/P